Joanna

by

Maria Rosaria Iuliano

CROWN OAK PRESS

To order more copies of this book,
call 1-866-909-BOOK (2665) toll-free.

I want to dedicate this book to my daughter Melinda.
May God keep her and bless her always.
Love, mom.

PROLOGUE

May 1982 – Pozzuoli, Italy. That particular night Maria had fallen asleep on the couch. She had been watching television late and had been too lazy to walk to the bedroom. Her then husband George, an American sailor, and daughter Elizabeth were asleep in her bedroom.

Around three o'clock in the morning, she woke up suddenly, feeling someone in the room staring at her. A figure was standing by the couch, his head covered by a white towel. In his hand he had a flashlight and was pointing it towards the corner of the room. He wore a white T-shirt, military-green pants, and around his waist he had a multicolored belt. He said nothing, just stood there. Maria was terrified. She tried to scream but no sound came out of her mouth. She tried to move but she was paralyzed. She tried with all her might to free herself of the paralysis that was holding her down and slowly she was able to move.

She tried to scream again "George! George!" This time the slur became clearer. She saw the figure turn around and walk out of the room; a few seconds later her husband came into the room. He turned on the light and sat on the edge of the couch, where she was laying.

"A man was in the room," she said to him.

"It was just a dream," he said, holding her hand. " There is no one here!" She got up from the couch and went to the front door to

see if the chain was swinging. She was so convinced that someone had really been there that she thought that if he had walked out of the door the chain would be still swinging, but of course the chain was not. It had been a dream, but you could not convince her of it.

CHAPTER ONE

San Diego, California, 1999 - Maria opened her eyes slowly. It was hard for her to wake up in the morning. She kept her head on the pillow for ten more minutes trying to remember what she was dreaming about, just before she woke up, but could only remember bits and pieces, so she stopped trying. It always upset her when she could not remember the dreams from that magical world she had been living in for the past seventeen years. It all started when she bought a Bible for the first time in her life. She didn't know it at the time, but later on she made the connection. That apparition in Pozzuoli happened just after she had bought one.

She rubbed her eyes and looked at the watch. 8:30 a.m. Rolling over she told herself that it was still early. It was Friday morning and she didn't work on Fridays. She rolled over again and pulled the blanket to her chin. She mentally went over the things that needed to be done around the house but she told herself that they could wait.

She lived in one bedroom apartment, on Sixth Avenue, by Balboa Park. The apartment was big and roomy and she liked to have space around her. The floor was covered by a blue carpet, which reminded Maria of a calm sea on a sunny day. The building used to be a hotel, many years back, but had been converted into apartments, one bedrooms and studios. No children lived there, only adults. During the day it was empty, while everybody was at work. Maria had felt the presence of two ghosts since living there.

Once inside her apartment she could hear no noise, even if there was loud music playing in some other apartment, because the apartment was located in the corner of the building. The only noises that she could hear were those from the cars in the street, and from the airplanes landing at the nearby airport.

Maria lived alone in the apartment. She had lived alone for the past seven years, since Elizabeth left. Her daughter, in fact, had decided that she wanted to go live with her dad and his new family when they relocated from San Diego to Louisiana. Maria fought it in court but she lost because George told the Judge that she had tried to commit suicide, a year earlier. That was back in 1992. She was crying and desolate, at first, but she got used to it. "You get used to anything," she told herself, "when you have no other choice." But she still missed her daughter. To go to court, she had borrowed money from her employer and had hired a lawyer that he had recommended. The only good thing that came out of it was the fact that the Judge ordered George to pay for the legal fees, which he didn't like, of course.

They had been divorced since May 1985. The divorce took place in Honolulu, Hawaii where they had been transferred from Italy. After that George was transferred to San Diego and Maria joined him and Elizabeth after about a year for three months until she found a job and moved on her own. Elizabeth moved in with her few months later.

****

9:30 a.m. said the clock sitting on top of the television. "Just a little bit longer," said Maria to herself. "I will stay in bed until ten o'clock and then I will get up!" So she rolled on her side hoping ten o'clock would never come. She tried to stretch it out as long as she could, neglecting the housework, which needed attention badly.

The neglect, more than to laziness, was to be attributed mainly to the great loneliness and despair that she felt, being so far away from her family. All her family, in fact, lived in Italy. She found that hard to cope with and remained unmotivated and without desire to tidy-up, even if it was just for herself. She had left her family in 1975, when she married. She was fine while she was married but since her divorce she had felt like a leaf on God's breath.

Ten o'clock came around and Maria let out a sigh. She said: "Darn it!"

She pushed her blanket away, got out of the bed and went into the bathroom to take a shower. She mentally said a prayer requesting protection for the day, and thanked the Almighty God for all that she had. The Catholic nuns had thought her about a severe and punishing God so every time she thought about Him, she felt anxiety and fear grip her stomach. She concentrated on the shower and tried to forget the way she felt, by thinking of the errand she was about to make.

****

The trolley for San Ysidro left just as she was arriving at the Trolley Station. But that wasn't the one she needed to take. She needed the El Cajon trolley and had only a few minutes wait until it came. As she boarded the trolley she noticed it was crowded for that time of the day. *I wonder why. Shouldn't all these people be at work?* she thought to herself, but she was not at work either so maybe all those people had a valid reason also. She sat next to a blonde woman, in one of the few seats available, and thought herself lucky.

The woman moved over to make room for her and Maria thought it was a nice gesture. She said "Hi," and the woman answered her with "Good morning!"

Her tone was friendly and so was her smile. She had long hair, blue eyes, all the opposite of Maria who had short brown hair and brown eyes. The hair needed to be combed, and it was, in part, sun bleached. She wore a T-shirt, which said "Away with It" and blue jeans, which had seen better days. At her feet was a large bag filled so tight that the zipper was about to explode.

"How are you doing today?" asked Maria.

"Ok I guess, how about yourself? Do you know what time it is?" asked the stranger while fidgeting with a strand of her blonde hair.

"It is eleven-thirty. Isn't it crowded for this time of the day?

Shouldn't this people be at work or something? Where are you going?"

"I am going to visit some friends. How about you?"

"I am going to a religious store in El Cajon, to buy a booklet for my daughter Elizabeth about how to pray the rosary. She bought a rosary three years ago but she doesn't know how to say the prayers. She asked me for another copy of a booklet that I once sent to her, as she had lost that one and I promised that I would buy her another one. I was raised Catholic and I should have thought it to her but I never really knew it myself. So here I am!" Maria felt a little annoyed with herself for having to explain all this to a stranger.

"It sure is far for you to go to buy a booklet. Isn't there another store closer to where you live?"

"There is one in La Mesa but it is just as far. At any rate I rather go to this one because is run by nuns and it has a certain mood to it. When you enter into it is like entering a church and you can feel the atmosphere of prayer. This one I am going to, used to be close to my house but they moved. I liked the store a lot because it had a chapel in it and I used to go in there and pray. When they moved, I was very disappointed."

"Do they have a chapel in this store too?"

"I don't know. I have never been there before. What is your name?'

"My name is Joanna, but you can call me Joey, that's what everybody calls me!" She was fidgeting with her hair again and Maria guessed she was nervous.

"My name is Maria! Nice to meet you! I think that I will call you Joanna if you don't mind. I like it better than Joey. How old are you?"

"I am twenty-eight years old. How about yourself?"

"I am forty-five! You don't look twenty-eight! I hope you don't get offended but you look older, I'd say about thirty-five. Maybe it is because you are not wearing any make-up!" Maria held her breath waiting for her reply.

"I'm not offended! I've had a rough life and I guess it shows! The reason that I don't wear any make-up is because I can't afford any! And the reason I am not working today is because I don't have a job. I am unemployed!"

"Sorry to hear that! I hope that you find a job soon!"

"Thank you! So do I!"

Being engrossed in the conversation they were not aware of people going on or off the trolley. Maria kept her eyes opened for her stop but there was still time, she could tell. There was silence for a little while, then she said: "Why don't you give me your phone number Joanna? If I hear of a job opening, anywhere, I'll give you a call!"

"I don't have a phone at the moment! I will get one in a little while!"

"What kind of job did you do before you became unemployed?"

"I was a cashier in a supermarket. Right after high school I worked in an office for two years, but I was bored to death. So I went to work in the supermarket. I like serving people! It makes me feel good! Plus the time goes by faster, talking to people and what have you!"

"Maybe I can give you my phone number," exclaimed Maria. "Yes, let me do that! You can call me every once in a while and I'll let you know if I hear of anything!" She dug into her purse and took out a business card. It was one she had made for one of her various money- making deals she got involved in, without success. She handed Joanna the business card and said,

"Here is my phone number. Don't pay attention to where it says 'Independent Contractor' because I am not involved in that anymore, but the phone number and the address are still good!"

"Thank you, Maria! It is very nice of you to do this for me!" Joanna was touched and gave Maria a very grateful smile while putting the card in her pocket.

"Don't mention it! I would do it for anybody who needs a hand. You make sure that you call me though, okay?"

"I sure will! Oh! Here is my stop. It was nice talking to you Maria. I hope that I will see you again soon!"

"Same here! You take care of yourself and good luck, Joanna," said Maria regretfully. She liked the stranger and she was sorry to see her go. It was so hard for her to make friends. She was already disappointed because she thought that Joanna was not going to call her, just like so many others she had given her phone number to. She watched her pick up the heavy bag, and slowly walk out of the trolley. She was taller than Maria, and her figure was slim and trim. She was attractive, overall, even if her face looked drawn and tired. Maria felt sorry for her, because she looked so lonely and wearied. And so young! What a pity!

She waved goodbye from the window, while she sat where Joanna had been sitting before. Joanna responded, while lowering her head, a little bit bashful. The trolley resumed its course and she was out of sight.

Once in El Cajon she soon found the store that she was looking for, very near the trolley stop. As soon as she entered, she was aware of the religious nature of the business as Christian music filled the air and there were three nuns, busy working. She recognized one of the nuns from the other store. It was the same one who had gone into the chapel to pray, one day that Maria had been crying while visiting the store. She had seen her swollen eyes, but hadn't said anything to her. Instead a few minutes later she had disappeared. When Maria had gone into the chapel to pray, there she was, praying. Maria had not told anyone but she was convinced in her heart that she was praying for her. She was moved. She didn't recognize the other two nuns in the El Cajon store. They were young and innocent looking, but they also looked business-like and Maria was full of admiration for them. Not knowing why, she also felt a sense of envy; maybe she longed for the peace they seemed to have. She felt a sense of emptiness inside. She asked one of the nuns if they had a booklet about the rosary and she quickly found one for her. Maria asked for two copies as she had misplaced her copy as well. She also asked if, per chance, they had a chapel in this store and to her surprise the nun directed her to a door at the side of the counter. Maria entered quietly and sat in one of the chairs. After few minutes she knelt and prayed fervently,

"Dear God, I come before you in humbleness of heart and contrite in spirit. I pray that you forgive me my sins. I pray that Joanna finds a job soon, that she will call me and that we can become friends. Close friends. Please help her with whatever is bothering her and making her sad. I pray for my daughter Elizabeth, for my family in Italy, and for the whole world, Lord! Lord, you know my heart, my every thought. Please give me the peace that I long for. Help me to be good to others but also to be good to myself. And please, oh please, help me to endure the loneliness that I feel in my heart! Maybe something wonderful will happen to me. It's all in your hands. Amen!"

CHAPTER TWO

It was Friday again and Maria woke up depressed. She'd had a nightmare about losing her job that made her think about what her supervisor, Linda Suarez, had told her at work that week. Linda was a Filipino four-feet-eight inches tall, slender with black hair that came to her shoulders. That week, she took Maria aside to tell her that their boss, Diane Lock, had mentioned she was planning to eliminate a couple of positions from the accounting department. Immediately, Maria felt that her job was in jeopardy. She told her co-workers, who also felt their positions were in jeopardy. Each of them thought that they would be the ones to go. It definitely created an atmosphere of uneasiness in the department.

Still in bed, Maria was thinking about her future. All she could see was the loss of her job and her failure to find another one. Everywhere she turned, in her mind, she saw closed doors. She feared losing her apartment, living in the street and worse still, having to go back to Italy. It would be a personal failure having to rebuild her life from scratch. She remembered how unhappy she had been while living in Italy and how happy she was to get away, when she married George. That wasn't the only reason she married him. She loved him. When he asked her to marry him after only knowing each other one week Maria said "yes" without fear. She felt safe with him. Going back to Italy for her would be a step backwards. Here in the United States, at least for now, she had a career.

In Italy all she could do was baby-sit or be a companion to an elderly person. Those positions didn't pay nearly enough. She would have to depend on her parents and she loathed that idea. Besides both her parents lived on meager pensions. Her father, on a disability pension, and her mother on a teacher's aid one.

Living in the small town of Onofrio, about thirty minutes from Naples, public transportation was almost non-existent. In Naples, where she would have to work, there were buses, but they were always crowded and never on time. She remembered the time she caught a man with his hands on her wallet. The bus had been so crowded. She just happened to turn her head and saw him as he was trying to take the wallet out of her purse. But Maria didn't lose her composure, she simply said "If you don't let go of my wallet I am going to punch you in the face". That worked, because the man got off the bus at the next stop.

Italy was out of the picture. She was not going back there. But how was she going to survive, if no one would give her a job? She totally believed that in her heart and anguish would grip her soul. Whenever she looked to the future, all she saw was an overwhelming darkness.

Once again, as she had many times before, Maria fell victim to this thought pattern. She decided she was going to kill herself but how? How was she going to kill herself? Not with pills. Pills would only make her sick, they would not kill her. She would just get stuck with hospital bills and the embarrassment, and then she would have to face all her co-workers. They already thought there was something wrong with her. No, she was going to use a gun. One bullet through the head. That should do it. But she didn't have a gun, so she would have to buy one. She got up from the couch and looked through the yellow pages. She looked under "Guns" and went through the list. Scrolling down the page, she found a store on the same street where she lived. She dialed the number listed and asked if they had guns.

"What kind of guns?" asked the clerk.

"Hand guns," she replied.

"Yes, we have them. Do you have the certificate?"

"What's that?" replied Maria.

"Why don't you come over and I'll tell you all about it?"

"Okay. Thank you."

Maria got dressed and walked toward the gun shop. On her way there, she thought about what she was going to do and she determined in her mind that she was going to kill herself. If she had a gun right then she would have already killed herself, she was so sure about it. Twenty minutes later she arrived. When she entered the store, there were two men behind the counter. They were both serving other customers, so Maria looked at the revolvers on display. Lots of them were used ones. She choose one that cost $75, because it was cheaper than the others and also because it was not bulky.

When one of the clerks was free, he approached her.

"How can I help you today?" he said, looking at her with an inquisitive look on his face.

"I want to see this used gun for $75. Can I hold it?" Maria made a conscious effort to control the tone of her voice so it wouldn't betray what was going through her head. The clerk took the gun out and showed it to her. He also showed her how to load and unload it.

Maria was fascinated. "A bullet from this gun can really kill a person?" she asked in disbelief.

"Yep. It sure can. That's why we have to screen people who want to buy one. Why do you want to buy a gun?" He looked at her intently while asking this question. Maria didn't look in his eyes when she answered.

"I live alone and I need a gun to protect myself."

He seemed satisfied with her answer. Then he told her that in order to buy the gun she would have to take a test. The law required it. It was called the BFSC, the Basic Firearms Safety Certificate. She could test for it, after she studied the booklet he was going to give her. The test cost $14 and if she failed she had until twelve the next day to retake the test, at no charge. After she passed the test she would have to fill out an application for the police to do a background investigation and if she passed that, she could buy the gun. Maria, disappointed, took the booklet, thanked the clerk, and left the store.

Back at the apartment, in her mind she went through the process of her suicide. She felt so alone and so hated. She saw herself dead, with a gunshot through her head. Before she killed herself she would have to do few things to make sure that her daughter would not suffer more than she needed to. She would have to write her a goodbye letter where she would leave instructions regarding her funeral. She wanted to be cremated. She would have to give her instructions about the money in the bank, about the change of address for her mail, the sale of the furniture, and so on. She saw her daughter distraught over her death, trying to take care of all the lose ends; she saw her crying and depressed over her death. She felt bad about it, so bad that she was having second thoughts. She didn't want her Elizabeth to suffer. If she killed herself Elizabeth would carry the pain the rest of her life, wondering why, asking herself why her mother killed herself without seeking help, and why she didn't have the courage to go on.

Just as it had happened before, and without her conscious knowledge, when the outlook on life got dark, she withdrew inside herself, shutting others from her completely. She lost hope and even though she was a very intelligent woman, she'd let irrational thoughts and fear get the best of her. Maria also thought that even if she passed the handgun BFSC test, she would not pass the police investigation. They would probably question her about being on medication and suffering from depression and Maria had a long history of depression. She had been taking medication for many years and the police would certainly find that out. Her records with the County Mental Health specified that she was chronic schizophrenic. They would never sell her a gun. But mostly it was the thought of Elizabeth in tears that she could not bear. So she decided that she was not going to do it, that she was going to face whatever came in the best way that she could.

Although she was unaware of it, at the time, this was a big step forward in her growth process. She was starting to look outside of herself, being considerate of herself and others while before she'd grab the first pills available and swallow them not thinking about the consequences.

She wanted to die and that was it. She was fearless.

Now, thirty years older, she was afraid of dying, of the afterlife, and of God's judgment. She asked God for forgiveness and decided that she was going to work on her faith and trust Him more. She had gone through so much already, she felt too tired to start all over again, but if that was God's will, so be it.

During all her married life she never had to work outside of the house. Being in the Navy, all her needs were taken care of: Food, housing, dental, health, entertainment. She could get up anytime she wanted in the morning and do the house chores according to her own schedule. Her life was stress free.

Ever since her divorce her life had been a constant struggle, full of fears. This created lot of stress, which affected her mental health, and this explained her deep, depressing moods. What would her future hold?

CHAPTER THREE

Maria was in the kitchen washing dishes when the phone rang. She dried her hands to answer the telephone.

"Hello?"

"Hi, Maria? This is Joanna. How are you?"

"I am fine, Joanna. Where are you?"

"I am downtown. May I come see you?"

"Yes, of course you may. Let me give you directions to my place." After hanging up, she finished washing the dishes and waited for Joanna to arrive. She was surprised by the call and wondered why she had called her. About twenty minutes later the phone rang. It was Joanna. She was downstairs.

"I'll be right down," Maria told her. She went downstairs and led her to her apartment.

"How are you, Joanna? It is so good to see you again. I wasn't expecting to hear from you. Is everything alright?"

"Everything is fine! I need to talk to you about something. You see, I am not from San Diego. I just drifted here from Minneapolis because it's warm here all year long and you don't suffer too much at night if you are homeless like me. I didn't say anything on the trolley when we met because you were a stranger and I didn't know you, but now I think that I must tell you the truth. I didn't have any friends to go visit that day. I don't know a soul. I don't have anywhere to go and I thought that maybe I could stay with you for a couple of nights. That is, if you don't mind. After all I am a stranger to you and if you say no I will understand. "

Maria was taken by surprise. She didn't know what to say. She looked at Joanna as if to read her character and see if she really liked her as a person, enough to let her spend the night or nights at her place.

"Well, let me think about that for a minute. This is such a surprise!"

"Take your time. I am a bum. I don't have anywhere to go or anything to do!" Joanna took a strand of her blonde hair and twisted it between her fingers. Maria had noticed it before on the trolley and came to the conclusion that she must be nervous even though she was trying to appear cool.

"Well, I guess you could stay here for a couple of nights. Let's give it a try and see what happens! In the meantime we need to talk so that we can get to know each other better. Where in Minneapolis are you from?"

"From the old part of the town. My parents were not rich, so when I was eighteen I found a job and left. But it wasn't much. I could barely make ends meet, so I stayed in the neighborhood; it was cheaper there. I didn't like my job, so I quit and got me a job as cashier in a supermarket. I left it when they accused me of stealing money from them, which I didn't do. You've got to believe me. Because of it I was not able to find another job so I started drifting and I have been homeless ever since. I came to San Diego because, like I told you before, it's sunny and warm all year around and that's nice when you have to sleep in the street. Nobody wants to give you a job if you're homeless, and you don't wear nice clothes, and aren't well groomed. So, basically, this is my story. I would like to settle down, get a good job, and support myself. I am penniless. I had to beg for the money to call you and that was not easy to do. People here don't respond well to begging. Is there anything else you like to know ma'm?"

"Yes, I like to know if you use drugs. Sorry to ask you this question, but I don't know you and I hope you understand my reason for asking it."

"My answer is no. I don't use drugs and I have never used them.

Besides where would I get the money to pay for them? Look, if you have doubts, I understand. And I understand if you say no. I didn't mean to put you on the spot. Sorry!" Joanna's face had turned red and Maria couldn't tell if she was bashful or angry at her for asking those questions.

"No, it's quite all right. You can stay, like I said. Let me fix the bed for you. You can sleep in the living room and tomorrow you can take a nice, long shower and go job hunting while I am at work. I would lend you my clothes but we wear a different size, so that is not possible. I will fix you something to eat if you are hungry. Are you hungry?" As soon as she said it Maria felt stupid for asking that question. Of course she was hungry.

"If it isn't too much trouble, yes, I am starving. I haven't eaten since this morning and it is eight o'clock at night. Thank you for your kindness!"

"Don't mention it. Jesus said we should feed the hungry. How does a couple of cheese sandwiches sound?"

"That would be fine. Thank you!" *This isn't easy for her,* thought Maria, *she's got pride and she hates to beg. Her life must be hell and I was feeling sorry for myself.*

While Maria went to the kitchen to fix the sandwiches, Joanna sat in the living room watching television, waiting. She couldn't wait to eat; she was really starving. She almost grabbed the sandwiches out of Maria's hand. Maria also gave her a glass of milk and it felt wonderful to gulp it down. She was finished in no time. She helped Maria fix her bed and she felt a knot in her stomach. It was so kind of her to let her stay that she was overwhelmed with thankfulness. She tried to put herself in Maria's place. Would she let a stranger spend the night in her house? Somebody you met only once and who showed up out of nowhere? She didn't know what to answer. Thank God for Maria, she told herself.

"Well, the bed is done. You can go to sleep anytime you want or you can watch television if you like. I go to sleep early because I have to get up at four-thirty in the morning to go to work. I'll give you some spare keys so you can get in and out when you need to. Here is a towel for when you take a shower in the morning or if you prefer you can take a shower before you go to sleep. It's up to you!"

"I really need to wash-up tonight. I haven't had a bath in so long I feel so dirty. All the gunk of San Diego must be stuck to my body."

"Make yourself at home, Joanna!"

"Thank you so much Maria. I really appreciate it!"

Joanna went to the bathroom and took a long shower. It felt so good she wanted to stay in the shower for hours, but she didn't want to abuse Maria's kindness, so she stepped out. She put her clothes back on since she didn't have a nightgown but to her surprise Maria was waiting with a nightgown in her hand and gave it to her as she came out.

"I have this large nightgown that my aunt gave to me when I went to Italy last time. It is too big for me, so it will probably fit you. You're welcome to keep it. It is a gift!

"Thank you! I don't know what to say!" Joanna looked at the nightgown. It was too big for her too but she didn't mind.

"You're welcome! Now I am going to bed. Sorry but I need my sleep. I will try to be real quite in the morning so I don't wake you up. Good night, Joanna."

"Good night, Maria!" Joanna was thankful but fearful at the same time. After all she didn't know Maria either. What if she was a cuckoo and stabbed her in the middle of the night? She pulled her bag close to her pillow and made sure her knife was handy, in case she needed it.

CHAPTER FOUR

When Maria arrived at work in the morning, her supervisor, Linda Suarez, had more bad news. She said that her boss, Diane Lock, told her that she would be trying a different billing system enabling the computer to automatically send out invoices eliminating the need to type them up anymore. That was part of Maria's job. She felt anxiety building up in her. Sweating she wished her supervisor would just quit talking to her about it, though she was too polite to say so. She tried to concentrate and not to think about it, but it was hard.

In the meantime, at Maria's apartment, Joanna was just waking up. She stretched out, still not believing her good fortune. Nothing had happened during the night. It was so nice to wake up in a bed with clean sheets and a warm blanket that she lingered in bed for a while before getting up to make coffee.

There was no coffee maker, but she did find instant coffee. She sat in the living room, sipping her coffee with delight. Going back to the kitchen, she found some eggs in the refrigerator, which she scrambled, and toasted two slices of bread. She also found some strawberry jelly to spread on the toast. She was elated.

She went through her mind thinking about what to do that day. She was supposed to go look for a job, *but later* she told herself. *Right now I want to enjoy this.*

After she ate breakfast she gave a look at the apartment. It was a one-bedroom apartment, with large rooms and a very soft carpet. She stepped into the bedroom and saw that the mattresses were on the floor with no base. One mattress was covered with books while the other must have been the one that Maria slept on. It was unmade. The room was lined by bookshelves, which were completely filled by books. She read the title of the books and saw that the majority were textbooks. No novels of any kind. *She must be a brainy person*, she thought.

A notebook lying on the floor caught her attention. She picked it up and opened it. It was a college notebook with essays for an English class. She debated whether to read them or not, but her curiosity won. The first essay was titled:

"The Winning Ticket"

The iron gate bordered the cemented sidewalk, standing guard to a congregation of nuns and numerous young girls. I felt so small walking along the pathway leading to the convent, so large and high-sided, made even higher by the rows of cypresses planted along the way. This was my home now and I had to let go of my mother's hand. The convent was self-contained and was very large and comfortable, but it did not have a school within its structure. Every morning the nuns gathered us in rows of two and the daily procession marched towards the middle of town where we had to cross the main street to arrive at the newly completed elementary school. The inside of the school was bathed in spurts of white light coming from the several large windows. Once inside, we would scatter to other groups and form new lines each leading us to our assigned classrooms.

Serotti Adele was the name of my elementary teacher and she was "My Beloved Teacher" for five years, lovingly guiding me along the path of knowledge and taking special delight from my willingness to learn. She would exhort me into reading for our daily exercises and I enjoyed it so much I would always offer myself to read whenever she asked for a volunteer. She was not married and for some reason I remember liking that; maybe possessiveness? I remember wondering about her private life and where she lived in the small town, maybe somewhere on the same street we had to cross every morning. The outer world held a fascination for me, being cloistered within our fenced world and I'd try to picture her inside her home doing various things, living all alone. That really fascinated me because being a little woman myself I was very atten- tive to the woman's role within our society. At that time in my life she was a symbol, a symbol of freedom surpassed by no one else I knew. All the females I knew had binding ties: The nuns to their reli- gion, my mother to my father, my aunts to their families, little girls to their siblings and their parents, all except her. For all I tried, I couldn't even imagine what kind of private life she had once away from us children.

That particular day something exciting was going to take place at our school. A lottery was going to be held in the huge atrium and we were all out of our seats, feeling the excitement of the event, walking around, meeting with our friends from other classrooms, enjoying the anarchy of the moment.

"If you want to participate in the lottery you have to buy the tickets, children," Ms Serotti told us – and the children went to their seats to get their money – "the prize is a wooden clock with compartments for jewelry at the bottom. Very beautiful," she explained further.

I had no money so I did not buy any ticket and I had resigned myself to my fate when Ms Serotti came towards me offering a ticket she had bought just for me. I was exhilarated at my good fortune and my heart was filled with happiness for the kindness of my teacher who had not forgotten that I lived in the convent and that I had no money of my own. To the little child that I was, the price of the ticket seemed to be a small fortune and my hand held the ticket tightly inside the pocket of my white school uniform, afraid that I might lose it.

It was time to get ready for the drawing of the "Wooden Clock" and all of us, children and teachers alike, left the classrooms like a storm of bees, all converging at a certain point in the atrium where, held on a pedestal, was the magnificent prize. A basket full of tickets lay nearby and we were eagerly waiting for the drawing to take place. It was presided over by the principal of the school. We all had a close peek at the prize while waiting and when the principal arrived, the drawing took place. "The number of the winning ticket is..." the official announced, and my teacher checked the number on my ticket. Like in a dream I saw her raising her hand saying, "Here is the winning ticket, right here! Congratulations," she said, excited to me. I felt very fortunate and very unique because out of about four hundred tickets, my ticket won. The eyes of all the children were on me and that made me feel very important. Ms Serotti's eyes were shining too because it was as if she had made a little miracle happen that day with the kindness of her heart. My classmates all congratulated me on our way back to our classroom. "What are you going to do with the clock?" they asked me. "I am going to give it to my mother," I replied imagining the clock sitting proudly on my mother's buffet while my mother would wash the floor and dust the room, being proud of her daughter for having given her such an important gift.

I don't know what happened to the clock because I don't remember carrying it back to the convent with me; I don't even remember holding it once; my teacher must have brought it to the convent or given it to one of our escorts. They knew about it for sure because Sister Adele (our guardian) approached me that afternoon as I was walking from the dining room to the courtyard to meet my friends for recreation. "Congratulations," she said to me. "I heard that you have won a beautiful wooden clock today." Her tone was very deferential as if she was talking to an adult and that aroused conflicting emotions within me because I felt important and suspicious at the same time. This was the nun who beat me when I misbehaved. What kind of trick was she playing on me? I thought anxiously. "You know, I thought that the Mother Superior would be very pleased to receive that clock for a gift; what would you say if we gave it to her?" she asked in a suave tone. The thought of my mother cleaning the room, proud of her prize possession crossed my mind for an instant. Mother Superior was like a mother to me also and I was her favorite one because she invited me often into her apartment to help her clean up or read something to her. "All right," I said to her and ran away eager to meet my friends for our games, forgetting everything about the matter by that evening. I can buy my mother many beautiful clocks now so I don't regret my decision; I just know that a little love and kindness goes a long way, but it strikes me as odd giving a jewelry holding clock to a nun who wore no jewels. Maybe she put her hairpins in it if she had any hair under her veil. I would never find that out!

CHAPTER FIVE

The next essay was titled *"In the Middle of August"*. It read,

The day of my marriage is memorable to me also for reasons other than the obvious ones. I was married in Naples, which is located in the upper southern part of Italy, in the middle of fiery August, around midday (see: "Spaghetti Western"). The man I married, an American sailor, was supposed to meet me at the altar and, traditionally, the bride cannot see the groom prior to the wedding. Around nine a.m. I went to make my confession in the Catholic Church, which was located at the street level, adjacent the hundred or so long, stony steps that led to the four hundred years old building I lived in. As I was leaving the coolness of the church, I saw between the columns in the large entranceway, my fiancé, squinting in the sun, walking to his parked car. I almost called him but remembered the tradition that the groom is not supposed to see the bride before the wedding and furtively hid in the darkness, behind the colonnade. I had my hair in rollers underneath a silky scarf and I was glad he didn't see me. What a way to start that day! After he left, I quickly went home and started to prepare myself to meet the photographer for the customary photographs with the immediate members of the family prior to the wedding.

That particular day was in the middle of "Ferragosto" week, a week in which, customarily, most businesses and self-employed

people in Italy take a vacation and hordes of people desert the steamy cities to find relief at the beaches. One of those people was my hairdresser. I had decided, therefore, to have a perm two days before. That morning I shampooed my hair and put on rollers. I was eagerly taking off my rollers, already envisioning myself with a beautiful hairdo; as I was unraveling the last roller a horrible vision was staring at me from the mirror: Oh no! It was a disaster. Things got worse when I combed my hair. What used to be shiny, nicely curled hair, had become a straw-like, pointed, stiff mess. Fortunately I had to wear a bonnet-like cap with a long veil trailing behind, so I did my best to hide the "horror" under it.

I was the last one to leave the apartment; I was almost late. Everybody was waiting for me below at the top of the steps. I nervously put my hand on my father's arm and we led the procession to the church. Everything was happening as I saw it happen so many times to so many people, but this time it was I and it felt almost unreal. As we entered the church the organ started to play to accompany a voice singing the "Ave Maria". The altar was full of fragrant flowers, and one could smell the wax of the lit candles, whose light, combined with other lights, gave the scene the appearance of a theatrical stage. The gold embroidery of the priest's attire shone intermittently while he recited the wedding mass. My legs trembled under the long gown and I was so preoccupied that I paid no attention to the ceremony until, of course, the moment came when we had to recite the vows. The groom was very nervous also and accidentally switched the rings by putting his ring on my finger, which was too large, and my ring on his finger, which was too small.

Once on the outside of the church we exchanged the rings while the guests looked anxiously towards us wondering why we were taking our rings off.

As the guests left for the reception at the restaurant, we went on a photographic expedition through the most panoramic areas of the deserted city. One of the stops was by the sea, on the little beach I used to sunbathe on every summer. Hardly anyone was there except for a group of little girls in bathing suits who started chatting with me. I asked the photographer to take a picture of all of us together and it turned out to be one of my favorites because of the oddity of the contrasting attire and the steam rising from the seawater. The smell of the ocean was so strong I started to think about seafood and that thought made me hungry. Fortunately we were almost done. After a short while, we drove away to the restaurant owned by my uncle, located on top of a hill in the suburbs of Naples.

Clusters of purple wisteria, intermingled with vines full of ripening grapes, adorned the rustic portico, welcoming us with its pleasant shade as we strolled to the restaurant. Applause welcomed us as we took our place at the center of the long table, reserved for us. More picture taking followed, this time with all the guests as a memento for all to cherish and to enrich the family photo-albums.

Later, as the bride, I, escorted by a couple of female family members, went to change into formal clothing to readily depart for the honeymoon, the wedding cake and champagne were being prepared by the bartender (my bearded cousin). I dreaded taking the cap off and I did the best I could to make myself presentable.

After cutting the cake and drinking the champagne we departed showered by confetti, which covered my hair making me want to "run" away.

Joanna finished reading the second essay. Putting the notebook where she found it, she felt a twinge of guilt because the contents were personal but she reassured herself thinking that the essays were written for a school assignment. She thought of what she was going to do for the day and decided to get ready and look for a job. Realizing how lucky she was to have found a place to stay, at least for a little while, she was very thankful to Maria for giving her this opportunity. Maria was a kind and caring woman, she decided.

Unzipping her bag to see if she could find something suitable to wear, she put away the knife and scolded herself for being silly. She found a pair of black pants and a turquoise shirt. They were all wrinkled so she looked around the apartment for an iron. It was on the floor by the couch. She couldn't find the ironing board so she ironed her clothes on the couch.

She got dressed, combed her hair, put on some of Maria's make-up that she found in the bathroom and, grabbing the spare keys that Maria had left her, she left the apartment hoping for the best.

CHAPTER SIX

Maria got home from work at six-thirty. Joanna was sitting on the couch watching the news on television. She greeted Maria with a big smile, feeling uncomfortable at being caught doing nothing.

"How was your day?" she asked.

"It was depressing. My supervisor keeps telling me that my job might be eliminated. I just wish that she'd stop talking about it. It makes me nervous and I can't relax. I am always uptight when I am at work."

"I hope it won't happen!"

"So do I. I had to work hard to get to where I am now. I'd hate to have to start all over again. I hate going to job interviews, filling out applications. Speaking of which, how was your day? Any luck in your job hunting?"

"No, unfortunately! I walked so much today, my feet are killing me. I went downtown and applied at all the stores where I saw 'Help Wanted' signs. On the applications I put your address and phone number. I also put you down as reference, I hope you don't mind."

"No. Not at all! Are you hungry? Silly me, why do I ask? Of course you're hungry. Have you eaten anything today?" Maria was tired and all she wanted to do was sit down in front of the television. If she'd been by herself she'd just grabbed something but with Joanna there she had to cook a full meal.

"I had some breakfast this morning. That's about it."

"Well, let's see what I can come up with! How about spaghetti and a salad?"

"That sounds pretty good. May I help you?"

"Sure. You fix the salad and I fix the spaghetti. How's that?"

"Great!"

They both went to the kitchen to fix dinner.

Maria took a can of tomato sauce. She put some oil in a pan, some garlic and let it cook for a little while, only until the garlic was brown. She removed the garlic and poured in the tomato sauce. She added salt, pepper, and some basil leaves and let it cook. She asked Joanna, who was busy washing the lettuce for the salad,

"Tell me more about yourself. Your childhood! Did you always live in Minneapolis?"

"Yes, my brother and I were adopted, but by different families. I was seven years old when it happened. We went through foster homes before that. I haven't seen my brother since then. He was six years old. I loved him so much. It broke my heart when we were separated."

"It's a sad story. You really had a hard life, didn't you? What about your biological mother, do you remember her at all?"

"Oh, yes. I do. She was beautiful but she had a drinking problem and I think that she also used drugs. My father left her and she was taking care of us on her own. He didn't pay any child support. But her lifestyle was what got her in trouble with Social Services. I think some neighbors called and reported that she was neglecting us. She would go to work at night and leave us alone at home. I was very scared, fearing that she might not come home every night and would leave us like my daddy did. It was very frightening."

"You didn't have any relatives that could have taken care of you while your mom went to work?"

"We did but my mom was too proud to ask for help. They were not talking to her because she got married to a guy they didn't like and they had warned her that he was no good, my mom told me. In fact he left her."

"And how old were you when your father left?"

"I don't remember. Around three years old I guess, by what my mom told me."

Maria put spaghetti in the boiling water and stirred them so they wouldn't stick. Joanna was almost done with the salad. She offered to set up the table. "Sure," replied Maria.

The dinner was very good, the best spaghetti Joanna had ever eaten. She dipped some French bread into the spaghetti sauce and licked the plate clean. They washed the dishes and put them away, then sat on the couch. The television had been on all the time but Maria turned it off. She wanted to talk some more to Joanna.

"Would you like some coffee?"

"No, I better not drink any otherwise I won't be able to go to sleep."

"How about some ice cream?"

"That would be nice. I haven't had any ice cream in about six months. I love ice cream!"

They had some raspberry and cream ice cream. Joanna savored each bite with delight. You could tell she really loved the stuff. Maria offered some more and she accepted. Food was always on her mind because of all the times she didn't have enough to eat, or money to buy food. She felt sorry for herself, but ever so thankful.

"Tell me about the family who adopted you. What were they like?"

"They couldn't have children, that's why they chose to adopt me. But they only wanted one child even though the Social Service worker offered to have them adopt my brother as well so we wouldn't be separated. They refused because they could only afford to adopt one child. My adoptive father was a postal worker and my adoptive mother did not work so their finances were limited. I never lacked anything though. Occasionally they would buy me toys and there were always presents under the Christmas tree for me. My adoptive mother was always loving towards me and did her best to make me happy. My adoptive father is another story but I don't want to go into that right now. Maybe when I get to know you better I will tell you about it. It is very delicate in nature and very personal."

"It's okay! You don't have to talk about it if you don't want to. When you're ready to tell me you will and I promise to respect your privacy. I promise that I won't tell a living soul about anything you tell me."

"Thank you!"

"Let me ask you something. Are you saved?"

"What do you mean saved? I don't understand."

"Have you accepted Jesus Christ as your Lord and Savior?"

"No, I don't believe that I have. Why?"

"Because it is important for your soul. When you accept Jesus Christ as your Lord and Savior you are immediately forgiven for your sins and you are guaranteed to go to Heaven when you die. You repent of your sins and the blood of Jesus washes you clean. God gave His only begotten Son for us so that we might be saved. What kind of religious upbringing have you had?"

"I don't have any. My adoptive parents didn't go to church or read a Bible and they never taught me anything about it. They were good people, at least my adoptive mother was, but they were not religious."

"Would you like to learn about it? It is for your own good. I go to church every week, maybe sometime you'd like to go with me. How does that sound?"

"Can I take a rain-check on that? I am not into prayers. I don't even know if I believe in God. Religion has just not ever been part of my life."

"Well, prayers really help. In fact, even if you don't believe in it I want to pray for you tonight. Let's just hold hands and pray that you find a job tomorrow."

Maria took hold of Joanna's hands. She could feel reticence in Joanna but she didn't care; she knew she was right and nothing would stop her.

"Dear Lord," she said bowing her head. "We come to you tonight because we have need of your love and forgiveness. Please cleanse us from all ungodliness and impurity. We lift up Joanna who is in need of a job. We ask, Lord, that you will guide her steps tomorrow and put people in her path who will be kind to her and offer her a job. Anything honest will do, Lord, for the moment, because she is trying to get off the streets and be able to support herself. We pray that you'll give her strength and courage to go out with a positive attitude. We ask all this in Jesus' precious name. Amen!"

Joanna didn't say anything. Her hands were limp in Maria's hands. She just sat there, uncomfortable. Maria was not discouraged by her reaction. She had witnessed the power of prayers and was sure in her heart that the Lord was going to answer her request. A long silence followed the prayer. Finally Joanna spoke.

"I have a confession to make. This morning I was looking around the apartment and I found a notebook on the floor in the bedroom. I read some of the essays that you wrote for your English class. I hope you don't mind, Maria." She seemed really sorry and Maria was moved by it.

"I am trying to remember what I wrote. If the essays were for an English class I am sure it was all right for you to read them. Don't worry about it, Joanna. In fact, there is one essay that I would like you to read. I wrote it for my psychology class. I want you to read it because it is about a time in my life that was very difficult and if I try to tell you, it might not be the same thing. I prefer it if you read it. Don't worry about it being late, tomorrow is Friday and I don't have to go to work. Let me get the essay so that you can read it."

Maria went to the closet were she kept the box with all her school papers and came back holding some papers stapled together.

"Here Joanna, read it!"

Joanna took the papers that Maria handed her and began to read. The essay was titled *"Who Am I?"* It read,

"Who Am I?" I am a specimen of the human race, who at the moment inhabits the planet "Earth". Of course I am talking about someone I should know better than what I actually do, namely myself, which is a pity because I could have saved myself and others a lot of the difficulties I have encountered so far, out of plain ignorance. But this is one reason I voluntarily choose to work on this topic: To solve the endless mystery of one's self.

My "Self" has been waiting eagerly, patiently and painfully to be discovered. So far I have walked in a daze, mystified by other's perception of me, becoming attentive to every little clue that I could get, by the way they treated me or responded to the outer projection

of myself. I have decided to step aside and observe this phenomenon of my persona. I see myself walking, talking, smiling, thinking, crying, studying, and doing many other things, trying to be objective and kind. Mostly kind. There is a reason for that; sadly I have realized that, over the years, I have not been very good towards myself. Ever since I was fourteen years old I have continuously tried to put an end to my life, mostly by means of ingesting pills of every kind. I am one of the luckiest people I know, a walking miracle, because Fate has been merciful towards me. I suffered no major consequences, at least physically, from the abuses I have inflicted to my poor system. Mentally is a different story. Mentally, I should have found a good and kind therapist at the age of fourteen, when my depression started.

I remember everything so clearly. I don't think that I will ever forget it. The saddest part is that for years I carried this huge amount of guilt and feelings of inadequacy while there were sound, medical reasons for the way I was feeling. I had never had the opportunity to understand this until recently while undergoing clinical therapy. It is amazing how simple life can become and problems begin to dissolve, like a fog in the warmth of the sun.

At fourteen I went to live with a family other than my own. The reason? I volunteered for a position of house helper, secretary. The lady of the house was ill and she needed someone to clean and do the cooking, while her husband occasionally had need of a typist. Their family came from nobility – the husband being a Duke. I was truly impressed by this, coming from a poor family with roots in the peasantry. I grew up with the "Cinderella Syndrome" and up to that age life was such a novelty and so full of wonderful possibilities.

I considered others above me, gave them more esteem than they deserved, out of innocence and feelings of inferiority. Several times I have walked back into my past and comforted the beautiful, unhappy child that I was. Pure, clean, and so totally ignorant of how the world was, who suddenly found herself exposed to a whole repertoire of emotions and behaviors for which she was totally unprepared. I had lived in a convent for about five years, until the age of eleven, then lived in the country until I was twelve years old. My family later moved to Naples, which is a big city where one learns a different perspective on life than living in the country.

The family I was working for was composed of a husband, a wife, a son, and a daughter. Plus, very often, especially for meals, the wife's brother would join us. I remember him particularly well because he was huge, totally unsophisticated, and used to clean his fingernails with a fork at the end of the meals. That totally disgusted me. I used to sleep on the couch in the living room and for a little while everything was fine. Then, suddenly, someone was touching me in the morning, under my pajamas, stroking my breast. The very first time I didn't realize what was happening. I was asleep and it took a little while before I awoke to the realization of what was happening. Later I would pretend to be asleep and when the duke would see me rouse from my sleep he would withdraw his hand and pretend that nothing had happened. The swine. I didn't know how to react. I was afraid that he would mistreat me if I showed him that I was aware of what he was doing and did not like it, so I kept silent. It only lasted for a short time because I began getting up before he came to wake me up, therefore resolving the dilemma.

I was angry, though. I was also blaming myself and having feelings of shame. I felt betrayed, dirtied. I also felt disgust for the man because his wife was laying in the next room, ill and unaware. That was my first experience with the hypocrisy of high society where everything seems to be perfect and smooth on the outside but where putrid waters lay just beneath the surface.

What I realize now is that that particular event triggered my long depression. I remember writing a journal of how I was feeling and a passage comes to my mind,

"What is the purpose to go on living? The same endless story, day after day, step after step, without any real reason." All of a sudden life had lost its shine. I wasn't waiting for something wonderful to happen to me, but something dreadful, and the waiting became unbearable. I carried this feeling with me every day, without confiding to my family nor to my host. The son and daughter of the Duke were both older than me. She was an art student who confided to me that she had a lover. He was married and had two daughters. She made me swear not to tell anyone. The son was

aspiring to become a journalist and wrote a sport's column for the daily newspaper. The mother and daughter did not get along very well; one day I witnessed them fighting, pulling each other's hair. I don't know if the mother knew that her daughter had a lover. He was an art dealer and I suspect that she made copies of famous art works for him.

The son and daughter had always been nice to me. On that unforgettable day I had cooked, washed the dishes, and had a little time off in the afternoon. The daughter was on the phone, making soliciting phone calls for a part-time job she had. The son was in his room resting on the bed. Since he was not sleeping I went in to chat with him. The door was open and we just talked for a little while. I had no idea that this was going to trigger the reaction it did from Marianna, the daughter. I was gaily going to chat with her in the dining room when she called me a whore. I was deeply hurt because my conscience was clean and whatever made her say that must just have come out of her disorderly life and the conflicts she was having about herself.

They both left after a while. I was all alone in the house. Very calmly I went to the bathroom medicine cabinet and grabbed two containers full of pills and I swallowed them all. I wrote a little note to my host, put on my coat and left. Walking the streets I approached a church. The priest was closing its gate: "Father, I want to confess," I said to him. "The church is closed now. Come back later," he replied sternly as if to say: "Don't bother me now!" This is a conspiracy, I felt in my heart. I kept on walking. The thought never occurred to me to call my family. I didn't think they would have understood, I was afraid they would have called me a whore also just like Marianna did because I had been in the bedroom talking to the son. Whatever I did it must be terrible or she wouldn't have said those things to me. What did I know about life? Nothing. I knew nothing about life. I was pure. I was still a virgin. I had never hurt anyone. Just like that day in the convent when I was crying on the bed, in the huge dormitory, thinking that no one loved me, I was crying inside. Who cares though, right? The priest had just told me to come back later. The pills would not wait; Father I want to confess!

I went to a pharmacy and I bought some more pills, eighty of them. I swallowed them all, one by one, without water as if they were candies. I had gotten to a busier part of town. The city was busy and lively; people shopping, working, meeting friends, searching for fun things to do. I saw a friend go by on the motorcycle; I thought about calling to him; it would be nice to go for a ride, but I remembered the pills. No, too dangerous, I might fall off the bike, how would he feel? A little ahead there was another church. The door was open so I went in. A quiet refuge, a shelter for my poor, lonely soul. I looked around: The church was empty except for one lady. Walking to one of the niches dedicated to the various saints, I chose Sainte Lucia, who is the Sainte of the eyesight. It was so silent I could hear my heartbeat.

I sat quietly for a while, thinking that it would soon be over. What a lonely way to die. Did I think how it was going to be after I died? No. Did I think that God was going to punish me? No, there was no God. There was nothing, only the end of my pain. I lit a cigarette. Oh no! That was a sacrilege! Ask me if I care? It doesn't matter. It soothes my pain. I calmly finished my cigarette pushing the butt under the bench so no one would see it and beat me up while I was dead and then I lay down on the long bench. The timing was just right. I closed my eyes and it was the end.

My eyes are shut but I am screaming. I am screaming and jerking my body upwards. I am tied up. Somebody has tied up my hands and feet. My eyes start to open, I see a blur: A woman in a white dress with something white over her head.

"Marianna, why do you hate me?" Those were the first words I said. She didn't answer, she kept on going about her business. I start screaming again. Someone slaps me in the face.

"Where am I? Is this hell?" No, it's just the hospital. Later on I was told that a lady from out of town had gone to the church to pray to her favorite Saint; she had found me and called the ambulance. I never met that lady nor did I seek her out. They also told me that I had been in a coma for five days and the doctor, seeing how young I was, did not want to scar me by drilling a hole in my throat as it was customary, but decided to insert a tube down into my stomach. I am glad she did.

Marianna came to see me in the hospital; she asked me what I wanted her to bring me. I said "shoes" and she agreed to buy them for me. I never saw her again except once, walking downtown. Her father, a lawyer, came to see me with his lawyer. The two culprits were trying to unload their guilt and giving me no rest. A doctor with blue eyes came to see me. I only saw him once. I was the youngest in the room of four or six, I don't remember. My mother came to visit every day. I did not tell my parents anything for some time and when they brought me home I would not even talk to them. One night, my mother and my sister came in and sat by my bed and we started to talk. That's when I told them what had happened to me in that house. They were not angry at me, but they were angry at them, so it helped me to get things off my chest. Eventually I started to come out of that state I was in and made quick progress. But I should have received some kind of counseling, which at that time I didn't. We were poor people from the country, we didn't know any better. Even if that option had been available, we would have thought it probably was not for us. We were second-class citizens.

Now I am living here in San Diego. I am waiting. Waiting for answers, answers to tell me what happened this past seven years. I feel at times that everybody knows me, but when I walk the street I am just another person people don't know. After my divorce, seven years ago, my ex-husband left all my belongings in the street. I had no home, no family, no job, no money. I thought I had no rights. I didn't even know there was a constitution because I was not a citizen and once again I ended up in the hospital. People were nice to me and I to them, but I was screaming inside. It hurt so much I thought my heart was going to break. The doctors wanted me to sign some papers stating that I was schizophrenic. Are you crazy? I am not signing that. I am just hurting. I am not crazy. I don't even want to take any medication. Doctors laugh, they seem to have fun. It confuses me; I think that everybody knows me and that it is all a joke. They will tell me what is really going on and everything will make sense. One day it will all make sense. I had no idea that others could know so much about me without me knowing anything about them. People intrude on my privacy and they never ask for permission. I became mistrustful and defensive towards everyone. I sought for God but I found nothing; just a floor and nothing. I felt "nothing". It was terrible!

I think that my depression reached a peak a couple of years ago and now I am definitely coming out of it. The magic click happened when I realized how my depression has been getting the best of me all of these years. Now I am on my way to complete recovery and I am never going to be depressed again, hopefully! Amen to that!

CHAPTER SEVEN

Joanna had tears in her eyes by the time she finished reading the essay. She handed it back to Maria and said: "It's a very sad story. Too bad you had to have such an experience. Did anything happen to that man for what he did to you?"

"No. My mother never pressed charges against him. They just forgot about it and so did I, at least I didn't think about it anymore until I had to write the essay."

A long silence followed. Maria was thinking of something to say when she heard Joanna sobbing. She was puzzled and concerned. She seemed really distressed, in pain. All of a sudden Maria had a revelation.

"You have been molested, haven't you? Tell me who the slime, the scum bag was that did that to you!"

"It was Raul, my adoptive father. He started molesting me soon after I was adopted, when I was seven years old. He had a drinking problem and would go out to drink almost every night. When he'd come back he would come to my room and start touching me, my private parts, my breast even if I didn't have any at that time. He would tell me that horrible things would happen to me if I ever told anyone about it. My clothes would catch on fire, or they would put me in prison because I was a bad girl. He said I was making him do those things to me and that I liked it and wanted him to do it."

Joanna took the Kleenex that Maria was offering her and wiped the tears from her eyes and face. She seemed to be breathing a little better now, almost relieved that she had told her. Maria's story had really touched her and had brought up all the pent up emotions. Emotions she had not allowed to come to the surface before, but that now felt like a river overflowing.

"I never told anyone before. I am so relieved that I did not catch on fire. He really had me scared all those years when I lived in his house. I wanted the molestation to stop and I asked him several times, but he would always come back, at night and do those things to me. He would just touch me. He never had actual sex with me, but that was wrong anyway. He would get aroused with me then he would go in his bedroom and have sex with his wife. She would not even wake up from sleep. She slept like a log. He knew that, he told me, and that's why he was able to get away with it for so many years. She never once woke up. Her name is Felicia.

She and Raul are children of immigrants from Cuba. They spoke Spanish but only when they got into arguments so I never knew what they were arguing about. They never taught me to speak Spanish but I would catch a word now and then that I thought I recognized. I think that the majority of their fights were about money and his drinking problem. I sure don't miss him, but I do miss Felicia a lot. She was so motherly and down to earth. I still call her every now and then but I never told her that I was homeless. I always tell her that I have my own place or that I am staying with friends."

"You can call her from my phone, if you like. You'll pay me back when you find a job, which I am sure you will. I am very positive about it. So, how long did the molestation last? How old were you when he stopped?'

"He never stopped. Not until I left at eighteen. He came into my room the last night I was there and I begged him to leave, but he wouldn't. He said that he would call his wife and tell her that I had tried to entice him. So I let him do it to me but I was crying. The thing that I am most ashamed about it is the fact that I sometime enjoyed it so I told myself that I was a bad girl. That he was right and I was really afraid that they would put me in prison."

"Don't worry and don't be ashamed. It is natural to enjoy it.

That's what most women feel when they are fondled. He is a scum bag and I am sure that in his heart he knows that. He has put all his blame on you for all this years. You must get rid of that. You are not at fault. He is. He was supposed to take care of you, protect you, instead he choose to molest you. If he had been a Christian he would not have done that. That's why it is so important that you give your life to Jesus Christ. He redeems and frees us from all guilt because he forgives all sins, except the blasphemy to the Holy Spirit. Let Jesus come into your heart and pray to him. Put all your problems at His feet and let Him take it from there. Of course you need some counseling because what happened to you caused you a lot of problems. Problems you need to deal with if you want to have a more balanced and healthy life. It might take you years of therapy, like me, before you heal, but it is worth it. The guilt that you feel, I have felt too. I can relate to what happened to you because I carried an enormous amount of guilt for a long time, but when I came to Jesus it all left. Now when I feel some guilt I tell myself 'I forgive you' and I immediately feel better. Tell the Lord tonight that you are sorry for all your sins and He will accept you into His fold. Trust Him and Him only."

"That's easy to say and hard to do. I really would like to go to counseling but it is so expensive that it sounds like luxury right now. I can't even buy clothes for myself, where would I get the money for therapy?"

"There are agencies that will treat you according to your income. Once you find a job you can apply and they will charge you according to what you make. Maybe you can go to County Mental Health like I did. They have very good therapists there and they don't charge you a lot."

"Maria, this all depends if I find a job and if I have a place to stay. How long are you willing to let me stay with you?"

"As long as it takes. Until you get on your own two feet. I must warn you though that if you talk to anyone in the building you must not tell them that you live here with me but that you are just visiting, otherwise they will increase my rent. Maybe, when you find a job and have regular income, we might tell them and pay the increase but not until then. I only shared a place once since my divorce and it sure is a lot cheaper that way, let me tell you. Well, thank you for confiding in me. It's time for me to go to bed now. I'll see you in the morning. Good night Joanna!"

"Good night Maria and thank you! For everything."

After Maria went to her bedroom Joanna unfolded the futon and made her bed. She was really exhausted and couldn't wait to lie down. She thought about what Maria had told her about Jesus Christ but couldn't bring herself to believe in it. Of course she had heard other people talk about Jesus Christ before but she never related it to herself; she was a bad girl, remember? She was not worthy of anyone's love. Why would Jesus Christ love her? But she silently said a prayer in her heart anyway, even if she didn't believe in it. She closed her eyes and was soon asleep.

Next morning Maria woke up at eight-thirty. Joanna was already up and ready to go. She asked her how she had slept and got busy in the kitchen to fix some breakfast. She took the cereal box from the top of the refrigerator and offered Joanna some. Joanna accepted and poured some cereal in a cup. Taking the milk out of the refrigerator she poured it on the cereal and she passed the milk to Maria who was waiting with her cup. She also poured some orange juice for both of them in two glasses. They both sat in the dining area at the table and ate their breakfast.

"What are your plans for today, Joanna?"

"I am going to look for a job. I also want to go to the Department of Motor Vehicles to see if I can get a California identification card. Can I put down this address?"

"Sure you can!"

"Well, I better get going then. It's already nine o' clock," she said taking the cup to the kitchen and the glass with the orange juice. She washed the cup and put the glass with the orange juice in the refrigerator, saving it for later. Maria asked her if she was coming back for lunch and she replied: "Yes, if you want me to."

Once Joanna left, Maria sat at the table thinking about her. The revelations from last night came to her mind and she felt a lot of love and compassion towards her. She hoped that their prayers would be answered and that she was going to find a job that day. She tried to imagine what it was like to be homeless and thanked

God that she had a place to stay. She wondered what it was like having to lay down on the hard cement with only a blanket to protect you. Wasn't she afraid that she might get assaulted or raped? How had she survived all these years? These questions kept running through Maria's mind. She decided that she was going to ask Joanna when she had the opportunity. She really cared. She felt that God was answering her prayer to become Joanna's friend, a close friend. She felt a little less lonely and she was glad she had someone to talk to. Someone as nice as Joanna was.

She took a shower and got dressed. She cleaned the apartment, did the dishes and finally sat down to think things over. Was it a wise decision to let Joanna stay with her for an indeterminate period of time? What if things didn't work out? She couldn't bear the thought of sending her back on the streets. She really wanted to help. She felt this was an opportunity for her to do good, to be a good Samaritan. She hadn't studied psychology for no reason; she really cared about people and Joanna seemed so vulnerable. She just wanted to protect her, guide her. She promised herself not to be too pushy or demanding just because Joanna didn't have anywhere to go. She would give her room to grow and adjust. She would not treat Joanna as a guinea pig for her psychological studies. She would treat her as a person who had lot of problems and needed a helping hand. She would act like a Christian. She took the Bible and read for some time. She then prayed and thanked the Lord for everything, renewing her strength and faith in Him.

She lit a cigarette. It was the first she had that morning. She felt guilty about smoking. Her daughter Elizabeth was always asking her to quit and each time she would tell her that she enjoyed smoking and that she was not ready to quit just yet. But she felt really guilty about it. Elizabeth had asthma so when she was visiting, Maria would always go in the kitchen to smoke. She'd sit by the window and blow the smoke out.

She wondered about her daughter. She hoped that she had adjusted to her new job, and that she liked it a little bit better as she always told her how much she hated it. She was working in Panama City, Florida with the phone company and living with her aunt Stacy who was her supervisor. Maria was very thankful to her for letting Elizabeth stay with her. She wasn't even charging her to stay there. Elizabeth was just paying the cable bill and something else she didn't remember. Her car payments were high and so was her car insurance but Maria told herself that Elizabeth had to realize that we all have to work for a living and no one is going to give us anything for nothing.

She felt in part responsible for how Elizabeth felt because when she was little she had filled her head with fairy tales about how everything was wonderful and that they were going to win the lottery, and have lots of money. Well, that just didn't happen *and it probably never will*, she told herself. That's why she respected people with money because it is so hard to come by, and she knew most people with money worked hard to get it.

She went to the kitchen and made herself some espresso coffee. She loved the aroma that filled the house and poured herself a small cup, one that her mother had brought her from Italy.

Looking at the clock she saw it was already noon and Joanna would be back soon. Opening her refrigerator she found some sliced ham and some cheese. She would toast some sandwiches and fix a salad to go with them. She decided to wait until Joanna showed up so that the sandwiches would be hot. They wouldn't take long to fix anyway. The phone rang. It was Joanna letting her know that she was downstairs waiting to come up. Maria opened the door to let her in since she had forgotten to take the keys. She waited, excited, at the apartment door, hoping to hear good news.

"So, how did it go? Anything exciting happen?"

"No. It was the same story as yesterday. I just walked and walked and filled out applications. I hope something will come up soon because it sure is tiring. So stressful! But I will go back after lunch. I might have better luck this afternoon."

"Well, let's have some lunch and fill our stomachs. We will feel better afterwards. How does a ham and cheese sandwich with a salad sound to you?"

"Wonderful! I am starving."

They had lunch, quietly. After lunch Joanna took off again in her search for a job. Once alone, Maria went to bed to take a nap. She always took a nap in the afternoon when she was off from work. But this afternoon sleep would not come. Her head was filled with questions about Joanna. *"I should have asked her more about her living in the street,"* she told herself. *"I want to know more about it and what better person to ask than her? Well, I'll ask her more about it tonight."* She tossed and turned. Since she could not sleep she got up. She tidied the apartment some more, went to the kitchen for a snack of crackers and cream cheese and finally settled in front of the television waiting for Joanna to come back.

CHAPTER EIGHT

"I have found a job!" Joanna said all excited when she came back that afternoon.

"Praise the Lord," said Maria. "Tell me all about it. Where did you find it and what kind of job is it?"

"It's a dishwashing job at 'Giovanni's', a restaurant, night club in Hillcrest. It's from Wednesday through Sunday from 6 pm to 2 am. The pay is $5.15 an hour but Giovanni, the owner, said he would pay me under the table. He doesn't want to mess with taxes and paperwork. I told him that I would let him know by tonight. I first wanted to talk to you about it. So, what do you think?"

"I think that it is wonderful, aside from him not paying taxes; that worries me a bit. He could get in trouble for doing that, but you shouldn't have any problem. I think that you should take the job, for right now, and look for another one, in the meantime. Why don't you call him now and tell him that you will start working next week?"

"Yes, I'll do that!" Joanna called the restaurant and told Giovanni that she would accept the job. She was beaming, still not believing her good fortune.

"I guess our prayers from last night worked. It's amazing! I can't believe it. I got a job! Now I will have some real money in my pocket. I will be able to help you, Maria!"

"We should celebrate. How about tomorrow? We could pack some lunch and go to Balboa Park. It is a beautiful place and we could have a nice, pleasant day!"

"Whatever you want to do is fine with me, Maria!"

Maria looked at her. She was very beautiful, she thought, especially when she was excited. Her hair needed to be cut, though. It was bleached and it had lot of split ends. A nice cut would make her features stand out, especially her beautiful blue eyes. Her teeth needed some work too, but she could take care of that as she became financially independent. They were nice and even, but they needed some cleaning and maybe some bleaching.

"Well, it's already six o'clock. How about some dinner; I am hungry!"

"Dinner sounds fine. What are we going to have?"

"What about some fish, mashed potatoes and green beans?"

"That sounds wonderful!"

"Let's go in the kitchen and get busy, then."

They both went to the kitchen and fixed dinner. They were like old friends, chatting and laughing. Joanna set the table and they had dinner. Joanna couldn't contain her excitement. She talked through the whole dinner, making plans and looking forward to the money that she would have. How her life was changing for the better. You'd think that she had found a job for $100,000 a year by the way she was talking about it. Maria smiled while listening to her. She was very happy and couldn't wait for the changes that were going to happen in Joanna's life.

After dinner they had some vanilla ice cream and settled in front of the television. Maria told herself that she was eating too much ice cream. She should stop because it was making her gain weight, which she didn't need. She was already forty pounds overweight. She knew she had to go on a diet and eating ice cream wasn't helping her any.

"Joanna, do you mind if I turn the television off? I want to talk."

"No, by all means. Go right ahead."

Maria turned the television off and turned towards Joanna who was waiting a little apprehensively wondering what she wanted to talk about.

"I'd like to hear about life on the streets. What it's like and how you managed to survive all these years."

"Well, for starters it isn't fun. It's a very scary and hard life. Everyday could be your last one. From the moment you wake up till you lay yourself down on a hard pavement at night you wonder if you are going to make it through the day in one piece. There is no money except for the few cents you manage to collect from people on the street. With that you buy whatever food you can afford to buy and if you have any left you save it for your next meal. Sometimes you can go to public kitchens where they feed you a meal. There are some here in San Diego and I have gone there a few times. The food is not great but it fills your stomach and keeps you alive another day. There you meet people homeless like yourself and you try to stay in a group, for the night. There are some shelters where you can sleep for so many nights but when you have exhausted all you are allowed you are back sleeping in the streets. That's why it is so important to stay in a group. It is very dangerous to sleep alone, especially for a woman. Anything can happen to you. You can get robbed while you sleep. I know these sounds amazing but there are people out there who would steal from a homeless person. That's why I always sleep with my bag under my head and I carry a knife. Do you want to see it?"

Joanna went to her bag and took out a knife and showed it to Maria. It was a short knife with a very sharp edge. Maria shuddered.

"Did you ever have to use it?"

"A couple of times. One time because a man wanted to rape me. The moment he saw the knife he fled. So I have to be thankful that I carried it with me. A friend gave it to me. Actually he wasn't really a friend, just someone I'd met for the day. He had a spare one so he gave it to me, for my own protection. You are not scared, are you?"

"No, of course not!"

"Well, after all the things that Raul did to me for all those years I don't want any man to touch me. I would have killed that man if he had tried to rape me. He knew that I meant it and that's why he fled. I am still a virgin."

"You are still a virgin? At twenty-eight? How did you manage to do that? Didn't you ever meet someone that you liked that way?" asked Maria in disbelief.

"It wasn't easy. Many times I had to fend men off of me because they wanted sex. I'd tell them that I had a venereal disease and that has worked so far. The moment it stops working I'll use the knife."

"What's the worse part about living in the street?"

"I guess it is having to go to the bathroom, especially for women. Men can just unzip their pants and pee anywhere they like, but women can't do that. That's why I always pick a spot close to the public restrooms to spend the night. I can normally stay a whole night without going to the bathroom but in the morning I need to wash-up otherwise I feel dirty all over. Here in San Diego the public restrooms are on Third Avenue and lot of homeless people sleep there. Dozens. Sometimes a good soul would bring us some blankets or some food, you know, people from a church but they would start preaching to us. When that happened we would normally keep quite and let them finish, then we would just thank them for whatever they'd brought and they would leave. I guess that's where I heard about Jesus Christ, from their preaching."

"And what did you learn about Jesus Christ?"

"Not much, because I always half listened. But one thing I have learned and that is that He loves us."

"That's right! He does love us, so much that he gave His life for us, to cleanse us from our sins and bring us to the Father, spotless. Joanna, what about at night, before you went to sleep, what were your thoughts? Did you ever think about God?"

"At night, before I'd go to sleep, I'd think about my life and what I could do to change it. Occasionally I'd think about God, yes, but He was always touching me like Raul did. I couldn't put my trust in Him, you see! Raul is still free; nothing is ever going to happen to him for all the things he did to me. I hate him!"

"Well, once you'll go to therapy you will be able to get rid of all these feelings that you have about Raul, I guarantee! But did you ever think about Felicia? Do you feel like she didn't protect you?"

"Sometimes. But I assure you she had no clue. And she was always so loving towards me. Sometimes I feel that she should have known, but how could she? It wasn't her fault that she slept soundly at night and her husband was always making love to her. How could she have suspected? Unless I'd told her, but I never will. I'll never tell. You are the only person in this world to know about it."

"Well, that's a start. In time you will realize that talking about it is good therapy and that's the only way to get rid of all those feelings of hatred and betrayal that you carry with you. The important thing is that you talk to the right people about it. I am not a psychologist, so I cannot treat you, even though I have a two years degree in psychology. You'll see, a good therapist will do miracles and you'll be like a new person. Your whole life will change."

"I hope so, Maria, because my life until now feels like the bottom of a pit. But one day I will come out of it and I will see the light. Right now I am really excited about my new job. I can't wait to start and have some real money in my pocket. I want to help you with some expenses, food, utilities, and so on. Let me know how much. I love you Maria! Thank you for taking me in!"

Maria was moved when she heard Joanna say "I love you" and she saw that Joanna was a little embarrassed for saying it, but she was glad she did.

"I love you too, Joanna. I hope that one day we can be sisters in Christ. I really do! Jesus is awesome, full of love and compassion. Once you get to know Him your healing will begin, you'll see!"

"You're bringing so many new things in my life I am starting to feel like I am riding a roller-coaster. I need time to adjust and take it all in. One thing at a time."

"Yes, of course. I apologize but I am excited for you and want to help you as much as I can. To me you're like a flower who is about to bloom and I am anticipating all the beautiful colors that might come out. I promise I won't push you and please tell me if you feel that I am. Can we talk more about your life in the streets?"

"I told you most of it. There isn't much more to tell."

"When was the last time you slept in a house?"

"Aside for sleeping in the shelters, you mean?"

"Yes."

"It was about six months ago, in Chicago. There were six of us and we all slept in one room, because my friend rented a studio apartment. Besides me there was one other girl, the others were all guys. We felt like we were rich. We had lot of fun for three months then the landlord found out we were there and we had to move out."

"Did the guys make passes at you, while you were there?"

"Oh yes! But I showed them my knife and they quickly understood to leave me alone about that. The other girl was messing around with them and that made it easier for me. I would hear them at night and that bothered me, but I never said anything."

"You know, your sexual molestation was a terrible thing and it shouldn't have happened, but it might have been a blessing in disguise because you are still a virgin. Nowadays it is almost impossible to find a woman virgin at twenty-eight years old. When you will meet the right man it will be wonderful to offer him your virginity on your wedding night. I was not a virgin when I got married, but George, my ex-husband, said he preferred it that way so that I would not get curious about other men and be unfaithful to him since I already knew.

Ever since I have become a Christian, though, I asked the Lord to forgive me for my promiscuity of when I was a young woman and I have really wished in my heart that I could have been a virgin the night I got married. But it's no use crying over spilled milk, is there? Besides, George was not a virgin himself. When I met him he was dealing with prostitutes."

"I guess you're right. But the reason I am still a virgin is because I don't want any man to touch me, especially my private parts. It's not because I am saving myself for the man I am going to marry. I probably will never get married."

"Never say never!"

"Let's talk about what we are going to do tomorrow. Where is this Balboa Park and what it's like?"

"You can see it right from my window. But to go to where I want to take you we have to walk a while, about twenty minutes. The Balboa Park is very old, more than 100 years. It hosted the Panama-California Exposition of 1915-1916 and the California-Pacific International Exposition of 1935-1936. Its architecture is Spanish Colonial and its very beautiful buildings have been turned into museums. But you'll see it all tomorrow. We're going to have fun. Would you like to watch some television now since it is still early? Let's see if they have some movies on."

Maria turned the television on and they sat silently watching a movie. After the movie Maria took Joanna's hand and looking in her eyes she asked her if she wanted to say a prayer before they went to sleep. Joanna said yes so they held hands, bowed their heads and prayed:

"Heavenly Father we come before you in humbleness of heart and contrite in spirit. We thank you so much Lord, for your help in finding Joanna a job. We hope that everything will go well for her and that eventually she'll find a better job. We pray that she will get along well with everyone at work and that it won't be too hard for her. We ask you Lord to protect everyone in our lives and a special prayer goes for Raul. We pray that the Holy Spirit convicts him and make him repent of all the ugly things he did to Joanna. We pray that you put your loving arms around Joanna and help her heal from all the abuses that she suffered at his hands. We pray also for Felicia and for all our relatives and friends. Protect us and keep us in the shelter of your arms. Amen."

Joanna lifted up her head and looking at Maria said:

"Thank you for praying for me. I am not very good at praying but I must tell you that I like it. It gives me a sense of peace. I hope that in time I can have the faith that you have. I really mean it."

"I hope that you will too. The main thing is that you accept Jesus as your Lord and Savior in your heart and put your life in His hands. He will teach you everything you need to know. You will be saved. You also need to repent of all your sins. We all have sinned. We are born sinners, but we don't have to live in sin. Jesus can change us. Once we repent, He is just to forgive us and cleanse us. You'll see, it'll be a new life for you just like it was for me. Well, let's go to bed now and tomorrow we'll have a very nice day. Good night, Joanna."

"Good night, Maria."

CHAPTER NINE

Next morning Joanna and Maria woke up around eight o'clock. They had a leisurely breakfast and then got ready for their expedition to Balboa Park. They prepared tuna fish sandwiches, packed potato chips and sodas, took two towels to sit on and departed. The park started right across from Maria's apartment. They walked for about ten minutes coasting the park then turned right on Laurel Street, crossed the long bridge and arrived at the museum section. They went past the Museum of Man, the Sculpture Garden Café then went to visit the Art Museum, which had free admittance. That month the museum had an exhibition of Russian icons depicting mainly religious scenes.

From there they went to the Botanical Garden with its display of exotic plants in a cool, refreshing atmosphere. They sat down and enjoyed the peaceful calm and luxurious vegetation. Maria said a silent prayer. From there they went past the History Museum, the Space Theater. They sat on the grass by the water fountain where they had lunch.

"Well, how do you like the park, Joanna?"

"I think it's great. What a beautiful place. Thank you for bringing me here! Maria, why don't you tell me a little more about you. Where were you born, how was your childhood?"

"I was born in Onofrio, in the province of Naples, in Italy. I was born inside the crater of an ancient volcano, of which I am very proud because it makes me feel special. My mom had six girls of which I am the third. The first is Amelia, then comes Sara, then me, Marta, Serena, and Susanna. I get along with all of them. Amelia and I used to fight a lot when we were growing up. I remember one time I threw a knife at her that got stuck in the back of her knee. It scared me to death but she pulled it out and it wasn't that serious. One time she threw a small plate at me, which hit me right on the head and split it open. My father didn't have a lot of patience with all of us and was often violent. My mother's excuse for him was that he had suffered a head injury at work and that was the reason why he behaved the way he did.

My parents were very poor when we were young and for this reason my mother put us all in different convents to be raised by the nuns. All six of us went. We didn't like it and didn't want to be there. In the convent where I was, the nun who supervised us, Sister Adele, was very violent when she got angry. I remember one time she got angry at Quercia, an orphan. She dragged her to the floor, sat on top of her, grabbed her hair and kept banging her head. I felt so sorry for her. One time she got angry at me because I wouldn't stop talking while we were napping. She grabbed me, brought me away from the benches where we were sitting and gave me the beating of a lifetime. I screamed so loud all the nuns came in to see what was going on, but no one said anything. One day, as I was playing with my friends, a nun told me that I was going home. I asked her why. She said it was because I had said that if they didn't send me home I would jump out the window. That was a lie but I didn't contradict her because I wanted to go home. Now I think they must have come into my dreams and told me something like 'You either eat this soup or you jump out the window' which is to say 'You either do this or else'. I must have told them I would jump out the window. That's why they thought best to get ready of me. So I was sent home. Besides, they were jealous of me because Mother Superior liked me."

"What was your mom like?"

"My mom was always busy. She had lot of cleaning, laundry and cooking to do. She never beat us but she was not very affectionate. She has never said 'I love you' to any of us. That's one reason why I always say 'I love you' to my daughter. I want her to be able to express love without any embarrassment. I feel that's very important."

"I agree. Felicia told me that she loved me a couple of times but she wasn't very affectionate, either. I always longed for my real mother, though. She was very affectionate, even though she left us alone at night. She was a good mom. What about your dad? Tell me more about him."

"Like I told you he was very violent. He used to get crossed very easily. He used to beat my mother all the time. I remember one time that my mother came to get me from the convent. We had just arrived home. As my mother stepped into the door he attacked her with a broom. He beat her with that until it broke. He then took an umbrella and kept poking her with that. He made her black and blue all over. My mother spent a month in the hospital and my father went to jail. I took care of my younger sisters while my mom was in the hospital and I remember that as something very rewarding. When my mother came back home she kept receiving love letters from my father so she took him back and he left the prison because she didn't press charges anymore. The love letters, I found out later, were written by someone else because my father didn't know how to write."

"It sounds like you had a sad childhood. I feel sorry for you!"

"I feel sorry for myself too. When my father called you'd better run. I remember one time I wasn't fast enough. He grabbed me by the arm and dragged me on the ground. My face was hitting the ground as he was dragging me and by the time we reached our porch my face was all swollen and bruised. My mother was angry at him for that. Another time he told us that he was taking us to see a movie. We all got very excited and started to run all over, all six of us. He got cross and told us that we weren't going anywhere. He wanted us to get in the house and as we got inside he gave each of us a kick in the butt. Needless to say we spent a very sad night."

"Didn't your father get medical treatment when he had the accident on the job?"

"I don't know. My mother said a beam that was supporting the excavation that he was helping to build for a railroad gave way and hit him on the head. The skin didn't break and the blood coagulated in his head and was putting pressure on his brain and that was why he would get those violent fits. He was obsessively jealous of my mother and very insecure. He was also very uneducated having received very little schooling. Anyway he used to whistle when he wanted us to go home. We were terrified of that whistle because if we didn't get home right away we would get a beating. We used to play in the neighborhood and sometime you couldn't hear the whistle."

Maria offered Joanna another sandwich.

"What about your other sisters. Did they get beatings too?"

"Amelia and I were the ones who got most beatings. Especially Amelia. I remember when she was in the convent. One day she ran away and hitched a ride with a man who was driving a horse-drawn wagon carrying hay. Half an hour after she got home, one of the nuns from the convent arrived and she told my father what she had done. My father kicked her like a dog while the nun watched. She never said a word to stop him. I suppose she thought that the beating was well deserved. Another time he hit Amelia with a stick with sharp corners. He split her head open. He got very scared at the sight of blood. He took her by the fountain and washed the blood away while his hands were shaking a lot. She needed stitches but she never got any. He would have gotten into trouble if he had taken her to the hospital. My father built our house all by himself, I have to give him credit for that. He designed it and built it stone by stone. He was on the roof of the house, one day. He told my sister Amelia to do something for him. She didn't move fast enough for him so he threw the pot full of cement at her and missed her by an inch. It would have killed her if it had hit her. Well that's my father for you."

"What was he like, before the accident?"

"He was very loving. I loved him very much and I used to wait for him to come back from work. He always brought us cookies or candies. I loved him so much I used to imitate him. One day I took his shaving brush, soaped it and got on a chair. I stood in front of the mirror and soaped my face. I was about to shave my face when my mother stopped me. Good thing, too, or I would have a beard today. He used to ask me what I wanted to be when I grew up. I'd tell him an actress, a singer, a ballerina. He used to laugh at me, in a very loving way."

Just then a man in raggedy clothes approached Maria and

Joanna. He stood by them casting a shadow over them. He asked them if they had any food because he hadn't eaten anything in two days. Maria and Joanna both said yes at the same time.

"Why don't you sit down with us and eat one of these sandwiches? They're fresh. We just made them this morning. What is your name?" asked Maria.

"My name is John Grey, ma'm!"

"Oh, don't call me ma'm. It makes me feel old. My name is Maria and this is Joanna. How old are you, John?"

"I am thirty-six." Maria offered him a sandwich which he took eagerly taking a big bite. He was at one time a handsome man, but his life on the street had affected his looks. His teeth were all decayed and his blond hair needed a wash. He had wrinkles on his face, which made him look a lot older than thirty-six. He was tall and slim. His clothes needed a good wash, too.

"I know you John," said Joanna. "You use to sleep on Third Avenue, by the public bathrooms. That's where I have seen you. What brings you to Balboa Park?"

"I needed to be around normal people, people with a normal life. Beside I was hungry and even though you can't beg in the park I thought I could find something to eat with so many people around. And I got lucky because I found you. Do you come here often?"

"This is my first time here, but Maria comes here often. I am staying at her house for a little while, until I get back on my two feet."

"Lucky for you. Say, Maria do you have a place for a stray dog like me?"

"I am sorry John, but I don't. I am not supposed to even have Joanna with me, because of the landlord. If he finds out he will raise my rent and I can't afford that. But I wish you the best of luck. Here, have a soda before that sandwich chokes you!"

"Thank you, ma'm! Well, I'll better get going. I am supposed to meet some friends soon. What time is it?"

"It's exactly twelve-fifteen. Good-bye John. We will pray for you!"

As John left, Maria and Joanna watched him walk away then, without saying a word, they both lay down on the towels and closed their eyes. The park was full of people. Some were talking noisily, calling their children; some were strolling enjoying the sunshine; others were sitting on the grass. They lay there for a while then Joanna said,

"I am still curious about your father. Did he ever get better?"

"No, he got worse. One day when he went to visit some doctors he got into a fight with one of them. They put him into a mental institute. I remember that I went to visit him with my mother. I noticed his hands were smoother with nice, clean fingernails. He pointed to a man in the room and said that he had swallowed his tongue because of the treatment they had subjected him to. I was fascinated. Anyway, he got out and they gave him a pension, which he still collects to this day. Later on he started drinking and it really got bad for us. He would get very upset and violent when my mother hid the bottle of wine from him so my mother stopped doing it.

We never took any of our friends home with us with one exception or two, because we were not sure whether he'd be drunk or not. When he got drunk and got into a fight with my mother, he would spit on her face and I felt very sorry for her having to be subject to such a barbaric treatment. His spit was foul smelling. He never brushed his teeth his entire life and they were all decayed. One time we found him peeing in the closet because he thought that it was the bathroom. His behavior didn't help me much with my self-esteem. I always felt ashamed to mention my family to my friends. They had it all: Cars, clothes, loving families. What did I have? A drunken father, a poor family, a few clothes that I managed to buy with my babysitting money, earned since I was fourteen, because my mother couldn't afford to buy them for us. Not much to brag about."

Maria sat up, shielding her eyes from the sun.

"I wish I had brought some sun-screen. This sun is very hot today. I feel my skin burning. Why don't we move into the shade?"

"Okay, Maria. I am not even supposed to be in the sun. My fair skin burns easily. I am glad you mentioned it. I forgot with all the excitement."

"Are you really enjoying yourself? I am so glad, Joanna!"

They moved their stuff under a tree, in the shade and lay back on their towels. They dozed off for a pretty good while. When they woke up the sun had moved and they were again exposed to its hot rays. They decided that it was time to go back to the apartment. They gathered their things and left.

CHAPTER TEN

The walk back to the apartment was peaceful. Maria was meditating and remembered the vision of her church which was to WIN a person to Jesus Christ according to Mark 16:15 "And He said unto them, 'Go ye into all the world and preach the Gospel to every creature.'" To DISCIPLE a person in Jesus Christ according to Matthew 28:19, 20 "Go ye therefore and make disciples of all nations, baptizing them in the name of the Father and the Son and the Holy Spirit. Teaching them to observe all things whatsoever I have commanded you." To SEND a person for Jesus Christ according to Acts 1:8 "…and you shall be witnesses unto Me both in Jerusalem and in all Judea and in Samaria and unto the uttermost parts of the earth." She asked Joanna,

"Say, Monday night I will go to the church for our weekly prayer meeting. Would you like to go with me? We gather together and go over a list of prayer requests that people put in a box during the week and we just pray for them. It's a group of five or six of us. I would like you to experience that. It's quite rewarding."

"Okay, I'll go but don't expect me to say too much or nothing at all. I have never been involved with something like that."

"You don't have to say anything. Just come and listen, you'll see, you won't be disappointed. So that's a date. Monday, after I come back from work we'll go to church." "Yes. Thank you Maria for trying so hard to save my soul. I would like to learn more about

Jesus Christ. Do you think that I could borrow one of your Bibles? I've noticed that you have two or three around the apartment."

"Be my guest. If you want to learn more about Jesus Christ you have to read the New Testament. That's where Jesus' life and his preaching are talked about. To know Jesus, is awesome. It is not easy at first. You will find yourself convicted for your sins. Then you will start to understand God's plan and how He sent His son to save us from our sins through His blood and death on the cross. It is only through Jesus Christ that we can approach God and stand boldly in His presence. He absolves us from our sins and gives us eternal life. To know Jesus is to have a new life, being born again, free from sin."

They reached Maria's apartment building and went upstairs. It was now three o'clock in the afternoon. Having time on their hands they were deciding how to spend the rest of the day. Joanna asked Maria if she could do the laundry. Her clothes needed a wash real badly. Maria showed Joanna where the Laundromat was in the basement and she cautioned her not to tell anyone that she was staying in the building but that she was just visiting. Joanna told her not to worry.

While Joanna was doing her laundry Maria started to tidy up the apartment. She then remembered that it was Saturday. She didn't do any work on Saturdays because she observed the Sabbath. She had for many years. She mentally asked God forgiveness for working that morning when she prepared for the picnic in the park. She took the Bible and went to her little shrine in her bedroom.

She closed the door and sat on the floor in front of the shrine. She read from the Book of Romans. After reading she lit a candle and got on her knees to pray. The shrine was very simple with a beautiful, small Plexiglas cross on top of it. At the bottom of the cross there was a base with a red rose inlaid. On the wall there were a big rosary made of material that glowed in the dark and three pictures of Maria, her daughter Elizabeth and her mother. There were three candles, those big ones that you buy at thrift stores for 99 cents, with pictures of Jesus and the Virgin Mary. Even though she didn't attend the Catholic Church anymore since she started to attend the Christian, non-denominational church, she still liked to have around her things like the rosary and pictures of the Virgin Mary because they reminded her of her childhood and she felt some comfort in that. She didn't recite the rosary anymore but she would hold it in her hands, sometime, when she meditated. She also had a small one, made in Mexico, of wood and she kept that by the bed. She sat in the lotus position and meditated. Pictures started to come into her mind.

It was March 15, 1985. Maria was laying on the couch in her house in Wahiawa, Hawaii. She was suffering from another horrible headache caused by her sinus. She had taken some medication prescribed by her doctor, but it wasn't working. Her husband George was at work and her daughter Elizabeth was at school. She lay there watching "All My Children" on television. She didn't normally watch soap operas but that day she did. She fell soon asleep. She didn't know how long she slept when all of a sudden she saw herself dressed in a long, white, silk dress. On hers shoulders she had a silk, blue veil.

Her feet were bare. Under her feet there was a globe and wrapped around the globe twice there was a black snake. Maria's right foot was pressing on the snake while the snake was looking up towards her. There was a great heat in her foot and around her head. Maria woke up. She looked at the clock. It was exactly 3:15 in the afternoon. The soap opera was still on. She didn't know what to make of what had just happened. She thought that it was about the Virgin Astrea because she had been reading Nostradamus recently.

It took Maria nine years to connect that experience with Genesis 3:15 where God says to the serpent: "And I will put enmity between you and the woman, and between your seed and her seed; it shall bruise your head and you shall bruise His heel."

Maria felt the heat on her head for many years after that. It got to the point that she would have to put ice wrapped in a towel on her head, to cool it down. She was also very sleepy all the time and slept for hours sometimes going to bed in the afternoon and not waking up till the next morning. She was very disturbed mentally, having nightmares on a nightly basis. She told of the experience to doctors and two priests but they didn't elaborate and didn't enlighten her as to its significance. It was a real struggle. Then

Maria saw a statue of the Virgin Mary exactly as the vision that she had had only that the serpent wasn't black and he wasn't wrapped around the globe. She didn't want to think of herself as the Blessed Mother, but she had been Her in her experience. She had many conflicts about the sacred and the profane because of that. There had been times when she had cursed, blasphemed and burned sacred pictures, when she felt so angry and confused. She didn't know who she was anymore. She didn't want to think that she was the Virgin Mary, because she didn't believe in reincarnation. The Bible thought that there was no reincarnation, that man is appointed to die once and then the judgment. So who was the woman she had dreamed about? She found another passage in the Bible where she thought that there might be a reference to her. She had discovered it in 1985, the same year that she had had that experience. She had met two Italian women, two sisters from Naples. One of them had told her that if she knew the number of her name she would find a passage in the Bible that would speak about her. So she had searched the Bible for that reference. She thought she had found it in Revelation 12:1, 2 where it says: "Now a great sign appeared in heaven: a woman clothed with the sun, with the moon under her feet, and on her head a garland of twelve stars. Then being with child, she cried out in labor and in pain to give birth." She felt that she had found the passage that related to her. She felt comfortable for the fact that it seemed to describe the woman simply as a woman, not like the woman in Genesis 2:23 where the *w* is capitalized. But she thought that the great sign referred to the fact that she had seen herself as the woman with the globe under her feet. She did have a lot of pain during childbirth. She had been in labor for three and a half days. They had injected straight alcohol into her veins to stop the labor because she was only six and a half months pregnant, but that didn't work. She had the baby anyway and she was healthy. She didn't think that the male-child of Revelation referred to the same child that the woman was bearing.

She knew it wasn't the same because of what had happened with Michael's mother, when she was screaming at her over the telephone talking about her son: "He is a kid" she yelled. "He is a man, a man!" Maria yelled back. She knew that Michael was the man-child of Revelation 12:5. He looked like a god, and she had no problem seeing him as Jesus Christ. Maria had met him at college and she had fallen in love with him immediately. She didn't care that he was twelve years younger than she was and that she was married. She had the crazy idea that she could marry him. She would call him at his house, but his mother was very rude. That relationship went nowhere. But she thought about him night and day. For eight years, after her divorce from George, she didn't date anybody waiting for Michael. But Michael never materialized. Except for that night that he went to visit her, at her apartment. He brought with him a friend and they both spent the night there. Maria and Michael slept in the bedroom and his friend slept in the living room. For as much as she had wanted him she was surprised by the fact that she had no real sexual desire. She didn't have sex with him even though he slept naked, his gorgeous body lying next to her. He was six feet four inches tall. She slept in the hollow of his arm, with her foot on top of his and that's how she woke up the next morning. They both had not moved at all for the whole night. He had not slept and his eyes were puffy. He had to leave early to go to work. Before he left he said: "I will be back!" He never did. Liar. All men are liars, Maria thought, as she reminisced. He was her sun god, Jesus Christ, how could he stay away from her. He told her that he loved her forever, but never called her even though she had gotten a divorce and was free to see him anytime she wanted or he wanted. In her search for God and reading the Bible searching for Jesus Christ she had combined them with his image. He was in everybody and everything. She could not make the separation. It was devastating for Maria. He was tall, blonde and blue eyed. He worked out at the gym and his body was full of muscles. She could hear him in the love songs, read about him in the Bible, see him in people she met. She even stopped a man, one time, and asked him if his name was Michael just because he was blonde and had blue eyes. Eventually she had to get over that obsession because it was taking a great toll on her health. She was deprived of human relationships; her soul was dying. She started to go out and date again.

Maria came back from her reveries when she heard the door open and Joanna back from the Laundromat. She said a closing prayer and she went in the living room.

"All done?" she asked.

"Yes. I got all my laundry done. Now I am hungry. What are we going to eat?"

"Let's see. How about carne asada wrapped in pita bread and a salad?"

"That sounds wonderful! Let's start."

"Before we start, do you mind if we say a prayer to close the day? Today is the Sabbath of the Lord and I always say a prayer at the end of the day. I have already said a prayer while you were gone but I want to say a prayer with you."

"Sure, Maria."

Maria sat on the couch next to Joanna, took her hand and said a short prayer. When she was done they both got up and fixed dinner. After dinner they sat on the couch and watched television. Joanna was very tired, but she didn't say anything. Her yawns spoke for her, after a while. She couldn't keep her mouth closed, one yawn after another. She asked Maria for the Bible and Maria gave it to her. She lay on the futon, on the living room floor and started to read Genesis. Maria told her good night and she went to bed also.

CHAPTER ELEVEN

Next morning, Sunday, Maria and Joanna woke up early. They yawned and stretched lazily. They prepared a scrumptious breakfast of scrambled eggs, sausage, bacon, pancakes, orange juice and milk. They sat down at the table to eat. While they were eating Maria questioned Joanna about her Bible reading the night before.

"I am glad you asked," said Joanna. "I have lot of questions in my mind. According to Genesis God created the Earth before he created the sun. Also God never told Adam and Eve where the tree of the knowledge of Good and Evil was, yet the woman knew where it was when the serpent tempted her. Also, isn't God supposed to know everything? Then, why didn't He know where Adam was when he was hiding in the garden? Why didn't He know what had happened? He asked Adam and Eve for explanations but He never questioned the serpent."

"You sure do have lot of questions and I am sure you will have many more as you read on. The Bible is the Word of God and as such is complicated, but as you walk with the Lord the answers will come to you. When they don't, you just have to go by faith. God's thoughts are higher than ours and that's why it is difficult for us to understand, sometime. Just have faith and don't be discouraged. It is possible that God had showed Adam where the tree was and that's how they knew. God didn't ask the serpent for any explanation because He knew his nature and that he was quite capable to have done what the woman said he did. Don't worry, Joanna, I had the same questions when I read Genesis and I still have them, sometimes, but I am at peace knowing that God has all the answers and one day He will show us everything and we will understand and have no more questions. With Jesus, though, we don't need to worry about anything because he has fulfilled the law and has made peace between God and us. Nothing matters anymore, even what happened in the Garden. God put an angel to protect the Tree of Life so we know that no one can touch it. With Adam man fell from grace, with Jesus the grace of God abounds for every man that turns to God through His son Jesus Christ."

"I hope that I will come to have the same faith as you have, Maria. You must be very close to God, by the way you're talking. This is all new to me so I hope you will forgive me for all my questions and be patient. I really want to get close to God too, just like you."

"I am going to church this morning. Would you like to go with me?"

"Yes, I would like that very much!"

"You know, I still have lot of questions, too. I had lot more before, when I was reading the Bible all by myself. But ever since I have been attending church regularly and listening to the pastor explaining it, I have a lot less, and I realized that I had been wrong, sometime. Also, things that seemed so important are just not that important anymore. My interpretation was wrong. I feel a sense of relief when that happens, as if a burden has been lifted up from my shoulders; just like there is one less thing to worry about and I feel one step closer to God and His Son Jesus Christ. I had a dream that worries me, though. It was about God. But I can't tell you because it might affect you and your relationship with God. I wouldn't want that responsibility. Maybe when you accept Jesus Christ as your Lord and Savior I will tell you, but not now."

"Oh! You got me curious now. I can't wait until you tell me."

"It wasn't a good dream, believe me! I wish I didn't have it, but I did and I must live with it!"

"If we're going to church we must hurry and get ready. What time does it start?"

"At nine-thirty. We have an hour, plenty of time. The church is right in the next block."

"How convenient!"

"Yea. That's another reason why I go there."

Maria and Joanna finished their breakfast and got ready for church. At nine-thirty they left. The church was located at the corner of Fifth and Fir. It was a square building of a light yellow color, with a cross in the top part of the front of the building. It was very old, about thirty years or so. There were greeters at the door when they arrived. They shook hands and walked up the steps into the sanctuary. Maria scanned the room to see if her friends Theresa and Penny were there. She saw them in the middle rows and walked towards them with Joanna on her tail.

"Hi Theresa, hi Penny. How are you? I want to introduce to you Joanna, a friend of mine from out of town, who's staying with me."

She gave them a hug and they shook hands with Joanna and gave her a hug also.

"Welcome to our church Joanna," said Theresa.

Maria and Joanna sat in the seats next to them. Theresa was a black woman of sixty-three years old. She looked a lot older. Her skin was wrinkled and full of scars. Her hair was short and curly. She had a very friendly disposition and always gave hugs to all of her friends and acquaintances. Penny was originally from Puerto Rico. She had come to the United States when she was twelve years old. She was fifty-three years old and a little bit overweight. Her hair was very short and silver. She was as tall as Maria while Theresa was about four inches taller. Both Theresa and Penny were part of the prayer group that met every Monday night at church.

The worship started with songs and praises. The band played soft rock Christian music. The congregation, which filled three quarters of the church, stood up and clapped their hands at the tempo of the music. At the end of each song they would clap their approval. Joanna was a little intimidated and she felt a little out of place. She watched everything and everybody with new eyes trying to figure out if this was right for her and if it was something that she wanted in her life. She liked the music. She observed the other people; how they raised their hands to heaven; how they clapped with enthusiasm; how they kept their eyes closed and their heads bowed down. She wondered if she would ever act that way or feel the same way they felt. She felt something stir inside of her. A yearning, a desire to belong, to be part of something; she wanted to put roots someplace, not to wander around aimlessly. She was really tired of life on the streets. She envied people who had a stable life even if it was the same old job every day. She wanted some security, a home to go back to every night. She wanted to build a new life for herself. She silently thanked God for putting Maria on her path." Jesus," she said in her heart, "if you are real and if you came to save me from sin and destruction please help me. I want to be good and I want to be saved. Please, oh please help me."

A man came to the podium. He said "Hi everybody. My name is Allan. I have a few announcements to make. Next Saturday there is the single mom's breakfast. We invite all you single moms to attend. It starts at nine-thirty. We need volunteers to work in the Children's Ministry and we also need volunteers to help in the office here at the church. If the Lord puts it in your heart to serve, then this is the opportunity for you. Whether it is one day a week, or one day a month we will all be blessed. Working with children is very rewarding. You never know who the children are going to turn out to be. Maybe one of them will become the President of the United States, or he might become a great leader that will bring many to believe in the Lord. If you are interested please see Laura after the service, downstairs by the gazebo or call us here at the church. Now lets say a brief prayer while the ushers come forward to collect tithes and offerings."

The band played another song while the ushers came forward. Maria gave her usual dollar, Theresa gave a check of ten percent of her salary; Penny and Joanna didn't give anything. At the end of the song a tall, bulky man came to the podium. He was blond, six feet four inches tall, good-looking.

"Good morning, how's everyone doing today? My name is Don Jackson, for those of you who don't know me. I am substituting for your pastor Bob Priceman. He has been called on church business in the North County, but he will be here next Sunday. Before I start I want to give a testimony of my life, on how I was addicted to drugs and alcohol when the Lord saved me, ten years ago. My life was in a shamble. I lived day by day, not knowing where my next meal would come from, where I would get the money to buy the drugs and the alcohol that my body craved.

Then I met and old woman who started to preach to me about the Savior and how He died to save me from my sins. At first I didn't want to listen, but she was persistent and kept talking to me. Without wanting to I started to absorb a little of what she was saying to me. But I was skeptical. Who would love someone like me: A drug addict and an alcoholic, with no job and no reputation, nothing to show for. What impressed me most was what she said about God's grace and how we were forgiven of all our sins. She invited me to go to her church and I said I would think about it, thinking that most likely I wouldn't go, but I said I would think about it just to get ready of her. I was wandering the streets and thinking about her words. Who would love me? I was unlovable. Why would someone die for me, a scumbag? That night I didn't have anywhere to go and I kept thinking 'I might as well go, it can't hurt' so I went to the church. It was crowded and full of people. What hit me was looking at the people in the church. They weren't well dressed, they didn't look rich; they didn't look holy. I saw several people I'd seen wondering the streets, and I knew they were homeless, like me. I wasn't very impressed. I felt uneasy.

I patiently listened to the sermon and kept wondering as I did so, few words entering my mind and lingering in my thoughts. I went back to that church and the more I went, the more words would impress upon me the need to be saved, to be clean. I started to pray and I asked Jesus to save me. I finally went up to be saved and gave my life to Jesus. I have been sober and drug free ever since. I have a family now, two beautiful children whom I adore and nothing, I mean nothing, could take me away from Jesus. You can see for yourself how far I have come, but I could never have done it alone. My life began when I put all my cares at His feet and asked Him to take charge. Opportunities started to appear out of nowhere, doors opened and I knew why He said 'I am the way, the truth and the life'. He is the Way, the Truth and the Life. Now let's come to tonight's sermon. I am going to talk about God's grace."

Joanna was listening attentively to every word that was spoken. She felt a sense of hope as she considered Don Jackson's life and the parallel it made with her life. Her life was in a shamble too, she was homeless, hopeless, fearful and ashamed. Who would want to love her? Especially if they knew what Raul had done to her and how she'd complied and even enjoyed it some time. She was a sinner, a poor, wretched sinner. "Oh, Jesus, come in to my life too and save me like you saved this man," she thought. "I need you Jesus! Please save me!"

Maria turned towards Joanna and saw tears flowing down her cheeks. She put an arm around her shoulders to comfort her. She was happy because she knew that God's Holy Spirit was touching her heart, but she kept her joy to herself because Joanna would not have understood. She was starting to come alive in Christ and she didn't know yet. At the end of the sermon Don Jackson asked the congregation to say a prayer. They asked for forgiveness and for salvation. He then invited those who wanted to accept Jesus as their savior to come forward and talk to a counselor. To her surprise Maria saw Joanna step forward. She offered to go up with her and she agreed. So Joanna went up accompanied by Maria and formally accepted Christ into her life.

When they were through Maria was beaming as they walked back to where Theresa and Penny were waiting for them. They congratulated and hugged Joanna for having accepted Christ. Theresa suggested that they needed to celebrate and invited Joanna and Maria to go out for the afternoon. They would go have lunch somewhere and then maybe go see a movie. Maria and Joanna accepted since they had no plans for the afternoon. All four got into Theresa's car and decided to go to Anthony's for lunch. The restaurant was right on the water with a view of the harbor with all the sailboats parked in the bay. Sea gulls were flying looking for fish in the water. The hostess seated them at a table by the window where they had a view of the bay. Their specialty was crab accompanied by rice and shrimp. They ordered their lunch and settled to wait for it to be served. Theresa and Penny were curious about Joanna. Maria had never mentioned her in their previous meetings and they had no clue about who she was. Theresa was the first to speak up:

"So, Joanna, tell us about yourself. Where are you from?"

"I am from Minnesota. I just got here few days ago and Maria is graciously letting me stay at her place until I get on my feet. I found a job and Wednesday will be my first day."

"I am so excited for you for having accepted Christ. Be ready for a real change in your life. He is faithful and will lead you to good things. I know because He has done wonderful things for me. After my divorce I didn't know what to do. So I put my trust in Him and He has seen me through ever since. I don't even receive any financial support from my ex husband, I am totally independent and self-supporting. I have a good job and I tithe faithfully every month."

"Excuse me Theresa, but what is tithing?"

"Tithing is giving ten percent of what you earn to the church. It's in the bible."

"Wow! You mean that every month you give ten percent of what you make? You must earn a lot."

"I don't earn a lot, but I'll make do with what I have. So far I have never lacked anything so I'll keep on doing it."

"What job are you going to start on Wednesday?" asked Penny.

"Oh! It's just a dishwashing job at Giovanni's. Just for right now. I will look for something better after I am settled in. It's a real blessing for me so I am not complaining. What do you do Penny?"

"I work for the City of San Diego. I am a clerk. I evaluate claims for people on welfare."

"And what about you Theresa, what do you do?"

"I work for the County of San Diego. I review contracts. Maria and I started working for the County of San Diego the same day; it's matter of fact. We were together at the orientation meeting. But Maria is a Senior Account Clerk at the Environmental Agency as you probably know."

"Yes, I know. I love San Diego, don't you?" Joanna asked the group.

"Yes, we do," Maria replied. "But it wasn't always like this. When I first got here there weren't all these nice buildings that you see today. There were drug addicts and homeless people everywhere, especially outside Horton Plaza. And it was dirty. But no more."

In the meantime the food arrived so they all ate with gusto

neglecting conversation for a while. Maria had ordered Fettuccine Alfredo with a salad. Joanna had ordered rice with scampi and a salad while Theresa and Penny had ordered the house special. Joanna felt a little shy and she was worried about paying for the food; she had no money, Maria knew that. So was she going to pay for her food? She quietly asked Maria about it and Maria reassured her telling her not to worry and to enjoy her meal. Maria excused herself and told them that she was going outside to smoke a cigarette. She always had to smoke after a meal. Sometime she ate something just so she could enjoy a cigarette more. Her daughter Elizabeth was always after her to quit smoking. She couldn't stop herself because she heard Maria breathing heavy sometime, while they were talking on the phone. Maria would tell her that she didn't want to stop smoking just yet because she enjoyed it, but still every time they talked she would tell her.

She walked outside the restaurant and went to sit down by the water's edge. There was a light breeze and some seagulls were perched near by. She had to cover her hand to light the cigarette. She finally did and took a deep breath, inhaling the smoke. She got in her meditating mood and felt at peace. The view was beautiful, the sky was clear and people passing by were chatting, or skating on roller blades, or riding bicycles. She wondered about Joanna and how her life would be changed from now on since she accepted the Lord. She knew from personal experience that it wouldn't be easy at first. There is doubt, uneasiness, guilt for having been a sinner. But she also knew that the Lord is strong and His hand is firm. She thought of Psalm 23 and she felt comforted. She would be there for Joanna; she would be her best friend and her sister in Christ. Joanna was a good person, she could tell, and really deserved a break. She finished her cigarette and went back inside the restaurant. Theresa was talking to Penny and Joanna about her vacation. She went to New York to visit her son who was institutionalized because he was handicapped. She didn't say what was really wrong with him and nobody asked. When she finished talking Penny said,

"What are we going to do now? Would you like to go for a walk, to see a movie or go to the mall and just look around?"

"I myself am for a walk to burn up the calories I just ate and then go to a movie," said Maria. "Does anybody have today's paper? We can check out the movies listed."

"I have the paper in the car," said Theresa. "Why don't we pay and then go check it out?"

They asked the waitress for the bill. When she brought it Maria, Theresa and Penny reached for their purses. Joanna didn't even have a purse and she shifted on the chair, uneasy. Maria said that she was going to pay for Joanna's meal but Theresa and Penny said they wanted to pitch in as a present, so they did. Joanna was moved almost to tears and thanked them profusely. They merrily walked out of the restaurant to Theresa's car. They had a little trouble finding the section where the movies were listed but they finally did. After going through the whole list everybody agreed to go see *Forrest Gump* but the movie would not start till 3:15 and it was now 1:30. So they decided to go for a walk, to Seaport Village to kill time.

Seaport Village is full of shops and eateries appealing mostly to tourists and weekend wanderers. Also to families and little children. Joanna was taking everything in, enjoying every moment, glad to be with such a nice group of people. Rows of luxury boats lined the pier and shops filled with souvenirs, books, ceramic magnets, glassware, handmade sweaters lined the promenade. They passed an ice cream shop and decided to stop there, to get some ice cream.

After that Penny started to lead them in every store. She was especially fond of bracelets and would try them on as if she was going to buy them, but of course she never did, wasting the clerk's time, while the others waited patiently for her to finish. They went inside another store where they sold souvenirs from Sweden. They had beautiful hand-knitted sweaters, which Maria admired. She checked the prices and found that they cost over $150. If she didn't know how to knit she would surely buy one, but she could make herself one if she wanted to. The thought of making sweaters and sell them crossed her mind, but she realized that she would have to sell them for about $50 each for the store to make a profit and she decided against it. It would take her about two weeks per sweater, not counting the money she needed to spend for the material.

At 3:00 they headed back to Theresa's car and went to Horton Plaza to see the movie. They barely made it. They all agreed it was one of the best movies they had seen in a long time. Tom Hanks gave a brilliant performance. After the movie they went home. Maria and Joanna were dropped off first, then Penny. Before they left they said a prayer.

Once in Maria's apartment they sat on the couch and were silent for few minutes. Maria spoke first. "So, how do you feel Joanna? I feel great, I enjoyed myself a lot. I always do when we go to these outings. Who needs men. Give me girlfriends any day. Did you notice that we didn't talk about men at all?" Maria wasn't being sexist. Since she was working and supporting herself she felt self-sufficient and independent. She also had learned to rely on herself and no one else, since she hadn't met anyone to replace Michael and since Michael was nowhere to be found.

"Yes, I did. I enjoyed myself a lot too. I haven't felt like this ever. Do you believe me?"

"Of course. Why wouldn't I believe you?"

"Oh, maybe you could think that I am just saying that, but it's true."

"How about this morning. How do you feel about giving yourself to the Lord?"

"I feel committed. I am also scared. How will I measure up, I wonder?"

"You don't have to measure up. You just have to read the Word on a daily basis, fellowship with other believers, pray, and meditate. It will all fall into place, you'll see."

"I want to be good, do good and be worthy of His love."

"You can never be good enough to earn His love. You just have to admit that you are a sinner and repent of your sins. We all have sinned and fall short of the grace of God. It is only through Jesus that we are forgiven and made worthy of standing in God's presence and petition for what we need or desire. Without Jesus we cannot go into God's presence. Above all we must love, because love fulfills the law."

"I guess I just have to be patient because I have the feeling that it's going to be a long time for me to accomplish all these things."

"Yes, but don't worry, just stick with it. I am not very hungry. Are you?"

"Not very much."

"Then why don't we fix a cup of tea and have some cookies with it? Do you think that will be enough?"

"Yes, certainly."

Maria went to the kitchen to fix tea and she came back bringing a tray of cookies while the tea brewed. She laid two napkins on the table and two dessert plates. There were some flowers on the table, which gave a nice look to the setting. Joanna turned the television on and chose CNN.

The news was grim as usual. An airplane had fallen and all people aboard died. Some nut had gone to a fast food place and shot people down and so on. She changed channels until she found something that she liked. She asked Maria if the channel she picked was ok with her. Maria said it was fine. The tea was ready. Maria brought some honey to the table and called Joanna to join her. As they were drinking the tea and eating cookies Joanna asked Maria if it was okay for her to call Felicia. She hadn't called her in a long time and she really felt that she needed to. She said she would like to call her tomorrow, while Maria was at work so that she could have some privacy. Maria said it was fine, to be her guest. Joanna promised to pay for the phone call as soon as the bill came through the mail. Even though she hadn't started working yet Joanna already felt a sense of independence. Independence that only money can give. She was planning to save as much of her money as she could. Maria had plans for her money too, but Joanna didn't know that yet. They finished eating and cleared the table. They spent the rest of the evening watching television until they got ready to go to bed. Maria said good night and went to her room. Joanna took the Bible and started reading.

CHAPTER TWELVE

Monday morning. Starting another week. Maria jumped out of bed to turn off the radio so that Joanna wouldn't wake up. It was four-thirty. She felt wide-awake and ready to go. It was funny, she thought, how she didn't feel sleepy at four-thirty in the morning while when she slept later she had a hard time waking up. She was not a morning person possibly because she was born at seven in the evening. But she wanted to be a morning person. Desperately. She imagined herself getting up early and by nine to have finished all her chores around the house and have the rest of the day to do as she pleased. Maybe now that Joanna was staying with her she would be able to do that, on her days off. Wait and see, she told herself. The thing was, though, that Joanna would need to sleep in the morning since she wouldn't get home until two-thirty in the morning. So scratch that, she thought, while getting in the shower. After the shower she tiptoed to the kitchen to fix herself a cappuccino and smoke her first cigarette of the day. Normally she would have the television on and watch either CNN or the Mass on channel 12, but she couldn't do that anymore because Joanna slept in the living room. Maybe after they got to know each other more she could sleep in the bedroom also since Maria had two single mattresses there. Right now she didn't feel comfortable with that. Plus she snored so maybe Joanna wouldn't be able to sleep. Well, we'll see, she thought. They both would need to make adjustments once they got on a schedule.

Maria left the apartment at five forty-five and walked for fifteen minutes to get to the bus stop where she caught the number 20A going to Kearny Mesa. There were the usual people catching the bus. Maria knew them all by sight and knew at which stop they would get off. Through the years she had seen many people catch the bus at the same time, then, suddenly some of them stopped being there. She thought that maybe they had found jobs elsewhere.

Maria's stop was the very last one on the line. She got off right across from the building in which she worked. It was very convenient having the bus stop there. And for that, she thanked Jesus every morning. She was very thankful for everything: The shower, toilet, clothes, food, bus and many other things that we all take for granted and stop noticing. She was full of wonder when she considered all the steps involved in making a product and how many people were involved in the process: From the inception of the idea, to the final product that we buy in the store. Amazing. Clever. She really admired humanity and how far we'd come in the physical evolution. All the discoveries made and the luxury items available. When she looked at bridges and skyscrapers, she thought with amazement that it took lot of intelligence and courage to make them. She was afraid of heights so she was in awe of tall buildings and how it must have felt to put the last building block to a skyscraper. The joy, the pride, the celebration.

She was the first one to arrive in her department. She took out the keys and opened the door to the accounting section. She turned on the printer and went to weigh herself on the scale. The digital reading gave her 176 pounds. She subtracted about two pounds for her shoes and clothing and she told herself that she wasn't going to have any lunch that day. It was ten minutes to seven; enough time to go smoke a cigarette outside. It was prohibited to smoke inside the building. She sat at the round stone table and smoked her cigarette while she observed people arrive and park their cars in the parking lot. She finished the cigarette and went inside. Her co-workers had arrived. She said hi to everybody and went to her office. At the moment she had the office all to herself but later on she would have to share it with someone else because they were planning to hire another worker to process the receipt of checks and to do the daily deposit. Her office was located right next to Linda Suarez, her supervisor who would frequently walk by on route to the other office shared by three workers. So Maria was always on the look-out, keeping busy or seemingly so, not to give the impression that she was not working. She would get tired occasionally and needed a break from the routine. They were allowed to take two breaks of fifteen minutes each, one in the morning and one in the afternoon. Plus they had half an hour for lunch, but Maria only took twenty minutes because she left a little earlier at night so that she could catch the bus.

Her supervisor was in a good mood that morning as usual. She giggled a lot and made jokes about other people in the department. She knew a lot about their personal lives because she frequently stopped and talked with people. A good sixty percent of her work-day was spent talking with people and gossiping. A lot of what Maria knew about other people she had found out from Linda. People talked to her because she had good manners and knew how to ingratiate herself to them. Since she was a supervisor, she could more or less dictate to her people what to do while she herself did as she pleased. She herself had very little supervision as her supervisor, Diane Lock, came down from her office only about twice a week. And most of the time she didn't find Linda in her office. Linda could do what she wanted; in fact she did do what she wanted. She had people wrapped around her little finger. Maria was lucky because Linda had sympathy for her. She had been lobbying with Diane Lock to have Maria's position upgraded to Accounting Technician from Senior Account Clerk and gave Maria updates on the outcome as she did so. There was a constant flow of people flocking to Linda's office and sometime she had to close her door to keep people from interrupting her when she was working on some project for Diane. Linda was afraid of Diane. If Diane would come looking for Linda and didn't find her when Maria would tell Linda she looked all worried and asked what she wanted, which of course Maria didn't know. So she would call Diane on the phone to find out. She was also angry at Diane because she refused to give her overtime pay for when she came in on weekends, to work on projects that had a deadline. There seemed to be many of those projects on her desk, but if she had cut down on her conversational time Maria was sure she would have had the time to finish them all.

This morning she was wearing a purple dress with a white, embroidered collar that she had bought in the Philippines. Her size was so small she could have gone into a children's store to buy her clothes. As she passed by Maria's she commented on her sweater, since it was new and she hadn't seen it before. "Is it new?" she asked.

"Yes. I bought it at J. C. Penney. I bought three of them, in fact: One white, one black, and one red. They were on sale."

"I spoke to Diane Lock, Friday, your day off. I asked her again about upgrading your position to Accounting Technician and I think that I might have convinced her because she said 'We'll see, I have to think about it.' I asked her again about her eliminating some positions from accounting and she wasn't sure so I don't know what to make of it."

"Well, Linda, I thank you for all the effort you're putting into trying to upgrade my position. But I put my name on the transfer list so if anything comes to pass about eliminating some positions from our department I won't be out of a job. I sure hope nothing happens, though, because I like working here. It is so peaceful."

"You know, Mark has a job interview tomorrow for a computer company in Orange County that pays fifty dollars per hour. He has been going to computer school at night, so this is a big opportunity for him."

Mark was a Junior Accountant. He was Filipino also. He was slim, about five-eight and very quiet. He would be making a lot more money if he were hired than he did at the County, which would be great for him. He had just gotten married, had purchased a house so he could surely use the extra money. Maria didn't blame him in the least. Everybody in accounting was looking for a job elsewhere, ever since Linda had mentioned the conversation she had with Diane Lock about eliminating some positions from accounting. All together, in the accounting department, there were five employees and one student worker. Three of them were from the Philippines; Linda, Mark and Zaida. Maria and Tanya were from Europe; Maria from Italy and Tanya from Finland. Tanya was very slender and her hair was colored with streaks of red and yellow. She badly needed a color job, but for months her hair looked like that and she hadn't done anything about it. She spoke five languages: English, Spanish, Italian, German and Finnish. She had been married twice and divorced twice, but she still maintained a relationship with both ex-husbands. One of them lived in Spain and she would go visit him in the summer. The other was Mexican and he visited her often, taking her out for dinners. She was a Senior Account Clerk, but she could have had a much better job with all her knowledge. She also had a Bachelor degree in accounting. She had put applications in as Junior Accountant and was on the hiring list but nobody had called her. She was buying her own place and she badly needed income. She had put her name on the transfer list also. She handled accounts payable, petty cash and refunds.

Zaida was from the Philippines. She was slim, a size eight, and very quiet and intelligent. She did her work thoroughly and had excellent customer relations. She was in charge of supplies; reconciliation of fixed fees applications, and petty cash also. Zaida, Mark and Tanya shared one room divided by partitions; Maria had her office by herself as did Linda. Maria was in charge of accounts receivable, reconciliation of deferred revenue applications, and petty cash for travel reimbursements. Mark was in charge of reconciling bank accounts, department of motor vehicle accounts, inventory, and other various duties. Zaida, with her husband, rented a room in a house, to save money. Her ten-year old son was still in the Philippines, waiting to come to the United States. Zaida missed him a lot but there was nothing she could do about it. She and her husband were still immigrants, without citizenship because they hadn't been in the United States for five years yet. Her and her husband took turns in going to the Philippines to visit their son. They saved money this way.

Maria heard laughter come from the other office and went to see what the joke was all about. Linda was making fun of one of the engineers who, according to one of the other engineers, had a crush on Zaida. She thought the idea very amusing and was giggling. The engineer had come to ask for reimbursement from petty cash from

Zaida and as soon as he left Linda started making fun of him. Maria was not amused and thought that Linda was just being silly. She went back to her desk and proceeded to do her work. The rest of the day went by slowly, painfully so, and Maria couldn't wait until it was over.

Joanna woke up around eight. She made herself a cup of coffee and decided that she was going to call her foster mother around 9:00 am. She didn't want to call too early, as she wanted to prepare herself for the phone call. She hadn't called in over a year so she wanted to be clear headed and think about what she was going to say. The hour went by slowly but eventually came around. She picked up the phone and dialed Felicia's number.

"Hello, Felicia? This is Joanna, how are you?'

"Oh my God! Joanna how are you doing? I haven't heard from you in ages!"

"I am fine Felicia. How are things over there?"

"I have bad news Joanna. Raul has been arrested!"

"Arrested? Oh my God. Why?"

"Child molestation. He molested our neighbor's little girl. There are witnesses. I am afraid it is true. This is so embarrassing, I haven't gone out of the house since."

"How did this happen, please tell me more!"

"Jackie, a neighbor's child, was playing in the yard with some other children and Raul enticed her into the house with candy. He brought her into the kitchen where he did inappropriate things to her. Her friends saw the whole thing from the kitchen window. Jackie went home with the candies and told her parents what had happened. They called the police who took him into custody. That happened two days ago. The judge has set bail at ten thousand dollars but I don't have that kind of money so he's going to have to stay in jail. The trial is set for next month. He is looking at five years in jail. I can't afford to get a lawyer so we have to use the services of a public defender, one appointed by the court."

"What are you going to do Felicia, how are you going to survive financially?"

"I am not worried about that because Raul receives retirement checks every month. He retired last year after thirty-three years of service and the money goes straight into our joint account so I have access to the money. The house is paid for so I don't have to worry about that. I don't know what got into him. What a disgrace!"

"Felicia, this is going to come to you as a shock but Raul molested me too, while I was living at your house. That's the reason I left as soon as I turned eighteen. I never told you before because I didn't want you to hurt, but Raul is a sick man. He needs psychiatric help."

"Would you be willing to testify about what he did to you?"

"Well, I don't know, Felicia. I have to think about it. It is very painful and disturbing for me to remember. I have been scarred for life by it. Maybe I will, I don't know. Why would you want me to testify against him anyway, wouldn't that make things worse for him?"

"I want you to testify to prove to the judge that he is a sick man, who needs help. I also want him to be punished for what he did to you. I am sorry, Joanna, I hope you don't hold it against me for not seeing it. How did it happen, please tell me!"

"He would come to my room, at night and he would touch me and make me touch him. I am just now starting to talk about it. You are the second person in the whole world I have told it to. It is not easy, but I need to talk about it to begin healing. I am planning to go to therapy in a clinic. Group therapy so other people will know about it, but that's not important. I am not afraid of Raul anymore. He cannot hurt me anymore."

"The slime, I hope he rots in jail. I am so sorry Joanna!"

"You are not at fault Felicia. You have been like a real mother to me and I do love you, but you do understand now why I haven't come home since I left. However, now that he is in jail, and it looks like he might stay there for a while, I might come to visit you. I just need a little time to save up the money. Guess what? I found a job as a dishwasher in a restaurant and I am starting this Wednesday. I have found this wonderful woman, her name is Maria, who is letting me stay at her place until I get on my feet. As soon as I do I promise I will come to visit you. If my plans don't work out I will come back and live with you. Would you like that, Felicia?"

"I would love it, Joanna. You could keep me company in my old age. I hope he rots in hell, the bastard. I am so angry I could kill him. No, Joanna, you have to come and testify. They will give him more years in jail and that's what I want. Plus I want to see you. I haven't seen you for so long I have almost forgotten what you look like. Tell me how you look now."

"Older, ten years older. I haven't kept up my appearance much during these years, but it will change, I promise you. I will start to take better care of myself. I tell you what, I will take some pictures and send you one, what do you say?"

"That would be lovely, dear. Do it soon."

"Okay. Felicia I have to go now. I will call you again, soon. Bye for now. I am glad it came out about Raul. He is finally going to get what he deserves. Bye, I love you!"

"Bye, dear. I love you too!"

Joanna put down the receiver. She did a pirouette around the living room. She was elated. What news! Wait till she tells Maria. That filthy, lousy bastard. Oh, to see his face now, it would be payment enough for all those years of fear, anguish and shame. She was going to heal, she was going to be a normal person, finally, and hope that she'd find a man she could love and give herself to. She knew it wasn't going to be easy for the scars were too deep, but this was a start. She wondered if the prayer that she prayed with Maria to Jesus had anything to do with Raul being arrested, but she was starting to see the power of prayers at work. She said a thank you to Jesus and a silent prayer. Maria had candles by her shrine. She took one candle and lit it, she then knelt in front of the shrine and remained there for a long time, just mesmerized, her mind racing; she was so excited that her thoughts went in all directions. Would she go and testify against him? Yes, she would. He could not harm her anymore; he was in jail. Her clothes would not catch on fire and the police were not going to blame her for the molestation. Nobody would say it was her fault, that she liked it, and that she was making him do it. Oh, the slime! She was suddenly very hungry so she went to the kitchen and fixed herself a good breakfast. Food had never tasted so good to her. This was the beginning of her walk to freedom.

Joanna had the rest of the day in front of her. She remembered that Maria had left her a telephone number to call, for the County

Mental Health Clinic. She found the number and dialed. If she was to testify in court against Raul she needed a support group to see her through. The woman who answered the phone was very polite. Joanna told her that she was interested in being in a group, and did they have group therapy. Yes, she replied but she needed to talk to a doctor first and he would decide what therapy to follow. Joanna asked her about paying for the visit. She told her that they had a billing system where you pay according to how much you earn. Joanna told her that she didn't work yet but that she would be starting this week and would be making five-fifteen an hour. How much would she have to pay? "Twenty dollar per visit," she replied. They had an opening for that day, would she be able to come? "Yes," replied Joanna.

She got off the phone and got dressed. The appointment was for 1:00 pm, she was to see Doctor Steinman, George Steinman. The clinic was three blocks away from Maria's place so Joanna didn't have to catch a bus or walk a long distance. It was in a small building at the corner of Sixth and Cedar. Joanna walked inside. There was a small reception room where a young, nice looking girl of about twenty years old was the receptionist. She asked Joanna for her name and told her to wait in the waiting room and Dr. Steinman would be right with her. The waiting room was small, also. There was a man waiting there as well. He looked as if he was sedated and was talking to himself which threw Joanna off and she kind of had second thoughts about being there. She hoped the people in the group weren't as obviously sick. A door opened and a young doctor called Joanna's name.

"Hi, Joanna how are you doing today? I am Dr. Steinman, please come in."

"Hello, Dr. Steinman. How are you?"

"What can I do for you today?"

"I have some emotional problems I have to work through and I need a support group around me, to help me deal with molestation issues. I was molested by my adoptive parent from when I was seven years old until I was eighteen and I am just now starting to talk about it. A couple of days ago he got arrested for molesting a little girl and is now in jail. I've decided that I am going to testify against him in court and I can't do it alone, I need help. Can you put me in a group or individual therapy?"

"Have you ever taken medication, Joanna?"

"No, never. Why, do you think I need to?"

"Not unless you can't cope or have feelings of depression that last more than two weeks. How is your sleep? Do you sleep well at night?"

"Dr. Steinman, to be honest with you I have nightmares every night. I have had them since I was four years old, that I can remember. If there was a pill that could stop me from having these nightmares I would gladly take it."

"I can prescribe some pills for you that will make you sleep better. I'll schedule you for individual therapy, at first and after you've resolved this issue of sexual molestation I'll put you in group therapy. How does that sound?"

"You are the doctor. You know best. I'll do whatever you suggest."

"The therapist I'll assign you to is Jill Thompson. She is very experienced, especially in sexual molestation issues. Plus, her being a woman will help you feel more open and relaxed. Here is the prescription for the pills. Ask the receptionist for the address of the pharmacist, on Sixth Avenue. I'll see you next month, Joanna; I hope everything works out for you."

"Thank you, Dr. Steinman. Good bye!"

Joanna left the doctor's office and stopped by the receptionist. She scheduled the appointments for Joanna. Joanna asked for a Monday appointment because she was off from work then. When it came time to pay the bill she told Sara, the receptionist, that she didn't have the money and asked if she could send her the bill. Sara agreed and gave Joanna some forms to fill out. When all was done Joanna left. It was 2:00 pm. Still four and a half hours until Maria came home. She decided to go for a walk to Horton Plaza where she could spend her time looking through the many, many stores. She went to the bookstore on the third level, and spent at least an hour there. There were many books that she liked, but of course she didn't have any money. She was hungry but she couldn't buy any food, so she decided to go back to Maria's place and get something to eat there. She'd have to wait to buy the prescription the doctor gave her until the next week, when she had her first week's pay. She was elated.

She arrived at the apartment and fixed herself a sandwich. She then sat in front of the television waiting for the time to go by. Six-thirty finally arrived and as Maria entered the door Joanna, all excited, told her about Raul being arrested. Maria was in shock. She couldn't believe her ears. She said aloud that she was wondering if their prayers to Jesus Christ a couple of days before had anything to do with him being arrested. Joanna said she had wondered the same thing. She also told Maria of her intention of testifying against Raul in court and Maria approved wholeheartedly. Since it was Monday night Maria asked Joanna if she wanted to go with her to church to pray for people who had requested prayers. Joanna said yes, so they both went. Theresa and Penny were already there and they greeted them happily with a hug and a kiss.

Maria introduced Joanna to the rest of the group, which was comprised of Joe, Rick, Christine, and Paul. Joe, Rick and Paul were black men. Joe was in his forties, had a neatly trimmed moustache and a nice smile. He was retired from the Navy and lived on his pension. Rick had a slim figure, a nice handsome face and was in his thirties. Paul was a very tall man, six-five, always wore sports clothes and walked with a limp because of problems to his left knee. Christine was an older, white haired woman who walked around with a respirator because of breathing problems. Maria didn't like Paul very much because he talked a lot and liked theatrical gestures. He shouted when he talked and once he started talking he wouldn't shut up anymore. Some nights there were no prayers recited because of that. He took too much time. Maria hoped that he wouldn't do that tonight because she really wanted Joanna see what the prayer meeting was all about.

Everybody was given a list of names and prayers requests. To those were added other names and requests from the participants of the prayer meeting. Before Paul had a chance to start talking, the meeting was underway. Each, in turn, read some of the requests and recited a prayer to the Lord to save or to grant what the requestor wished. Joanna didn't pray, she just observed and kept her head bent most of the time. When the list was over Paul started to preach and read from the Bible. He was very emphatic about asking Jesus Christ for anything our hearts desired and we would receive it. And that Jesus Christ has given us a power of attorney to use to ask the Father in His name. How easy it is for us to access our Father in heaven, through our Lord Jesus Christ. At eight o'clock Maria and Joanna left and went home. Maria asked Joanna what she thought of the meeting and Joanna replied that it was fine, and that it was very generous, and very Christian of them to do that. Maria confided that she might stop going because most of the time there wasn't time to pray because of Paul and that they had to bring the list of prayers home.

Once in the apartment they had dinner and settled themselves in front of the television. Joanna told Maria about her visit to County Mental Health. Maria was very pleased to hear that and she congratulated Joanna.

"So tell me more about Raul. How did it happen?"

"I don't know much, I was in shock when Felicia told me. All I know is that he invited our neighbor's little girl into the house with the excuse of giving her candies and then he molested her. They have witnesses. Her little friends saw the whole thing through the kitchen window. He has no excuses. The pig!"

"When is the trial?"

"Next month. I have decided to testify against him. Felicia is aware of what he did to me and she wants him punished too. I'll have to ask for some time off to go to the trial, but I am sure it will be alright."

"I am sure it will be alright too. What do you say about praying to close the day, would you like that?"

"Yes, I would like that. Can I pray?"

"Oh, yes, it will be great. I am glad you volunteered."

Joanna took Maria's hands and held them in her hands. They were facing each other on the couch, their heads bent.

"Dear Lord, I want to thank you for taking me into your fold. I am new at this but I hope that you will listen to my prayers, anyway. I pray for everyone we know, good or bad. I am thankful for Maria and I ask you to bless her for her kindness to me, and that you also bless her daughter Elizabeth. Please put a shield around them and protect them always and forever. I pray for myself and for this trial that is coming up. Give me strength and courage to face Raul in court; don't let me be afraid of him anymore and guide me on what I will say in court. Forgive us for our sins and help us not to sin anymore. I pray all this in Jesus' name. Amen!"

"So, how did I do, Maria?" asked Joanna."

"You did splendidly, Joanna. That was a good prayer."

"You know, Maria, I have doubts. What if we believe in Jesus and it turns out that He does not exist, that we believed in vain."

"I have doubts, too Joanna. But the more the doubts, the more I pray. Even if it turned out that we believed in vain we have certainly not lost anything, but gained a lot. Christianity teaches us to love, and love fulfills the law. By loving and forgiving, by believing in Jesus Christ we have access to God and to His kingdom. But if we don't believe and it turns out to be true we can be lost and damned forever. Would you like to take that chance? Joanna, you can keep believing, without doubts and without fears. Now what do you say we call it a night and go to bed?"

"I vote yes. Good night, Maria!"

"Good night, Joanna!"

CHAPTER THIRTEEN

Tuesday was very slow for Joanna. It seemed to her that time never passed. She straightened out the living room, did the dishes then sat in the living room not knowing what to do with herself. Her anxiety was growing. Tomorrow would be her first day at work and she was very nervous about it. She tried to picture herself at work. She had confidence that she could do the job well. She worried whether she would be accepted by the people in the restaurant; how big was the workload; and about being paid under the table. She selected the clothes that she was going to wear: A pair of jeans and a red shirt. The shirt had the logo *"Coors"* on its front and it needed to be ironed so she proceeded to do that. She fixed herself a sandwich because she was hungry, and then decided to go for a walk. She directed her steps towards Horton Plaza, where she looked for hours, browsing through clothes neatly arranged on racks, thinking that soon she would be able to afford to buy some of them. At Nordstrom she left quickly because the prices were astronomical but browsed longer at Mervyn's as the prices were more affordable and the clothes more to her liking. Daydreaming about what she would buy if she had the money she passed by a store clerk who was giving free T-shirts if you applied for a Mervyn's credit card. She completed the form and received a free T-shirt. Not bad, she thought. She knew that her application would be denied because she had no credit, but in the meantime she made out with a T-shirt that she could wear to go to work and look more decent.

On her way out of Mervyn's she passed by Starbucks. The smell of coffee made her linger, breathe in deeply. Seeing a customer walking out with a *Caramel Macchiato* she wished she had the money to buy herself one. For a minute she thought about standing at the corner and beg for enough change, but she changed her mind, feeling a little ashamed. There were tables and chairs outside so she sat down for a while observing people passing by. A man with blue and purple hair tied in a knot in the back of his head was sitting at the table next to hers. He was in his thirties and cleanly shaven. Joanna kept looking at him without being obvious. What in the world could make a man paint his hair in such colors, she asked herself. An old man passed by. He was walking with a cane in one hand and a disposable camera in the other. He was wearing a suit that resembled a paramilitary uniform, had a moustache and a pointed beard that, together with his felt hat, made him look alpine. He was wispy with mischievous eyes, observing everything in his path. Turning around he stopped by the man with blue and purple hair. "Can I take your picture? I love the blue hair," he said. "I would rather you didn't," replied the man. Without regards to what the man said the old man proceeded to snap a picture. The younger man was about to get up but changed his mind. "You were about this close to having your camera taken away from you," he said. "Well, I asked you," replied the old man. "But obviously you didn't hear me say that I said I'd rather you wouldn't." The old man shrugged his shoulders and walked away. A few feet ahead, he stopped to take a picture of a couple passing by. They gave him hostile stares, but he kept on walking as if nothing mattered.

Joanna had been enjoying the scene with her legs crossed and laid back. Soon after the man left she got up and walked towards the center of the Plaza. She went past the big Jessop's clock and the selling booths, looking avidly at the merchandise. When she reached Victoria's Secret she walked into the store. A sales clerk approached her asking if she needed help with anything. "Just looking," she replied. The front of the store had creams, lotions, and various fragrances. Trying some on she decided that her favorite one was the apple scented body lotion. She would definitely come back when she had the money to buy one. She walked to another section of the store that displayed underwear. The bras were beautiful and sexy and she lingered there for a long time trying to choose one that she'd be able to afford in the future. *Better to buy one of good quality even if it costs more*, she told herself, *it'll last longer.* The panties were on sale but she thought they were a little expensive. Sexy nightgowns and baby-dolls caught her eyes but she knew she didn't want any of them because it wasn't her. She was more the type for flannel nightgowns like her grandmother would wear; anything not to show her body to a man. She felt sadness in her heart thinking about how Raul had tainted her life with his libidinous acts. A wave of shame came over her and she walked out of the store almost in tears.

****

Wednesday. Why was time going so slow? Joanna's anxiety grew to a high pitch. She paced the floor restlessly not knowing what to do with herself. When four-thirty came around she fixed herself a sandwich and ate it very slowly. She didn't know if she was going to eat at Giovanni's so she ate even though it wasn't dinnertime yet, and she wasn't hungry. At five-thirty she left the apartment and walked all the way to Hillcrest since she didn't have the money for the bus. Twenty-five minutes later she was at Giovanni's, perspiring and hot. She hesitated at the door but she took a deep breath and went in. Giovanni was there. As he saw her he said,

"Ciao, carissima. How are you doing? You made it!" He sounded very enthusiastic and real glad to see her.

"I am fine. A little hot, that's all. I walked all the way here."

So far so good.

"Here, let me show you where the kitchen is," said Giovanni, extending an arm towards her. He led the way to the back of the restaurant to a large room. In the middle of the room there was a table covered by pots and pans, fresh herbs and spices, bowls full of cooked spaghetti and other types of pasta. On the left of the table there were two stoves where the two cooks, Emilio and Franco, were busy cooking, stirring food in the pots. In one corner of the room was the oven with wood chips burning to keep it hot for the pizzas. Mario, the *pizzaiolo,* was taking a pizza out. He was covered in sweat because of the heat emanating from the oven. On the right side of the table there were two large sinks where dishes were being washed by Alfredo. He would wash in one sink, rinse in another, and put the dishes on a shelf on the right side of the sinks, to drip dry. The first impression that Joanna had was that of chaos. Not dirty, just messy. Giovanni introduced Joanna to all of them:

"This is Joanna, everybody. You treat her right, you hear? She is our new dishwasher. She'll be helping Alfredo. Alfredo you show Joanna what to do. I'll go back in the front now; I am needed there," he said and walked out.

Alfredo went to a closet and took out a white overcoat.

"Here," he said. "Put this on, Joanna, so you won't get your clothes wet."

Joanna took the overcoat and put it on. It was too big, hiding her slim figure. She started to wash dishes while Alfredo would rinse. This is easy, she thought, giving sideways glances at Alfredo. She refused to wear the gloves that Alfredo handed her. She could get a better grip with her bare hands.

Alfredo was forty-six years old. He was of medium height, maybe five-feet-four inches tall, about two inches shorter than Joanna. He had a gold tooth in the front of his mouth that would shine every time he smiled. He looked slim though Joanna couldn't tell for sure because his overcoat hid his figure.

"Are you married?" asked Joanna.

"Yes, I am. I have been married for twenty years and I have two kids, one boy and a girl, but they are not here in the United States. They live in Caserta, Italy. I send them money every month and go visit them every two years. What about you, Joanna, where are you from?"

"I am from Minneapolis," said Joanna. "How can you afford to send your family money? This job doesn't pay very much!"

"I have two jobs. In the mornings I work at the Convention Center. I do a little bit of everything: Set tables and chairs, distribute flyers, clean, etc.. I don't make a lot there either, but every little bit helps."

"How many hours do you sleep every night?"

"Well, I finish here at eleven and I am in bed by midnight. I'd say about seven hours per night, which isn't bad. I don't wake-up tired in the morning. I am fresh as a rose. Are you married, Joanna?"

"No, I have never been married and I probably never will."

"How come you've never been married? A pretty girl like you. I am sure lots of guys would like to marry you."

"Well, it's a long story. I just don't want to go into it right now."

"I am a very good listener, Joanna. If you ever need a friend, a shoulder to cry on, I am here. Don't forget."

"Thank you, Alfredo." Joanna was moved by the offer and decided that she liked Alfredo. Her anxiety diminished a little because of his kind words.

Giovanni's restaurant had a large room with about twenty tables and a smaller room with about five tables. One wall of the large room was covered by wine bottles, imported mostly from Italy. The cash register was right by the door, where the hostess-cashier stood. About ten tables and chairs were set outside, on the patio, which was covered by vines, providing a nice shade in the summer. Inside the restaurant, on the walls, were antique photographs of places in Italy. The tables were covered by white and red, checkered table-cloths. On each table there was a vase with a fresh rose in it. Two waiters and two waitresses served in the restaurant, plus the cashier-hostess. On the right of the large room there were six steps descending into the nightclub. In the dimly lit nightclub, was a bar and the room was filled with tables. Two large couches were by the piano. The nightclub opened at ten-thirty. It was frequented mostly by homosexuals who lived in the Hillcrest area, but straight people, mostly friends of Giovanni, went there as well. The nightclub closed at 2:00 am.

Giovanni Grimaldi was fifty-five years old, five-feet-ten inches tall. His hair was jet black with splashes of gray at the temples. Thick eyelashes framed his green eyes. He was slim and didn't look a day older than forty-five. He was the only son of two immigrants from Taormina, Sicily. He had been in the restaurant business since he was twenty-five years old. His first restaurant had been located downtown, in the Gaslamp Quarter but he moved to this location after ten years due to pressure from mobsters who had tried to run him out of business because he refused to pay them a cut from his earnings. He had been at this location for the past twenty years. Mobsters were still after him to get a share of the business and he agreed to pay them a smaller portion of his earnings. In exchange they made sure that supplies were delivered on time, that they were fresh and they even sent customers to eat at the restaurant. Sometime they would hold meetings there by dining in the smaller room, which had doors that could be closed, assuring them of privacy.

Giovanni Grimaldi's wife had died five years earlier of breast cancer. Giovanni was devastated and had not remarried. They had no children. After the death of his wife he had sold his house and moved in with his mother. He put all his energy in the business and barely had any recreation time. On his time off he would stay at home and relax, except on Sunday mornings when he would accompany his mother to church. He was not much on dating and there really wasn't anyone he was interested in even though there were plenty of women interested in him. He was very successful and very handsome, but he never let it go to his head. In fact, he was very humble and that quality made people like him right away.

Giovanni found himself thinking about Joanna, and what he felt when he saw her, all sweaty and out of breath. He felt a stirring in his loins but disregarded it thinking that it was only because he hadn't had any sex for a very long time. Joanna was very attractive, but she needed a major makeover. Her hair was bleached and stringy looking, her clothes were second-hand, and when she smiled she lost points due to stains on her teeth. He wondered how she was doing and when he had a few minutes available, he walked to the kitchen to check on her. She was washing dishes and talking to Alfredo. He saw her laughing in response to something Alfredo said. She threw her head back and laughed a hearty laugh. *I hope she is not the type who throws herself at every man she meets*, he thought. That could cause trouble with the men in the kitchen and he needed his men to pay attention to what they were doing, without the distraction of a pretty woman.

"So, how's everything going?" he asked everyone.

"Oh, just grand, boss," said Alfredo.

"Joanna, you are not tired, are you? Around nine o'clock you can take a break. Half an hour. I'll pay you also for your dinnertime. Ask for anything on the menu. It's on the house," Giovanni told Joanna. He felt compassion for her, seeing that she was all sweaty; in fact she had hair sticking to her forehead and her face was flushed.

"Thank you, Giovanni," said Joanna shyly. She was a little intimidated by him. He was the boss and he was so good-looking; also very generous. She wondered if he was married. Later she would ask Alfredo. She hoped they could have dinner together and talk. It was eight-thirty and she was tired. She had never seen so many dishes in her life. How she was going to last till 2:00 am she had no idea. Giovanni left after asking the cooks if everything was alright.

At nine o'clock Alfredo told Joanna that they could go on break. Joanna looked at the menu to see what she wanted to eat. She chose lasagna while Alfredo chose ravioli. Emilio, the shorter cook, gave them a generous portion each.

"This way, bambina," said Alfredo to Joanna while pointing to the closet. Joanna thought he was joking but when she entered the closet she saw that it was furnished with a table and four chairs.

"Our very own dining room," said Alfredo and he explained that this was where the employees took their meals. In fact, they'd better hurry up because the waiters and waitresses were next, followed by the cooks.

"Would you like some wine?" Alfredo asked and before Joanna had a chance to answer he was pouring her a half glass of red wine. "Not too much. We still have a ways to go. We don't want to get drunk and sleepy, do we?"

"Thank you, Alfredo, for everything you're doing for me," said Joanna. "Say, is Giovanni married? I noticed that he didn't wear a wedding band."

"He is a widower. His wife died five years ago from breast cancer. One moment she was fine and three months later she was dead. It was a shock to all of us. Poor thing. She was so beautiful and so kind to everybody. I don't know why the good Lord took her but let His will be done."

"Are you a Christian, Alfredo?"

"I am Catholic. I go to church every Sunday. What about you?"

"I am a very new Christian. I just gave myself to Jesus last Sunday. So you can say I am a babe in Christ."

"Maybe we can go to church together some time," said Alfredo while eating his ravioli. Joanna was enjoying the lasagna immensely and after they were through eating she complimented the cooks. They all beamed.

Emilio was a short, plump man in his fifties. He came from Salerno, Italy. He had been a cook all his life and enjoyed it very much. He had been at Giovanni's for three years.

Franco was related to Giovanni. He was a second cousin. He also came from Taormina, Sicily, like Giovanni. He was in his thirties and was very masculine and handsome. *It must run in the family*, thought Joanna. Lastly, Joanna asked Mario where he was from. Mario was from Naples, Italy *where they make the best pizza,* he said. Tomorrow she should try one of his pizzas. Joanna said she sure would and she and Alfredo went back to work. *These people are so nice*, thought Joanna. *I sure like working here.*

At eleven o'clock all the dishes, pots and pans were clean. The cooks had left at ten-thirty since they weren't serving any dinner after that. All that remained to be done was to mop the floor and Alfredo told Joanna that he would do that since the mop was very heavy. Joanna was relieved as her back hurt and her feet were aching. She was wondering what she was going to do till 2:00 am when Giovanni walked in. He told Joanna that she would be downstairs, in the nightclub, washing glasses and cups for the bartender. But she needed to wear a uniform. Joanna looked puzzled. She hadn't expected this. She felt more comfortable in the kitchen. Plus she looked a disaster. What were the customers going to think? And what about the uniform? She hoped it wasn't the miniskirt she had seen the waitresses wear. Yes, that one. Giovanni handed her the uniform complete with black panty hose and told Joanna to go change in the bathroom, then go downstairs and the bartender would show her what to do.

The uniform consisted of a black, very short miniskirt and of a white, cotton blouse. Joanna put them on and looked at herself in the mirror. She'd never have the guts to go out like that, she told herself. She was lingering when she heard a knock on the door. It was Giovanni wondering if she was all right. She opened the door and he looked at her. She had a knockout body but she was so self-conscious. And what about her shoes? She was wearing sneakers and looked ridiculous. Good thing she'd be working behind the counter so customers wouldn't see her feet. Joanna felt incredibly shy and uncomfortable. She wanted to run away. Giovanni asked her again if she was alright and she said yes, everything was fine while asking Jesus to forgive her lie. Giovanni escorted her downstairs and introduced her to Philip, the bartender. Philip was Irish, in his twenties, and about the same age as Joanna. He spoke with a British accent and sometime it was hard to understand what he said. But he was the best bartender in the neighborhood, *coming from a family of drunks*, as he said jokingly. He was good-looking and had to fend off advances from gay patrons on a nightly basis. He was straight, married and his wife was expecting their first child.

A few heads turned when Joanna walked in but everybody went back to what they were doing before. Introductions finished Joanna walked behind the bar quickly and started to wash glasses. There were so many already. Giovanni went to sit down at a table with three other men and a woman. Joanna kept her head down, embarrassed and feeling on display. When she dared to look up she noticed two men holding hands and she winced. She saw another man sticking his tongue in his boyfriend's ear. She came very close to quitting right then, but she told herself that she needed the job and what did she care what people did anyway. She wanted to cry. Around midnight the place was filled with people and the air was full of smoke. Joanna was so busy she barely thought about her discomfort anymore. One time she looked up and saw Giovanni looking at her. A few regulars said hi and welcomed her. She answered politely and went back to her business.

When two o'clock finally came, Joanna went to the bathroom to change her clothes. Coming out she found Giovanni waiting outside the door.

"How are you getting home, Joanna? Is someone coming to pick you up? Your husband maybe, or your boyfriend?"

"I am not married and I don't have a boyfriend. No one is coming to pick me up. I guess I'll just have to walk home."

"You don't have to do that. I can give you a ride home. Where do you live?"

"I live at the corner of Sixth and Elm."

"Great. That's near my house. I live at the corner of Front and Ivy. So let's go."

Giovanni extended an arm around Joanna and escorted her towards a Jaguar parked in front of the restaurant. Joanna was really impressed by the car. It was black with gray, leather interior. The inside of the car smelled new and fragrant. She sat a little uptight and put the seatbelt on.

"You're ready, Joanna? You're all set?"

"Yes I am, thank you Giovanni."

"Well, let's go then. You tell me when we arrive at your place. It must be an apartment because there aren't any houses where you live."

"Yes, it is an apartment. I share it with a friend of mine, Maria, for right now. Later on I will get my own place, maybe." Joanna didn't want to tell him that she was homeless. It was none of his business. Plus she didn't know him yet, so until she found out if she could trust him, just to be on the safe side, she was not going to volunteer any information, in case he was a snob. That's not the impression she had so far but she was cautious.

"So, how did you like your first day on the job? Was it tiring?"

"Yes, very tiring. My hands look like prunes. But I am sure that with time it won't be as tiring. It's also the stress of the first day, all the new people I met, and not knowing what to expect."

"You're right, the first day is very stressful. You did great, by the way. Everybody had a good impression of you. They like you."

"I am glad. I like them too."

They were silent the rest of the way. When they were about to approach the building Joanna lived in, she said: "Here, you can stop in front of the white and blue building, please."

Giovanni parked the car and turned around to face Joanna. All of a sudden, without any warning he grabbed Joanna's head and gave her a kiss on the mouth. With his left hand he fondled her breast. Joanna was under shock. She hadn't expected anything like that to happen. She tried to free herself of Giovanni who had a strong grip of the back of her head. She also tried to push his hand away from her breast. She had to try really hard but she finally succeeded. She slapped Giovanni hard on the face. She was furious.

"How dare you?" she yelled. "Just because you are my boss and gave me a ride home doesn't mean you can do what you just did. Nobody kissed me before, ever. I quit." She was hurt and frustrated and she was really angry with him.

"Are you serious? Nobody kissed you before? How old are you?"

"That's none of your business," replied Joanna. She was sorry she mentioned it. She didn't want to look like an inexperienced schoolgirl, a teenager. This was a grown man she was dealing with and she wanted to be a woman.

"I am really sorry, Joanna. I don't know what got into me. Ever since my wife died I haven't dated anyone but that doesn't make right what I just did. So, how old are you? Will you please tell me?"

Joanna's anger lessened a bit when she heard him mention the death of his wife. She saw him as a lonely man and felt sorry for him. His left cheek had red marks where she had slapped him and she wondered if she had hurt him. He didn't seem hurt but pleased even though he had said he was sorry. Joanna wondered what he was smiling about and that made her angry again.

"So, do you do this to all the women you give rides to? I am really sorry about the death of your wife, but that doesn't make it right. You shouldn't do things like that. I trusted you and you betrayed my trust. I guess you realize that I can't work for you anymore and I am really sorry because I needed the job badly."

"Oh, please don't quit. I promise I will be a gentleman from now on. I won't even touch you with a finger if you don't want me too. We really need you, Joanna. Will you please reconsider?"

Joanna was really confused and didn't know what to answer. One minute he was acting like a horny beast and the next minute he was imploring like a little child. She was wondering how old he was and didn't realize that she said that out loud.

"I'll tell you how old I am if you tell me how old you are; is that fair?"

"Okay, I am twenty-eight years old."

"And in twenty-eight years you have never been kissed? Where have you been living, on a mountain all by yourself?"

"Like I said before, it's none of your business. I don't care to discuss my sex life with you. So, how old are you?"

"I am old enough to be your father," Giovanni said, serious all of a sudden. "I am fifty-five years old."

"Well, you don't look fifty-five, maybe forty-five, but not fifty-five."

"Thank you for your kindness. So, will we see you tonight?"

"I have to think about it. I'll let you know." Joanna was about to open the door to get out but Giovanni stopped her. He got out of the car, went to her side and opened the door. "You see, I can be a real gentleman," he said embarrassed all of a sudden by the thought of what he had done.

"Thank you, Giovanni." Joanna was not impressed anymore even though she had never before been in a Jaguar and no one had ever opened a car door for her. She was too angry for that. She took her keys out of her pocket and walked towards the building leaving him there like a fool. She heard him get in the car and drive away as she was climbing the stairs to Maria's apartment. *The louse*, she thought, with tears in her eyes. Why did he have to go and do something like that? She didn't encourage him in the least, so what was his problem? She wished Maria were up so she could talk to her about it, but Maria, as expected, was sound asleep. She could hear her snoring. She made her bed, and exhausted, fell asleep right away.

CHAPTER FOURTEEN

Joanna was in an empty room, all by herself. All of a sudden hands appeared out of nowhere. The hands were touching her breasts, taking her shirt off. She tried to stop them but the more she tried more hands appeared. They were squeezing, caressing her. She didn't want to succumb to the pleasure they gave her and she was yelling to leave her alone. As she looked at her breasts she saw milk come out of them. She screamed and woke up. The first thought that came to her mind was that of Giovanni and what he did to her. She felt a great sadness come over her. She looked at the clock on the cable box. It said eleven-thirty. She had slept eight-and-a-half hours. She had been so tired when she went to bed that she fell asleep the minute her head hit the pillow. But now she was wide- awake and she couldn't help but think of what had happened. She was not angry anymore, but she needed to talk to Maria about it. She wanted a second opinion before she made up her mind whether to go back to work or not. She dialed Maria's phone number at work.

"Maria, can you talk?"

"Yes, Joanna. What's up?"

"As you know, I went to work last night. Everything was fine and everybody was nice to me. I was dead tired by 2:00 am and couldn't wait to come home. Giovanni, the owner of the restaurant, gave me a ride home. Before I left he kissed me and fondled my breast. I slapped him and said that I'd quit. He begged me not to quit and I told him that I'd let him know. He was very apologetic about what had happened and seemed really sorry even though he was smiling at that point. Now I don't know what to do. What do you think I should do?"

"I wouldn't quit if I were you. Italian men are like that. They make a pass at you to see if you are easy or not. They do it on purpose. If you let them fondle you, you are labeled easy and they won't respect you. If you resist them and slap them, like you did, they think you are a saint and they will worship you, put you on a pedestal. I don't know which is worse, to tell you the truth. So, in my opinion, you have scored big and now you don't have anything to worry about. Actually, you have to guard against him putting you on a pedestal, like I said before, because in that case it is much worse. You will have to act saintly all the time and possibly lose your freedom. Just be yourself and shrug it off. I know this is shocking to you because of what happened with Raul but don't be afraid. He won't touch you anymore. What does he look like, anyway?"

"He is very good-looking but he is fifty-five years old. He could be my father. But that doesn't matter because nothing is ever going to happen between us. I know that. Especially now, after what happened he won't have anything to do with me."

"You might be wrong there, my friend. Who knows? Just don't be afraid, okay?"

"Okay, Maria. I'll do as you say."

"Joanna, I have to go. I can't talk anymore, my supervisor just walked in. Bye."

Joanna put down the phone and went to the kitchen to make herself some instant coffee. She sat on the couch to drink it and think. What was she going to do? She didn't want to give up her new job; she felt comfortable there, except working in the nightclub. She didn't like that at all but she hoped that with time she'd get used to it. She was thinking about calling Giovanni and telling him that she wouldn't quit, but the thought of what happened made her hesitate. She didn't want to admit it to herself but when he was kissing her she felt a twinge in her stomach. But she also felt pleasure after that. Why? Was it normal? She didn't know. She liked

Giovanni and felt attracted to him, but he was so much older than she. *Age doesn't matter*, she told herself. He doesn't look fifty-five, anyway. But she was running way ahead of herself. Nothing ever was going to happen between them, she knew that.

She grabbed the phone and dialed Giovanni's number. One of the day waitresses answered the phone. She left a message that she would be there at 6:00 pm and hung up. She felt disappointed that she hadn't talked to Giovanni, but just as well. She fixed herself some scrambled eggs with toast and ate them, thankfully. When she got paid she would give Maria some money to pay for her food, but right now she couldn't so she'd have to wait. She thought about asking Maria for bus fare yet knowing her, she was surprised that she hadn't offered it to her. She must not have thought about it, she thought. What was she going to do until four-thirty? She looked around the apartment. Maria's bed was unmade, the floor needed vacuuming, the dishes needed to be washed. The thought of washing dishes almost made her ill but she told herself to get over it because she had just started and it wasn't good that she was feeling that way. She got busy and by the time she was finished the apartment looked nice and clean. It was 3:00 pm.

****

Maria was thinking about what Joanna had told her. So typical, so Italian. *They are all the same, it doesn't matter where they are, here or in Italy. It must be in their genes.* She was curious about Giovanni and she thought that she'd like to meet him and see for herself what kind of man he was. He must like Joanna, or why else would he have kissed her. She was glad that Joanna had slapped him. If it had been her, she would have done worse than that, maybe punched him. But she didn't have to worry about anything like that happening to her. Men didn't exist in Maria's life. She didn't have the sugar to attract the flies. Plus she was overweight and that didn't help her appearance.

The last relationship that she had was with Eric, a black man, a year older than Maria. He was very handsome and sexy looking. Maria was attracted to him physically. She didn't love him because she was still in love with Michael but she enjoyed having sex with him. When she seriously became a Christian she stopped having sex and he stopped seeing her. He didn't love her either, it was just sex for him too. He used to call her his *"Italian Pepper."* He was a bus driver, had been for seventeen years. Maria would catch the bus and ride it back and forth just to be near him. He was pleasant with the passengers and had many friends and acquaintances.

There was another woman who would ride the bus just to be in his company. She was black also and a Christian. Maria wasn't happy and she would have jealous fits, but Eric would tell her that the woman was just a friend. He also told her that she was a minister and Maria was very cynical about that. Eric never took Maria out. Their relationship was restricted to their bedroom. It wasn't Maria's choice. That's how Eric wanted it. They never did what other couples did: Go see a movie, go to dinner, go for a walk. They only had sex. He would go to Maria's apartment after work, which was always around eleven-thirty at night. They would have sex and after a while he'd leave. Maria felt a little bad about the whole situation but she was just thinking about herself. She hadn't dated anyone for eight years hoping that Michael would come back into her life. When he didn't, Maria decided that she needed to be with somebody or she would die of emotional starvation. It wasn't just the sex part, it was also companionship, even though all she was getting was crumbs.

Eric confided that he had a fantasy woman in his mind and wished that Maria were like that. His fantasy woman was sexy, slender, wore miniskirts and high heels. So Maria bought herself a pair of black shoes and modeled them for him in her bedroom. The heels were so high her legs ached after a while. No, she could never be his fantasy woman. When he told Maria of his fantasy, the picture that came to her mind was that of a hooker, but she didn't tell him that. She also thought that if the Holy Spirit didn't restrain him he would be a pimp. Their relationship never ended formally. He just stopped coming and she just stopped calling him. They were still friends.

****

Joanna watched television until four-thirty. She then got on her way to Giovanni's. She felt trepidation in her heart all the way there. When she got there Giovanni was at the door. He welcomed her and told her that he was happy that she had decided to stay. Joanna went to the kitchen.

"Ciao, bambina. How are you today?" Alfredo welcomed her with a smile. She went to the closet and put on her white overcoat. She started to wash the dishes but Alfredo stopped her.

"No, bambina. Yesterday you washed and I rinsed. Today I wash and you rinse. Is that fair?" Joanna was very pleased with the arrangement and told him so. Emilio, Franco, and Mario said hi to her and asked how she was doing. She wanted to hug them all, she felt so much affection for them already. As they were washing dishes Alfredo told her stories about Italy. He also told her about his family. His wife Maria was a custodian at a school, in Caserta. She lived in a small apartment attached to the school with her son and daughter. They didn't pay any rent. That, and a small salary, coupled with the money that Alfredo sent every month gave them enough to just get by. His son Carlo and his daughter Sabrina were nineteen and twenty years old. They were both attending the university. Carlo wanted to be an engineer and Sabrina wanted to be a teacher. No sacrifices were big enough for their parents. They wanted to see them complete their studies and find decent jobs.

What Joanna didn't understand was why was Alfredo here, in the United States. Why wasn't he in Italy with his family? Couldn't he find a job as dishwasher there? She asked Alfredo. Alfredo told her that in 1980 there was a big earthquake in Caserta, which killed over a thousand people and destroyed many houses. As a result, many people lost their jobs and many were homeless. That's when he decided to expatriate. Originally, the plan was that he would come to the United States and become a citizen. He then would have his wife and children reunite with him. However, so far it had not been financially possible. Besides that, the children were studying at an Italian university and eventually planned to get jobs there. They spoke little English and because of that it would be very hard for them to find employment here. His wife didn't speak English at all and she didn't have any particular skill or much schooling, for that matter. So they decided that, for now, they would see their kids through school, wait until they found jobs, and then his wife would join Alfredo in the United States. Maybe. Maybe he would go back to Italy. He didn't know for sure.

He was a very loving and understanding father. He would call his family once a month and he always wanted to cry by the time he said goodbye. The only thing that kept him going was knowing that, with his sacrifice, he was able to provide for his family.

Going to church every Sunday also helped him. He would talk to the Italian priest afterwards or during confession and felt restored. He suggested she should go to church with him one Sunday. He would like that. Joanna said that she'd love to do that, because he asked her, though she was not Catholic. She was a Born Again Christian.

At a quarter to nine Joanna and Alfredo each ordered a small pizza from Mario. Mario suggested to Joanna that she try the *Margherita*, one of his specialties. It was the simplest of the pizzas, made with mozzarella cheese, tomato sauce, garlic and fresh basil. Joanna said she'd love it. Alfredo chose the vegetarian pizza because he wanted something light. They went to the closet and Alfredo poured Joanna half a glass of red wine. There was always a bottle there for them. Giovanni was very good to his employees and that's another reason why his business was so successful.

"Alfredo, tell me your last name," said Joanna.

"My last name is Esposito. What is yours?"

"Mine is Ruiz. It's Cuban. I was adopted when I was seven-years-old by a couple whose family was originally from Cuba. They gave me their last name."

"No kidding, you were adopted?"

"Yes, I was."

"What about your real parents? Where are they now?"

"I don't know. My father left my mother when I was three-years-old so I haven't seen him since. In fact I don't even know what he looks like. My mother I haven't seen since I was five-and-a-half-years-old. I don't know where she is today. I miss her a lot and I wish that I could see her, but I don't know if that will ever happen."

"Poor bambina. You had a rough life, didn't you?"

"Yes, I did. But I am stronger because of it. Alfredo I need to talk to you about something but you've got to promise not to tell anyone."

"I promise, bambina. What is it?"

"Last night Giovanni gave me a ride home. When I was about to leave, he kissed me and fondled my breast. I slapped him and left my handprint on his face. He apologized and said that he wouldn't do it again. Should I trust him?"

"I have known Giovanni for the past ten years. He has always been good and kind to me and I have never heard any rumors like that before. As far as I know he has always been a gentleman with all the women he knows. Are you sure you didn't do something to lead him on?"

"No Alfredo I wouldn't do that. I have never been kissed before in my life. Last night was the first time. I wouldn't even know how to do it. You don't believe me?"

"It's hard to believe. Not being kissed before. Where have you been living, under a cabbage? Next thing I know you're going to tell me that you are a virgin."

"I am. I swear to you. It's true. What I want to ask you is, if he wants to give me a ride again tonight, should I accept?"

"Yes, of course you should accept. He would get offended if you don't. Take-it-easy on him, kid, will you? He's had a rough time these past five years. I'd hate to see him hurt."

"Well, all right. If you say so."

Joanna ate the pizza with gusto and drank the wine in little sips. She wished they had more time for their break but it was over and they had to return to washing dishes.

****

Maria arrived home at six-thirty. Today it was Thursday and it was Home Fellowship night. She didn't have time to eat anything, just enough time to grab her Bible and be on her way again. She walked for fifteen minutes to Ivy Street where the Home Fellowship was held. She was the first one to get there. The host was Nanette. She managed the beautiful building she lived in, in exchange for free rent and a small salary, which she supplemented every month by house sitting for people she knew. The apartment was small and consisted of one bedroom, a living room, and a small kitchen. Yet she managed to host about ten people every Thursday. Outside the apartment, in the hall, she'd prepare snacks for people to eat before and after the Bible study. She was about five-feet-four-inches tall, had long hair, which she'd tie in a pony tail, was a little overweight, and wore very casual clothing. With her, lived her divorced daughter, Samantha, and her grandchild Jessica.

Samantha was very tall, with short, brown hair and looked nothing like her three sisters, which Nanette had by another man. Samantha was going to college at night and held a job during the day. She was in the living room when Maria arrived, while Nanette was in the kitchen getting the snacks ready. Maria said hi and Nanette came out of the kitchen to give Maria a tight hug. She was always pleased to see her and her hug showed that.

Samantha was busy with her daughter Jessica trying to get her to eat before everybody arrived. There were six chairs around the living room, a couch, love seat, and a rocking chair in which Maria would always choose to sit. That had become her chair and they would always save it for her.

Sitting in the rocking chair, which was covered by a warm blanket, Maria watched television while waiting for the other members of the group to arrive. Jessica had cartoons on. It would soon be turned off. Ten minutes later Peter and his wife Sara arrived followed by Andrea and John. They said hi and took their seats. Then came Martha and her husband Jim. The fellowship leader, Brian, his wife Ruth, and son Richard came at about seven-thirty. Jessica was sent to the bedroom to play there and read some of her books. She already had on her nightgown. Maria went to get some coffee and snacks outside before the meeting started and others did the same.

When everybody was ready, a prayer was said by Brian to start the meeting. They were reading from the book of Romans and Brian went over the last verses from chapter one that they had read the week before. He then assigned passages for everyone to read out loud from the second chapter. When everyone had read their assigned segments, the discussion began. It went on for about an hour and fifteen minutes. A prayer was then said to close the meeting. Brian asked everybody if they had someone or something they needed a prayer for. Peter needed prayers for a job interview that he had the following day; Martha needed prayers for her daughter and grandchildren, because one of them was ill; Jim needed prayers for a test he had the following week; Maria needed prayers for her daughter Elizabeth that she might come to accept Christ in her life. When everybody expressed their requests, prayers were said and the meeting was over.

Everybody stood up and went outside to get coffee and more snacks. Martha had brought some homemade cookies that she had baked herself. Every week someone would bring something. Those who didn't want to bring anything could put money in a coffee canister so that Nanette could use it to buy snacks. Maria would give a dollar every week because she didn't have the time during the week to go to the store and buy something and she didn't like to cook anything herself. Small groups formed. Everybody was chatting and the atmosphere was very cordial. It went on for about half an hour. Brian and his wife would always give Maria a ride home but they were the last ones to leave because Brian helped Nanette to clear the snack table. When all was done everyone left.

It was nine-fifteen by the time Maria got home. She turned the television on to watch the Italian news, which started at nine. It made her feel closer to her family and to her old country. The apartment was deserted, as Maria expected but wasn't one-hundred-percent sure, since receiving the phone call from Joanna that morning. There had been a chance that she might have quit. She was happy to find out that she hadn't. She wondered how things were going for Joanna. She hoped that she would reconcile with her boss.

****

At two o'clock Joanna went to the bathroom to change her clothes. When she got out she found Giovanni again waiting for her. He offered her a ride home, afraid that she might refuse. But Joanna said yes. Once in the car they drove in silence the few miles to where Joanna lived. When they were about to arrive she told Giovanni that her roommate Maria was Italian. Giovanni was very surprised and said to Joanna that she should introduce her to him.

Maybe she could take her to the restaurant, and they could have dinner there. Free of course. Joanna thanked him for the offer and said that it was very generous of him to do that. After talking with Alfredo Joanna's feelings toward Giovanni had mellowed out some and she wasn't angry with him anymore, but she still was a little anxious and embarrassed. She didn't want to bring the subject up anymore as she thought she would. She looked at his profile and was again surprised at how handsome he was. He certainly didn't look fifty-five to her and he had such distinguished features.

His clothes were impeccable and he looked like those fancy advertising in some fancy magazine. He wore Italian-made suits and shoes and she wondered where he bought them. They looked expensive. Joanna felt very poor and inferior in his presence, but he was so humble and kind towards her and to everybody else. She felt very attracted to him but she knew that he would never consider her as a potential mate. Especially after what happened the day before. He was probably looking for an older woman, closer to his age. One who was refined, wore expensive clothes, and had lots of money like him. Maybe one who had a business of her own. Joanna felt very depressed. She wished he would say something but he was silent and didn't mention the day before at all. When they arrived she looked uncomfortable not knowing what to say and since he wasn't saying anything she quickly thanked him for the ride. She thought that he was going to get out of the car to open the door for her but he wasn't moving. Confused she opened the door and got out. Giovanni waited till she got inside the building, then left.

Joanna found Maria up, watching an old movie on channel 33. Maria asked her how it went at the restaurant and what happened with Giovanni.

"Nothing happened. He was nice and cordial to me as if nothing had happened. He said he was glad that I had decided to stay and then I didn't speak to him until he offered me a ride home. By the way, I told him that you were Italian and he said he'd like to meet you. He invited you to the restaurant for dinner, free of charge. Maybe we could go this Monday or Tuesday. I really want you to meet him. He is special and I like him a lot, but he probably won't have anything to do with me, anymore, after what happened yesterday. He was so polite and so quiet that you'd think I imagined it all. Alfredo told me that nothing like that has ever happened before, as far as he knows. Do you think he likes me?"

"He probably does," Maria said. Joanna perked up, her hopes rising. Maria knew Italian men; what if she was right? "Like I told you this morning, Italian men test women. He wouldn't have done it if he didn't like you at least a little. Now it's up to you. Don't flirt with anybody; don't be easy. If he likes you he'll come around. Of course you need to do something about your appearance. A stylish haircut, a visit to the dentist, some new clothes, and some therapy, don't forget that. When you get the money this Sunday we'll make plans on how to spend it. We'll make a budget."

"I have an appointment this Monday with Jill Thompson at County Mental Health. I can't wait till I tell her everything. I hope that she can really help me. Dr. Steinman said she's very experienced in sexual molestation issues. I'll have to tell Giovanni about it too when I ask for a couple of days off to go to the trial. God, I hope it's on Monday or Tuesday so I won't have to tell him. I don't really want him to know. It's so embarrassing."

"My advice is that you don't tell him. Just tell him that Felicia is sick and that you need to go for a couple of days to help her. Joanna, I have a book that you can read. I meant to tell you but I forgot. It's titled '*The Courage to Heal*', *A Guide for Women Survivors of Child Sexual Abuse*, by Ellen Bass and Laura Davis. I have only read a little but it is very good. You can read it while you go to therapy.

I am sure it will help you a lot. Also, continue to read the Bible, that will help you too, especially the New Testament."

"Yea, I have been reading it, but it's like stepping into another dimension when I read it. Plus it scares me when it talks about trials and tribulation and hell fire. It's like a bad omen."

"That's why you need to go to church and hear the pastor explain it to you. He makes it more relevant and more realistic. What about Sunday, do you want to go to church with me again? I know you come home at two-thirty so you won't get a lot of sleep but for one day only it'll be worth it."

"Okay, I'll go. But you'll have to wake me up."

"I will. Joanna before we go to bed I think that we should pray. Do you want to pray or do you want me to?"

"I think I'd like to pray, if you don't mind." They held hands together as Joanna recited a prayer. She prayed for her job, that Giovanni would respect her in the future, that her testimony at the trial would be convincing. She also prayed for Maria and her daughter. "Well, I am getting better at this all the time," she said when she finished. Now is time to go to bed. Good night, Maria."

"Good night, Joanna."

CHAPTER FIFTEEN

Friday morning. The ringing of the phone woke Maria up. She quickly picked it up so that Joanna wouldn't wake up. She looked at the radio clock on top of the television, in her bedroom. It was ten-thirty. It was Joseph. Joseph was a black man, in his early thirties that Maria used to date before Eric, the bus driver. Her relationship with him was very short because he was a misfit. He was very poor. In fact he didn't have a dime or a job. He was very unrealistic in his expectations. He wanted to be a disk- jockey. Maria loaned him three hundred dollars to buy a used car, after he destroyed the one that he had. He still had not repaid her.

He was six-feet-four- inches tall, was very well built and had dread locks. He was very handsome. He came from Chicago where he told Maria that he had shot a man, and didn't know whether he had killed him or not because he ran away. Maria was not scared of him because he didn't seem violent to her and he seemed to love her. A few months earlier he had been making collect phone calls about once a week. Maria would refuse to accept them so he finally stopped. She imagined that he was broke, as usual. She also thought that he might be in jail.

"I am sorry I called you collect," Joseph said. "I was in jail and that was the only way that I could call you. I hope that you are not mad at me."

"No, Joseph, I am not mad at you. Why were you in jail?"

"Burglary."

"So, what did you steal? Oh, never mind. How long were you in jail?"

"For almost a year. I did lot of thinking while I was there. I have changed. I am really sorry for things that I did to you. I always think about you. Ours was the best relationship that I have ever had. And I remembered your phone number; thank God you haven't changed it."

"Where are you staying, Joseph?"

"In a motel, in Old Town. It's cheaper this way. I'll wait until my financial situation changes before I move into an apartment. I am going to school to become a computer programmer. I have some grants. I also have been putting applications in and I have a couple of job interviews next week."

"Don't they ask you if you have been in jail on the job applications?"

"Yes, some do, but not all of them. Anyway, I went for a job interview for the transit company and they didn't seem to mind. Are you sure you are not mad at me?"

"Yes, I am sure. I have forgiven you. But I still want my money."

"You'll get your money back if it's the last thing I do."

"You don't have to pay me all at one time. Whatever you can afford, like fifty dollars a month. By the way, since you are into computers you might be interested that I have an extra computer I was going to sell for $150. I'll sell it to you for $100. It's really good. It's got Windows 95, Word, an internal modem for the Internet. Think about it and let me know. You know Joseph, I am really happy that you are getting your life together, like going to school and looking for a job. Do you pray?"

"Yes, I do."

"Do you believe in Jesus?"

"Yes, I do. I went to church a couple of times while I was in jail."

"There is a church right next to my building that I attend. They have services on Wednesday at 7:00 pm and on Sunday at 9:30 am. Their Bible is read and explained to us. You should go sometime."

"Yea, it sounds like something I might want to do. I am really glad that you are not angry with me, Maria. I've changed a lot. I'm not the same Joseph anymore."

"Well, it's nice to hear; just stay away from bad company and pray a lot. I'll be praying for you too."

"Thank you, Maria. Bye now."

Maria hung up and pulled the covers to her chin. Why was Joseph still calling her? She wondered about it and decided that he might have been fishing for a place to stay. She let him stay with her for two months, when they first met but after two months, Maria threw him out. He had the gall to say: "What have you done for me?" after she had fed him, sheltered him and taken care of him. But like she said, she wasn't angry with him anymore, just cautious. And she did want her money back, but she didn't hold much hope.

She threw the covers back and got up. Hearing noises from the living room she gathered that Joanna was awake.

"Rise and shine," she said to Joanna who was still lying down on the futon. The futon had belonged to Joseph. Maria had bought it from him for $70.

"What time is it?" asked Joanna.

"Eleven o'clock. Get up, sleepy head. We're going somewhere. It's a surprise."

"What surprise?" Joanna was wide-awake now. "Why do you do this to me Maria? You always make me curious. Like when you told me about the dream that you had about God. Can you tell me now that I have become a Christian?"

"Okay, I'll tell you. But don't say I didn't warn you. In the dream I was laying on the floor and there was someone next to me who was my friend but I don't know who it was. Across from me there was a man with long hair, sitting down. God was there also. He was in His thirties and had a glow on His face. He was very ill. I lifted him up and laid him down on my right. Without looking at Him I knew that He was dead. The man sitting across from me kept staring as if he was studying me and thought that I was being very cold and unfeeling. He brought God back to life and God emitted a sigh of relief. As He did so He turned into a serpent. The other man went to His rescue and he turned into a serpent also. That's when I woke up. I was very saddened by the dream because it showed God as a mortal. But the more I thought about it the more I realized that it must have been a false dream. Demons can come into our dreams, you know, and even the Bible says that there are false dreams. The one I dreamed about couldn't have been God because God is eternal and immortal. He doesn't get sick and die and He certainly wouldn't turn into a serpent. So, now I told you. Are you happy?"

"Yes, I am. Where are we going?"

"That I won't tell you. It's a surprise."

Maria and Joanna showered and left the apartment. Joanna was puzzled but she resigned herself to the fact that Maria wasn't going to tell her. They walked on Cedar Street going towards the ocean. They turned right and walked until they arrived at the corner of Date and State Street. They stopped in front of *Our Lady of the Rosary* Church. The doors were open and they went inside. The church was mid-size with two rows of benches. It was consecrated on November 15, 1925. It had been built with the financial support of the immigrants, a population of fishermen mostly from Genoa, Italy and Sicily mixed with Portuguese families. Stained glasses adorned the walls, each depicting one of the fifteen Mysteries of the rosary. On the ceiling and on the side of the altar there were paintings from a Venetian artist named Fausto Tasca. On the right of the altar there was a statue of Saint Joseph holding the baby Jesus. Behind the altar, in an alcove, there was a statue of the Virgin Mary in a pink dress also holding the baby Jesus. On the left of the altar there was another statue of the Virgin Mary wearing a white dress and a blue veil on her shoulders. Under her feet there was a globe and on top of the globe, under the Virgin's feet, there was a snake.

Maria brought Joanna to the feet of this statue. Below the statue there were electric candles and an offering box. Maria put twenty-five cents in the offering box and lit a candle. She said a prayer and turned towards Joanna who was looking around with a curious look on her face, still wondering what the surprise was. She was surprised all right.

She had never been in a Catholic church before but she liked what she saw. It was so peaceful and so beautiful but she didn't dare to move or talk. She waited for Maria who was praying at the foot of the statue. Maria started to walk outside and Joanna followed her. When they were outside Maria told her that the statue she was praying under was the statue of the Virgin Mary, who was the mother of Jesus.

"Now, are you ready for the surprise?"

"Yes, what is it?" replied Joanna.

"I was the Virgin Mary. I had a vision where I was dressed in a white, long, silky dress, just like her, and on my shoulder I had a blue veil. Under my feet there was a globe and wrapped twice around the globe there was a black snake. With my right foot I was pressing on the neck of the snake with all my strength. He had his head raised and was looking up towards me. There was a great heat in my feet and around my head. When I opened my eyes I looked at the clock and it was three-fifteen in the afternoon. It happened March fifteen, 1985. It has taken me nine years to connect it with Genesis 3:15 where it talks about the enmity between the woman and the serpent. You read Genesis. Do you remember about that passage?"

"Yes, I remember reading it. But are you sure that the woman was the Virgin Mary?"

"No, I am not sure. The Bible says that there is no reincarnation so I couldn't be the Virgin Mary. God said those words five thousand years ago and it came to pass. I don't know how the Catholic Church even knew about how I was dressed. The only thing different was the serpent. Mine was black and it was wrapped twice around the globe. Maybe someone else had a vision about it too. I don't think that my subconscious made up that vision because I had never seen the statue before. So, how did they know? God knew five thousand years ago, isn't that amazing? And isn't it amazing to find yourself talked about in the Bible? Another passage in the Bible where it talks about it is Revelation 12:1. I don't know if you read it but it mentions a great wonder appearing in heaven: 'A woman clothed with the sun and the moon under her feet'. Read it when we go home. I am an American citizen and America has gone to the moon and walked on it, so that came to pass too. I think my vision was a milestone, a sign of the times that tells us that we are in the last days."

"Well, this was a surprise. So you are a very important person. Should I get on my knees and worship you?" said Joanna, half joking.

"No, silly. You only kneel in front of God. I was just a tool in God's plan. I am flattered because He called me a great wonder but it plainly states in Revelation 12:1 that I am simply a woman but yet I have defeated Satan with the help of Jesus. I couldn't have done it without Him. He forgave me my sins and gave me strength to endure the persecution, forgive myself and get rid of all that guilt I was carrying around, even for things that I hadn't done. It's all very exciting because it means that soon Jesus will come back and rule the world."

"I hope Jesus comes back soon. I would be honored to meet Him."

"I am afraid though, because I think that someone, incited by the Devil, would try to kill Him. I know though, that He will be victorious. Actually I think that He is already here. In Revelation 12 you will read about the man-child. I think I know who the man-child is."

"Who? Tell me. This is so exciting."

"It is Michael. He is the man-child. He is gorgeous. He is tall, blond, blue eyes, and full of muscles. And American. Not Jewish. I don't know if he is a Christian, but to me he is God. I wish that I could have spent more time with him to get a feeling of who he really is. I think that he has some supernatural powers that he needs to develop. He told me that he wanted to be a physical therapist because he had healing powers in his hands. I don't know what he is doing because I haven't seen him in long time. I met him when he was eighteen and I was thirty. You can imagine how his mother felt when I would call his house. She yelled at me all the time because she didn't want me to see him. One day she said she was going to call the police and told me that her son was just a kid. Well, he didn't look like a kid to me and I told her that he was a man. That's why I think that he is the man-child of Revelation 12. That happened even before I read about it. Also I made a drawing of a book and on the book I wrote 'Book of Life' and I didn't read about it in the Bible till later. To me the Bible is a magic book.

All this supernatural experiences didn't start happening to me until I bought the Bible and brought it in my house. I didn't really started to read it until I was thirty-one years old though. Since then it has been one revelation after another. You should read it all like I have done."

Joanna and Maria had been walking while talking. Without realizing it they had arrived at India Street, a section of town called Little Italy because it had restaurants and grocery stores owned by Italians. The church was also part of it. Since they hadn't eaten before leaving the apartment they decided to stop at one of the restaurants with tables and chairs outside, to eat their lunch. A waiter approached them and handed them two menus. As they were scanning them Maria explained to Joanna that they were in the heart of Little Italy, a section of town that had been built and inhabited by fishermen from Italy who, at the beginning of the century, had settled there because it was near the ocean. In recent years some of them had moved elsewhere, but the majority remained. Also, most of the hired help nowadays was not Italian but Mexican. Their waiter was Mexican too. Maria asked what his name was and he told her that it was Jose'. They ordered lasagna for Maria and *Parmigiana di Melanzane* for Joanna. The *Parmigiana di Melanzane* was a type of lasagna but made with eggplant slices instead of noodles. Maria strongly recommended it and she took some from Joanna when it arrived. It was delicious. They drank red wine and were very happy through the whole meal.

At the end of the meal they ordered espresso coffee, which is an Italian custom. Joanna didn't like it because it was too strong for her, but Maria loved it. She lit a cigarette.

"Maria, just after you had that vision what did you think? You said it took you nine years to connect it to Genesis 3:15."

"I didn't think anything. Actually I thought that it was about the Virgin Astrea because I was reading Nostradamus at the time, but Nostradamus fell out of favor with me because the Bible is what I believe in now."

"Who is Nostradamus?"

"Nostradamus was a seer. He was born in 1503 and died in 1566 in France. He was also an astrologer. He has written a book of prophesies which, according to some, have come to pass. Nostradamus mixed up the prophesies in order to protect himself so many of them are not clear, especially if you read them lightly. At the beginning of the book that I read, the instructions were that you had to really believe within yourself that the predictions were true. Not knowing what I was getting into, I swore that I believed. Silly me. I don't believe a word he said. Of the Virgin Astrea, the only thing that I know about her is that she is a heavenly figure who lived on the earth during the golden age. She was the only one that came to my mind when I woke up from that dream or vision. But I rather identify with the Virgin Mary, if you ask me. Besides, she is the one that comes closer to my vision."

"I find this whole thing fascinating. I wish that I had a vision like that. Which reminds me. I had a dream. Hands were touching my breast and milk was squirting out of it. What do you make of it? Do you think that what happened the other day caused me to have this dream?"

"Sure. I think that it's a very happy dream. I think that you and Giovanni will get married and have a baby. Mark my words."

"Oh, Maria. How can you say that? The hands didn't have a body attached to them and there were lots of them."

"Well, all that means is that Giovanni will touch your breasts a lot. You don't believe me?"

"I want to believe you because I like Giovanni a lot, but he is never going to be interested in someone like me."

"Never say never. I have to tell you something before we go. Don't tell anybody about the dreams that you have because they are going to label you as schizophrenic. Just like they did with me. But I have to say that they might be right in my case. I did have lucid dreams, visions, I did hear voices and I was paranoid. The minute I started to take Zyprexa all this symptoms disappeared. They also have diagnosed me as having major depression because of my suicide attempts. I don't scare you, do I?"

"No, Maria. You don't scare me. But I am going to take your advice. I won't tell Jill Thompson of my dreams, only you. I know you won't label me or think that I am crazy."

"You're right on that. Besides, I like having visions and hear voices. It makes me feel closer to God. The only bad thing is the paranoia, the thinking that people can turn into dogs and can read your mind. I don't like that. You know, if the prophets had been living today they would have been labeled schizophrenics too. They heard the voice of God and they had visions all the time. They thought that I was schizophrenic when I told them about my vision. So I am not going to tell them about it anymore. I keep my dreams to myself."

"And so will I. Thank you for your warning. What do you say we go home and take a nap? It's two o'clock now. I can still grab a couple of hours of sleep."

"Good idea. I can use a nap myself," said Maria asking Jose' for the check.

Maria paid and left a nice tip for Jose' who thanked her in Mexican, thinking that she was Mexican too. Lot of people did that, confuse her for Mexican, and they were always surprised when she told them that she was Italian.

****

At five-thirty Joanna was ready to leave the apartment. Maria asked her how she was going to get to Giovanni's. Silly her, she hadn't thought about it. Would she like the money to catch the bus? "Yes," replied Joanna. *Thank goodness*, she thought. *I knew she hadn't thought about it or she would have given me the money before*. But Joanna had been too shy to ask her. She gave Maria a hug and left.

Giovanni was at the door as usual when Joanna arrived at the restaurant. He greeted her cordially and put a hand on her shoulder to escort her to the kitchen. He noticed that she wasn't red on the face or sweaty as she had been the past two days.

"Did someone give you a ride?" he asked.

"No, I caught the bus," replied Joanna.

"No wonder. You should catch the bus every day. I hate to see you tired even before you start working. Poor thing, walking so far." Joanna didn't say anything. She didn't want him to know that she was homeless and penniless for fear that he might form a bad image of her in his mind. *The less he knew, the better*, she thought. She went in the kitchen where Alfredo greeted her with a big smile, his gold tooth shining as he did so. Tonight was her turn to wash. She wore her white overcoat and started to wash. Friday night was a busy night and there was already a big pile of dishes. They worked ceaselessly until nine o'clock when they took their break. Joanna ordered another *Pizza Margherita*, and Alfredo *Spaghetti alla Puttanesca*. They had their usual half a glass of red wine.

"So, tell me bambina. How did it go last night? Did the boss give you a ride home?"

"Yes, he did. Tell me: What does 'Bambina' mean?"

"Bambina means baby girl. Don't get off the subject, did anything happen?"

"No, nothing happened. He was the perfect gentleman. Alfredo, I like him. Do you think that I have any chance with him? I mean is he dating anybody?"

"Not that I know of. Don't you think you're going too fast? I mean you've only met him two days ago, how can you be sure that you like him? How old are you?"

"I am twenty-eight and he is fifty-five. I know, he's old enough to be my father, so save yourself the sermon. I like that though."

"What is it that you like?"

"The fact that he is so much older than me. It makes me feel more secure. He is a man, a real man. He is capable, intelligent, industrious, and according to you, a real gentleman. Plus he knows how to make money and that is a big plus in today's world. It takes a lot of work and perseverance to do that. I admire anybody who can make money because it is so hard. The hardest."

"You should see your face when you talk about him. It glows. Boy, you really like him, don't you? Well I give you my blessing. If you catch him I'll give you an A+. Other women are after him, you know and they have money, which you don't have. They are sophisticated, have college degrees, and some of them are real beauties. I don't know why he hasn't married one of them yet. Maybe he is still grieving the loss of his wife."

"I feel an inch tall, Alfredo. I am nobody. He is never going to pick me. Why would he when he can choose from so many sophisticated women? I give up."

"Wait a minute. Don't give up so soon. There must be a reason why he hasn't married yet. I guess we have to find out before we rule you out. You ain't bad. Just because you're a dishwasher it doesn't mean that he wouldn't marry someone like you. You're pretty, intelligent, young. Let's give it some time and see what happens."

"Thank you, Alfredo. You're a real pal. I didn't tell you about my roommate. She is Italian, from Naples or near Naples, I don't remember."

"No kidding. A paisano. When are you going to bring her over to meet us?"

"I told her that we could come Monday, on my day off but silly me, we are closed on Mondays. I guess she'd have to come during a day when we're open and I just have to take some time off to dine with her. You won't mind, Alfredo?"

"No, I'll be happy, bambina. Anytime. Well, back to work. Time is so short when you're having fun." They went back to washing dishes.

Joanna didn't see Giovanni again until she went downstairs to help Philip with the glasses. Her uniform was sticking to her body like a glove and she was very self-conscious. Occasionally she would look up and see Giovanni looking at her while shaking his head, listening to what someone was saying. He looked very comfortable in a social setting. He would talk to the customers, sitting with them, offering them something to drink on the house. Joanna could tell who were his friends and who were just acquaintances. Tonight he was wearing a black suit with a white shirt. He looked like the king of Spain. His beautiful green eyes were so magnetic. It made Joanna ecstatic when he looked at her. She should get a hold of herself, she thought or she'll be in a lot of trouble. She was already in a lot of trouble.

She studied the women in the nightclub. They looked so sophisticated, all made up and with fancy clothes. It took a lot of money to look like that. She didn't have any money and she felt like Cinderella, but maybe she could do something to improve her appearance. She was planning to follow Maria's advice and go get a haircut; she would go to the dentist and to the therapist, anything that would improve her life. She was also going to buy creams and perfume, fancy bras and fancy clothes. But where was she going to wear them, to wash dishes? Yes, she told herself, because when Giovanni would give her a ride home he would realize that she wasn't just a dishwasher but a woman. She needed to study him more, to ask him questions, to be alluring.

She could never tell him about Raul. He would feel horrified and maybe reject her. She'd have to be really careful about what she said about herself. But was she being unrealistic by aiming at such an important man? Only Maria and Alfredo knew how she felt about him and both of them were friends, so maybe they were being unrealistic also, wanting good things to happen to her, bless their souls. Only two weeks before, she had been homeless, begging at a street corner. Would Giovanni have hired her if he had known? What if he found out? All this thoughts were going through her mind as she kept washing and rinsing glasses automatically. Thank God Philip didn't talk much or he would have asked her if anything was wrong. She was so self-absorbed she didn't notice anything going on right under her nose. She didn't pay any attention to the homosexuals, even when one of them made a pass at Philip. "Do you believe that guy? The nerve," said Philip. "Uh?" replied Joanna. She was falling from the sky.

When two o'clock finally came, Joanna went in the bathroom to change. When she got out, she found Giovanni there as usual. He didn't say anything, just escorted her to his car. After they had driven a short distance Giovanni spoke first.

"You know that Joanna means Giovanna in Italian? So we are Giovanni and Giovanna. I might start calling you that if you don't mind."

"No, I don't mind." *You can call me anything you want*, Joanna told herself.

"You know, I got to ask you a favor Giovanna. I would really appreciate it if you don't tell anybody about what happens between you and me. Thank God you told Alfredo and not somebody else. It would be all over the restaurant by now if you had spoken to someone other than him."

Joanna felt like somebody had stabbed her heart with an icicle. Alfredo had told on her. How could he? She considered him a friend. He told her to go to him if she needed a shoulder to cry on. I guess you cannot trust anybody in this world. She was going to face him tomorrow and ask for an explanation. Of course she wasn't going to confide in him anymore, that's for sure.

"What did Alfredo tell you, exactly?" Joanna asked.

"First of all he was very impressed with the fact that you are still a virgin at twenty-eight. Not even in Italy you find a virgin at that age. Then he just wanted to warn me that you were talking about what happened the other day and since he doesn't know you he thought best that I'd be informed. Don't be mad at him. He just wanted me to know because he cares about me and I think that he cares about you too. He is very loyal, as you can see. I am glad he came to me tonight and told me. So, that's a deal? If you have something to say about me you come to me, okay?"

Joanna felt like a foolish schoolgirl being reprimanded by her teacher. She didn't know what to say so she quietly agreed. *How could things get any worse than this*, she thought. Now look what you've done. They had arrived by her building but Joanna hadn't really noticed, being so embarrassed about being scolded. Her face was hot and she couldn't wait to get out of the car. She thanked Giovanni for the ride and left.

"Good night Giovanna!" yelled Giovanni.

"Oh stuff it!" Joanna said under her breath.

CHAPTER SIXTEEN

Saturday morning. Joanna hated waking up. She always had whenever she had a problem she didn't know how to deal with. Her first thought was what happened in the car with Giovanni early that morning. How was she going to face him in broad daylight? What about Alfredo the Snitch? Wait till she talked to him. Right now she hoped that Maria was awake so she could tell her all about it. She knocked on her door and Maria told her to come in. Joanna went in and sat cross-legged on the other mattress. She told her everything that had happened and Maria listened patiently. When she got the whole story Maria said,

"I am not taking Giovanni's side but I think that he is right. You shouldn't tell anyone at work because people talk and gossip all the time. Alfredo seems like a nice guy, from what you've told me. I think that he told Giovanni because it was a very delicate matter and he wanted to find out for himself whether it was true or you were just making it up. He has known Giovanni for the last ten years and you have known him for the past three days. Whose side do you think he would take? Plus he doesn't know if you are going to tell someone else. What if you do? That's going to ruin Giovanni's reputation and he is very attached to Giovanni. He doesn't want anything bad to happen to him so he tells him. Plus you got both their attention by saying that you are a virgin. Being a virgin is a big thing for Italian men. They might be screwing around with ten women but when they marry, they want their wife to be a virgin. When I was fourteen I ran away from home. I went on the highway and hitchhiked a ride. Some Sicilian men stopped and picked me up. They were carrying oranges to Bologna, Italy. There were three trucks all together. The guys I was riding with were the youngest. I happened to mention that I was still a virgin. When we stopped in Bologna I saw my driver and one of the other drivers argue. My driver came in the truck and told me that the other driver had threatened to stab him if he wouldn't turn me over to him. The reason being, I was a virgin. Apparently that just drove him nuts.

My driver offered to drive me out of town and when he did he stopped by the interstate and had the guts to question the fact that I was a virgin and wanted to see for himself. I thought that all men are crazy and ran out of the truck as fast as I could while crying. I hitch-hiked a ride and that's the last I know about them. On my way home I ended up in Florence. There I met a policeman who took me to see a movie. I told him that I was a runaway and a virgin. During the movie he made a pass at me. I resisted. He didn't try again. When we got out he took me to the station where he worked. He told me to wait for him, that he was going to talk to his friend who was standing guard outside the station. I saw him talk to the guard, not suspecting anything. They approached me and lifted me up, one hand under each arm. They took me to the station, went through everything I had in my purse, questioned me and send me in a police car to a girl's home until they could accompany me to Naples.

The policeman that turned me in was a Sicilian. It had impressed him so much that I was a virgin and that I resisted him that one year later he came to my house in Naples to see how I was doing. But I wasn't home and he didn't come back. To him, turning me in was the right thing to do, to protect me. If I had given in to his advances he would not have turned me in. He would just have taken his pleasure and left me. Is Giovanni Sicilian? Most Italian families in San Diego are Sicilian. I bet his father was a fisherman."

"I don't know where Giovanni's family is from. As soon as I get a chance I will ask him. Alfredo is from Caserta. Is that in Sicily?"

"No, that's near Naples. Well, kiddo I don't know about you but I am going to spend the whole day in bed reading. I will only get up to eat, if I eat at all. I have been trying to fast so that I'll lose weight, but I don't know if I am strong enough to do that. I am a weak, wicked woman. I am joking."

"So Maria, what do you think I should do about Alfredo? How do I deal with him? We have our break together and talk. I can't stop talking to him. Should I mention to him that Giovanni told me?"

"Yes, you should. Tell him that you felt betrayed but that you understand his reasons. Then continue as you have been doing, just don't tell him anything personal anymore."

"This is getting too complicated for me. I think that I'll stay in bed all day too and read the Bible. Thank you Maria for your advice. I think you're right," Joanna said and walked back to the living room, to her futon. She started to read the Bible but she soon fell asleep again and didn't wake up till two-thirty in the afternoon.

She got up and went to knock on Maria's door. Maria told her to come in. Joanna wanted to talk some more. She was feeling really uneasy about the whole affair with Alfredo and Giovanni. She was thankful for Maria being there for her to talk to. She was growing really dependent on her opinion. She seemed so wise especially when it came to Italian men and Italian culture in general. It was odd, she thought, how many Italian people had come into her life in those past few days. Maria was her angel sent by God to protect her. She sat cross-legged again on the other mattress that was half covered by books and magazines and didn't say anything for a couple of minutes. "What's up?" asked Maria. "You look still sleepy. Maybe you should go back to bed, sister."

"No, I am awake. I just wanted to talk some more. By the way, are we going to eat anything soon?"

"You can, if you want to. I am fasting. Fasting and praying is good. It is the way to get the same powers that Jesus had to heal sicknesses and diseases, and also to do other miracles. I want those powers, and I want to lose weight."

"What are you reading?"

"I am reading *Religious Psychology* by Vincent Herr. I am almost done reading it. It is very enlightening. How are you doing with the Bible?"

Maria put her book down and looked at Joanna. She had puffy

eyes, still full of sleep. Her hair needed to be combed. She looked so innocent in her oversized nightgown. One shoulder was bare and she looked like one of those magazine advertisements, only you had to picture her in black and white.

"I have been reading Genesis again. I read Genesis 3:15 and you were right. God did know five thousand years ago about what happened to you. I do believe it was a sign that God gave the world. You must tell somebody trustworthy, somebody who doesn't think that you are crazy or schizophrenic, somebody who studies the Bible and the events in our time and how they relate to prophecies."

"Don't you think that I want to? But the people I told it to didn't take me seriously. The priest at Our Lady of the Rosary Church said 'We'll see, we'll see' but didn't treat me with a lot of respect because he rebuked me when one day I asked to talk to him. He told me rudely that he was busy and couldn't talk to me. Some people might think that I might be trying to make myself great or special."

"You are great and you are special, why else would God pick you?"

"I don't mind being great and special in God's eyes. That makes me very happy. What I don't like is the kind of notoriety that big stars have today. That would make me feel very uncomfortable. It's not me. I do want to be somebody and I think that I am somebody, especially now, but most of all I want to be treated with respect and not have my rights violated. I want to do something special, like writing a book or paint beautiful pictures. I don't think that I have the know how to do those things though, so I must resign myself to being just me, a government employee whom God has chosen to give the world a sign. I am still the luckiest woman in the whole world, so I am very happy with myself. If I deserve glory God will give it to me in heaven. His glory is the one I want because it is everlasting. The glory received from men is only temporary.

It would be very embarrassing to be in the tabloids as on a freak show, for a couple of weeks, and have everybody forget the whole thing as if it was not important.

While I keep it to myself, it is mine and mine only. Once I tell, people will speculate and have their opinions about it and some might not be very pleasant."

"That's not the point," said Joanna frustrated. "Since it was a sign from God to the world, I think that you don't have any choice. You have to tell."

"What else can I do? I told two Catholic priests and some psychologists. What they do with it is their responsibility toward God and toward men. I can't put a sign outside my window saying 'Here lives the great wonder'. People would think that I might just be trying to glorify myself, which I am not. But I'll see. If I meet someone in the church that I can trust I will tell him or her. Until then I am happy just the way I am."

"You know in Genesis 1:26 God says 'Let *us* make man in *our* image' and then proceeded to make man as male and female. Does that mean that God is male and female? If that is so then we could pray to a woman-goddess and not do offense to God. I think that I would prefer a woman-goddess instead of a man because of all the problems that I have had with men. I would feel more comfortable telling her my problems since she is a woman also. She would understand more and be motherly towards me. I love my mom, Felicia, and you, but I don't love any man except now I like Giovanni but I don't know if I love him yet so he doesn't count."

"I don't know how to answer that Joanna. The God I believe in is definitely a male God. He goes to war, judges people and angels, incarnates as a man in the figure of Jesus and will live among men as a God. There are women portrayed in the Bible but they are all human. The only one who found favor with God was Mary but nowhere in the Bible does it say that she was a goddess even though the Catholic Church worships her as the Mother of God. I person-ally think, sometime, that God is a woman or that God is male and female, or that the Holy Spirit is the female essence of God and Jesus. Sometime, when I pray I say 'Mother God' or 'Father God' but most of the time just 'Father in heaven'. I think of God as a man so much that I have adopted Him as my father. My earth father is not a father to me at all. I can't count on him for anything. I can't ask for advice, guidance, or insight so I just divorced him, in my heart. God is my father now. I trust Him for everything, from the smallest to the biggest. Occasionally I pray to the Virgin Mary but because of the vision that I had, I feel sometime that I am praying to myself so I stop doing it. What's the point?"

"So you do think of yourself as the Virgin Mary?"

"Yes and no. I can't deny the vision. I was she. What am I supposed to do, throw away the whole thing? It did happen and it's not my fault. It's just a mystery that God is going to have to solve in the afterlife. When I'll die I'll know. But who knows, we may never die. If Jesus comes back, as I think He has, then He will change us in the blink of an eye and we will have eternal life, in these bodies. The Bible says that a man one hundred years old will be as a baby, so that means that we will live, if not forever, for a very long time. Don't you find this exciting?"

Joanna stretched her long legs and passed her hand through her hair. She thought for a moment, then said: "I don't know as much as you do, so lot of things I am just hearing about now. I don't know. I guess it would be exciting to live a long time, if life was good to you. Otherwise I would prefer my eighty years on earth, then pass on to a better life. If we reincarnate after we die, I would like to come back as a man. Men have all the privileges in this life, it's not fair."

"The Bible teaches us that there is no reincarnation. That it is appointed to man to die once and then the judgment. Personally, I like the idea of reincarnation. I hope that we will be able to, if the story of Jesus doesn't work out, that is. I would like to come back as a beautiful woman, with a beautiful singing voice. I would like to be an actress, to star in Christ centered movies and sing Christian songs. For parents I'd like to have two successful and talented individuals. I would love for my mother and father to have college degrees and have lot of money. I would like to have everything that I don't have now. I am thankful though to my parents for sending me to school, especially since they had very little schooling themselves. I love my mom. She is so nice. She's had such a hard life with my father being sick, alcoholic and abusive. Thank God that I had a better life than she."

Maria looked pensive as she said that. She was feeling homesick and missed her mother very much. Joanna picked up on her mood and felt compassion for her. She was homesick too, but she could never see her mother again nor her father. She felt sorry for herself as well as for Maria, two sisters in distress. She put her hand on Maria's knee. Maria pulled the blanket to her chin and smiled at Joanna.

"Sorry," she said. "I get homesick occasionally. Every time my mother comes to my mind I think of home, food, holidays spent together and so on. I wish we weren't so far apart. What about you, Joanna? Do you miss your mother a lot?"

"Oh, yes very much. There is a spot in my heart that's always empty and only being with my mother could fill that. But I know that it is not possible. As for my father, I don't know him at all so I don't miss him. Maybe I should ask God to be my father too. Tell me everything you know about God, please," she sounded like a little girl. Maria loved the opportunity to talk about God, especially to Joanna who had just recently become a Christian. She reached inside herself to find the right words.

"God is awesome. When I look at the moon and the stars I am amazed. That's when I reach for God the most and I can almost sense Him. I remember one time when George and I were married. We lived in London, England. We were going squirrel hunting on the queen's land. A policeman friend of George was our host. We left very early in the morning when it was still dark outside. The sky was full of stars and I spent the whole two hours' drive looking upwards, gazing at the stars. I felt such a longing in my heart, as if my home was up there and not down here. I really longed for God in my heart. God is very creative. Everything we see He made: The sky, the land, the sea and all things alive. He made us in His image, to bear His likeness. I believe that God drew us before He created us. I can tell that He drew us freehand because one of our eyes is smaller than the other and so is one breast in the female. I saw a photograph of a fish. It had beautiful colors and it looked like a watercolor or an acrylic painting as if an artist had drawn it first. So God gets an idea in His mind, draws it then He creates it. Isn't it fascinating? It must be a lot of fun. God owns the universe yet He is so humble and gentle, forgiving and compassionate. But He is also a judge. As a judge He had to condemn us to death because of our sins, but as a father He stepped down and incarnated Himself as our Lord Jesus Christ to pay the death penalty for us so that we could be reunited with God. Isn't it loving? No one loves us more, not even our mothers.

God could have chosen to incarnate Himself into a well-to-do family. Instead He chose a carpenter, Joseph, and his wife Mary, two simple people with simple means. He had to work to earn a living. We should follow His example, to work without grumbling, be meek, obedient and full of grace. I love Him as God and I love Him even more as Jesus. As far as a woman-goddess, I leave myself open to that too. It has to be a motherly figure, there is no other explanation."

Maria was very animated as she spoke and her face was very expressive. Joanna listened intently not missing even a word. She was hungry for God and everything connected to Him. She had really meant it when she gave herself to Jesus and wanted to know more. Maria's words inspired her and brought her a step closer in her walk with God.

"Now from the holy to the profane. How about a ham and cheese sandwich? You don't even have to get up. I'll bring it to you in bed," Joanna said to Maria.

"No, Joanna, but thanks. You go ahead and eat. I'll just lay here and keep reading." Maria picked up the book from the floor and opened it where she had marked the page.

"Say, today you are off. How about coming to the restaurant, have dinner there and meet everybody?"

"I'll take a rain check on that. But I am willing to come tomorrow. How's that?"

"You're on. I can't wait!" Joanna stretched her legs and got up. She looked around. The bedroom was a mess. Not dirty, just messy. There were books everywhere. On the mattress, on the floor, lining three bookcases. She stepped on a book on her way to the kitchen. She fixed herself two sandwiches and drank a glass of milk. She was feeling groggy when she got into the shower, but her grogginess soon left under the nice warmth of the water. She stayed in the shower longer than usual. When she got out she checked the clock. It was four-thirty so she had plenty of time to go to work. She got dressed and went back to Maria's room. "I am being a pest today. Forgive me but I like talking to you. You're so easy to talk to. You never pass any judgment and I feel that I can tell you anything. Can we worship? I have this great desire for God today. I can't explain. Did it ever happen to you?"

"All the time. Mostly I worship alone but it is better to have company. Jesus said that if two or more are together praying He is in the midst. Let's light a candle by my shrine and turn off the light. That will get us in the mood faster, without distractions."

Joanna went by Maria's shrine and lit a candle. She put it by the plexiglass cross with a red rose inlaid at the bottom. They turned out the light and sat cross-legged at the foot of the shrine. Their heads bowed down Maria said the opening prayer. "Dear Lord, we love you so much. We ask you to please be in our midst as we dedicate these few minutes of our time to worship you. We ask for forgiveness of our sins and for you to bless our loved ones and us. Thank you."

They sat in silence, their eyes closed, with their hands resting on their legs with the palms upwards. About ten minutes later Joanna spoke: "Dear God, I have a great desire in my heart and that is to find my mother. Her name is Jane Hampton. If you know where she is will you please let me know? You can make our paths cross and if that is not possible, you can give me directions on how to find her. I trust in you Lord. I want you to be my father also, like you are to Maria. Amen."

Joanna almost choked on her words. Tears were in her eyes but she was trying not to cry. When it came to her mother she was six years old again. All the fears, frustrations and heartaches were renewed again, full force, and she would lose control of her emotions. It hurt so much she thought her heart would break. The longing for her mother and the part of her childhood when she was with her was so intense she'd be spasmodic, restless, and angry. Those feelings were all with her and she mentally turned them over to the Lord. She entrusted her life into His hands. It was a big commitment. She just hoped it would work.

Maria felt a sensation on her cheek as if a hand was caressing her face. She didn't say anything out loud. She just enjoyed the experience thinking that it was the Lord. She experienced those feelings often. Sometime it was her belly, other times it was her heels or the soles of her feet or the top of her head. She always held her breath when that happened not wanting it to stop. But of course it did.

Those sensations never lasted longer than a minute and they

were very enjoyable, very gentle except the ones on her heels, which sometime were painful. She'd try to remember what she was thinking about just in case she was triggering the sensations with her thoughts. She was trying to control the situation, while she should just relax and open up. She had read about chakras but she wasn't knowledgeable enough about them and what to do to release that energy. She had also read about the kundalini and how dangerous it could be to awaken it if not done the right way. So she steered clear. She had also stopped studying astrology since she had become a Christian because in the Bible God is opposed to astrologers, wanting everyone to trust in Him only. They sat meditating for a good long while. When they were done they said a closing prayer and put out the candle.

It was time for Joanna to go to work. Maria gave her the money for the bus and she was off. When she arrived at Giovanni's he was at the door as usual. The thought came to Joanna's mind that he was there waiting for her, but she told herself that he was there to greet the customers. He was wearing a gray vest on top of a white shirt and black pants. It was more casual than what he'd wear at night in the nightclub. He would change later for that. Joanna was greeted by a warm smile and a pat on her shoulder. She went to the kitchen where Alfredo was already washing dishes. Tonight it was her turn to rinse. She went to the closet and put on her overcoat. She was cordial and nice to Alfredo the whole night, not showing any of the feelings of ambivalence that she felt towards him.

He acted the same as usual and you couldn't tell by the way he was behaving that anything had happened at all. During the break Joanna almost assaulted him. "Alfredo, why did you tell Giovanni what I told you in confidence, last night?"

"Oh bambina, don't be too harsh on me for that. I wanted to see what his reaction was going to be when I told him. I wanted to see for myself if it was true or not. He didn't deny it. He just told me not to tell anyone about it. So now I believe everything you told me is true."

"So, you didn't believe me? You thought I was making it up?"

"I didn't know what to believe. I just met you. I wasn't sure. You can't blame me for it. I was trying to do good for both of you."

Alfredo looked like a little boy caught with his hand in the cookie jar. He blushed and stammered on his words. He hadn't thought about Giovanni telling Joanna and he regretted talking to him. He liked Joanna and didn't want to lose her friendship. She looked so innocent, so naïve that he felt like he had to protect her.

"C'mon bambina, take it easy. It's not that bad. You can still count on me; you can still talk to me. I promise I won't tell anybody what you tell me, not even Giovanni."

Joanna watched Alfredo squirm and thought that it served him right, but that didn't last very long. All of a sudden she saw humor in the situation and gave out a little laugh. Alfredo was puzzled. "What's so funny?" he asked.

"Nothing. It's just your face; you make me laugh. C'mon, it's not that bad. I guess it is my fault too, for not being more discreet, but I feel better that I told you even if you divulged it. I forgive you, Alfredo but you must promise not to tell anymore on me."

"I promise you again. Cross my heart and hope to die." Alfredo was greatly relieved and gave out a sigh. "What about attacking the food and eat it while it is still hot? We have to celebrate. Tonight we drink one full glass of wine. Here, to your health, Joanna. Don't let any man touch you, ok? If somebody bothers you, you tell me and I'll take care of it." What Alfredo wanted to say, really, was for her not to lose her virginity but he was too embarrassed to say so. Joanna was moved by his words and she felt like a jerk for attacking him. She was glad that they had made peace.

"So tell me, what was Giovanni's reaction when you told him?" Joanna was eager to know and she hoped that Alfredo wouldn't be stingy on words.

"He didn't say anything. He just wanted to know everything you said and made me promise not to tell anyone. So don't tell him that I've told you or you'll get me into trouble. Capisci?"

"Yes sir. We are the Secret Brotherhood. It's me and you against the world," replied Joanna attacking her *Spaghetti alla Puttanesca*. Alfredo gave her a big smile, his gold tooth giving him the look of a pirate.

"What advice can you give me, Alfredo? How do I make him like me?" Joanna was glad she had made peace with Alfredo so she could get information from him. She didn't have any friends except for Maria so she was happy to have a friend in him too.

"Just be yourself bambina. His wife was down to earth and very nice to everybody. She was also a very capable businesswoman. She practically ran the business. Her death was a great loss for Giovanni. She is going to be hard to replace."

"What did she look like?" asked Joanna.

"She was shorter than you, about five-four. She was slender and had black, curly hair. She had beautiful black eyes with thick eyelashes and she didn't use any make-up. She didn't need to. She was Sicilian too, like Giovanni. I think they were both from the same hometown of Taormina, Sicily. Their families arranged their marriage when they were very young. Giovanni brought her over when she was eighteen and they were married in Our Lady of the Rosary Church, in Little Italy. Anita, that was her name, used to tell me stories of when she first came over to the United States. She felt really lost because she didn't have any friends or relatives. She had to work hard in making her mother-in-law like her and once she did, she became like a mother to her. Of course she was a virgin when she got married.

Her family gave her a dowry, which they used partially to start the business, so she was part owner. They were very sorry they didn't have any kids but the business took all of their time. They loved each other very much. They were a team."

"I can't compete Alfredo, can I? I don't think that I have any chance." Why was it that Joanna felt depressed every time she thought of Giovanni or talked about him? She was falling in love with the man, that's why! Her insecurities would come to the surface and hit her full force. She couldn't wait for Sunday to come around so she could have some money and improve her appearance.

"You have chances Joanna. Don't put yourself down. I think that he likes you. That's the impression that I had while talking to him."

"Do you really think so?"

"Yes, I do. Now, how about going back to our dishes? The break is over kiddo." They went back to the kitchen, to the sinks, and spent the next hour and a half washing and rinsing while talking amiably. When eleven o'clock came around Joanna went to change into her uniform. She was still wearing sneakers and felt goofy. The first thing she was going to buy with her money next week would be a pair of black shoes. It would be a good investment, she thought. Next she was going to buy a purse where she could put a comb and some make-up. She could then fix herself up a little before going to the nightclub. Right now she looked a mess, with hair sticking to her face and no make-up. She hated going to the nightclub looking like that, but she had no other choice. Giovanni was at the foot of the steps talking to a very elegant, well made-up woman. Joanna flinched and lowered her head, embarrassed by her appearance. Giovanni moved aside to let her pass and said hi while giving her a big smile, which she missed. She went behind the bar and said hi to Philip. "Hi lass, how's life treating you?"

"It could be better, but I am not complaining because it could be a lot worse too," said Joanna shuddering at the thought that she could be laying on a hard pavement at this very moment. She knew, though, that life could be just grand and that there were people in the world who had so much, not ever having need for anything. Why shouldn't she have the same things, the same opportunities? She mentally said a prayer to Jesus and started washing the glasses. She had gotten more used to the crowd in the nightclub and started to recognize faces. There was an old man, in his sixties, who was openly gay and Joanna would watch him as he'd try to make conquests of the younger gay men. So far he had not been successful. He must have been loaded with money because he wore very elegant clothes and had an enormous diamond ring on his little finger. Joanna noticed the ring when he sat at the bar to order a whiskey and was eyeing Philip. Philip, as usual, pretended not to notice, while being very polite.

Philip had a great body. He exercised and lifted weights and you could see the muscles under his silk shirt. He was always on the alert as his wife was almost due to have his baby and he was waiting for a phone call telling him it was time. Every time the phone rang, beads of sweat would form on his forehead and he seemed disappointed when he realized it was someone else. The air was already smoggy and Joanna's eyes were burning. She noticed another old man who was not gay. He was one of the regulars. He would look at her with lusty eyes. Joanna would squirm when she'd look up and meet his gaze. She felt really uncomfortable being eyed like that but there was nothing she could do about it. He would just sit by the piano player, sipping his drink and staring. He was well dressed and Joanna thought he must be loaded with money too as all the other patrons seemed to be. He was skinny, had a moustache and receding black hair. He reminded Joanna of a bird. Occasionally he'd come to the bar and would ask for a whiskey or a gin and tonic. He would turn towards her and smile but Joanna would keep her head down and pretend not to notice. This would be the perfect occasion to get a sugar daddy, she thought to herself; she could get fancy clothes and jewelry, a place of her own and be a kept woman. She would never have to wash dishes again. Her fingernails would be manicured and painted and she would have a car. Joanna looked at the "bird" and thought to herself, "no thanks". Better homeless. Just then Giovanni came to the bar and hugged the "bird" whose name was Joe Bellagio, an Italian name. They were speaking Italian and Joanna didn't understand a word they were saying. She should ask Maria to teach her Italian so she could understand. She eyed Giovanni and gave out a sigh. Philip saw her sigh and understood.

"You got a lot of competition on that one, lass. If you want him you better do more than sigh."

"I am a virgin. Does that help?"

"Yea, and my wife is the Virgin Mary," said Philip, ironically.

"Really, it's true." Joanna was offended. She should have kept her mouth shut. Hopefully Philip wouldn't advertise it. She saw the bird look at her while talking to Giovanni and Giovanni looked at her too. She had the gut feeling that they were talking about her and wondered why. She found out when Giovanni gave her a ride home.

"You have an admirer, Giovanna," said Giovanni glancing at her to see how she'd react.

"Oh yea? And who might that be?"

"Joe Bellagio. He is in construction and very wealthy. He said he likes you and wanted to know if you were interested. What do I tell him?"

"Tell him 'no thanks,' I am not interested."

"Why? Do you have someone else?"

"No, I don't have anybody else. At any rate I'd like to keep my private life private."

Joanna could not believe her ears. Was he trying to push her towards Bellagio? What if he was? Would he suggest she'd flirt with customers? She didn't know what to say so she remained silent.

"You know, Bellagio is not the type to take no for an answer. He might get cross or he might try to approach you himself. If he does, I want to know. I might have to talk to him myself to get him off your back. You're my employee and I'll take care of it if I have to. You don't need to be frightened, Giovanna. Big daddy will watch over you."

Joanna was so relieved she almost kissed him. She was also moved. In one instant he had changed from a pimp to a knight in shiny armor. "Big Daddy" she liked that. She was happy and her eyes were shining as she left the car to go home.

CHAPTER SEVENTEEN

"Wake up sleepy head," Maria said, coming out of her bedroom. Joanna lifted up her head and rubbed her hand over her eyes.

"What time is it?" she asked.

"It's eight-thirty. Come on, let's have some breakfast and get ready for church. Remember, you said you'd come?"

"Yea, I remember. I'll be up in just a second." Joanna was fighting sleep. She rubbed her eyes some more and got up to help Maria fix breakfast. She got a cup of coffee and sipped it slowly. They fixed scrambled eggs, toast and jelly.

"Don't forget about tonight, Maria. You said you'd come eat at the restaurant."

"Don't worry. I haven't forgotten. I am looking forward to it actually."

"It will be fun, you'll see. One thing, though, I haven't told Alfredo and Giovanni that you were coming. I hope it's alright."

"I am sure it will be Joanna. Don't worry."

"I am not worried. It's just that I should have told them. Alfredo will have to wash the dishes all by himself while I dine with you. I hope he doesn't mind. Tonight is going to be very crowded and he'll have a lot of dishes to wash."

"You worry too much. If it bothers you why don't you call around five tonight and let them know that I am coming?"

"That's a good idea. That's what I'll do."

"Now that we have that settled why don't we wash these dishes and get ready for church?"

"Right on. Let's do it."

They quickly washed the breakfast dishes and in turn took their showers. At nine-thirty they were ready to go. They each took their Bible and left the apartment. Once in the church they soon spotted Theresa and Penny and went to sit next to them after each had a hug. Maria was so thankful for their friendship she always thanked the Lord for them. She considered it a real blessing. The songs of worship started and they all stood up and clapped their hands including Joanna. Joanna seemed more relaxed and at ease and Maria was happy for her. Ever since she had moved in with Maria and ate regular meals, she had changed dramatically. She didn't seem thirty-five anymore but started to look her age of twenty-eight. The dark circles under her eyes had disappeared and her skin was more translucent, without wrinkles. She was very beautiful, in a delicate way. With a little fixing up she'd look like a model. Her body was slender, a size eight and she had full breasts. Men would turn their heads when she'd walk by which they never did for Maria. Maria was not jealous. She was actually happy. Happy to be her friend and happy to help her.

When the first song was over Maria sat down. She would get real tired standing up and never lasted too long. She felt a little embarrassed but she did it anyway. She loved the Christian songs. They were light rock and very beautiful, not like the usual, boring songs that you'd hear on some Christian radio shows. When she'd listened to them she thought that God would be very bored and annoyed if He had to listen to them all day long. Today's lyrics were very beautiful and you could actually understand them. Maria looked at her friends. There was a frown on Theresa's face. She thought that she must be worried about her mother who was eighty-six and in poor health. Theresa also worried about her handicapped son who was in an institution up in New York and about her other son who was not saved. She prayed a lot for all of them. Maria loved Theresa. She was so friendly, so warm. She'd always give Maria a hug and make her feel loved and welcome no matter what.

Maria admired capable women. In Italy, especially Southern Italy, women were not so emancipated. Here in the United States women could do anything, even go up in space. She said a prayer in her heart for all the women in the world; that they might all, one day, be equal with men and not be battered and abused. Growing up with the nuns, Maria's growth had been hindered. She had been either restrained in a seat or in a line and couldn't move unless the nun had said so. She remembered one time when the nuns put all of them in a line in the courtyard. They were going to give them some grapes. As the nun called out your name you were supposed to go forward and get your grapes. Maria was distracted and she accidentally stepped out of the line, out of turn. Suor Antonietta slashed her neck with an electric cord that left a mark for four weeks. She had come prepared to do just that as she already had the cord in her hand. Maria's mother took her home for the holidays. One afternoon she was searching Maria's head for lice. She saw the mark on Maria's neck and asked her how she got it. When Maria told her, she was very angry and cursed the nun.

Because of the way she was raised, Maria was always afraid that she was going to be beaten if she spoke up or did something wrong. Because of that she was not daring and would not take any chances and her potential remained dormant. Maria didn't hate the nuns but she doubted in her heart that Jesus was married to them. Some of them were so mean, so rigid, so self-righteous not even a man would marry them, let alone Jesus.

Half an hour had passed and the worship was over. Tithes were collected and Maria gave her usual dollar. The pastor, Bob Priceman came to the podium and started the Bible lesson. The lesson had its emphasis on meekness and various passages throughout the Bible were cited. Penny was restless in her seat. She was hyperactive, always moving, always doing something. Her daughter was in Europe, by herself and she prayed for her. Last time she had gone to Europe someone had stolen her backpack. Penny had to send her money so she could come home, but this time everything was going smoothly. She was having fun in Paris. She had already been to Italy and she was on her way to London. Lucky her, Maria thought.

Joanna was following her Bible at every passage the pastor

mentioned. She was feeling so much better than the week before. She was glad she had become a Christian and she was starting to feel like she belonged. So many things had happened in one week that she had hard time remembering them all. The lesson was not complicated and she understood everything. It was good to be reminded to be meek and humble because it was so easy to become proud and arrogant, so she treasured the preaching.

When the lesson was over Maria and Joanna said goodbye to Theresa and Penny and left. It was eleven-fifteen. Maria suggested to Joanna that they go to Our Lady of the Rosary Church for the service that started at noon so that she could learn also about Catholicism. Joanna agreed even though she wanted to go back home and go to sleep. They walked to the church. When they got there it was eleven-thirty. The Mass wouldn't start for another half hour. A group of people in the front pews was reciting the rosary, together with one of the priests. Maria joined in, on her knees, while Joanna remained seated not knowing what to do. She didn't know the prayer. In fact, she didn't even know what it was. Joanna was having so many new experiences it was hard to absorb them all. She told herself to keep an open mind and not to pass any judgment. Things were happening for a reason and that, with time, she would understand. During the Mass Joanna repeated all that she saw Maria doing. Maria, on her part, repeated all that she saw the other people doing. She didn't know all the prayers and she didn't know when to kneel, get up or sit down so she just copied and Joanna copied her. When it came time for Communion, Maria got in line with the others and so did Joanna. They both took Communion, went back to their bench and kneeled.

When the Mass was over they walked out. At the door they shook hands with the priest. It was a beautiful day; there was not a cloud in the blue sky. Maria suggested they go to Horton Plaza to get something to eat. So they did. They went to the Steakout and ordered a sandwich, French fries and a small soda and sat on the patio outside to eat their lunch.

"Tell me Joanna, what did you think of the Catholic Mass?"

"It was all right, but all that sitting, standing and kneeling made my head spin. I don't see how you can ever remember all of it."

"I don't remember it at all. I just do what I see other people do. You know when we went up to take Communion? What that means is that we eat the body of Christ and when the priest drinks the wine he is drinking His blood. Strange, don't you think? But it says so in the Bible. They're the words of Jesus at the Last Supper. He drank the wine and said that it was His blood; He then broke the bread and said that it was His body and for us to do that in remembrance of Him.

This part I have hard time understanding, but I have to go by faith knowing that He knows best and if He said that's what we should do, then we must. This sandwich is good, don't you think?"

"Yes, very good. Thank you Maria. Guess what? Tonight I get paid and tomorrow I am going shopping. It won't be much, just two hundred-six dollars but it's a start. Tomorrow is going to be a busy day for me and I can't wait. After we eat I'd like to go home and catch a few hours of sleep, if you don't mind Maria."

"Oh, it's quite all right. I think I'll do the same."

They finished their lunch and walked back home. They slept all afternoon. Joanna woke up at four-thirty. She woke Maria up and reminded her that she was going with her at the restaurant. Maria prepared herself with special care. She wanted to make a good impression on the people she was going to meet in an hour or so. She applied make-up and chose a black and white outfit, which hid the extra pounds. When she was done she found Joanna waiting for her in the living room. She took her purse, the keys, and they were off. They didn't have to wait long for the bus. They caught the number 3 going to Hillcrest. When they arrived, Maria asked Joanna how she looked. Joanna reassured her saying that she looked beautiful. They did look like an odd couple with Maria all dressed up and Joanna in jeans and T-shirt.

When they arrived at the restaurant Giovanni was at the door as usual. Joanna made the introductions. Maria was pleasantly surprised by Giovanni's looks. He looked like an actor. He told them that he had reserved a table just for them and directed them to a table by the inner wall, unless they preferred to eat on the patio, he said. They both said inside was fine and sat down. Giovanni left as they seated themselves, only to come back a couple of minutes later bringing a bottle of red wine with him. He took a chair from a nearby table and sat himself with them.

"This is the best wine in all of San Diego," he said. "It comes from Sicily. I have some relatives there who produce it and they send it to me."

He filled their glasses. "Taste it and tell me what you think." Joanna and Maria tasted the wine. Maria compared it to her grandmother's wine and noticed that it had the same texture. She could drink glass after glass and not get drunk.

"This is very good," she said. "It reminds me of my grandmother's wine. It has the same richness."

"Where are you from, Maria?" asked Giovanni.

"I am from Onofrio, a small town near Naples. My grandmother and my uncles own a slope of a hill where they grow grapes and other things. They make their own wine but only for their own consumption. They don't sell it. They should because it's very good, but I guess it is not enough to sell." Maria could not look into Giovanni's eyes for more than a second at a time. His green eyes mesmerized her. She was afraid she'd get hypnotized so she would shift her glance from him to Joanna to the glass. He was very handsome and very well dressed. He was also very kind and polite. She was not surprised that he smote Joanna. He had a certain humbleness about him which made you want to be kind to him and tell him all of your problems. He was approachable and sensitive. Maria noticed that Joanna was watching every move that he made and had a look of wonderment in her face. It was plain to see that she was in love with him. *I don't know*, she thought to herself. It might be harder than what she thought. Joanna would have to be a lot more sophisticated to catch him. It was obvious that he had good taste; you could tell by the clothes he wore. So he wouldn't settle for a woman in jeans and T-shirt and no education. She'd have to work with Joanna on her looks.

Just then a party of six people entered the restaurant. As he saw them, Giovanni quickly excused himself and went to greet them. He embraced and kissed one man and shook hands with the others. The man he kissed was older than the others. He had white hair and was wearing a pair of dark glasses. Giovanni was very deferential with him as he escorted the group into the smaller room.

Maria was all excited as she said to Joanna: "Do you know who that is?"

"No," replied Joanna.

"Angelo Bonifacio. They say he is the godfather of San Diego. I know because he goes to Our Lady of the Rosary Church. One day I heard some people behind me say so when they saw him enter the church. I wonder what the connection is between him and Giovanni. I hope he is not in the mafia. Have you noticed anything unusual since you've been here?"

"No. I don't notice much since I am in the kitchen most of the time and in the nightclub Giovanni talks to everybody. Besides I don't know how to tell if one is in the mafia or not. But I'll keep my eyes open."

Giovanni remained in the small room for few minutes, until everyone was seated, engaging in small talk. As he left, he closed the door. Maria thought that he did it to give them privacy so no one would hear what they were talking about; a secret meeting, perhaps. They were the only ones occupying the room. Giovanni talked to a waiter, briefly, gesturing towards the small room and when he was done he came back to their table.

"So, how is the wine?" he asked Maria and Joanna very casually, as if nothing had happened. Maria was biting her lips so she wouldn't come out with the wrong questions. She was dying to find out more about Angelo Bonifacio and what Giovanni's relationship with him was.

"Are those your friends?" she asked. Giovanni was breathing a little heavier since he'd been back. He took a deep breath. "Not really, just good customers." "I have seen that man with the white hair before. He goes to Our Lady of the Rosary Church. Is he Italian?" "Yes, he is." Giovanni was not going to elaborate on the subject and Maria thought best not to push the issue.

"Thank you so much for this dinner, Giovanni. It is very nice of you. I appreciate it very much."

"So do I," said Joanna.

"Oh, it's nothing. I'll leave you two to have your dinner," Giovanni said getting up. He put the chair back to where he got it and got busy attending to business. It was very crowded. Many diners knew Giovanni and he would stop by their tables to chat and to inquire if everything was all right with their meal. The food was delicious. Maria and Joanna ordered a medium pizza to share and a salad each. They were tempted to order the most expensive item on the menu but decided not to be impolite and take advantage of Giovanni's kindness. While they were waiting for their order to be served Joanna suggested they go in the kitchen and she would introduce Maria to the crew. Maria happily followed her. Everybody was busy in the kitchen cooking and washing dishes. As Maria and Joanna entered the room they stopped what they were doing to say hi. They were very warm towards Maria, happy to meet an Italian person. Franco, Emilio and Mario went back to what they were doing. Only Alfredo remained to talk with Maria. He asked her in Italian where she was from; what she did for a living; was she married; did she have any kids and so on. Joanna stood by, patiently, not understanding a word they were saying. When they were through Joanna and Maria went back to their table to enjoy their meal, which had been served.

Giovanni fascinated Maria. He had acquired, in her mind, an aura of mystery after seeing him with Angelo Bonifacio. All kinds of wild thoughts came into her mind. She kept looking towards the small dining room. The doors were closed. Only the waiter went in and out. He stayed briefly each time. She wondered what kind of tip he was going to get. She saw that they ordered pizza and wine. Nothing else.

Angelo Bonifacio was a very enigmatic man. He was mellow but he could also be stern when the need arose. The rumors about him were true. He was the godfather of San Diego. The police knew it and so did the District Attorney but they had no proof against him. He led a very private life and was surrounded by devoted people. His white hair gave him a grandfatherly look and people respected him. He was very old fashioned and avoided violence. Only in extreme cases he would resort to it. He refused to deal in drugs and didn't like those who did; they were not allowed in his clan. He had connection with the New York mafia and would meet with them at least twice a year. Once a month he would meet with his closest associates to discuss business. That's what they were doing that evening at Giovanni's.

He chose Giovanni's because he was one who paid the monthly dues and was considered one of the clan. His presence in San Diego deterred crime, especially from Mexico. Mexico traded heavily in drugs and illegal smuggling of Mexicans across the border but Angelo Bonifacio's men knew those who did and very often would tip the police to their whereabouts and they would get caught. Because of that, Angelo Bonifacio had enemies who wanted to see him dead and replaced by someone who would get involved in drugs and other crimes. But Angelo Bonifacio was powerful and had powerful friends who would not hesitate to kill if any harm came to him. The other older godfathers in New York and the West Coast supported him in his hate for drugs. They all saw the devastating effects drugs had on people and some of them had either children or grandchildren addicted to them. They were at a loss as what to do, as drugs were so foreign to them, a plague of modern society. They could only oppose drug trade, not very successfully, to tell the truth. There was just too much money involved and if they got rid of some dealers, others would quickly take their places.

Most of the revenue for Angelo Bonifacio came from gambling and protection money, which was enough for him. He had a daughter, two sons and eight grandchildren. His wife died two years before.

The agenda that evening included talking about a couple of businesses who refused to pay protection money. Angelo Bonifacio told his associates to spread the word to boycott them. Everybody knew what to do. It was like a well- rehearsed routine. Goods would not be delivered or they would be delivered damaged. Employees would quit and others could not be found to replace them. Customers would not materialize. Suddenly they were out of business. The smarter ones would change their minds and agree to pay. Magically everything would start working right and they were back in business.

They could talk freely at Giovanni's because, as far as he knew, there were no bugs. The police had no clue where the meetings would take place and Angelo Bonifacio never chose the same place twice in a row. Maria would have loved to eavesdrop on that meeting. Everything she knew about the mafia was true that evening, with the exception that there were no murders involved tonight.

The next item on the agenda was to discuss finances. Antonio Accurso, the accountant, started to brief Angelo about the revenues and the expenses. Business was good and everything was done legally on the surface. They had many legitimate businesses where money was laundered. Their most successful enterprises were public relation firms where most of the protection money went. Antonio, a fifty-year-old man, was Sicilian like Angelo. He had been with him for twenty-five years and was trusted implicitly. Angelo paid him $70,000 a year and he was worth every penny. He was honest in his dishonesty and was very loyal to Angelo. He was married and had two children. His family knew nothing about his connection to the mafia. He never discussed his work at home. One of his children, Peter, had a drug addiction so, understandably, Antonio had the same hatred for drugs as Angelo did. His son was presently in a rehabilitation program. Antonio briefly told the group about the progress his son was making and asked them if anything could be done to get rid of the dealer who provided Peter with the heroin. They asked for the dealer's name but Antonio didn't know. Hopefully his son would one day tell him he was clean for good and realize how damaging a drugged life can be. Antonio said he would let them know. He didn't want the dealer killed but if it came to a choice between his son's life and the dealer's he would have no regrets in doing so. Of course he wouldn't do it personally. There were those in the clan whose job was to kill and they did it expertly. Most of the people who were killed were nothing but rejects anyway, worms who even their mothers would have spit on, so they were doing society a favor. The other four associates each had a chance to speak and each talked about various business problems and asked the godfather permission to go ahead with what needed to be done. Once they got his blessing they all continued to eat the delicious pizzas and drink the Sicilian wine.

When the waiter came in to bring more wine, Angelo Bonifacio asked him if he could ask Giovanni to come in. As soon as the waiter delivered the request, Giovanni immediately left what he was doing and went in the small dining room.

"Is everything all right?" asked Giovanni with a little anxiety.

"Everything is just fine, Giovanni. Come, sit with us for a little while and tell us how is your business doing," replied Angelo.

"As you can see, my business is thriving. God is blessing me. I can't complain, godfather. You should know by the money I pay every month." Giovanni surprised himself with that statement. He hadn't meant to say it but now it was too late. He looked at the godfather a little worried but Angelo was smiling.

"Oh, yes. I want to thank you for that, Giovanni. You always pay on time and we appreciate it. If there is anything we can do for you, don't hesitate to ask. Anything and I mean it. Do you need more business?"

"Oh, no. I have all the business I can handle. Thank you for sending customers. How is your family, godfather?"

"My family is doing fine. My children and grandchildren are all prospering, God bless them. What about you, Giovanni, anything new in your love life? Are we going to see you married soon? It's been five years, you know."

"Well, there may be someone but it's too soon to tell. I might have more news the next time you honor me with your presence."

"Let's hope so, Giovanni. You know we want the best for you. Well, we're finished. Here, put everything on my credit card," said Angelo handing him the card.

"Let me treat you, godfather. You don't come here often enough. It'll be my pleasure."

"Nonsense. You already pay enough. I won't have it." Giovanni took the credit card and went outside. He gave it to the waiter and told him to process the payment. When the waiter gave the card back to Angelo, he gave him a fifty-dollar tip. The waiter thanked him profusely and got busy clearing the table. Giovanni accompanied the six men to the door. He kissed the godfather and embraced him; as before he shook hands with the others. When the party was gone he went to Maria and Joanna's table.

"So, how was your dinner?" he said.

"Delicious," said Maria. "If you promise me that you'll let me pay, I'll come here again. That was the best pizza in San Diego. Make sure that you tell Mario that I said that."

"I sure will. Well, Joanna, it looks like it's back to the kitchen for you, Cinderella. Make sure you don't loose your slipper on your way there. If you do, I'll know where to find you." Giovanni was smiling at Joanna and Joanna blushed furiously. She got up.

"Yes, boss, anything you say. Your wish is my command," she said. She went to Maria and gave her a hug. "I'll see you tomorrow night, Maria. Thank you for coming. Giovanni, thank you so much for this dinner, it means a lot to me."

She went to the kitchen; a little light-headed for the wine she had drunk. Maria was left alone with Giovanni.

"So, Giovanni, tell me, was the white-haired man Angelo Bonifacio, the godfather?" Maria asked.

"How did you know his name, I didn't tell you," replied Giovanni, suspicious and surprised.

"I heard it in Our Lady of the Rosary Church."

"In the church? How in the world…," he was speechless.

"Someone behind me knew him and his name and he commented loudly about it; that's how I know. So, is he really the godfather?" Maria would not relent.

"Oh, those are just rumors. I don't know that he is. I try to stay away from things like that. To me he is just a good customer, nothing more," lied Giovanni.

Maria intrigued Giovanni. He liked her and thought that she was a very nice person. He was glad to make her acquaintance. He was also glad that she was Joanna's roommate. He was starting to care about Joanna but was being cautious about it because of the difference in age. Also because he didn't know whether she'd be interested in him.

"How long have you known Joanna, Maria?"

"Not too long. We met on the trolley. We liked each other and decided to become roommates," lied Maria. She didn't want to tell him about Joanna's homelessness. She didn't know how much she had told him so she didn't elaborate. She was afraid to say the wrong thing.

"Giovanni, do you believe in Jesus Christ? Are you a Christian?"

"The answer is yes, and yes."

"Where do you go to church?"

"I go to Saint Joseph Cathedral on Fourth and Beech. I take my mother every Sunday. Maybe you and Joanna could come with us this Sunday." Giovanni was taking the opportunity of Maria's friendship to get to know Joanna better. He didn't want to commit himself just yet but was aware of his feelings for her. She moved him to tenderness and he wanted to protect her. He liked her serious attitude and the fact that she didn't flirt with men. Quite a few men were interested in her, he could tell by the way they looked at her but so far only Joe Bellagio had come out and said it. He was jealous and was glad that she had rejected his offer. He wanted to kiss her again but her reaction the first night he kissed her made him desist. By inviting her to church he could also see his mother's reaction to her, whether she liked her or not. It was important to him that his mother liked her. He adored his mother and valued her opinion.

"We would love to come to church with you and your mother, Giovanni," replied Maria. "I am sure Joanna will say yes. What time will you come to pick us up?"

"Eleven-thirty."

"Well, it's been a wonderful experience meeting you, the kitchen crew and to have this wonderful dinner, but now I have to go. I have to get up at four-thirty in the morning and it's almost passed my bedtime. Thank you again, Giovanni."

"How are you going home, Maria?"

"I am catching the bus, why?"

"Why don't I give you a ride, it's not far and I'll be back in no time."

"Thank you so much, I really appreciate it. Boy, you are a Godsend. I am so happy to have met you. I'll be back to eat here for sure."

"Anytime. You're always welcome."

Maria was really impressed by Giovanni's Jaguar. On their way to Maria's place Giovanni asked: "What kind of girl is Joanna, Maria?"

"What do you mean by that?"

"I mean is she always that serious? What about men, is she dating anybody?"

"Well, she is pretty serious most of the time, but she is also a lot of fun. Anything I suggest that we do, she gladly goes along with it. She is kind and gentle and no, she is not dating anybody. Are you interested in her?" Maria was holding her breath, waiting for Giovanni to answer. *Wait till I tell Joanna*, she thought.

"Promise not to tell her but, yes, I am interested in her. I don't want to rush into it, though, because of the age difference and also because I don't know anything about her except that she is a virgin." Maria blushed as he said that, but waited for him to continue. "Ever since my wife died I haven't really been serious about anyone. Joanna is the first one to arouse my interest but, as I said, it is too soon to tell."

"Believe me, if you marry Joanna you won't regret it. She is loyal, faithful and dependable. I wouldn't want to see her hurt and I am glad you are being cautious about it. If it helps, and if you don't tell on me, she likes you very much. She just doesn't feel that she's the type you'd go for, with all those sophisticated women that surround you, in the nightclub. Go easy on her, okay?"

"Yes, ma'm, don't worry about it. Thank you for your help." Giovanni left Maria off at her place. On his way back he was jubilant. So she liked him. To know that, took away lot of the anxiety that he was feeling. Ever since he kissed her that first night he had wanted to do it again, but remembering how she had reacted kept him in line. With her, he decided, he had to act the old fashion way like bringing her flowers, taking her out to dinner, going to church and so on.

CHAPTER EIGHTEEN

Monday was going to be a very busy day for Joanna. She woke up at eight-thirty having determined to wake up early that morning. Her first thought was the money, which she had put under her pillow. She couldn't believe the kindness of Giovanni. He had paid her even for the time she had spent with Maria having dinner. She took the $206 and spread them out on the futon. Her own money. She was exhilarated. Her mind was full of ideas. She knew she had to be careful on how she was going to spend it because it wasn't going to be enough for all that she needed. She grouped the money together and got up to have breakfast.

She remembered the happiness she had felt that morning when Giovanni had given her the money on her ride home. She had waited to count it till she was in the apartment. Giovanni had seemed very pleased with her as he handed her the money and told her that she was doing a great job, which pleased her almost as much. *Oh Giovanni, I love you*, she thought to herself.

So, what was she going to do first? While eating the eggs she tried to organize the day ahead in her mind. She decided that the first thing she was going to do was to buy a bus pass; that would give her mobility for all the errands ahead. She quickly showered and dressed. She walked downtown to the check-cashing place and handed the clerk the $49 for a bus pass. The bus stop was right at the corner. She boarded the bus going to Hillcrest at Fantastic Sam, the same hairdresser that Maria used. In fact, she had recommended it. She said it wasn't very expensive and they cut hair decently. Well, she was soon going to find out for herself. When she walked in, there was nobody at the counter. They were all busy cutting hair. She noticed a sign-in sheet at the register and signed her name, she then sat down, waiting. It wasn't very long before one of the hairdressers called her name. Once she was seated Joanna told Sandy that she wanted her hair cut and colored. She wanted it cut straight just below the ears and she wanted to color it the same shade as her natural color because right now it was all bleached out. She was all excited; she expected miracles.

Oh, the magic of money.

Sandy shampooed her hair and cut it just as Joanna wanted it. It took her a little time to find the right shade for the coloring but she found it and went to work applying it to her hair. When she was finished she handed Joanna the mirror so she could also look at the back of her head. Joanna could not believe the change. She looked beautiful. She had a big smile on her face when she paid the $40. She gave Sandy a $2 tip and walked out. While she was waiting for the bus a couple of men went by. They both whistled when they saw her. Joanna blushed but she was immensely pleased. She was thinking of Giovanni, of course, and how he would react at the change in her. Giovanni was all she could think about lately.

Joanna didn't have to wait long for the bus. While in the bus she mentally went over the things she had to do. They were many and she hoped she had time to do them all. She got off at Cedar Street and walked to County Mental Health for her appointment with Jill Thompson, her therapist. She was fifteen minutes early so she asked Sara, the receptionist, if she could pay for the visit then. She also paid for the previous visit with Doctor George Steinman. She then went into the waiting room. A couple was there also. Joanna guessed that the woman was the one in therapy by the slight slur in her speech, which indicated that she might be on medication. They said hi to her and gave her inquisitive looks, especially the man. They were wearing worn out jeans and T-shirts. The woman's hair needed to be combed and she was wearing too much make-up on her eyes, which made her look older than she was. Joanna guessed that she must be in her late twenties, while the man in his early thirties. The man had his arm around the woman's shoulders and would kiss her on the cheek every so often. Joanna thought that was very romantic and she thought of herself and Giovanni. How nice it would be if he kissed her like that while embracing her. She sighed and a feeling of depression washed over her. *What's the use*, she thought, *he is not interested in me, a dishwasher, a poor and unsophisticated woman. Good thing he doesn't know I was homeless and sleeping on dirt or he might not even have hired me. He must never find out.*

Something the woman said brought Joanna back from her reveries and out of curiosity she started to listen to their conversation.

"Last night I went to a bar with my friend Samantha and I had a little too much to drink. We both did. There was a drunk who kept buying us drinks all night long and…" the woman was saying.

"So you went to a bar without telling me," said the man taking his arm off her shoulders. He looked offended and a little angry. "You could have told me. I would have liked to go myself."

"We decided on the spur of the moment, that's why I didn't tell you. Anyway, all I did all night long, beside drinking, was playing darts and shooting pool."

"You know I don't like Samantha and that I don't want you to hang out with her. What's the matter with you, why do you always do things that upset me, why can't you be a better girlfriend? At any rate, you are not supposed to be drinking because of the medication. When are you going to become more responsible? Grow-up, will you?"

"I am sorry, honey, will you forgive me?"

"I suppose. You know I worry about you. I never know when you are going to get yourself into trouble. I can't relax when I am away from you. How did you get home? Don't tell me you drove."

Just then the door opened and Dr. Steinman called the woman's name. She quickly got up and followed the doctor into his office. Her boyfriend remained in the waiting room. As soon as the door closed behind the woman and the doctor the man tried to strike out a conversation with Joanna. Joanna was noncommittal and answered in monosyllables. She didn't really want to talk to him being a little anxious about the next hour with her therapist. She tried to think of what she was going to talk about and Maria's advice came to her mind. *I am not going to talk about my dreams,* she thought. *I am just going to talk about Raul and being homeless.*

Joanna was still thinking about what she was going to say during therapy when the door opened and a woman in her sixties called her name. She asked Joanna to follow her upstairs. Joanna got up and followed her. She was filled with anxiety. This was all dramatically new for her and she took a deep breath. While going upstairs Joanna looked at who she thought was Jill Thompson, her therapist. She was about five feet, four inches tall, had short, gray hair and a curvaceous body. She was wearing a floral print shirt in blue and green shades and a black, tight skirt. Her manners were very amiable and Joanna liked her immediately. She looked motherly and in fact she was, as she found out later on.

Jill Thompson had five daughters, all grown and with families of their own. She had divorced late in life and had put herself through college to obtain a master degree in social work. Despite some opinions from one of her teachers that she was never going to make it, she graduated with honors and was now working as a social worker. She had a vast experience with sexual molestation issues and Joanna knew immediately that she could trust her.

Jill Thompson entered a room to the right of the upstairs floor and invited Joanna to take a seat. "Hi Joanna. I am Jill Thompson, your therapist. Since this is your very first visit I don't have a lot of information about you, except for this note from Dr. George Steinman, which states that you have been sexually molested and have to appear in court to testify against the perpetrator. Good for you, I hope that whoever he was gets what he deserves. Why don't you tell me the details so that we can work on a strategy to put you through the ordeal?"

"I was adopted when I was seven years old. My adoptive father, his name is Raul Ruiz, is the one who molested me. The molestation started a little after they adopted me and didn't stop until I left at eighteen. He never actually had sex with me, but he would touch my body and made me touch him, his private parts. I was too scared to say no because he would threaten me and he has put so many fears in me that I always have nightmares. For years I didn't tell anyone about it because I was too scared and ashamed, but recently I told Maria, a friend of mine and she is the one who suggested that I come to therapy."

"She was right. You need a lot of therapy. Your situation is one, which is not solved overnight. You have years of abuse to deal with and this monster is now in jail, is he not, and cannot touch you and do you harm, so you can relax. In fact I want you to do breathing exercises everyday and as you breathe out imagine you are expelling all the abuses and filthy things he made you do. Imagine you are expelling him out of your system with every breath. Cleanse yourself and do it without fear."

"That's easier said than done. I am twenty-eight years old and I have carried these fears in me for all these years. I will need your coaching every step of the way. I can't do it alone."

"And you shouldn't do it alone. That's why therapy can be helpful. I don't advise you to tell people at large. This friend of yours, Maria, is she trustworthy? Do you know if she will keep it to herself?"

"Oh yes she will. She promised me she will not tell anyone and I believe her. I was homeless and she took me in. She has given me a place to stay and she will let me stay at her apartment until I get back on my feet. I found a job as a dishwasher and I have just completed my first week at Giovanni's restaurant. Do you know it?"

"Yes, it's in Hillcrest. I have gone there during my lunch hour a couple of times. They have the best pizza in San Diego. I always order it when I go there. Let's get back to your molestation. What do you want to talk about today, what bothers you most?"

"What bothers me most is the fact that sometimes I enjoyed when Raul touched me. I didn't want to, but I did anyway. I want to deal with that because if I enjoyed it, it makes me an accomplice in what he was doing. I want to get my innocence back, of when I was seven years old and no one had touched my body except my mother. I also want to talk about my biological mother. I think about her everyday and I feel empty inside. She was so loving and gentle. Nobody will ever be able to replace her in my heart. I need to get strong for when I will go to court to testify against Raul. He has threatened me. He said that if I ever told anyone I would be sent to jail. He said that I was a bad girl and I was making him do those things to me. He also said that if I told anyone my clothes would catch on fire. I know now that it is not true, but when I was seven years old I believed him and I guess a part of me is terrified. I wish I could go today and testify because the anxiety is killing me."

"What is the date of the trial?"

"I don't know for sure, sometime next month. I am waiting for Felicia, my adoptive mother, to let me know."

"I don't know if I will see you before then. I will try to give you an appointment two weeks from now. We usually see our clients on a monthly basis, but I guess I'll make an exception in your case. I will talk to Sara, the receptionist, when we're done. Tell me Joanna about when you were seven years old and were adopted. Whatever you remember; how you felt."

"I was staying at a foster home, together with my brother John. The social worker from Social Services came to pick me up, just me, not John. She said that we were going to her office to meet a couple that liked me very much and wanted to take me to their home to live with them. She said they were very nice and would treat me as if I was their own daughter. She also asked me to be nice to them. I asked her about my mother and I told her that I wanted to go home to her. She told me that it was not possible because the judge had decided that she was not a fit parent, so I couldn't see her anymore. She told me to forget about her and learn to love the couple that was coming to pick me up.

We had been in the office for ten minutes when a dark-skinned, dark-haired couple was let in. They said hi to the social worker and I gathered they knew her; then they came towards me, smiling. 'Hi Joanna,' the woman said. 'My name is Felicia and this here is Raul, my husband,' said the woman. 'We've come to pick you up and take you home with us. What do you think about that, aren't you happy?'

I didn't reply, just stared with wide eyes. My heart was beating really fast and I was scared. I hugged the stuffed bear really tight and I wanted to crawl out of there, away from them. I wanted to run away to my mother and to my brother but a sense of defeat took hold of me and I started to cry. They seemed very concerned and gave the social worker a worried look. Felicia came over and hugged me gently. She took a handkerchief and dried my tears. I felt then that she was a kind woman and some of my fears subsided. I wasn't sure about her husband. He remained silent and apart and I felt intimidated by him.

The social worker got up and came over. She said 'Now, now, there is no reason to cry, baby. Felicia and Raul want to be your mom and dad. They don't have any children and that's why they want you. They want you to be a real daughter to them. They will be loving towards you so let's dry those tears, ok?' She spoke briefly to them about some final papers that they needed to sign before they could take custody of me and once that was taken care of I left that office with Felicia and Raul. The social worker came to see me at the house a couple of times to make sure everything was fine but after that I never saw her again. I never saw my brother John again, either."

"What happened after you left the office?"

"Felicia was holding my hand and talking to me gently. She asked me if I was hungry and I said yes. She wanted to know my favorite place to eat and I told her McDonald, so they took me there. Raul didn't say very much, but he tried to cheer me up when he spoke. He was nervous, I could tell, maybe more nervous than I, even though he was trying not to show it. When we got to their house I waited in the car until they opened the door to let me out. The house was one story, and it had a nice garden in front with lots of flowers, which I later found out was tended by Felicia. We went inside and I was escorted to my room. My attention was caught by a huge, stuffed giraffe standing in one corner; next to it there was a big, white, fluffy bear with a red heart on his chest. A handmade quilt, in pastel colors, which continued the color patterns of the room, covered a single bed. On the wall there were framed pictures of clowns, three or four of them. Under a large window there was a desk with a chair, which I would use to do my homework. An assortment of other toys was hanging in a net suspended from the ceiling in another corner of the room.

I liked the room and felt an easiness come over me. I was slowly accepting the idea that this was my home now whether I liked it or not, and I realized that it was in my best interest to like it and like it fast. I gasped as Felicia took me to a small walk-in closet where there were hanging half a dozen new dresses, in my size. She opened a chest of drawers and showed me underwear, socks, and sweaters that were contained therein and she gave me instructions for when I would be dressing myself up. She pointed to a wicker hamper and told me that I should use it to put dirty clothes into it. After that she gave me a tour of the rest of the house.

It was a two-bedroom house with one-and- a-half baths, a dining room and a spacious kitchen that faced the backyard where there was a swing for me there, she told me. I noticed that she had vegetables growing and I was pleased by that because I have always loved gardening, growing things, especially vegetables. I would often help her and she was so impressed that she gave me my very own plot, to grow whatever I liked.

The first night I spent in the house was terrifying. I was afraid to go to sleep. I was alert and would hear even the faintest noise. I cried most of the night, missing my mom and my brother John. Felicia had to wake me up the next morning. She sat on my bed and gently stroked my hair till I roused from sleep. I was confused and didn't know where I was for a while. When I realized where I was I gave her a faint smile.

It was a Sunday and I didn't have school that day. That was another thing I needed to adjust to: Changing school. The school I would attend was within walking distance from the house but Felicia always walked me; she was afraid I'd get kidnapped, with my blonde hair and blue eyes. She said someone might mistake me for the daughter of rich people and ask for a ransom. She was proud of my looks. I love Felicia; she has been like a real mother to me and I miss her sometime, but my real mother is the one I miss most. I will always love her best and I don't care if the judge said she was an unfit mother, to me she was the best mother in the world. She made me laugh but she would also correct me when the need arose. She was easy going and carefree and spoiled my brother and me something awful but unfortunately that didn't last very long.

She was beautiful; blonde, blue eyes like me, slender with beautiful long hair. My recollection of her is that of a small child so she probably is bigger than life in my memories. She worked at night and she would leave my brother and me alone at the house. I used to be worried for her and every night I'd be afraid that she might not come back. I also think, but I am not sure, that she drank and used drugs. Sometime I'd hear noises coming from her room, early in the morning, and I knew that she had a man in there with her. Eventually some of our neighbors called Social Services and that's when they took us away from her and started to send us to foster homes."

"Did you ever search for your biological mother?"

"I always wanted to but I didn't know where to start. I asked Felicia if she would help me, but she wasn't too keen on that. She has Cuban blood and she is very passionate in her affections. She was afraid that I wouldn't love her anymore. Besides, she had no clue either of where she might be. I will hire a private investigator as soon as I can afford to and I will find her. My last name now is Ruiz but my real last name was Stanford, but I don't know if that is my biological father's last name or hers. This makes it much harder. I might never find her. I also want to find my brother John, but for that I'd have to get in touch with Social Services in Minneapolis and I don't know if they will give me the information. They are pretty funny about that."

"Well, Joanna, it seems to me that you did have a certain amount of affection in your life with the Ruiz'. When did the molestation start?"

"It started about three months after I was adopted. Raul had gone to the bar at the corner after work and he came back late and drunk. He sneaked into my room and reached under the covers. I was asleep so I didn't realize what was happening at first. His hands reached into my pajamas and I woke up fully. I froze. I didn't dare to move. He was touching my private parts with one hand and rubbing the front of his pants with the other. As he realized that I was awake he whispered that he was trying to make me feel good, grabbed my hand and put it on his penis, moving it up and down. I didn't say anything. I didn't know what was happening. I was only seven years old and I had no knowledge of anything sexual, but somehow I knew there was something wrong with what he was doing to me. I wanted to call Felicia and I asked him where she was. He said that she was asleep and for me not to make any noise. He said again that he wanted to make me feel good and would I be a good girl and make him feel good also. As he said that he increased the rubbing. He was very excited, I know that now, but I didn't know it then. Then he suddenly stopped and that's when he started to tell me not to tell anyone, that it was our secret, and that if I told anyone my clothes would catch on fire. Then, just like that, he left the room.

I remained awake for long time after he was gone, afraid that he might come back and start touching me again. I had visions of me burning alive and I was terrified. After a while I could hear noises coming from their bedroom and I was wondering if he was telling Felicia what he had just done, but somehow I knew that it was unlikely. Years later I realized that the noises coming from their bedroom were Raul having sex with his wife. After a while it seemed to be a pattern with Raul. He would go out drinking, come home, get aroused with me, go to his bedroom and have sex with his wife.

As time went by the threats grew worse and the molestation got more sophisticated. He would unzip his pants and pull out his penis. Later on he would force me to give him oral sex. All I know about sex I have learned from Raul; I have never been touched by another man. I am still a virgin. I don't want any man to touch me except, maybe, my boss Giovanni. He is the first man I have felt attracted to in my whole life. He kissed me and I got mad at him and slapped him really hard on the face, but now I wish he would do it again. I think I am falling in love with him, but I don't think anything is going to come out of it. I am not his type."

"Let's stay focused on Raul because of the trial. How are you going to feel being in the same room with him and recounting all the things he did to you?"

"I am going to be terrified, but I won't recant. I am not going to be intimidated into silence. I am going to tell the whole truth. I hope he goes to jail for the rest of his life, the pig."

"I don't have one thing clear in my mind. Help me to understand: Why is he in jail? Is it because he molested you?"

"No. He also molested a little girl, the daughter of one of their neighbors. They have witnesses."

"Well, I am glad he was caught. It serves him right. I see from the chart that Dr. Steinman prescribed some medication for you, because of your nightmares. I suggest you take it every night; it will help you sleep better. Let me ask you something, Joanna. How was Raul during the day, how did he treat you?"

"He was always nice, caring, and that would confuse me. It was as if he had a change in personality. If I had told anyone about what he was doing to me, they would not have believed me because of the way he'd act. He was the same even when we were alone and there was no one around to see it. But those times I'd catch him looking at me and my heart would grow cold from fear. I didn't want to be alone with him but I couldn't tell Felicia or she would have become suspicious. I have been so ashamed for so many years. I want to get ready of all the feelings that that situation has created for me. I want to start to live again, to be free."

"I agree. The breathing exercises that I mentioned earlier will help you do that. In the meantime just think that he is behind bars and cannot do anything to harm you. He might get violent in his feelings towards you and give you hateful stares when you testify in court, but don't let that deter you. Just say the truth and don't be afraid. Any problem that you will have we will discuss during therapy. The worst has passed; there are only good things for you in the future, just be assured of that. We're almost out of time. Let's go downstairs and make an appointment for two weeks from now. When are you going to see Dr. Steinman again?"

"In a month, to get a new prescription and to let him know how I am doing."

"Don't miss it. I am glad you came to see me Joanna. We have a lot of work to do, but we'll make it, girl."

They left the office and went downstairs to make an appointment, which Joanna requested for a Monday, since she didn't work on Mondays. She said goodbye to Jill Thompson and walked out of the clinic.

Joanna left the building overwhelmed by emotions. As usual, when she thought of all the years of molestation that she had endured she felt like choking with unshed tears. Right then she wanted to cry but pushed back the tears and concentrate her attention on what she needed to do. She followed the directions that Sara had given her for the pharmacy and directed her steps there. It wasn't hard because it was located a little ways down on Sixth Avenue. McGills Pharmacy was on the left side of the street. The door was small and she almost missed it. She had her prescription filled and found out that she only had to pay $5 for it. The plan she was enrolled in paid for the difference. She put the container in her front pocket, since she didn't have a purse.

Next on her agenda was the dentist. Again she was lucky because the Downtown Dental Clinic was at the corner of Sixth Avenue and Broadway. They advertised on their window that they had a payment plan. She walked in and took a number. She then sat down in one of the comfortable chairs of the waiting room and hoped that it wouldn't take too long. Fortunately it didn't. When the receptionist called her number she quickly got up and explained to her that she wanted to be on the payment plan. She could only afford $20 per week. The receptionist gave her some papers to fill out. When Joanna had completed them she handed them over and waited eagerly for the answer.

The receptionist, after consulting with a co-worker, came back and called her name. She told Joanna that $20 per week had been approved, would she show them an identification card. Joanna took her new ID from her front left pocket and handed it to her. When the receptionist was satisfied she asked her what dental work she needed to have done. Joanna told her that she needed a check-up and a cleaning. She was told to take a seat and wait for someone to call her. *Thank God they approved the payment plan,* thought Joanna, while taking a seat once more.

There were about ten people in the waiting room, some of them being children, moving around noisily or playing with toys in a corner of the room. Joanna got in a reflective mood and started to think about Giovanni. I wonder where he is right now, she mused. She imagined him in the restaurant, busy with the supplies, with the bookkeeping; in his office, overseeing the smooth restaurant operation. She felt an ache in her heart thinking about him. *I wonder if he likes me,* she thought, *even just a little. I wonder what he'll think when he sees me Wednesday night. I want to be pretty for him. I am going to buy a dress so he'll see that I am a woman and not a tomboy. I am going to wear make-up as soon as I can afford some, in the meantime I'll borrow Maria's; I am sure she won't mind.*

Her mind was going round and round ruminating on thoughts of Giovanni, daydreaming and fantasizing about their imagined relationship. A woman wearing a white lab coat was calling her name. She had to call twice before Joanna heard her. She quickly got up and followed her in the lab room. She was asked to seat down and was covered by a thick, protective coat. She was asked if she was pregnant to which she replied that she was not married. The lab technician took many x-ray pictures of her teeth. She worked silently and efficiently and was done in no time. Joanna was sent to the waiting room to wait for the results of the x-rays.

Twenty minutes later the lab technician escorted her to see the dentist, Dr. Gonzales. He was Mexican. His face was tanned and he had beautiful, white teeth of which he was well aware because he flashed his smile often. He examined Joanna's teeth after he looked at the x-rays. He found three cavities and a tooth that needed bonding. He also pointed out that her teeth needed cleaning. He was done in five minutes. His assistant escorted Joanna to the reception area and gave her file to the receptionist to schedule the appointments for future visits. Joanna asked if she could have her teeth cleaned that same day and the receptionist looked at her logbook. She said she was lucky because there was an opening in one hour. They scheduled two more appointments: One for the cavities and one for the bonding.

She was asked for payment of the first installment of $20.

Joanna left the Downtown Dental Clinic and walked to Payless Shoes located at the corner of Fourth Avenue and Broadway, so she only had to walk two blocks. She was looking for black shoes with medium heels to wear with her uniform at night. She was very embarrassed having to wear her old sneakers. It was totally unsophisticated. She looked for the isle that displayed her size, 8 ½, and found it very quickly because the store was not very big. She looked at the selection available and tried on various shoes. She found a pair that she liked and went to the cash register to pay for it. Joanna was beaming as she paid the $15 for the shoes. To her it was well worth the price. The clerk looked at her and a smile crossed her face as she gave her the change. "Thank you, and come again," she said. "Oh yes, I will," replied Joanna leaving the store.

She still had half an hour to kill before her appointment. What was she going to do? Horton Plaza was right across the street. She remembered looking at someone who was drinking a Caramel Macchiato from Starbucks and she got a craving for it, but she decided to wait because she wanted to sit down and savor it. Besides she needed to have her teeth cleaned so she didn't want to put anything in her mouth. She spent the next twenty minutes window- shopping and making plans for the rest of the money. She then directed her steps to the Downtown Dental Clinic.

When she got there she took a seat and started to think about Giovanni again. She remembered that the restaurant was closed on Mondays so he wouldn't be there, or would he? What did he do in his free time? She wished she knew. She wished she were part of his life. *But I am part of his life*, she thought; *a little part right now, but maybe it'll change. Who knows? Be optimistic and don't worry.* She took a deep breath and thought of Raul.

What would she feel when she saw him in a court of law, hand-cuffed and escorted by a guard? She was going to cringe and she was going to be ashamed, but she resolved within herself that it wasn't going to deter her from saying the truth. How he had molested her for all those years, without remorse, relentless and without merci. So she had enjoyed it sometimes, but did that make her an accomplice? She never showed Raul that she was enjoying it, she always pleaded with him not to do it. She decided that she was not going to mention it; it was better for her. Why should she? She was the victim. She felt sorry for herself and was on the point of tears when she heard her name being called. It was the hygienist who invited Joanna to follow her. She pointed to a dental chair in her small office and invited her to take a seat. She took one look at her teeth and exclaimed that it was going to take her a long time to clean them.

"How long has it been since you had them cleaned the last time?" she asked.

"Maybe ten years," Joanna replied. "I know they're in bad shape. Just do the best you can." The hygienist went to work on her teeth. While she was cleaning them she told Joanna about a bleaching gel to whiten the teeth in ten to fourteen days. Would she be willing to try it? "Yes," replied Joanna.

She was staring at the ceiling where a picture of Brad Pitt was looking at her. She tried to relax but she was too excited and her mind was racing with thoughts of Giovanni and thoughts of Raul. She wondered what kind of man was Giovanni in bed. Would he ask her to do the same kind of things Raul did? How would he touch her? She didn't have a full comprehension of the sexual act since Raul had never had straight sex with her so when she thought of herself and Giovanni she imagined it only up to a point and then her mind would draw a blank. She would let him teach her everything. She would do the breathing exercises that Jill Thompson had recommended and get Raul and the molestation out of her system; she would start anew. She had no idea that Giovanni was interested in her so she was tormented by doubts and insecurity. What was she going to tell Giovanni when he inquired again about her virginity, which she was sure he would? She was going to tell him that she had saved herself for the right man. No reason for him to know about Raul.

Joanna was right, in that Sicilian men were very jealous, like God. He wouldn't have liked it at all and would probably have hired a gun to kill Raul, even if he was in jail. He must never know, she determined in her mind and she would ask Maria to keep the secret too. When she was going to court to testify against Raul, she was going to tell Giovanni that Felicia was ill and that she needed to be with her. She wasn't happy about the secrecy and the lies but she was thinking smartly and wisely. She was going after what she wanted the best way she knew how. She had suffered too much. She was not going back on the streets again. Life was giving her opportunities and she was going to take them. She was going to have no scruples. Scruples were for losers and for those who could afford them. She was going to fight, her own way. She was going to get what she wanted.

Merciful God, dear Jesus, my Lord and my King, let me marry Giovanni, she prayed silently, *I'll be a good wife and a good mother, I promise*. The hygienist asked her to turn her head slightly so she could clean the other side of her mouth. It was taking her a long time because Joanna had lot of plaque on her teeth. Joanna turned her head without stopping her thinking. The hygienist's face was inches from hers. She closed her eyes so she wouldn't have to look at her. That made her uncomfortable. *I want to get married and have children, by Giovanni,* Joanna thought, *no other man would do. I will become sophisticated like the other women in his life. He won't be ashamed of me.*

Joanna was exhausted by the intensity of her thoughts. She decided to give her mind a rest and she started to drift into a light sleep. Her whole life seemed to pass in front of her eyes; all the pain that was in it overwhelmed her. Images would overlap images, without her even trying to recall. You just can't stop your mind at will, she realized. Thoughts, thoughts, thoughts. She recalled a verse of the Bible that warned man to guard his thoughts because life was shaped by them. Very good advice indeed. She would start having positive thoughts about everything. Maybe this way her life would change for the better. She would just have to wait and see. She decided to start right then and there. She saw herself in a bridal gown marrying Giovanni. Maria was the Maid of Honor and Alfredo was the Best Man. She saw herself pregnant and having a little boy. His name would be Giovanni Jr. She would work side by side with Giovanni taking little Giovanni Jr. to the restaurant and watching him grow into the business, which he would inherit one day, when his father retired. She saw herself wearing nice clothes and jewelry. She would learn how to drive and have her own car.

Jesus, what a new world is opening in front of me, she thought. *I hope it works. I am going to make it a daily exercise from now on. I will spend at least thirty minutes a day having positive thoughts and breathing exercises. I am so excited. Forget about sleeping, I feel like I just won the lottery. I can shape my life anyway I want. What an incredible thing.*

"Okay, I am all done," said the hygienist. "Lot of the stains have come off, but your teeth still have a yellowish color. I am going to take an impression of your teeth. With that we will build a whitening tray where you will put the gel in and keep it on every

night for fourteen days. Your teeth should be white by then and you should have a beautiful smile." The hygienist took an impression of Joanna's teeth then gave her a mirror to look at them. She was pleasantly surprised to see that lot of the stains had come off.

Her gums were red and that made her teeth look whiter. She was all excited and wished she could start using the gel right away, but she had to wait another week until the whitening tray made from the mold was ready. She didn't need to make an appointment for that. She should come in a week to pick it up and then she would be given everything she needed with the instructions for use.

God forgive me, but I love money, Joanna thought. *Money can change your life. Without money I couldn't do any of the things I am doing. I hope and pray that I have lots of money one day. Lots of it. Money is power; money is freedom; money is independence; money is self-respect; money is life.*

Joanna left Downtown Dental Clinic with a smile on her face and rightly so, because her teeth were clean and lot of the stains were gone. She was lucky because she had straight teeth and a beautiful smile that made her face look radiant. She passed a homeless person sitting on the ground and she gave him a dollar. He thanked and blessed her. *How peculiar life is,* Joanna thought. *Now I am the one giving money.* She happily walked to Longs where she bought a comb. She needed one badly for when she had to go to the nightclub, at night. She paid $3 for it. She bought a short one that she could put in her pocket since she didn't have a purse yet. She couldn't afford one till next week. She counted the money left in her pocket. She had $36. She went to Mervyn's to look at the clothes. She wanted to buy a dress to wear Wednesday night, at work.

She went through every rack there was and tried on many dresses in the fitting room until she found one that was perfect for her. It was baby blue, like her eyes, with tiny white flowers that reminded her of a clear spring day. It had spaghetti straps and flowed smoothly down to her ankles. Its length made Joanna look taller than she was. In the front it had a V cut that exposed a little of her beautiful, firm breast. She looked at the price tag. It cost $46 but it was discounted. When she paid for it, including taxes, it came to $25. Joanna was so happy she couldn't contain herself. Her smile was a beam of light.

Starbucks was right next to Mervyn's so she decided now was the perfect time for her to buy a *Caramel Macchiato*. Finally. She paid $2.50 for it and went to sit at one of the tables outside. She counted her money again. She had $8.50 left. She decided she wasn't going to buy anything anymore since it wouldn't be another week until she got paid again. Next week, she decided, she would give Maria $50 hoping that it'd be okay with her.

The *Caramel Macchiato* was delicious. She sipped it slowly, watching people go by, relaxing and casting away from her mind all negative thoughts, feeling as if a door had been opened in front of her. In that room, full of light, there was happiness and the fulfillment of all of her dreams.

CHAPTER NINETEEN

Maria had a bad experience that morning, going to work. She was walking down Sixth Avenue going to the bus stop on Broadway, when a homeless woman who had been sleeping outside an office building approached her. She was taller than Maria, slender, in her late forties, early fifties. She asked Maria for money and Maria told her that she didn't have any. On hearing that the woman got angry and became verbally aggressive. Maria responded in tune and they had a word fight. She stopped talking to her when she threatened to kill her.

The woman, content that she had the last word, walked back to where she had been sleeping and Maria, very upset, continued to walk towards the bus stop. The street was deserted, except for them, and it was still dark, so she had no witnesses. When she got to work Maria called the police and told them what had happened, where it had happened. They took her phone number and name and told her that they would dispatch a car to the area. She never heard from them and soon forgot about it, being engrossed in her work.

Maria used to be very generous towards homeless people. She remembered one time, when she was living in Hawaii, that she had seen a man searching in a garbage can, looking for food. Maria was having her lunch; she had actually finished her sandwich, and was observing him. Moved by compassion she took $20 out of her purse and gave it to him. The man couldn't believe his eyes. He thanked her profusely and sat by, stunned. He was still sitting there when Maria left to go back to work. In San Diego there were many homeless people when Maria first arrived. Every time she'd walk downtown she would be assailed by them, at every corner, asking for money. Initially she gave money to everybody whether it was a quarter or five dollars, but she soon realized that she could not keep doing that because she was not a rich person. At any rate, most of those homeless people just used the money to buy alcohol or drugs; you could tell by the way they looked. Also, some of them received financial help from the government, but would squander the money and be forced to beg to make it to the end of the month.

So she stopped giving.

Maria still did charity deeds, though. She'd try to commit herself to one per year. One year she volunteered to call a homebound, elderly woman, every day to make sure that she was all right and to keep her in touch with another human being. Maria even called her on weekends, even though she didn't have to, and would spend over an hour on the phone with her. Her name was Grace. She was in her seventies, partially blind. Maria formed a strong relationship with her through those phone calls and she even met her, one day, when she drove her to various stores to buy things she needed for herself and for the house. She didn't have a picture of Grace in her mind before she met her so she was neither pleased nor disappointed when she did meet her.

She was short, a little chubby, with her hair totally white. Maria liked her even more, if possible, after meeting her. She was a character. She was not totally alone, though. She had a daughter who lived in another city and she had two granddaughters who would keep frequently in touch with her. Her health was not very good, because of her heart. In fact, she had a pacemaker, which she had to have replaced. Through daily contact with her she became her best friend. She would confide in her and tell her about things that were happening in her life. She became her confidant for a year, after which her assignment was over. Actually, it was over because Grace went to live with her daughter otherwise Maria would have continued past the one-year deadline.

That experience had been very rewarding for her and she

missed that daily connection.

Another charity project she undertook for one-year was the sponsorship of a child in Peru. She would pay a certain amount of money every month. That money was used for that child only, to provide for her needs. At Christmas time she received a letter from the child, thanking her for her support, and that was the only contact she had with her. There was no return address on the letter so she was not able to communicate with her, but she was moved by her childish handwriting on the note. When the year was over Maria stopped sending the money. After that she sponsored the local, public television, KPBS, for one year and after that, it was the turn of a Christian denomination. To that she contributed $25 a month. In the last few years she had donated to the best charity she knew: Herself. In fact she was saving money to buy the house that belonged to her parents in Italy. She had managed to save $30,000. Her plan was to buy out two of her sisters. Her parents owned two houses that were attached one to the other. They had a total of six rooms altogether, which amounted to one room each for them since there were six daughters who would inherit the properties at her parents' death. If she bought the share of two of her sisters, that would give her ownership of one of the houses. She didn't know how much the property was worth because it had not been appraised yet, but hopefully her mother would have it appraised so she would know how much to pay two of her sisters who were willing to sell their share.

She preferred the newer house, which was few feet higher than the older one. In that one she would have more privacy since it was standing further back from the street. It had been her mother's idea for her to buy the house. In fact Maria had not given it any thought. One day she told her mother that she had money saved and that was when her mother suggested that she'd buy out two of her sisters. Maria accepted that idea happily and now that was her mission. She would have a place to grow old into and once she had her pension from the County and her Social Security from the federal government she could grow old without financial worries.

She really looked forward to her retirement, but it was quite a few years away. She needed at least ten years of service with the

County and she needed to be fifty-five years old before she could start collecting the pension. But Maria was always hoping that she'd win the lottery before that. A part of her, though, didn't believe that she would.

The morning was going to be really slow, Maria noticed, while looking at the clock. It was barely ten-thirty and it felt like she had been working for hours. Linda Suarez, her supervisor, had told her that Mark, the Filipino worker, had been hired by the computer company he had interviewed with, and his last day would be in two weeks. Maria was sorry to see him go, but this was a great opportunity for him. The pay was much higher and the location was much closer to his new home. Right now it took him one hour to drive to work every morning and one hour to drive home, at night. So Maria went to Mark and congratulated him. She noticed that he was quite happy about it, and who wouldn't.

Now they would have to interview to find a replacement for him and Linda told Maria that she wanted her to be on the interviewing panel. Maria was pleasantly surprised by her request and agreed. She had always been interviewed so it would be quite an experience to be on the other side deciding who would be getting the job. Maria liked Linda and Linda liked her. She had a lot of personality and she was not afraid of anything except of Diane Lock, her supervisor. She was so tiny that the few times Maria had hugged her she had felt as if she were hugging a little girl. She was easy going but she could be severe if the job wasn't done right, and she wanted it to be done a certain way or else. She was independent and knowledgeable about her job, which she had learned all by herself. It seemed that the previous supervisor had left in a hurry so she had to take over the accounting section. No one had been there for her, telling her what to do and how to do it. So Maria admired her for that. She was also the only one in accounting who liked to socialize outside, except Tanya, with whom Maria had gone out a couple of times.

Linda gave her a ride to the company's picnic the year before; she also had invited her to her church since she knew that Maria was a Christian also. That's when Maria met her husband, a Filipino quite older than she, and her little daughter Corinna. She seemed much in love with her husband because they were holding hands during the service. The congregation was made mostly of Filipinos. The church's pastor called Maria home a couples of weeks later. He wanted to visit her, together with his wife. Maria asked him why and he said to talk about Jesus, our Savior. Maria told him that she was already saved and that she was a Christian and already had a church she was going to, so thanks but no thanks.

Linda told Maria that she might be leaving the job also, because she had applied for an analyst' position with another branch of the County. She said that Diane Lock had told her about the position and that she had encouraged her to apply. Maybe she wanted to get rid of her. Why else would she have told her about it? So that was the second bad news of the morning. Maria told Linda that she hoped she wouldn't get it because she didn't want her to go. What were they going to do without her? She knew everything. Every problem they had she knew how to solve and anything new that came up she knew how to deal with. They'd be lost without her. Linda replied that she had made up her mind and if they hired her she would go. She said she felt stressed out at that job; that Diane was taking advantage of her and that all that stress was giving her a rash to her face. In fact she did have a bad rash and she was always scratching her face because it itched.

The rest of the day was uneventful and when five-fifteen finally came around Maria left thanking Jesus for another day on this Earth. She always thanked Jesus at the end of her workday. Now she was doing better, mentally. Ever since the doctor had put her on Zyprexa all the paranoia had left her. She didn't feel anymore that others were reading her mind and that made it easier for her to do her job.

Mondays were always hard on her, though. On Mondays she had to switch gears, get in a working mode. After three days off she would be too relaxed and having to readjust was sometimes a problem. She looked forward to her ride on the bus. The time she spent on the bus belonged to the Lord. She would meditate and think about God; the meaning of life; why are we on this earth; how was she improving; the thoughts she had during the day; and the thoughts she hadn't had. Because of her mental illness she had been paying close attention to her thoughts. Also, thinking that others were reading her mind, she had tried not to have any thoughts at all. That had worked out to her advantage because she had found a sense of peace within herself. She wouldn't pass judgment or be too opinionated so that people felt more relaxed around her and treated her better.

Another reason she tried to control her thoughts was the realization that ninety-nine percent of them were negative. So, since she believed that life was shaped by our thoughts and perceptions she came to the conclusion that by eliminating those negative thoughts her life would get better. Being aware of her thinking pattern did her lot of good. Now she needed to consciously have positive thoughts; create them out of nothing and see how that affected her life. It was like a new world had opened up for her. So, controlling her thoughts had brought a certain stability to her life. It was uneventful most of the time but she preferred it that way compared to having negative things happening to her. She also had to make a conscious effort to have positive thoughts. That was enlightening her in regards to what her real desires were.

Did she want money? Yes.

Did she want a house? Yes.

Did she want peace on her job? Yes.

Did she want Elizabeth to go back to school and then get married? Yes.

Did she want a man? No.

Did she want to get closer to God? Yes.

Riding on the bus was an extremely positive experience for her. She was even glad when there was traffic so that she had more time to think. Unknown to Maria, Joanna had come to the same conclusion: Our thoughts shape our life and that at the same time. Amazing. The Holy Spirit was obviously at work in their lives but they didn't realize it just yet.

When she got home Maria had the surprise of her life. She knew the woman in the living room was Joanna, but what had happened to her? She was beautiful. Joanna was wearing her new dress, her hair was combed and she had put on some make-up. Her figure, size eight, looked very slender in her long dress. She looked like a movie star.

"Girl, what have you done? You look positively smashing," exclaimed Maria. "Wait till Giovanni sees you. His jaw is going to drop."

"Do you really think so, Maria? Is he going to like me?"

"If he doesn't he is a fool. Any man will like you. You're a knockout. And your smile! Have you been to the dentist?"

"Yes, I have. And I have to go next week to get a gel, which is going to whiten my teeth about eight shades lighter. You should do it too."

"I'll see how it works on you and then I'll do it. I am a little afraid to mess with my teeth because an Italian friend of mine had the whitening done and now his teeth are all black. He is very handsome but when he smiles he looks ugly."

"Do you know what kind of bleaching he had done?"

"I think they used laser, not gel."

"Oh well, I can relax then. So, who is this Italian friend of yours? How come I haven't met him yet? Tell me about him."

"His name is Vittorio Malatesta. I met him through my friend Concetta a couple of years ago. She had known him for many years. Anyway, he is a hairdresser in La Jolla and has his own business. He imports merchandise from Italy. When I first met him I had a crush on him and so, when he asked me to loan him $3,500 I gave it to him. That was two years ago and he still owes me $1,600. I am very upset with him and I get angry every month because I have to go all the way to La Jolla to get the money. That's a two hours bus ride. Have you been to La Jolla yet?"

"No, I don't believe I have."

"Well, I am going this Friday. You can go with me. He is probably going to flirt with you, so beware."

"What does he look like?"

"I think he is very handsome. He is about five-feet-six-inches tall, has jet black hair combed back, weighs about one-hundred-sixty pounds and has beautiful eyes. Sometimes they are blue and sometimes they are green. The only drawback is his teeth. My daughter doesn't like him. She saw a picture of him and she said he looks like a faggot."

"Well, is he?"

"Nooo! He is very straight. In fact he has a girlfriend and they share a house together. They also work together because she is a hairdresser too."

"How come he doesn't cut your hair?"

"He has a couple of times. Of course I didn't have to pay for it because we are friends and he didn't want to take anything from me especially since I loaned him the money. He is very good at cutting hair. He should do only that and let go of the importing business because he has not been very successful at it. He has a very rich clientele. He has a partner hairdresser. His name is Maxim. He is also Italian. He is homosexual but you couldn't tell by looking at him because he looks straight. He works at the salon only and he is very good. He cut my hair a couple of times."

"Well, I can't wait to meet them. You'll have to wake me up Friday so I can go with you."

"Yea, I will. Oh, that reminds me; we are going to church with Giovanni and his mother this Sunday. He'll come to pick us up at eleven-thirty. I hope it's ok with you because I've told him yes."

"When did he ask you?"

"Sunday, after you left the table, when we had dinner at Giovanni's. He sat down with me and we talked a while then he gave me a ride home."

"What did you talk about? Did he say anything about me?"

"I don't recall exactly what we talked about. I do remember, though, that he asked about you. He wanted to know if you were always so serious and what kind of girl you were. I got the distinct impression that he is interested in you. Why else would he ask me?"

"I can't believe I am going to meet his mom! I hope she'll like me."

"I am sure she will, Joanna. I can't see why anyone wouldn't like you."

"I forgot to tell you Maria, but there is this Italian guy who comes at the club. His name is Joe Bellagio. He told Giovanni that he likes me and if I was interested. I told him no and Giovanni is a little worried because he said he can't take no for an answer. What should I do if he approaches me?"

"Be polite and just say no. He can't force you. Tell him that you have a boyfriend. Giovanni is interested in you. He told me so. You should be available for him."

"Oh I am available for him all right; one hundred percent. You know Giovanni told me that Joe Bellagio is a constructor and that he has a lot of money. Maybe you should meet him, Maria. If you married him you'd never have to work again."

"What does he look like?"

"He reminds me of a bird. He is bold at the top of his head, skinny and about the same height as Giovanni. He is not very handsome and he is not my type. He has a thin moustache. I don't think he is your type either, but you could learn to like him."

"Well, I like money but I could never marry somebody just for that. I need to like the person too. I would be terribly unhappy and no amount of money is worth that."

"I see what you mean. It's the same way for me. I would be terribly unhappy too."

Maria remembered how unhappy she was the last couple of years she was married to George when she fell out of love for him. She spent days daydreaming about being free, at times even whishing that George would die because she was contrary to divorce. She even made an appointment with a Navy lawyer, since George was in the Navy, to find out what her legal rights were in case she did decide to divorce him. Somehow, though, George found out about the appointment and insisted that he'd go to the appointment with her. The lawyer frankly told her that since her husband was present he could not give her legal counsel, so Maria left with no knowledge whatsoever and when they did get a divorce, since she couldn't afford to get a lawyer for herself she lost some of her rights including a fourth of George's military pension.

Maria had told George, when they were married, "I will be faithful to you until I love you. The moment I stop loving you I won't feel bound to be faithful to you." Of course George had not been happy to hear that and he definitely would not have liked it if he'd find out that Maria had been unfaithful while they were married.

She had been unfaithful twice the last two-and-a-half years of their marriage. It happened in Italy, where Georgè was stationed for his military duty. Once with an American man who worked as patrol at the recreation park for the Americans stationed in Naples. He was tall, blonde and had blue eyes; all the opposite of George who was dark haired, dark eyed. Maria used to take Elizabeth to the park since they lived within walking distance and at the entry of the park there was Hugh. She would say hi to him and even though they never had a real conversation they became friends. She found out that he was married and his wife was enlisted in the military. Hugh was a civilian and helped out by working at the park. One day she walked up to him and said:

"I don't know why I am telling you this but I just know that I have to. My husband is working tonight. Would you come to my house to see me?" He said yes.

Maria gave him the directions on how to get to her house and she and Elizabeth left. Elizabeth was two years old and Maria pushed her in a stroller.

That night, at about nine o'clock Hugh came to her house. They didn't say very much. They went to bed right away. Hugh was nervous at first, sweating a cold sweat but soon relaxed. Afterwards he didn't stay very long. He had to go home or his wife would have become suspicious. That was the whole adventure. They didn't see each other privately anymore even though Maria kept seeing him at the park almost everyday. One day she brought her camera and wanted to take his picture but he refused because he was afraid that George would see it. Another day she asked him if he loved his wife. He said yes with so much passion that Maria was hurt and confused. She asked him why he had been with her, then, and he had no answer. She told him that she had been with him because she didn't love her husband anymore and that she had told him so, so she had an excuse.

She kept wondering about his reasons for a good while. He seemed to genuinely like her and Maria liked him a lot too, because he was very handsome, plus the way he looked at her made her feel very desirable. She was getting mixed signals from him, so she decided to ignore him because she didn't want to fall in love and get hurt.

One day Maria and George were inside the Navy Exchange. Hugh and his wife were there too. Maria pretended not to see him even though he kept looking at her as if to say "I am here, say hi to me."

A couple of months went by when Maria, out of the blue, had a call from him. She was taken aback with surprise because she hadn't thought about him in a while. George, her husband, was right next to her and was on the alert because he heard her speak English. All her calls were in Italian, from her relatives, so who was she talking to? Maria to this day doesn't remember what she told him. She just remembers that she lied to George making up an excuse so he would not suspect, which he did. She was not good at deceiving.

The other time she was unfaithful was with her landlord. He was dark haired, had the eyes of a rich mahogany color, was five-feet eight-inches tall and was very handsome, even though her sister Susanna said to the contrary when she showed her his picture.

Maria saw him once a month when he'd come by to collect the rent. She felt attracted to him because he reminded her of her childhood. He evoked in her images of when she was a little girl playing with her friends, and felt as if he was one of them because he was the same age as she. The attraction developed slowly, over a period of time.

Since she had told George that she didn't love him anymore she felt free to pursue other men. She slowly became flirtatious towards her landlord, whose name was Alfonso, to the point that he started to flirt back with her. One evening, while George was at work, she called him at home, her voice full of desire. By the time their conversation ended he had invited himself over to her house. He went over and they had sex on the living room floor. When it was over he told her it was not as he had imagined, and Maria, who was crying, asked him why. He didn't tell her how he had imagined it; just that it wasn't the same. He must have fantasized about her for a while, why else would he have imagined it?

Maria kept crying, overwhelmed by sadness and he tried to console her, puzzled by her reaction to their lovemaking. Did he fail her? Why was she crying? She did not know. He was very tender and understanding but he was not very quiet. The whole neighborhood must have heard him come and leave her house that night because he wore *zoccoli*, a pair of wooden sandals that made a loud noise on the pavement as he walked.

The next day, her neighbor upstairs, sent her daughter to ask Maria if her husband worked nights, to which Maria told her yes. The heck with the neighbors, she didn't care about her reputation. *You can't hide anything from them*, she thought. Sometime later, a neighbor friend of hers told her that people were saying that she had a lover, to which Maria replied that it wasn't true. She didn't think it was any of their business. She felt free to do it because she told George how she felt. She didn't tell him about the affairs because his male ego would have been destroyed.

Another part of Maria was doing it out of anger. George was always flirting with other women and he often told her that they turned him on. She got so tired of hearing him say that, that she told him to just go ahead and have sex with them, which he did.

One night he came home at two-thirty in the morning. He woke her up very excited and told her that he had done it, with one of his subordinate, at work. He went into great details about everything but Maria, who had been in a deep sleep when he came home, was mad at him for waking her up. She merely turned on her belly and went back to sleep. The next day she acted as if nothing had happened. She couldn't care less.

Maria's relationship with Alfonso, her landlord, continued on and off for two years and if George suspected anything he did not show it. It was easy for her to see him since George worked at night at least twice a week. When he did, Maria and Elizabeth went to stay in Naples with her mom who, at the time, lived in the city. It was on those occasions that she would meet with him. Her mother would baby-sit Elizabeth. Of course she didn't know that she was seeing another man or she would have forbidden her to go. She would just tell her that she was going out with friends.

Alfonso was very rich. He and his family owned many properties. He was the typical Italian lover. He had other girlfriends beside Maria but she wasn't jealous. She didn't know for sure but she suspected so. She was not at peace with herself during their relationship. She felt very guilty. At some point she stopped having sex with Alfonso; they would just go out as friends. She preferred it that way. She didn't enjoy being unfaithful.

Thinking back, after her divorce, she felt angry with herself for feeling guilty, wishing she had truly enjoyed it, because George deserved it. Especially since he confessed to her that he had been unfaithful before, while he was in Spain, during a Mediterranean cruise on the aircraft carrier the Saratoga. The pig. Later she thought that must be why she was so resolute and unafraid while she was unfaithful; maybe her subconscious had picked up clues from him about his unfaithfulness.

Well, that was then. She resolved within herself never to be unfaithful again and that's why when she met Michael in Hawaii she tried to avoid him, at first, like the plague.

He was truly the most gorgeous man she had ever laid eyes on. And he was eleven-and-a-half years her junior. But that didn't matter. He looked like a full-grown man, sexy, manly, and so very handsome. In few days Maria was hopelessly in love with him and stayed in love for the following ten years. She was obsessed. She thought about him all the time, day and night. During that time Maria had very powerful psychic experiences. She had nightmares all the time. She confused him with Jesus, the man-child of Revelation 12, since she was reading the Bible on her own. She saw him in every man she met; he was in everything and everybody. Curiously enough she didn't dream about him very often. When she did he was always kind to her but not in love. One time she heard him say very distinctly "Leave me alone. My mother doesn't approve." She was in Las Vegas visiting a friend when it happened.

Her dreams were very powerful. She would have out of body experiences. She would dream of flying and it felt very good, very liberating. At times she was alone but most of the time she was with other people. Mostly people she didn't know.

All those psychic experiences started when she bought a Bible, even though she didn't read it for the first couple of years. She bought one because she intended to teach her daughter about God. When she got married in the Catholic Church George had to promise that he would raise his children in the Catholic faith, but he did not do it. Maria remembered his promise and decided to buy the Bible for that purpose. Maria had been raised Catholic but she had never used the Bible. She was totally ignorant of what it contained because the Catholic Church, in Italy, didn't use it, using instead the

Vangelo. So, since she had heard in America about the Bible she decided to buy one.

Elizabeth was three years old and too young to be thought so she just put it aside until she was older and could be thought. She had no idea it would unleash those psychic occurrences.

Maria and George had never been to church the whole time they were married, except for the day they got married. George was not a religious person but Maria would pray every night reciting the Lord's prayer, concentrating on God as she said it quietly in her mind. She found that it calmed her and enabled her to go to sleep feeling at peace with herself and the world. She was then able to turn on her belly and go to sleep shutting everything and everybody off.

****

"Well," Maria said to Joanna, "it's dinner time. We should get busy preparing dinner. I have bought all that we need to make shell pasta with green peas. Why don't you come with me in the kitchen and I'll teach you how to fix it." Joanna followed Maria in the kitchen. Maria got all the ingredients out of the shopping bag and put them on the counter.

"First thing we do is chop an onion real thin, then we chop some ham in small pieces and we put both in a skillet with a little bit of oil, to soften and brown. When that is done we add a can of green peas with all the liquid. We add salt and pepper and let it cook until all the water evaporates. In the meantime, while the green peas are cooking, we put some water to boil and cook the shell pasta al dente. We drain it and add it to the peas, stirring and mixing it well. We turn the heat off, add heavy cream and voila', it's done. It's delicious, I can't wait to eat it."

"Can I do it?" asked Joanna. "You can go watch television in the living room. I'll call you when it's ready."

"All right. If you need anything just yell." Maria went into the living room and turned the television on, selecting channel 7 and watching *Wheel of Fortune.* By the time *Jeopardy* started Joanna was done. She served the dinner really pleased with herself. They said Grace and started to eat. It was delicious and Maria praised Joanna for her effort. They ate quietly while watching *Jeopardy*, trying to guess the correct answers. They were both lousy at it. Joanna looked lovely, Maria couldn't help but noticing. Her hair reminded her of the rich gold of wheat fields in the summer. Her teeth looked like small pearls and her complexion was nice and smooth.

"I can't get over how you've changed, Joanna," Maria said. "In one day. That's a miracle."

"The miracle is called money, Maria. Without money you can die, and nobody would even notice it."

"That's true. I get terribly worried when I think that I may lose my job. I see myself homeless, walking the streets, begging for money. It's sad, but it's the truth. Well, let's make a toast to money. May we always have an abundance of it."

"I'll second that," said Joanna, raising her glass.

When dinner was over they cleared the table and washed the dishes. Maria made herself some espresso coffee and joined Joanna in the living room. She lit a cigarette and smoked it in silence.

"Maria, can we go and sit by the shrine? This day has been so amazing for me, I've accomplished so much, that I want to praise God and thank Him."

"Sure thing," replied Maria, happy to oblige. They went to Maria's bedroom and lit the candle. They then turned the lights off and sat on the floor with their legs crossed.

"Heavenly Father," said Maria, "we come before you with thankfulness in our hearts. We want to thank you for the blessings you've bestowed upon us this day and we hope that you keep blessing us in the future."

"Dear God," said Joanna, "I want to thank you for my job and for the money I received. Thanks to it I was able to go to therapy, fix my hair, go to the dentist, and buy me this dress. That's a lot. I haven't had this much in years. I want to thank you for Maria, for putting her on my path. May you richly bless her for all she's doing for me. I hope that one day I'll have a better job. I want to pray for Giovanni too. I am in love with him and I hope that we can have a relationship one day. I pray that you reward him for giving me this job and that you increase his business tenfold. I pray for Maria's daughter, Elizabeth; may you watch over her and protect her from any danger. I pray for Felicia. May you give her the strength she needs to overcome this ordeal she will have to face pretty soon. I pray for my mother and my brother, wherever they are. May you be their guide and their protector. And, finally, Lord, I pray that I never lack anything, material or spiritual as long as I live. I put myself into your care, like a ship to a captain. May you lead the way for me to follow. Thank you Jesus, thank you Father, thank you Holy Spirit."

"Boy, you're getting good at this, Joanna. That was a beautiful prayer."

"Thank you Maria."

After a brief silence Maria prayed: "Our Heavenly Father, I want to pray for my sisters, for my mom, for my nieces and nephews. I want to pray for our leaders, that they may pass laws that are good for us and in harmony with your will. I pray for all the women and children of the world, especially the abused ones. I pray for the men, that they may act in a godly way to bring your kingdom here on earth. I pray all this in Jesus' holy name. Amen."

Maria and Joanna sat in silence for a pretty good while. The flickering of the candle cast wavering shadows across the room. It was a scented candle that Maria had bought at Victoria's Secret with a gift certificate from Elizabeth. She inhaled deeply with her eyes closed to enjoy the fragrant smell. Joanna did the same. Each of them was meditating on her life, her future, her hopes and her dreams. When they were through they opened their eyes and smiled at each other. There was peace on their faces and a deeper bond between them. They turned on the lights and blew out the candle.

CHAPTER TWENTY

Tuesday Joanna received a subpoena to appear in court on the seventeen to testify against Raul. She called Felicia to let her know. Felicia told her that she was going to send her the plane tickets, and for her not to worry. But Joanna was worried. She was panicking. She would have to face strangers and talk about very private things. The thought was overwhelming. She paced the floor, terrified, until she could not stand it any longer and called Maria at work. Maria couldn't stay on the phone very long, but she did her best to reassure her. Anxiety gripped Joanna's chest. She put out the futon and laid on it. She couldn't breathe. She felt herself blush by thinking about her court appearance- and seeing Raul. God, that was a nightmare. Having to look at his face and remember. She thought of ways to get out of it but it was too late. The court ordered it and she had to do it.

The anxiety stayed with her all through the day. The following day was even worse. She couldn't relax. She prepared herself to go to work but there was no joy in her. When she got to work Giovanni at first didn't recognize her. As she got closer he exclaimed:

"Giovanna, for the love of God, what happened to you? You look beautiful!"

"Oh, nothing," replied Joanna. "I just went to the hairdresser and bought me a dress. Giovanni, listen. I have a favor to ask you. My mother isn't doing very well. I need to go to Minneapolis for about a week, from the fourteenth to the nineteenth to help her out and spend some time with her. Is that all right with you?"

"Sure, doll, sure. Anything you want. Now go to the kitchen, Alfredo is busy already."

Joanna walked to the kitchen aware that Giovanni was looking at her. As she entered the room Alfredo turned around.

"Yes, can I help you?" He hadn't recognized her. As she got closer she said: "Alfredo, it's me Joanna."

"Joanna, bambina, you look like Barbie. What happened?"

"Oh, nothing. I had my hair cut and colored. Do you like it?"

"Do I like it? I love it. And that dress. You look like a movie star. Doesn't she look beautiful?" Alfredo asked the cooks. All three of them whistled in appreciation. Joanna blushed. She went to the closet to get her overcoat, put it on and started to wash the dishes, which were plenty. Her mind kept wondering about the trial and she could not concentrate on what Alfredo was saying. He was talking about his son Carlo, in Italy. Apparently, he had participated in a demonstration against the government and had been struck in the head by a stone. He had been taken to the hospital where they had to stitch him up, but he was fine now. Alfredo just kept on talking unaware that Joanna was listening with only one ear.

When they had their break at nine o'clock, Joanna just kept on nibbling at her *Calzone*. She finished her wine in no time and refilled her glass all the way to the top. Alfredo noticed it and was concerned. "What's matter, bambina. You all right?"

"No, I am worried about my mom," lied Joanna. "She is not doing very good. I asked Giovanni if I could take off from the fourteenth to the nineteenth to go visit her and he said it was fine. So I guess you're going to be by yourself for a week. Do you mind?"

"Gee, no I don't mind. I hope it's not serious. Is it her heart?"

"No, she has really bad arthritis and some days she can't even get out of bed. She just needs me to clean up the house for her, stock up on groceries and visit for a little while until I can go visit again. She asked me to move up there with her, but I told her no. I like it here in San Diego. Plus I am in love with Giovanni so I am not going anywhere."

"Doesn't your mother have a husband? Why can't he take care

of her? Why do you have to go all that way just to clean the house?"

"It's not just cleaning the house. She is not doing well and wants to see me. Her husband does take care of her; he does the cooking, the shopping, but he is getting old too and he suffers from other old age ailments. He can't do everything. Besides, I miss her and I want to see her too."

Joanna was feeling flushed from the wine and from all the lies she was saying, but by looking at her Alfredo didn't have a clue. He was savoring his spaghetti with clam sauce. He would dip bread in the sauce and make grunting noises while eating.

At eleven o'clock Joanna left Alfredo to mop the floor and went to the restroom to change her clothes and fix herself up. She took the comb out of her dress pocket and combed her hair. She then dried her face and her neck with a paper towel and put her other clothes on. She felt more confident, self-assured, at ease. She didn't feel like the ugly duckling anymore but a beautiful, vibrant, twenty-eight years old woman. Her face was radiant as she walked down the steps into the nightclub. As Philip saw her he greeted her with an excited smile.

"Congratulate me lass, I am a daddy."

"You are? Congratulations Philip. I am so happy for you. Is it a boy or a girl?"

"It's a girl. Her name is Leandra. She is beautiful. Eight-pounds-five-ounces. She was born Monday morning at exactly eleven o'clock. God, I am so happy I just can't describe it. You have to come by our place and see her. You must promise me you will."

"I promise, if you tell me where you live."

"I live just around the corner, on University Avenue, at 1915, on the second floor, apartment No. 2."

"You better write that down for me because I won't remember it five minutes from now."

"Sure. Here, let me write it right now before I forget it." He took a paper napkin and wrote down the address. Joanna took the napkin, folded it in half and put it inside her bra, since she didn't have any pocket in her uniform. As she did that she lifted her eyes and saw Giovanni and Joe Bellagio looking at her. They had been talking but stopped when they saw her putting the napkin inside her bra. Joe's eyes were lusty while Giovanni's were loving. Giovanni had just told Joe that Joanna had refused his offer and he was not pleased. Not pleased at all. Joanna saw him walking towards the bar and lowered her head. He ordered a gin and tonic and sat on a bar stool right in front of Joanna. He didn't say anything for a good five minutes. He just stared at her, which made her very uncomfortable. Joanna wished that Giovanni was there too and looked up to see if he was nearby. She saw him talking to a couple sitting on the couch by the piano. She noticed that he had his eyes on Joe Bellagio as he talked and felt a little reassured.

Finally Joe talked to her. "Hi beautiful," he said.

"Hello Mr. Bellagio," replied Joanna.

"Don't call me Mr. Bellagio. Just call me Joe."

"Ok, Joe. How are you tonight?"

"I am a wounded man. Giovanni just told me that you are not interested in my offer. Can you tell me why?" he leaned over as he said that, almost in a whisper so Philip wouldn't hear.

"I didn't mean to hurt your feelings by refusing, Joe. The fact is that I am already interested in someone else."

"Who is he? Is he someone I know?"

"I'd rather not talk about it, if you don't mind."

"Why don't you reconsider? I can keep you like a queen. You'd never have to wash dishes again. Look at your hands! Is that what you want for the rest of your life? I'll buy you a car, a house, jewelry, clothes; you name it, I'll buy it for you. Don't be a silly girl. Reconsider!"

"I've already made up my mind, Joe. This is what I want. If I can't be with the person I love I don't want to be with anyone else. Better washing dishes and catching buses for the rest of my life than being with someone I don't love."

"You'll learn to love me. I am a very lovable guy."

"No, Joe. That's final!" Joanna was annoyed and it showed on her face. She started to wash the glasses again and ignored him. He got the hint and, scorned, walked away from the bar. He was angry, very angry. He was more taken by her since the denial and liked her even more, especially tonight with her new haircut. The girl didn't know what she was missing. She must be out of her mind.

He'd find out who the man was she was interested in and beat him up. He'd ask Giovanni if he knew who he was. He'd bring her presents. No woman would say no to that. No woman had ever refused him or his presents. He looked around the room to see if anyone was watching him. Everybody was engrossed in conversation with someone and nobody was paying attention to him except Giovanni. He motioned to him. Giovanni excused himself and walked towards Joe.

"Is something wrong? You don't look too good."

"The girl must be crazy; she turned me down and God knows for whom. She said she was interested in someone else. Do you know who he is?"

"I don't have a clue," said Giovanni. He was sure she was interested in him but was certainly not going to tell Joe that. He might punch him out right in the middle of the nightclub, in front of everybody. Giovanni had seen him angry before. Even though he was not big he had a mean punch and didn't hesitate to use it when he was aroused by anger. Afraid that he would make a scene Giovanni tried to calm him down.

"Why don't you just forget about her Joe. You can have any woman you want. Look around. Half of the women in here would say yes to you in a heartbeat. She is just a dishwasher, not much, if you ask me. Look how sophisticated those other women are. Don't waste your time."

"I want her. And I don't care that she is a dishwasher. I am going to have her, you mark my words."

"Let me buy you a drink, Joe. What'll you have, a whiskey, gin and tonic, a vodka, what? I want to introduce you to this woman I just met. She is new to the club. She is a Russian countess or other and she is very wealthy. Let me buy you a drink first and then I'll introduce you to her." Giovanni led Joe by the arm, to the bar, far away from Joanna so that he would not get angrier.

Inside himself Giovanni was jubilant. He was proud of Joanna. She gave up a lot for him and he would make sure she didn't regret it. He couldn't wait for Sunday to come so that he would introduce her to his mother. Then, if his mother liked her, he would ask her out on a date. He gave Joanna a reassuring smile to tell her not to worry, that he had the situation under control. Joe didn't miss that, even though he was half drunk.

"What's matter Giovanni, are you in league with her? Maybe it's you she likes. Tell me, is it true?"

Damn, thought Giovanni, *you can't hide anything from this punk.*

"So, what if it is me she likes? What would you do; would you beat me up? I am not afraid of you, Joe. I would just be sorry that our friendship would end, that's all. Why don't you go home and sober up? Tomorrow you'll feel better and our friendship will be safe. Like I told you before you can find many other women so don't get hung up on this one. To be honest with you I like her too and if she likes me I am going to propose to her. But I am not going to buy her, like a kept woman. I am going to marry her."

"You know, you're just a dirty rat. 'I don't have a clue' you said when I asked you if you knew who the other man was while you knew all along. With friends like you who needs enemies. I am disappointed in you Giovanni. You should have been honest and tell me from the beginning. As it is I don't feel that I owe you any loyalty and if I can take her away from you I will, so beware." At that Joe Bellagio left the nightclub giving one last look at Joanna as he walked by her. *Damn she is pretty*, he thought. He was drunk but it didn't show. He held the liquor well. He was also furious and that showed. He had never handled anger very well. He got out of the nightclub with bloodshot eyes. He saw Giovanni's car parked in front of the restaurant and had an idea. He reached down and pulled a knife out of his right sock. With that he swiftly slashed all four tires of the black Jaguar. He looked around, the street was deserted and no one had seen him. *Good*, he thought, *that'll teach you, you bastard.* He got up, straightened his silky black jacket and walked to his red Ferrari, parked near by. He pushed hard on the accelerator and left.

Inside Giovanni walked up to Joanna. "Did Joe bother you, Cinderella?"

"Actually, he did. He wanted me to become his whore. He promised to buy me a house, a car, clothes and jewelry if I said yes."

"What did you say?" Giovanni already knew the answer but he

wanted to hear it from her.

"I said 'No thanks'. He got very upset with me and left. What did he tell you? I saw you two arguing. I hope it was not because of me."

"Actually, it was. He accused me of being interested in you and wanting you for myself. He was very upset, but I am sure he'll get over it once he sobers up. As it is right now, our friendship is over. But he'll be back. We've been through this before. The nightclub is his home away from home. Plus you are here. I bet you he'll be back tomorrow night and act as if nothing has happened."

"What did you tell him when he accused you of being interested in me?"

"I told him he was crazy for thinking that," lied Giovanni. He didn't want to reveal his feelings to her yet. He wanted his mother's approval first. Joanna was disappointed but didn't let it show. Giovanni felt like a worm but he told himself that he had reasons and that he was justified.

"I told you, Cinderella, that Joe wouldn't take no for an answer. Remember?"

"Yes, I remember, and you were right. Are all Italian men like that?"

"Yes, they are all like that. I am the only exception," joked Giovanni.

"Listen to him," she said. "Boy, I am lucky to know you, the one and only."

"You are right. Don't you forget it. Well, let me go and take care of my patrons. They are staring at us. We better keep our relationship a secret."

Our relationship, thought Joanna. *What relationship is he talking about? He is a little crazy himself, tonight. It's all Joe's fault, the bird. I hope he doesn't bother me anymore.*

"Hey, lass. What is going on?" asked Philip. "Looks like something is going on, why don't you enlighten me?"

"There is nothing going on, Philip. Joe Bellagio wanted me to become his whore and I said no. He promised to buy me a house, a car, clothes, and jewels if I said yes. He got very angry when he couldn't convince me and took it out on Giovanni."

"He promised to buy you all that and you said no? Girl, you are crazy. I wish somebody would propose to me. If I were a woman I'd be the best kept woman in the world."

"You mean you would give up your wife and your daughter for material things?"

"Ouch! You got me. No, I guess I wouldn't give them up for anything especially Leandra, my beautiful, precious daughter. I can't wait to go home and hold her in my arms. When I go home is time for her feeding. I'll watch her mother breastfeed her, then I'll get to hold her until she burps. I'll change her diaper and I'll lie down on the bed with her until she goes to sleep. The problem is that I am so tired that I will probably fall asleep before she does. But I am not worried because her mother will put her in her crib."

"You are very lucky, Philip. I wish I had a baby, especially with someone I love. There is nothing more beautiful in the whole world, to give life to another human being. Babies are so precious and they smell so good. I can't wait to see Leandra. Who does she look like, you or your wife?"

"It's hard to tell right now. I think she looks like me, but my wife says she looks like her mother. I guess we'll be able to tell better when she gets a little older."

"Well, my congratulations to you again."

"Thank you, lass. By the way, I have to congratulate you too."

"Oh yea? What about?"

"Your new look. You look smashing."

"That's what Maria said. My roommate. You don't know her. She is Italian."

"You have an Italian roommate? You might as well move to Italy, you like Italians so much. When am I going to meet her?"

"I'll ask her to come to the nightclub one of these nights. She doesn't go out at night, but maybe she'll come if I ask her. She came to have dinner at Giovanni's last Sunday, but she left early that's why you didn't meet her. Philip, I want to ask you something. Last Sunday, when Maria and I were having dinner, a group of five or six men came in the restaurant. Giovanni hugged and kissed one of them, an older, white haired man. Maria said his name was Angelo Bonifacio and that he is the godfather of San Diego. Do you know if that is true? And do you know if any mafia guys come in the nightclub?"

"Lass, even if I knew I wouldn't tell you. If you want my advice, stay away from all this. It's not good for you to know certain things. Working here I hear many things and see many things, and so will you. I mind my business, I am polite to everybody and as long as they pay and don't cause a disturbance everybody is my friend. You do the same."

"Can you tell if someone is in the mafia just by looking at them?"

"I can."

"Will you tell me? I am terribly fascinated by it; I want to know."

"Let's do this. When I see a mafia guy I will scratch my neck. That's my signal to you. But you mustn't tell anyone or we'll soon be in a lot of trouble. Ok?"

"It's a deal. But don't tell Giovanni. It's just for my own curiosity."

"Ok."

"You whore! That's why you don't want me, you like him. I saw you looking at him with those blue eyes of yours, flirting with him. But I got news for you. You can't have him, because he is married and just had a baby." Joanna almost jumped out of her skin. Apparently Joe Bellagio hadn't gone home; instead he'd gone to another bar and got more to drink. He kept ruminating over Joanna's refusal and couldn't digest it so he went back to Giovanni's and unknown to them had been watching Joanna and Philip talking. Taken as he was by his feelings of rejection he became furiously jealous. Immediately Philip became the other man and that caused his outburst.

Giovanni and everybody else in the nightclub heard Joe shout at Joanna. Some were terribly amused by it, those who knew Joe well. Others were curious but Joanna was terribly embarrassed. She blushed and turned her back to Joe pretending that he was not even there. Philip started to say something in her defense but Giovanni got there first and affably put an arm around Joe's shoulders and took him into his office. As soon as he closed the door he took Joe's arm and twisted it behind his back. "You punk," he said, "you don't come in here and talk to her like that, not now, not ever. I want you to go back in there and apologize to her. And do it so everybody can hear you, understood?"

"Gee, Giovanni, I am sorry man. You know how crazy I get when a woman says no to me. I saw her talking to Philip and the blood went to my head. I am totally in love with her. I am crazy about her."

"She doesn't want you, you got that? Go after somebody else. She is not a whore and if I hear you call her that one more time I go to the police and tell them few things I know about you. How you make your bids, how you threaten other contractors and some of the people you know. Plus I'll get a restraining order against you and won't let you set foot in here again. You'll go and do business somewhere else."

"No need to do that Giovanni. I'll go and apologize right now. We're still friends, ok?"

Joe put his hand in his jacket and took out his wallet. He counted five one hundred dollar bills and handed them to Giovanni. "What is this for?" "Man, you won't like it when I tell you, but I slashed all four of your tires. This is to pay for new ones."

"You son of a drunken whore. I guess I should have expected it from you. You rotten dog. Yea, this will pay for them all right. Don't ever do that again. After you apologize I want you to leave and don't come back for a week, you hear?"

"Yea, sure man. Anything you say. I apologize."

"Now smile and act as if we are best friend, you dog." Giovanni opened the door of his office and both of them walked into the nightclub, smiling and talking to each other. Joe went to the bar and loudly apologized to Joanna. Joanna blushed remembering the insult. She looked at Giovanni and he winked and smiled at her. She knew she was safe. She smiled back and graciously asked Joe if he wanted some coffee. Joe said he had to leave but he would take a cup to go. She took a paper cup, filled it with coffee and handed it to Joe. He apologized again and left.

Giovanni sat at the bar stool and asked Philip for a whiskey.

"How are you feeling, Cinderella?" he asked Joanna.

"A little shook up, that's all," replied Joanna. "Nobody had called me a whore before, just because I was talking to a man. I guess I've never seen a jealous man before. He is crazy."

"I know, crazy about you. I told him not to show his face in here for a week. I hope that gives you enough time to recover. If not, let me know and I'll keep him away longer."

"That should be enough time. I hope he doesn't bother me again."

"I have bad news, Cinderella. Joe slashed all four of my tires. I won't be able to give you a ride home. I will call a cab for you. I'll pay for it, don't worry."

"I have a better idea. Why don't you walk me home. I know it's a long walk but it'll be fun. We'll be the only ones in the street and we'll be there in no time." Joanna thought that it would be very romantic to walk with him and wished the distance be even longer, but she couldn't tell him that.

"If that's what you want, that's what we'll do," Giovanni agreed. The idea seemed very romantic to him too and he was eager for it.

All of a sudden two arms embraced Giovanni from behind. It was the Russian countess.

"Giovanni, darling, buy me a drink will you?" she turned Giovanni around and gave him a kiss on the lips. She was wearing a bright red lipstick, which got on Giovanni's lips. Joanna looked at him and laughed. She handed him a paper napkin to wipe it off but the Russian countess wasn't happy about it.

"So, who are you and what is your relationship with my Giovanni?" she asked.

"My name is Joanna and Giovanni is my boss. Who are you?"

"I am Countess Katrina Petrova from Moskow. Nice to meet you Joanna. Are you sure Giovanni is just your boss? The way you look at him says that you care for him as a man. I have been watching you. You can't fool a woman, especially me. Well, you can forget about him because I am interested in him and will take him away from you."

What's wrong with these people tonight, thought Joanna. *First Joe, now Katrina*. She looked at Giovanni to see his reaction. He shook his head as if to say it was not true, then turned towards Katrina and smiled at her. Joanna was angry about that. She looked at the clock. It was one forty-five in the morning. *Fifteen more minutes and then this hell will be over*, she thought. It was the strangest night. It must be a full moon outside.

Joanna asked Philip for a rum and coke so she could walk away from Giovanni and Katrina who where in what seemed to be an intimate conversation about the royal jewelry that Katrina owned. They had been given to her by her mother who had inherited them from her mother and so on, all the way to the Tzar of Russia. Giovanni listened to her intently and seemed captivated by her. She was a very strong, very beautiful woman. She knew what she wanted and went after it with gusto. She had just met Giovanni, yet she acted as if she had known him forever. She was wearing a black halter-top made of shining spandex and silk black pants that fit her beautiful figure like a glove. Her hair was black and she had it styled so that it was pulled back from her face and tied into an intricate knot on the back of her head. She must have had her maid or her hairdresser help her with it, Joanna thought, because she couldn't have done it by herself.

Katrina and Giovanni talked for the next fifteen minutes to the annoyance of Joanna.

A younger man approached the bar and asked Katrina if she was ready to leave. He was her escort for the night. He didn't seem to mind that she had left him to talk with Giovanni. He had black hair combed back, was six feet tall and had a very handsome face. He must have been in his late twenties, thought Joanna. His features were very aristocratic and by his clothes she guessed he was wealthy; either that or he was kept by the countess. That would not have surprised her one bit. They left arm in arm after Katrina gave Giovanni one last kiss that left more lipstick on his lips. Joanna gave him a napkin and again he wiped his lips.

Since it was closing time Joanna went to the bathroom to change. When she came out of the bathroom Giovanni was outside, as usual, waiting for her.

"Are you ready, Cinderella?" he asked.

"Yes, mighty prince," replied Joanna. "No royal coach tonight," she said jokingly.

"Just as well. Tonight is a beautiful night, perfect for a long walk. Good thing that I don't have a father waiting for me at home or I'd be in trouble."

"Well, if we are going to walk we'd better get going. Don't you have a sweater to put on? It's chilly outside at this hour of the night. Here, put my jacket on," said Giovanni. He removed his jacket and put it on Joanna's shoulders.

"What about you? You're going to catch a chill, Giovanni." Joanna was moved by his kindness and looked at him lovingly. They left the building and walked outside. The night was clear. The sky was full of stars and the moon was three quarters full. Perfect for lovers. They walked in silence for a good five minutes. Fourth Avenue was deserted at that time of the night except for few cars that drove by every now and then. Fourth Avenue was one way going south so the lights of the cars didn't bother them. A car with drunken kids yelling obscenities went by. They ignored them and kept on walking.

"Do you like the countess, Giovanni? She was all over you and you didn't seem to mind," said Joanna.

"She is a very interesting woman. As far as her being all over me you know how we men are. We love the attention. And she is beautiful, but I already have my heart set on someone else." He didn't elaborate and Joanna felt a stabbing pain in her heart. She wondered who the woman was and thought her very lucky. She wished it was she but didn't have a clue by looking at him.

They were walking side by side and Joanna could smell his cologne. Very masculine, very sexy. He would look at her as he spoke and Joanna would look right back trying to hold his beautiful, mesmerizing green gaze. She had never seen eyes as beautiful as his. His lashes were black and thick and made his eyes look greener. *Blessed be the woman who brought you into this world,* Joanna thought; *I love you so much I think I am going to faint. Lord, hold me still and let him fall in love with me, please.*

"Tell me Joanna, why are you still a virgin?" he asked suddenly.

Joanna gasped not expecting the question.

"I have been saving myself for the right man," lied Joanna. She felt guilty for deceiving him but she didn't want to reveal the horrible truth. How could she? If she told him the truth he would have felt disgust for her, maybe. He would not have understood. How could she tell this man, that she loved so much, that most of her life she had been sexually molested and had to perform sexual acts on a man who was supposed to be her father and protect her from the same abuses he inflicted upon her. Impossible. Sadly she was silent.

"You know, virginity is highly priced among Italian men. We have gone to war, killed, to defend the honor of our women. You are a rare flower among thorns. The man who'll marry you is very lucky indeed," said Giovanni. He could not believe his good fortune. To him she was a rare gem, a pearl. Again he felt a little anxiety thinking that another man might come along and snatch her away from him, but told himself to be patient, to wait nevertheless and don't rush into it. He wanted to take her into his arms and kiss her passionately, right in the middle of the street but remembering how she'd slapped him when he had kissed her that first night made him desist. *All in good time*, he told himself.

"So, you've never had a boyfriend?"

"Yea, I had a boyfriend a couple of times but we never had sex. They didn't love me enough to wait, or were not serious enough about the relationship, so they took off."

More lies. Joanna felt terrible. If she had said she never had a boyfriend he would not have believed her or he would have had serious doubts about her. *God help me*, she pleaded. She had to steer the conversation away from this subject because she didn't like to lie, especially to him who was so dear to her.

"So, Giovanni, tell me about your late wife. Was she a virgin when you married her?"

"Oh yes. I would not have married her if she weren't. Just like you, she had never been intimate with a man. I was the only man she knew her whole life. That's how it should be. Nowadays women sleep around too much. Freedom is okay but when it's misused it becomes a weapon. Most, if not all, of the women nowadays are not virgins and that, Cinderella, makes you very special."

"I don't feel very special. At times I feel discouraged and think that I am never going to meet the right man. Men sleep around too, you know. They only seem to want sex from a woman and they don't want any of the responsibilities. *Use her and lose her*, is their motto. Our freedom, like you said, has become a weapon. A weapon that hits us right smack in the middle of our values; it's destroying our society. Most marriages end in divorce, families fall apart. People are not strong enough to withstand the difficulties that come their way. I rather never get married than marry and divorce. When I get married is going to be forever."

"You are very wise, my pet. Again, the man who's going to marry you is very lucky. You told Joe Bellagio that you are already interested in someone else. Is that true or did you just say it to get rid of him?"

"Oh, it's true. I am interested in someone but I don't think it's going to work out because he doesn't seem to respond to me. He is very good looking and lot of women chase after him. He can pick and choose, so why would he choose me? I am just a dishwasher and he is very wealthy. I really am a Cinderella."

"Well, he is crazy, if you ask me. When I love a woman I don't care if she is a maid or a dishwasher. I look at the heart, at the personality. Does she flirt with other men or is she serious; does she care about me or is she just interested in my money; does she want to have my children; is she willing to work hard and does she have the same passion about my business as I do. You see, Cinderella, there are lot of things involved in a relationship. It takes real love and a lot of responsibility to make a marriage work. One more thing I didn't mention before, does she believe in God and Jesus Christ? That's the first thing. God is first in my life. I owe Him everything. He is the father I lost. Without His blessings I would be a poor man indeed."

Giovanni was surprising himself. He seldom revealed his feelings to anyone, except his mother. Talking to Joanna was easy and non-threatening. He felt a wisdom, a sadness in her, a maturity of spirit that he hadn't felt with anybody since his wife passed away. For some reason, he cared about what she thought about him. Joanna listened to him talk and was impressed by what he was saying. *I could be all those things to you*, she thought, *if you only give me a chance. I could make you so happy, Giovanni.* She was silent for a while.

"You know, Giovanni, I just recently became a Christian. I gave myself to Jesus a few days ago and I feel like a new person. Jesus is changing my life around. I still have long ways to go but it's a start. Jesus is revolutionizing my life. Where there was guilt and ugliness now there is hope and love. It takes a great soul to die for someone else and a great love. He sacrificed His life on the cross so that we might be saved and be reconciled with God. I couldn't do that. Could you, Giovanni?"

"I could die for you. I mean I could die for someone I love, like my mother, my wife, my children if I had any but I don't think I could die for a stranger. I don't even know if I could love a stranger let alone die for him or her. Yea, it takes someone great to do that and Jesus certainly is one. That reminds me, we have a date for Sunday. I am coming to pick you and Maria up to go to church with my mother. Do you mind?"

"No, Maria told me about it and I am very happy to go and meet your mother. What is she like?"

"She is in her late seventies and looks like an angel. I say that without any prejudice."

"I can't wait. You are Catholic, right?"

"Yes. I have been all my life."

"How is being Catholic different from being a Christian?"

"Catholics believe and pray to the Virgin Mary and the saints. We believe in Purgatory, Heaven and Hell, while the Christians don't believe in Purgatory. We celebrate the Mass, we have communion and holy water. We have the sign of the cross and other rituals that Christians don't have. Plus the Christians don't believe that Saint Peter founded the Catholic Church. They proclaim that nowhere in the Bible it says that, but we know he did."

"And how do you know that?"

"Why, you don't believe me? We know from historical facts. He was the first pope. Priests were the only ones who knew how to read and write and they have been very diligent through the years reporting in writing historical facts. If it weren't for the priests we wouldn't know about history. We'd still be in the Middle Ages."

"I am sorry, Giovanni, I didn't mean to sound as if I didn't believe you, it's just that I am very ignorant when it comes to religion."

"It's alright, Pumpkin." Giovanni got a little closer to her as he said that. He would have loved to put his arm around her shoulders.

Instead he took her hand. Joanna tensed. She didn't know how to react. She looked at him but he was staring straight ahead of him and looked very casual as if he'd done that all the time. He gave her hand a little squeeze. They walked hand in hand the rest of the way without saying a word. When they reached Joanna's building she took off his jacket and gave it back to him.

"Thank you for lending me your jacket, Giovanni," she said. "It was very sweet of you. I hope you're all right. You didn't get too cold, did you?"

"No, I didn't. I am fine. Don't worry about me Cinderella. Well, I guess you'd better go. I see you tonight; sleep well, will you?"

He took hold of her shoulders and gave her a light kiss on her forehead. He waited till she got inside the building then turned around and walked away.

CHAPTER TWENTY-ONE

S unday couldn't come soon enough. Joanna was excited at the prospect of meeting Giovanni's mother. She woke up around nine o'clock. Maria was getting ready to go to church at the corner of Sixth and Fir. She would be attending two services that morning. Joanna had realized that she couldn't wear her dress to church. It was not appropriate. She asked Maria for a loan of $50 so that she could go and buy herself a new dress and a purse. Maria loaned her the money and left to go to church. Joanna showered and dressed. She went to Mervyn's where she found a dress that she deemed appropriate. It was black, short sleeved and came to her knees. It had a collar and an opening in the front. The waist was elasticized with a smock stitch that wrapped tightly around her body for about three inches in height. The material was soft and clung to her body. She bought a slip to wear under it. Next on her list was a purse. She went to the leather goods department and purchased a medium sized, very simple purse that could be worn with fancy clothes and also with sports apparel. Satisfied she left the store. It was ten-thirty. She had better hurry if she wanted to be ready on time.

Back at the apartment Joanna put her dress and slip on. She looked at herself in the full- length mirror. She liked what she saw. Her figure was enhanced by the dress. Her breast was full, her waist slim and her hips nicely round. She looked like a model. She wondered if Giovanni was going to like her. She went to the bathroom and applied make-up on, not too much, just enough to give her face a special glow and her eyes a mysterious look. Very sophisticated. When Maria got back from church and saw her, she whistled. She couldn't believe the change in her. Her compliment made Joanna blush. *Giovanni is going to drool when he sees her*, Maria thought. *This is so exciting; I think he is going to ask her out.*

"Thank you Maria for all you're doing for me. None of this would be possible if it weren't for you. I hope God will bless you for it. I hope that one day I will be able to repay you," said Joanna.

"Oh, don't mention it Joanna. It's a pleasure to see you bloom. Anything I can do, anytime, I am happy to do."

"I wonder if Giovanni's mother is going to wear black too. You and I are both dressed in black. We're dressed more as if we are going to a funeral than to Mass. Do you think it is appropriate?

"I can change, if it bothers you," said Maria. "In fact I think I will." She went to her closet, chose a lavender shirt and changed into that. She left her black pants on deciding that changing the shirt was enough.

"I think we should wear some perfume, don't you? Here, wear this," Maria said handing Joanna a perfume bottle. It was Anais-Anais by Cacharel. It was very feminine, very light and very romantic.

"Uhm," Maria exclaimed, inhaling the scent. It was her favorite and she always made sure she had some. It reminded her of Paris, walks along a promenade, dinners by candlelight. Maria was getting more excited as the time drew near. She wished with all her heart that Giovanni and Joanna would get married and would do anything to make that possible.

"You look so nice, Joanna. You know, if you want you could be a model. In fact, why don't you go to a talent agency and see if you could get some work? You would need a portfolio of photographs taken by a professional photographer, but if you save some money you can do it. I'll go with you. What do you think?"

"I don't know Maria. Do you really think I could?"

"Would I say it if I didn't think you could? You're still young enough. It would sure be better than being a dishwasher. With your figure you could model clothes for catalogs, do commercials. The field is huge. You could be making lots of money. Promise me you will think about it."

"I promise you. I just have to convince myself that I have what it takes. Maybe after more sessions with my therapist I will feel better about myself and be more confident. It sounds like a great idea. Thank you for suggesting it. Look at the time Maria. I think we should go downstairs and be there when Giovanni and his mother arrive. We don't want them to wait, it would be rude."

"I agree. Let's go."

Maria was locking the door when Joanna remembered about her purse. She was so used to not having one that she had forgotten about it. She went back into the apartment, took the purse and put her comb inside leaving the papers that came with it since she didn't have anything else. She remembered her keys and put them inside also together with some change that she had left from her shopping. Again Maria locked the door and they both walked downstairs.

Maria lit a cigarette since Giovanni wasn't there yet. He arrived as she was taking the last drag. The Jaguar was beautiful, all clean and shiny. Giovanni was gorgeous. He was wearing a turtleneck the same color of his eyes on top of charcoal corduroy pants. His mother was wearing a black dress with a charcoal jacket on top of it. She had a pin fastened to the collar of the jacket in the shape of a rose with a real diamond on it. Her hair, all black, was tied in a knot on top of her head. She looked very elegant, all in silk. Maria and Joanna were very impressed as they got into the car.

"Maria, Joanna, this is my mother Amelia Grimaldi. Mom, these are Maria and Joanna. Joanna works at the restaurant and Maria is her roommate. She is Italian."

"Nice to meet you," they all said in a chorus.

"All ready?" asked Giovanni. "Let's go."

They drove the short distance to Saint Joseph Cathedral on Fourth and Beech. Giovanni parked the car in the parking lot in front of the cathedral and they all got out. Amelia Grimaldi waited for her son to open the door and leaning on her cane she slowly stepped out. Giovanni put her arms under hers and they all walked towards the side entrance of the building instead of climbing the stairs on the front.

The inside of the cathedral was huge with three large rows of benches. At the back an enormous organ took the whole wall on the top floor. Confessionals were on either side of the bottom floor but were never used. Statues of the Virgin Mary and other saints were located throughout the cathedral. On the front platform there was the altar, the podium and some chairs on either sides.

Giovanni, Amelia, Maria and Joanna took a seat in the middle row. Maria waited till Joanna passed by her so that she could sit next to Giovanni. She was doing all she could to get those two together. She prayed to that effect while looking at them with the corner of her eyes. They made a great couple. Giovanni looked so youthful that you could not tell that there were twenty-seven years of difference in age between them. Joanna looked so sophisticated and regal in her black dress, they could very well be married as far as others knew. All they needed now was a little baby in the picture and it would be perfect.

Maria felt like the poor relative in her simple clothes. She wished she had worn her silk dress instead of the black pants, but just as well. She had no idea that Giovanni's mother would be so elegant. Sunday was probably the only day she got out of the house so it was understandable that she'd wear such expensive clothes.

While waiting for the Mass to start Amelia Grimaldi took out her rosary beads and prayed quietly. Every once in a while she would look at Joanna and Maria and smiled gently. She really looked like an angel, thought Joanna. She was in her late seventies but she, like her son, looked a lot younger. Her skin was white with only few wrinkles and her hair didn't have any gray in it at all. Maybe she dyed them. She would ask Giovanni when she got the opportunity. She was slim and about five-feet four-inches tall. Her legs were covered by very expensive black panty hoses and she was wearing real leather shoes probably made in Italy.

Giovanni was very tender towards her and full of attention. You could tell that he was devoted to her. Joanna was galvanized by his nearness. She could smell his cologne and noticed that it was different than the one he used during the week. This was musky and light, you could barely smell it. They were sitting so close that their bodies touched. Joanna could feel the heat of his body. She didn't dare to move. She hoped they could stay like that forever, so close, so intimate, in the presence of God. She prayed with all her heart that he'd love her as much as she loved him, hopefully even more. She side- glanced at him. His profile was so perfect, so handsome she wished she could caress it. He seemed deep in thought and she wondered if he was praying. What could he be praying about? His mother, his business? What about her? She was suffering for lack of knowledge. All these important questions she had in her mind, all without an answer. What a torture that was.

Giovanni had suffered a small shock that morning when he'd seen Joanna in her black dress. She was a vision. He knew that she didn't realize how beautiful she was, because she was so humble, so insecure, and he had collected himself real fast so that she wouldn't know the impact she had on him. *I hope mother likes her,* he thought, *because I sure do. God, if it is your will, make our relationship grow in love*, he prayed. *Let me have her for wife and raise my children, I pray you.* He looked at her. Her profile was so gentle, so refined and so beautiful that he gasped. She was like a real pearl among fake jewelry. All of a sudden he was grappled by fear. What if someone else wanted her, like Joe Bellagio did. What if she said yes. He had to move on her fast, make her his, claim her. What if she didn't reciprocate his feelings? Maria had said that she liked him, had she not? But was that enough to go on? What a torture this was. Finally, exhausted, he put the whole matter into God's hands and so he was able to relax.

Amelia Grimaldi knew immediately that her son was taken by Joanna. She knew the moment she saw her. When Giovanni had told her that he had invited the dishwasher from the restaurant with her friend she had not imagined that she was such a great beauty. She had expected someone short, plump, unsophisticated, nothing like the truth. She saw them now, sitting close to each other. What a nice couple they made. She would ask Giovanni later if he liked her and she would give him her blessing. It was time for him to marry again. It had been five years since his dear wife had died, it was now time to move on with his life. She eyed Joanna. She seemed still young and able to bear children and that's what the Grimaldi family needed, new blood. So what if she wasn't Italian? Girls nowadays were not as they used to be. Their values had changed. There wasn't anymore the sacred respect for the family; traditions were not upheld. An American would do just as well. She hoped to live long enough to hold a grandchild in her arms, because she knew she had only few years left on this earth.

Her mind went back to when she was a young bride, just arrived in the United States with her husband. They had come on a ship to Ellis Island. The emotions she felt as she got off the boat and presented their papers to the immigration officer. A relative had been waiting for them. On their way to his apartment he had showed them around Little Italy, introducing them to the people in the neighborhood. His apartment was small. Waiting for them there was his wife and three children. As they entered the apartment the smell of tomato sauce and sausage assailed them. They were so hungry they almost fainted. They ate ravenously accompanying the meal with lots of good wine imported from Italy. They slept on a bed made for them in the living room. They stayed with them for a week, then they headed south to San Diego where there was another relative waiting for them.

They had to change train many times, going from one city to another in their long journey, but Amelia was ecstatic taking everything in. Her husband, Giorgio Grimaldi, was a very sweet, gentle man. He was amused by his wife's youthful enthusiasm about everything. Everything was beautiful to her even the desolate countryside they traveled through, with few houses here and there. By the time they arrived in San Diego she was exhausted having been perked up during the whole trip, which lasted for days. Their relative took them to his house, by the bay. It was a nice three-bedroom house with a large garden in the back full of ripe tomatoes, eggplants, peperoncini, lettuce and grape vines.

They settled in with them for few months until Giorgio could get a loan from the bank to buy his own fishing boat. When he did he took them all out to celebrate. And what a celebration it was. Their relative had a wife and two children, all grown. Giorgio hired them to work on the fishing boat with him. They found a small, two-bedroom house few blocks from theirs and moved into it. It had a large sized garden in the back and Amelia soon planted a large variety of vegetables. She would spend hours working in the garden. She had plenty of time to do that since Giorgio was away at sea for weeks at a time. What a celebration when he'd come home. She would treat him like a king, cooking his favorite dishes, shining his shoes. He'd never let her lack for anything. Oh, how she missed him, her dear, beloved Giorgio.

God really poured his blessing on the Grimaldis. Catches were plentiful and they soon paid off the loan only to get another to buy a second fishing boat and a third, and a fourth, and a fifth, and a sixth. They stopped at six because that was all that Giorgio could handle otherwise they would have had a bigger fleet. All of the fishermen were Italians. They knew their families and they all lived in the same neighborhood. When the fleet was in, they would all gather together at Amelia's and Giorgio's house to celebrate and give thanks to God for a good catch. On Sunday mornings they would all go to church. After church the men would gather together while the women would go home to do the cooking, which they would bring to Amelia's house. Long tables would be set in the garden and that's where all the food was laid. As soon as the men arrived they'd start eating. Wine was always plentiful, imported from their native town of Taormina, in Sicily.

Amelia was the one who controlled the finances in Casa Grimaldi. Giorgio was content to let her do it because he didn't have a head for math. His passion was fishing. Amelia had saved enough money to buy them a three-bedroom house in the same neighborhood and a couple of years later she had enough to buy a whole apartment building, the same she was living in now. She needed a loan to do that but with the money she had saved the loan was not very large. She paid it off in no time with the money from the rentals. After that it was another building, other houses, so many that she almost lost count. Her husband was amazed at her. She was a genius. He trusted her implicitly. She didn't even slow down after the birth of their only son, Giovanni. She was a dynamo. Even though she spoke broken English she was able to get loans from the banks. They had seen the genius in her too and she had a good credit with all of the banks. She never defaulted on payments and loans were paid off on time.

As soon as Giovanni was able to withstand it he accompanied his father on fishing trips, but as he grew older he realized that that was not his passion. His passion was cooking. He would spend hours in the kitchen to help his mother with the cooking. Giorgio Grimaldi was puzzled by his son' interest but he never argued with him about it thinking that it was just a phase he was going through and that he would grow out of it.   But he didn't. Instead he came to him one day and told him that he wanted to be in the restaurant business. Giovanni had married in the meantime and had to support his wife. That's when he thought about opening a restaurant. Giorgio gave him his blessing and even loaned him some of the money.

He didn't live long after that. He was killed by a heart attack during one of his fishing trips. They brought him home on a stretcher. Amelia's eyes were filled with tears as she remembered that sad day. She pressed hard on the rosary beads as she realized she had lost count of the Hail Mary's she was reciting. She looked at her son and felt comforted. He looked so much like her Giorgio, she was amazed. She was so proud of her son. In fifty-five years he had given her nothing but joy. He was so kind, so gentle. She thanked God for him everyday.

The priest approached the altar ready to celebrate the Mass. They all stood up. During the Mass Joanna and Maria did exactly as everybody did and neither Giovanni, nor his mother had any clue that they were not Catholics. During the collection of tithes and offerings Joanna took out the change that she had and put it all in the basket including the pennies. She was thankful that she didn't have to be embarrassed by not donating anything. When the Mass was over they all walked out heading for the car.

Amelia asked Giovanni to take them all to lunch at Giovanni's if it was ok with Joanna and Maria. Amelia used that excuse so she could spend more time with Joanna and observe her. If this woman was important to her son she wanted to know of what stuff she was made of before she gave him her blessing. Maria and Joanna happily agreed to go to lunch and Giovanni drove towards the restaurant.

They were seated in the small dining room where they were

alone with the exception of a couple with two small children who left a little after they got there. So now they were totally alone. It was unusual for Giovanni and his mother to be guests of their own restaurant. Giovanni was surprised by his mother's decision since she never went anywhere except to church on Sundays. He thought something was cooking and wondered if it had to do with him and Joanna. His hopes rose. *Maybe she approves of her*, he thought; *maybe she wants to know more about her.* How right he was.

Amelia Grimaldi might be in her late seventies but her wits were as sharp as those of a twenty years old. She didn't miss a beat. *How lovely Joanna is*, she thought. Her features were delicate and Madonna-like. She reminded her of one of those Madonnas in Italian paintings. All she needed was a bouncing baby boy sitting on her lap. It's going to be Giovanni's baby, she determined.

Even though she was studying Joanna she didn't ignore Maria. Maria seemed to be very kind and a very good friend. She smiled often and gave away the fact that Joanna and Giovanni were in love. Every time they looked at each other she would smile,

mischievously. *So it's true,* Amelia thought, while doing small talk. Maria was more talkative than Joanna, but Joanna didn't have to talk a lot for Amelia to find out about her. She noticed the sadness in her eyes and for a moment her heart stopped for fear of hidden danger; danger that could harm her son. *She has a secret*, she thought, but what that secret was she didn't have a clue. It would take a long time to find out, months or years perhaps. She managed to learn that she was from Minneapolis and that she was going there in a week to visit her sick mother. That led her to believe that she was a good daughter devoted to her parents.

How was Giovanni taking it? *Her leaving San Diego*, she thought. She would find out later, at home. She looked at her son who seemed to be deep in thought. *May God protect you*, she prayed in her heart. *May He shield you from any pain and bring you comfort when you need it.*

He was her only son, her whole life. She had not been able to conceive anymore after she gave birth to him even though she had visited many doctors. They all told her that there was no physical problem; that the problem was in her mind. So she and Giorgio had gone to therapy and when that didn't work they had sadly accepted the truth and dedicated their lives to their only son. That had proved to be worthwhile, but their hopes of becoming grandparents had been shattered when Giovanni's wife had not been able to conceive and the doctors told them that she would never have a child because of ovarian cysts and blocked tubes. So Giovanni and his spouse had dedicated their lives to the business, it becoming their child.

Amelia had been greatly saddened by that news and she had tears in her heart every time she'd go to the park and see children with their parents, until she accepted the situation and dedicated her life once again to her son.

Giovanni was pouring wine for all of them. He proposed a toast.

"To my mother, the most beautiful woman in the world," he said. "Also to Maria for being such a good friend and to Joanna for her upcoming trip to Minneapolis. Last but not least, to me, Giovanni, the most handsome devil in the neighborhood."

They all laughed. The food was being served and they all became silent as they started to eat. Amelia had ordered a chicken salad; Maria spaghetti with calamari; Joanna lasagna; and Giovanni a pizza. The food, as usual, was delicious. They ate and laughed at the jokes that Giovanni told. He was quite funny. Maria told him that if he ever needed a job he could be a comedian. His mother agreed with that and she said a couple of jokes herself to show that humor ran in the Grimaldi's family. When dinner was over Giovanni gave them all a ride home. When they arrived at Amelia's house she insisted that the girls come in and see her house.

It was one of four houses, two at the bottom and two on top all adjoining together. Hers was the bottom one overlooking the bay. There was no hallway. As you walked inside there was the kitchen, to its left the dining room, which was very spacious. Three bedrooms were located on the sides of the living room, one on the north side and two on the east side. Giovanni's bedroom was one of the two on the east side. He had converted the other into his office. Amelia's bedroom was the one on the north side, which included a full bathroom and which Amelia used as living room also. She entertained her closest friends there where she would sit on the couch with them and they would either watch television or just talk.

It's not that she had many friends but people in the neighborhood knew her from when they owned the fishing boats and they would stop in from time to time to talk about the past and share memories.

Joanna's interest perked up as she visited Giovanni's bedroom. It was here that her love slept. It was here he would come to after he'd drop her off at the apartment. She liked it because it meant that he didn't bring any woman home; he would not do that since his mother lived there as well. She was comforted by that thought.

The bedroom was very simply furnished. The bed had a mahogany headboard with intarsia in the shape of roses, very intricate. Two side tables were on each side of the bed with Tiffany lamps on each of them also with roses inlaid. A pipe, a clock and an ashtray were on top of one of the side tables and Joanna guessed that was the side he slept on.

"I didn't know you smoked," said Joanna.

"I don't smoke," replied Giovanni. "I only smoke the pipe every now and then. It calms my nerves, plus I like the smell." A closet ran the whole length of one wall and two chests of drawers were on the other two walls. All the furnishing was in mahogany, dust free and shining. *I wonder who does the cleaning*, thought Joanna aloud.

"A Mexican woman who lives in the neighborhood," explained Giovanni. "She comes twice a week to help my mother with the laundry and the cleaning. My mother used to do it all by herself, but since she turned seventy she realized that she needed help, especially since I moved in with her five years ago. I try to be careful but I still need to be picked up after, I am afraid. The woman who marries me has her job cut out for her," he said looking at Joanna and smiling.

Would she be willing to pick up after him, he wondered. Joanna returned his smile. It was a brief moment, very intimate and Joanna's hopes went sky high.

Maria was most interested in the artwork. All over the house there were paintings of Jesus, the Virgin Mary and other saints. On top of Giovanni's bed there was a huge rosary made of enormous mahogany beads with a wooden cross also in mahogany. On the sidewalls there were a painting of a woman breastfeeding her child with her breast exposed, and a painting of Jesus carrying the cross.

They seemed to be originals and had very expensive frames. *I wonder how much they are worth*, thought Maria.

The office was furnished with a computer table with computer, by a desk also in mahogany, by an antique escritoire and by filing cabinets. Giovanni shared the filing cabinets with his mother. There she kept the records of all her properties. She still did her own bookkeeping. An armchair in rich, brown leather was by the desk and a tall lamp was by its side. In this office Giovanni spent most Mondays and Tuesdays when the restaurant was closed. He didn't trust to leave his most important business papers at the restaurant for fear of fire and for fear of someone peaking in and minding his business. Too many people had access to his office and he didn't want to give the Devil an opportunity.

Giovanni was a firm believer in the Devil. He knew that he existed just as he knew that God existed. He should have shared that with Maria who had been molested by the Devil all her life. But Giovanni didn't know that. He saw the Devil in all the ignominious things that happened in the world: in rape; murder; lying; deceiving; child molestation; theft; lewdness; sexual immorality. One of his goals in life was to defeat the Devil, another thing he had in common with Maria but he didn't know that either.

When they finished the tour of the house Amelia offered them *orzata*, a drink made from almonds. It is an Italian custom to offer guests something to drink and pastries. She got out of a cabinet some *biscotti* and explained that she made them from a very old Sicilian recipe handed down to her by her mother. She said she would give the recipe to the woman who married her son. Both Maria and Joanna said the biscotti were delicious and so was the orzata. Maria had tasted the orzata before but the biscotti were new to her. She tasted orange in them and she wondered if Amelia had used grated orange peel to make them.

A painting on the dining room wall fascinated Maria. It was of Jesus at about the age of eight years old. He was wearing a white tunic tied in the waist by a cord. He was holding white lilies and there was light all around him. He had blonde hair and blue eyes. The face was most handsome and Maria wished that she had a son.

Giovanni looked at the clock. It was three in the afternoon. He told his mother that he needed to go to the restaurant and that he was going to take the girls home. Amelia invited them both to visit her anytime they could. There was so much more that she wanted to share with them. She liked them both.

The girls said goodbye. Maria gave Amelia a kiss on both cheeks Italian style and Joanna did the same. They got outside on the porch where there were many plants growing in pots, and waited for Giovanni who was kissing and embracing his mother.

The distance from Amelia's house to Maria's apartment was about three minutes by car. Giovanni left the girls outside the building and went back to his mother's house. His mother was surprised to see him again so soon. Giovanni lied and told her that he needed to change his clothes. Amelia knew that he was up to something because Giovanni kept clothes in his office at the nightclub. So she went to her room, sat on the couch and waited for his move, watching television.

She didn't have to wait long. He went to his mother and asked if he could talk to her.

"Sure," she said. "You know that I am here for you, Giovanni. Anytime, day or night. Are you having problems?"

"Yes and no. The problem is Joanna. I like her but I am afraid to ask her out. The first time I took her home I kissed her. She slapped me so hard she left the print of her hand on my face for hours. She told me she had never been kissed before and that she was a virgin. Mom do you imagine that? Twenty-eight years old and never been kissed? Come on, I thought, she is just pulling my leg. I can understand being a virgin but never been kissed? What do you think about her mom, should I trust her and ask her out?"

"I think you should, son. She'll make beautiful babies. Now if you don't mind I'd like to take my afternoon nap. I am quite fatigued and you know I need my rest or I'll be a Sicilian ogre. Go to work and treat her right, you hear? No sex before marriage and take your time; don't rush into it."

"I love you, mom and thank you for being so nice to her. It means a lot to me." So his mother approved. Giovanni was very happy about it and couldn't wait for when he would give Joanna a ride home so he could ask her out.

Joanna went to work in jeans and T-shirt. Giovanni's heart leaped when he saw her. Even in jeans she looked like a million bucks. He gave her a pat on her behind and immediately regretted it. Some of the waiters were giggling. He felt embarrassed and blushed like a teenager. Angry with himself he moved away from Joanna and busied himself with the business of the restaurant. Joanna was not mad at him. She was actually pleased that he had touched her.

She went to the kitchen and gave Alfredo a hug.

"What's matter, bambina, have you won the lottery?" he asked her, taken by surprise.

"No, but I feel like I have," she replied. "I am so happy because I met Giovanni's mom. She is wonderful and she likes me, I can tell. We, Maria and I, went to church with her and Giovanni this morning. We came here to eat afterwards and then we went to her house. Now I know where Giovanni sleeps. Their house is so nice; it's almost like a church with lot of religious paintings, and it is so clean. Have you ever been to their house, Alfredo?"

"Yes I have, a couple of times. I agree with you, entering the house is almost like entering a church. They have a lot of faith in God, you can tell."

"I have a lot of faith in God too. What about you, Alfredo?"

"Oh, you know I do. Without faith in God I couldn't make it. When I have a hard day I just look up and ask Him for help. He has never failed me, not even once. I praise and worship Him with all my heart. He is first in my life."

"Giovanni said the same thing. That's amazing. I am new at this but I hope I'll have the same faith as you both do."

"You will, bambina. If you've given yourself to Jesus you will grow in faith each day. The important thing is that you stay close to Him and He will be close to you. Read the Bible every day and let Him speak to your heart. I read the Bible every morning, the Psalms and the Proverbs, they are my favorites, full of wisdom."

"I don't have a favorite yet because I just started reading the Bible. I am most interested in passages that speak of God because I want to know about Him, what He is like, how He thinks. You know that you can reason with God and have Him change His mind?"

"No kidding. I got to remember that when I pray. So, tell me bambina, how are things going between you and Giovanni, has he made any advances to you?"

"No, he has been the perfect gentleman. He gives me a ride every night but he hasn't tried anything anymore since that first night. Sometimes I wish he would but I guess I scared him off with that big slap I gave him."

"Yea, that must be it."

Joanna and Alfredo were washing dishes as they talked. Joanna was wearing gloves now because she had been taking better care of her hands. She'd put on cream everyday and she had decided that as soon as she could afford it she'd go to a manicurist to manicure her hands.

"Tell me Alfredo, how is Carlo, your son. Anymore trouble?"

"No. He has decided to stay away from politics and demonstrations. That blow to his head put some wisdom in it, I tell you. I didn't even have to preach to him, he decided all by himself. All he wants to do now is study and get his degree."

"I am glad. How about your wife and daughter, how are they doing?"

"They are doing fine. My wife complains all the time because we're so far away. She always asks me to go home, but I tell you, bambina, that I am used to live here now and I wouldn't go back even if I could. Maybe in five to ten years I'll be ready to go but not now. I like it here."

"What do you like about living here, Alfredo?"

"I like the open space, the organization, the freedom. San Diego is beautiful, let me tell you. It's clean and people mind their business. You can't ask for more. I miss them, don't get me wrong, but I prefer to live here. Once my kids get their degrees and get married maybe my wife could come to live with me, but right now she needs to be there with them. Four or five more years that's how long is going to take. We'll see."

"I admire you Alfredo and I am glad you like it here. This is my country and I love it. This is the country of opportunities, you can be anything you want to be, with God helping you of course."

"It is my country too, you know. I have been a citizen for three years now and I feel like a new person. Being an American is a boost to my ego, especially when I go to Italy to visit. They call me 'The Americano' and I am so proud of it. It makes me stand out, different in a good way, you know."

"I wish the whole world was American. Just imagine what it would be like. No more poverty, everybody having what they needed, speaking one language, having the same money. And they wouldn't even have to give up their culture. It would be the American Planet Earth."

"Yea, keep dreaming. It's never going to happen. Too many people hate us. They hate what we have: our freedom, our money, our well being, our form of government. They wouldn't know how to handle it. I am glad I was born in Italy. There too we have freedom, especially the freedom to say what we think. Sometime more than here and to our detriment I have to say because we say things that hurt others. Here it is better. Here we have to think before we speak. I like that saying 'If you can't say something nice don't say anything at all'."

"It's hard to do Alfredo. I try to think before I speak but I still get in trouble sometime."

"I guess that's part of being human. We all fail. Without God's mercy and Jesus' sacrifice on the cross we would all go to hell."

"What do you say we place our order with the cooks and take our break? It's almost nine o'clock already. I am going to have a salad because I ate a lot today. I was nervous meeting Giovanni's mother and when I am nervous I eat more. What are you going to have?"

"Oh, just a pizza and a glass of red wine."

"A glass of wine a day is supposed to be good for you, so I think I'll join you."

The dinner was leisurely and full of laughter. Joanna was feeling closer to Alfredo as time went by. She told him most of her problems but she couldn't bring herself to talk to him about her past because she didn't trust him enough not to tell Giovanni. She knew that he was very loyal to him. She felt that if she told him he might concoct pictures in his mind about her wondering the streets, dirty and begging for money, which were all true but she didn't want him, or Giovanni for that matter, to think that of her. Her past belonged to her.

When all the dishes were done, at eleven o'clock, Joanna went to change. The nightclub was busy already and there were plenty of glasses to wash. Philip was in a very talkative mood, going on and on about Leandra, his new baby girl. Joanna's heart was filled with joy in seeing him so happy and wished she would have a baby also, Giovanni's baby. She was following every move Giovanni made trying to find out whom the woman was he cared for. Maybe she was someone who visited the nightclub. Many women came to the nightclub regularly and he seemed to know them all. He would spend time with them and they all seemed to be captivated by him even if they were with other men. That's because he is so cordial, Joanna told herself. He seemed to treat them all with respect and courtesy so it was hard to tell which one he preferred.

The Russian countess was sitting on the couch by the piano. At her side there was another handsome young man. She was slowly sipping her drink, listening to the music. She too followed Giovanni's every move. She looked beautiful in a silver sweater and black, silk pants. Silver earrings adorned her ears and her luscious black hair was loose around her face. The moment she caught Giovanni's attention she beckoned him to come and sit by her. Giovanni excused himself with the people he was talking to, got up and walked to the couch where he sat by the countess. Joanna felt a stab of jealousy in her heart and dropped the glass she was rinsing making a loud noise. Philip asked her if she was all right. He hadn't missed the fact that she was watching Giovanni like a hawk and that she was listening to him with just one ear. He was worried about her because she seemed so innocent, so vulnerable and wanted to spare her any pain. But he knew that it was impossible because we all have our cross to bear. He saw her blush and recoil and decided not to embarrass her by asking more questions. Instead he told her to take a break, which Joanna did, relieved that she didn't have to watch Giovanni flirt for at least fifteen minutes.

She went upstairs in the empty restaurant and sat at one of the tables. She lit the candle on the table and started to pray to calm herself down. She had her eyes closed and was practicing positive thinking. In her mind she saw Giovanni leave the countess and come to her. He told her he loved her and was asking her to marry him. She put her hand out and he put a diamond ring on her finger. She had a smile on her face.

She opened her eyes and screamed, jumping backwards. Giovanni was sitting across from her, looking at her with a smile on his face. How long had he been sitting there, she wondered.

"A penny for your thoughts," he said.

"You don't want to know my thoughts, Giovanni, it is not safe. They would just bore you, anyway."

"Try me." He really wanted to know.

"No, and that's final." Joanna would rather die than tell him what she was thinking about. She saw Giovanni lower his head with a sad look on his face. Joanna took his hand across the table and said: "I am sorry, Giovanni; I didn't mean to be rude, forgive me."

"I forgive you Cinderella. There is something I want to ask you, but if you are not in a good mood maybe I can ask you some other time. Oh, by the way, here is your weekly wages." He handed her the money for the past week. Joanna put them in her bra, since she didn't have her purse with her. She wondered what Giovanni wanted to ask her.

"By the way," he said, "why are you up here all by yourself. Did something happen between you and Philip?"

"Good heavens, no! Philip is a sweetheart. He saw me drop a glass and sent me on a break. Do you mind? I mean, is it all right with you? You are still the boss, you know."

"No, I don't mind. Are you feeling better now?"

"Oh, yes I do. So what did you want to ask me?"

"I want to ask you if you would go out with me on a date tomorrow night," said Giovanni blushing.

"Go out with you? Are you serious? What about the woman you're interested in, won't she mind?"

Giovanni was caught in a bind. He didn't want to reveal his feelings to her yet for fear that things might not work out between them, but he had to answer her question.

"Forget about someone else. Right now I am interested in you. Is that a good answer?"

"I guess, but it would be nicer if there wasn't anyone else involved. What about the countess, she is all over you, all the time."

"Don't worry about her. Like I said, now I am interested in you. I'll pick you up at six and we'll go out to dinner somewhere. Wear a sweater because it's chilly at night."

"I haven't said yes yet. I'll let you know when you take me home at two. Is that all right?"

"Yea, sure." Giovanni was disappointed. He thought she'd jump at the opportunity, but he'd been wrong. He felt insecure and foolish. Maybe she was thinking about his age, he could be her father. Maybe she didn't like him that way. He thought he was sure she would say yes but he wasn't so sure anymore. He felt his heart tighten and put a fake smile on his face as he waved at a couple leaving the nightclub.

"Well, we better get back to work Cinderella." Giovanni got up and went back to the nightclub. Joanna blew out the candle and followed him.

She washed the glasses automatically, absent minded. She was holding back, still in shock. Did she hear him right? She was not mistaken, was she? Why would he go out with her when he could have a real life countess? She desperately wanted to say yes but she kept her wits about herself. It would be good to make him wait, she was proud of herself for doing that because she wanted to say yes right away. She didn't know where she found the courage, but she did. Now she was tormenting herself for fear that he'd change his mind. Two o'clock was not far away. She felt anxiety in her chest as the time approached. She was going to say yes, yes, yes. Well, maybe just one yes. Who cares about the other woman, she probably doesn't even know about it. And even if she did, she would take him away from her. Try me, she said, talking to herself. Poor Cinderella.

Riding in his luxurious Jaguar, smelling his cologne, made Joanna dizzy. He wasn't talking. She was shy and insecure. She felt lowly and out of place. She turned towards him to look at his face. He was so handsome. She was crazy about his green eyes and his black hair. What a combination. She desperately wanted a baby from him, with the same green eyes and the same black hair.

"Yes," she finally said. "I will go out with you tomorrow."

"You will? Good. You won't regret it. You don't need to be afraid to go out with me, Joanna. That night I lost my head. I promise I won't even touch you if you don't want me too."

"I know Giovanni. Why don't we both forget about that night and start afresh? What do you say?"

"I say that's great. Let's."

He stopped the car in front of her building. He took her hand and kissed it.

"Good night Cinderella. I'll see you tomorrow or rather today at six."

"Good night Giovanni. Sleep well," and she was gone.

CHAPTER TWENTY-TWO

S leep would not come. Joanna tossed and turned. She wished she could talk to Maria about it but she wouldn't dream of waking her up. She was so excited she thought she would burst. A date with Giovanni. God was answering her prayers and her exercises in positive thinking were working. *Jesus, let me marry him, I pray you*, she asked fervently. Her mind raced for about an hour when finally, exhausted, she fell in a dreamless sleep.

Maria woke up at four-thirty as usual, to go to work. She moved around the apartment very quietly so that she wouldn't wake up Joanna. But Joanna woke up anyway.

"I am sorry, Joanna, did I wake you up?" Maria said apologetically.

"No Maria, you didn't wake me up. I am too excited because Giovanni asked me out on a date. Can you believe it? What am I going to wear? I think I'll go buy a new dress. Oh, by the way, here is the fifty dollars you loaned me and I am sorry I can't give you any money yet, but I will when I come back from Minneapolis. If things go well between Giovanni and me maybe I can repay you for all your troubles. Can we go to the shrine and say a quick prayer for tonight? I really want God's blessing on this relationship."

Maria and Joanna went into the bedroom and lit the candle. They knelt down and prayed for God's blessing. They then prostrated themselves with their faces on the floor for about a minute.

Afterwards they said a closing prayer and got up, blowing out the candle.

"I won't be here when you come home from work and I don't know what time I'll be back tonight so don't wait up for me, Maria. I am so excited. I wonder where he is going to take me. If he tries to kiss me should I kiss him back?"

"That's up to you Joanna. Follow your heart and use your head. You don't want to give him everything before he commits himself and asks you to marry him, and even then, you should wait till after the marriage. You've waited this long, you can wait some more. Remember that some men, especially Italian men, after they get what they want they lose interest."

"Thank you for your advice."

"Anytime. Now I better get ready or I'll be late for work."

Maria left at five forty-five as usual. Joanna tried to go back to sleep. She struggled for a little while till she fell asleep again. She slept till ten-thirty. She got up and made herself a strong cup of coffee. Being nervous made her hungry. She fixed a good breakfast of scrambled eggs, toast and fresh fruits. While she was eating she went over in her mind about what she needed to do. She needed to go to the County Mental Health to cancel her appointment for the following Monday since she would be in Minneapolis. She would try to see Jill Thompson and if that was not possible, to schedule another appointment. She also needed to go to the dentist and to Mervyn's to buy a new dress. She should receive the airplane tickets from Felicia within the week, so she didn't need to worry about it.

Thinking about the trial again gave her cramps to the stomach. *God help me to go through it, please*, she prayed. The thought of her date with Giovanni took her mind away from that unpleasantness. She really felt like Cinderella meeting her prince. The ugly stepmother was her past. She needed to be clear headed and watch what she said. It was going to be hard, especially during the following week when all the ugliness from her past would be revealed in front of strangers. She hoped they would believe her, and why shouldn't they. She would be saying the truth. She was nervous about seeing Raul but knowing that he was under police custody made her relax a little. He could not hurt her anymore and she didn't have to do anything to please him either; never, never again for as long as she lived. What a comfort this thought brought.

She wondered where Giovanni was going to take her. She imagined a restaurant by the sea serving fresh seafood, violins playing, a beautiful sunset. "Off we go," she said out loud. She took a long shower and dressed. She wore jeans and T-shirt.

County Mental Health was her first stop since it was located two blocks from the apartment. She explained her situation to Sara, the receptionist. Sara told her that Jill Thompson had a full schedule that day but maybe she'd be able to see her for about ten minutes since she was on her lunch break. She called her on the phone and Jill agreed to see Joanna. Jill had a worried look on her face when she came downstairs.

"Is something wrong, Joanna? Our appointment is not till next week. Why are you here today?" she asked.

"I have been subpoenaed for next Wednesday to appear in court so I can't make it for our appointment since I'll be in Minneapolis. I was just trying to reschedule for when I got back. Can we reschedule?"

"Oh yes, I am sure we can. We just make it for the following Monday, no problem."

"Can I talk to you for a little while? I am very nervous about the trial. I am afraid that I am going to breakdown and cry, or that I am going to be so intimidated by Raul that I won't say everything he did to me. Please help me."

"Calm down Joanna. Here, let's go sit down in the waiting room. There is nobody there so we'll be able to talk." Jill Thompson gently led Joanna in the empty waiting room. They seated next to each other. Jill put her hand on top of Joanna's.

"Tell me Joanna, have you been doing the breathing exercises that I suggested? They are very important, you know."

"Yes, I have and they did help, but the thought of the trial is making me a wreck. I start shaking when I think about it. I can't help it."

"Yes you can. You must. You want to put that man behind bars, don't you? Then you must be strong and get a hold of yourself. You'll see, when you'll get on the stand to testify, the anger you've repressed for all these years will come out and you will make mince meat out of him. You won't be afraid and you'll pour out your heart. I hope they'll give him the maximum of the sentence."

"I hope so too, Jill. Can you prescribe me some medication to take away the anxiety?"

"I can't but Dr. Steinman can. Wait here and I'll see if he can write you a prescription."

"Thank you, Jill."

Jill Thompson disappeared behind a door. Joanna took a deep breath. As she exhaled she mentally flushed out Raul and all he'd done to her. She felt a little better. She didn't have to wait long. Jill Thompson came back and handed Joanna the prescription for anti-anxiety pills. She took it and put it in her purse. She gave Jill a hug and went to the reception desk. She made an appointment in two weeks and left.

On her way to the dental clinic she stopped by McGills Pharmacy to have her prescription filled. She took a pill right away and swallowed it without water. Few blocks down the way she entered the Downtown Dental Clinic and went to the reception desk. She told the receptionist that she'd come to pick up the whitening tray and the whitening gel for her teeth. She was admitted to a room where the dental assistant was. The assistant gave her all that she needed to whiten her teeth with the instructions on how to apply the gel in the tray and slip the tray on at night for fourteen nights in a row.

Joanna was happy. She decided that she was going to start the treatment when she got back from Minneapolis. Right now there were too many distractions and she was afraid she might skip a night. She went to the reception desk and paid forty dollars, twenty for that week and twenty for the following week. She told the receptionist that she was going to be out of town. That done she proceeded to Mervyn's.

On her way to Mervyn's she couldn't resist. She had to stop at Starbucks and order a Caramel Macchiato. She sat outside and sipped her drink while watching people go by. No man with blue hair this time. Instead she saw a girl with purple hair tied in two pony- tails. She was probably fourteen years old and was wearing a leather jacket and leather pants. On her face she wore heavy make-up and purple lipstick. She was hugging what seemed to be a fifteen-year old boy also wearing leather jacket and leather pants. Joanna finished her drink. She tossed the empty cup in the trashcan and walked to Mervyn's.

There was a big sale going on, Joanna was happy to see. She went to the women section and scrolled over all the dresses on various racks. One dress caught her attention. It was a pale yellow, strapless with a built-in bra. The material was chiffon-like, very light and transparent, but it had lining underneath. She took two sizes to the dressing room, size eight and size ten because she wasn't sure which one would fit. She tried both on and size ten fit better. It looked real nice on her, the color almost matching her hair. She decided she was going to buy it. She also bought a necklace to go with the dress and some make-up to take with her to Minneapolis.

All her shopping done she went outside. It was two-thirty. She was a little bit hungry but decided not to eat anything since she had a big breakfast. She wanted to save her appetite for when she went to dinner with Giovanni, that evening. She was undecided whether to stay in the mall or go home. In the end she opted to go home and get more rest. She hadn't slept very well.

Back at the apartment she lay on the futon and tried to get some sleep, but she was too excited and sleep would not come. Instead of getting up she remained laying down with her eyes closed, doing breathing exercises like Jill Thompson had suggested. Slowly she felt the tension leaving her. She practiced positive thinking with images of her marrying Giovanni and having a baby boy. She saw her future bright with great happiness and contentment. Every once in a while thoughts of Raul and the trial would interfere, but she'd chase them away by replacing them with more positive ones. She saw herself helping Giovanni run his business, working side by side as a team, loving the togetherness. *It will come to pass,* she told herself.

Half an hour later she got up. She ran the bath water and took a bath. She breathed deeply the smell of the scented oil as she started soaping her body. She shampooed her hair the second time that day. She had perspired during her errands that morning and it felt good to wash it all away. She wanted the evening to be perfect and being clean was important. She had thoughts of her and Giovanni kissing passionately. She brushed and flossed her teeth for a good while. Now she felt completely clean. She sprayed Maria's perfume Anais-Anais by Cacharel, on her body and waited few minutes to let it dry before she put on her dress. She dried and styled her hair. She took the make-up she had bought that morning and applied it on her face and neck.

Looking at herself in the mirror she saw a beautiful woman, very different than few weeks ago. She looked very sophisticated. Any man would be proud to be seen with her. Gone were the wrinkles and dry skin. Her hair looked healthy and shiny, her face smooth.

It was fifteen minutes to six o'clock. She sat on the couch and worked on her fingernails removing all the cuticles and filing them smoothly. At six o'clock she went downstairs.

The Jaguar was parked in front of the building. A couple of passer-by turned to look at her as she stepped outside. Joanna was pleased. As he saw her, Giovanni got out of the car to open the door for her. He looked very handsome in an elegant black suit, Italian made for sure. Inside the car he took a bouquet of red roses and gave it to Joanna. She was so surprised and moved that she blushed like a schoolgirl. She was speechless. No one had ever given her flowers before. She kissed Giovanni on the cheek to thank him and she saw him blushing.

"You look beautiful, Joanna," he said.

"Thank you, Giovanni," she replied. He started the car and they drove in silence for a good ten minutes. Finally Joanna said: "Where are we going?"

"You'll see," replied Giovanni. "Have you ever been to Del Mar?"

"No, I don't believe I have."

"That's where we're going, to Antonio's. He is a friend of mine. I have reserved a table by the window overlooking the sea. It's beautiful, just wait and see."

"How is your mom, Giovanni?"

"She is fine. You made a good impression on her. She likes you."

"I like her too, very much. It's nice to have a mom."

"Why do you say that? You have a mom too, don't you?"

"I was adopted when I was seven years old. I don't know where my real mom is."

"Oh! That's too bad, Cinderella. Do you miss her a lot?"

"Yes, all the time."

"Would you like to find her? I have a friend who is a good private investigator. He specializes in finding missing people. Maybe we could hire him."

"Thank you for your kindness, but you see, I don't even know what her last name is. My last name before I was adopted was Stanford but I don't know if that was my mom's or my dad's. She could be dead for all I know."

"Think positive. If she is out there we'll find her. Have faith Cinderella. God works in mysterious ways."

"I have faith but it has been too long."

"If you were adopted when you were seven years old, that was twenty-one years ago. How did your adoptive parents treat you, where they good?"

"Oh yes, they were very good," lied Joanna, "especially Felicia. She has been like a real mother to me."

"What time are you leaving Sunday for Minneapolis?"

"At three o'clock in the afternoon."

"I'll give you a ride to the airport. Would you like that?"

"Oh yes, I don't know how to thank you Giovanni. You are so good to me."

"It's nothing. Before I forget, don't mention anything at the restaurant about us going out, not even to Alfredo. I know you talk to him. I don't want anybody to know. I hate gossiping."

"I promise I won't say anything until you say it's all right."

"Good."

The Jaguar ran smoothly on the I-5. Signs for Del Mar started to appear. Finally Giovanni took an exit and drove west towards the center of the town. Joanna was looking in silence outside the window observing the shops and the houses of Del Mar. The town was on the sea and it was a summer resort for many tourists. It had long stretches of beaches and it was the site of Del Mar Fairgrounds with many fairs throughout the year. Giovanni turned the car to a side street and stopped in front of a building with a lovely landscape all around it. Geraniums, impatiens, begonias, marigolds, adorned the building, which had large windows overlooking the sea below.

A host was at the door of Antonio's and welcomed them inside. Giovanni gave him his name and told him that they had a reservation for six forty-five. He checked his book and smiling escorted them to a table by a window overlooking the sea. Giovanni and Joanna sat opposite each other. White lace tablecloths covered the tables. A vase on each table held a red rose. Very romantic. A waiter came over and lit a candle. He gave them each a menu.

The restaurant was full and Giovanni was glad he had made a reservation. He asked the waiter if Antonio was in. The waiter told him that he was not in yet, but that he should be in soon. Giovanni asked him to tell Antonio to come to their table when he arrived. When the waiter left they opened their menu and read through it. Joanna noticed a big selection of seafood. That seemed to be their specialty. Spaghetti with octopus in tomato sauce caught her attention. She decided she was going to order it together with a mixed salad.

Giovanni asked her if she wanted some wine and she said yes. He gestured to the waiter and ordered some white wine and mineral water. He looked at Joanna, how lovely she was in her new dress. The more he saw her the more taken he was. Inside his heart he knew he was doing the right thing.

They sipped the wine in silence shyly looking at each other. The light of the candle gave their skin a soft glow. Outside the sun was setting. The sky was bright orange with streaks of red. They both looked at it in awe.

Joanna's hand was resting on the table by her wine glass. Giovanni couldn't resist the impulse of putting his own hand over it. Instead of retreating her hand Joanna gently squeezed his fingers. She had decided that she was going to encourage him if he made any advances, up to a certain point, of course. Holding hands was so romantic. The whole setting was romantic: the wine, the rose, the sunset, handholding and the music. The music was old Italian songs and was coming through speakers on the wall. Joanna couldn't understand the words but she could tell it was love songs. Giovanni's also played Italian music but this was different, more melodious, and more nostalgic.

"I have already decided what I am going to order. What are you having Giovanni?"

"I am going to have *'linguine al pesto'*," he replied, "with a side order of *'shrimp in lemon sauce'*, very delicious, you should try it."

"It's all right, I'll try it the next time we come over," said Joanna looking at him to observe his reaction. He smiled at the thought and took a sip of his wine. Their hands were still touching when the waiter came over to take their order. As the waiter left, another man approached their table. His skin was dark and his eyes and hair were black. He was wearing a dark, expensive suit. He shook hands and embraced Giovanni.

"Antonio, it's so good to see you, my friend. I want to introduce you my date Joanna. Joanna this is Antonio, the owner of the restaurant and a dear friend of mine."

"Pleased to meet you, Antonio. You have a beautiful place; I love it."

"I am pleased to meet you too, Joanna. About time you went on a date my friend. It's sure being a long time since I have seen you," he told Giovanni.

"Well, you know how it is, the business takes a lot of my time. It's hard to get away. I am happy to see you, how is your family?"

"The family is fine. I had a little boy since I have seen you last. I have now three kids and that's a handful, let me tell you. We've decided not to have anymore. My wife will be happy to hear about your visit my friend. How is your lovely mother?"

"She's fine, thank God; not a wrinkle on her face."

"Give her my regards, will you?"

"I sure will, Antonio. Thank you!"

"I'll let you two have your dinner," said Antonio, ready to leave since the food was being served. Giovanni ordered more wine.

The food was delicious. Joanna ate slowly wanting to spend as much time with Giovanni as possible. She savored every bite and she drank the wine, not enough to get her drunk, but enough to make her tipsy. It was dark outside and the sky was full of stars. The only light in the restaurant was that of the candles on the tables and that of four lights in the corners of the room.

What a magical night. Joanna thought that it was better than she had imagined in her positive thinking exercise. She made another wish to go for a walk on the beach after dinner.

"How do you like your food, Cinderella?"

"Unbelievably good."

"Better than mine?"

"Nothing is better than yours."

"Would you like some coffee and dessert? I want you to try the 'Tiramisu', they make it different than us, you'll like it."

"Okay, I trust you."

Giovanni motioned to the waiter. When he came over he ordered two Tiramisu and two espresso coffee with sugar. The waiter took their order and cleared the table. While waiting for the coffee Giovanni took Joanna's hand again.

"You don't have to be afraid of me, Cinderella," he said. "I assure you that my intentions are serious. I would never do anything to frighten you away. You have to trust me."

"I trust you, Giovanni. I think you are the sweetest man I ever met and I am not afraid of you. You're always looking over me at the nightclub, in my private life, when you give me a ride home every night. You're making my life easier and I am thankful for that. I don't know what I'd do without you."

"That's because I care about you, Cinderella. You're like a breath of fresh air in my life."

"Speaking of fresh air, it's getting chilly don't you think?"

"Yes, it's much better".

The waiter served them the coffee and the *Tiramisu*. They ate and drank slowly afraid that the night might end.

"There is a beautiful beach down below, would you like to go for a walk after we're done?"

"Oh, yes, I'd love to, Giovanni, what a lovely idea." Joanna was happy that her wish would come true. He must have the same thing in mind as I do, thought Joanna. His green eyes seemed even more alluring by candlelight. Just looking at them made Joanna shiver. She felt an animal magnetism coming from him. She longed to be embraced by that handsome man, to be kissed by him. Hopefully it would happen soon. She was willing to give him her heart if he had asked.

Giovanni paid for the dinner leaving a generous tip for the waiter. He put his arm around Joanna and escorted her outside. There was a full moon and stars lighted the sky. What a magnificent night. They walked down some stairs to the beach below. The sand was hard and wet under their feet. Giovanni took her hand and they slowly walked towards south.

"A penny for your thoughts, Cinderella."

"Why do you call me Cinderella?"

"I don't know, maybe because you are a dishwasher; maybe because you're poor, alone and insecure. But underneath all I perceive a beauty, a greatness in you that will make you a queen one day. Just wait and see."

"Tell me of when you were a little boy, Giovanni. What kind of life did you have?"

"I had the best life. I am not a mama's boy but I loved to spend time with my mom in the kitchen. Ever since I can remember I have always been fascinated by food. I'd help my mother cooking, cutting green beans, and slicing tomatoes. I would make mental notes of all the ingredients for the various recipes. I'd beg to cook. My father would take me on fishing trips hoping that one day I would take over the business, but my love was in the kitchen, and that's where it has stayed to this day."

"Didn't you like to play with your friends?"

"Yes, I did, but not much. Some of them even made fun of me for cooking saying that it was a woman's job, but I didn't care. Being an only child I was adored by my mother. She would have laid down and let me walk all over her if I had to. Thank God that I didn't. My mother is my best friend; no one will ever take her place. I enjoyed spending time with her so much that sometime I even helped her with the cleaning. She would sit by me night after night while I'd do my homework, quietly knitting sweaters for my father and me to wear. She'd go to bed at midnight and be up at the crack of dawn. She was a seamstress and had many clients, mostly women in the neighborhood. I truly enjoyed growing up with her. I don't think there is another boy in the whole world that was as lucky as I was. But enough of me," said Giovanni drawing her close to him and putting his arm around her shoulders. "Tell me about your childhood. What was it like being adopted?"

"You come to accept it; at first you are angry because you think that your adoptive parents are trying to take your real parents' place. I waited for my mom, day after day, to come and take me home with her. When it didn't happen I became bitter. It took me a long time to let go and start warming up to Felicia. She was and is really good to me, the best. All summed up I had a good childhood; I never lacked anything. It could have been much worse; I could have spent my life in foster care, but thanks to Felicia it didn't happen, that's why I am happy to go and help her out now that she needs me."

"I am going to miss you, Cinderella."

"Oh, you always have the countess to keep you company. Just remember to keep napkins handy so that you can wipe her lipstick off your lips. Is she very wealthy?"

"Yes, she is. Her family left Russia before the revolution so they were able to take all their wealth with them. They settled in France and much later they made their way to the United States. They own lot of land and oil; they knew how to invest their money. You know, though, if I had to choose between you and her, I'd have no doubt in my mind, I'd choose you. You know why? Because you are a virgin and she is not. She changes man as she changes underwear and she is not the type to be submissive to her husband. Plus, the way I make my money is debasing to her. Sell food? Puah! She just wants to get into my pants, that's all. The more I resist her the more she insists. It's a game she is playing; I am not fooled one bit by it. A marriage with her would last three months, that's all."

"I hear what you're saying but still, it is flattering to be wanted so much." They had arrived at the end of the beach where huge rocks separated one beach from the other. They sat on one rock and continued their conversation. Giovanni felt very comfortable talking to her. It almost seemed that there was no difference in age between them. Joanna surprised him with her maturity, her seriousness. He felt he could spend hours talking to her. One thing bothered him though: The sadness he'd seen in her eyes. He wanted to know why, but he was sure he might never find out. His only hope was to take it away from her, make her happy, give her a home, children, love.

Out there, in the cool breeze, he realized he was in love with her. He wanted to kiss her but he told himself that it was too soon. Better to wait. Maybe she would make the first move.

Joanna put her head on his shoulder and grabbed his arm, nestling close to him. They sat like that for a while, neither of them wanting to break the spell. It was a magical night; Joanna would cherish it forever. So he didn't kiss her; everything else told her that he liked her, why else would he bring her flowers, take her to dinner, and go with her for a walk on the beach? You don't do things like that for just anybody. She couldn't wait to tell Maria to see what she thought about it. She looked up and saw a shooting star. She quickly made a wish. She wished for a baby boy, Giovanni's son.

All of a sudden she screamed. Giovanni came out of his dreaming state and asked her what was wrong.

"Something was crawling on my arm. I threw it away. It must have been a crab. Let's go Giovanni, I am sleepy."

"Before we go I want to ask you out for tomorrow. I want to take you out to Torrey Pines. There is a trail for hiking, which is very beautiful and underneath it there is a beach. We could have lunch, go swimming, fish a little, and just have a day outside. Don't say no; say yes."

"Yes," said Joanna with a little laugh. He was just a big boy; she couldn't disappoint him.

"I'll pick you up at nine. Is that ok?"

"That's fine."

They slowly walked back to Antonio's where the Jaguar was parked. When they got there they both took their shoes off and shook the sand off of them. It was nine o'clock. Antonio came towards them asking them to wait.

"So you were going to leave without saying goodbye?"

"I looked for you but I didn't see you. You know I wouldn't leave without saying goodbye. We were just going to come inside to look for you. We went for a walk on the beach."

"How was everything?"

"Just superb as usual."

"I want to invite both of you to my house so you can see my little boy. Promise me that you'll come."

"We will but not next week. Joanna is going to be out of town. I'll call you to find out when it's the best time for us to come over when she comes back. How's that?"

"That's fine. I wanted to offer you a liquor that I received from Italy. It's called '*limoncello*'. It's all the rave there."

"Maybe next time. I have to drive and if the cops stop us I'd be in trouble."

"As you wish, my friend. I'll see you in a couple of weeks."

They hugged and patted each other on the back. Antonio kissed Joanna's hand and told her he was delighted to have met her. Joanna blushed. She and Giovanni got in the car and waved to Antonio as they were leaving.

Joanna took the roses from the back seat and smelled them. They were fragrant. She found a little envelope. She opened it. It said: "To Joanna with love. Giovanni" Joanna took a deep breath; she was afraid that she'd wake-up and find out that it was all a dream. She bit her lip really hard. She was not dreaming, it was all true. On their way back to San Diego they didn't say much. Giovanni played a tape by Kenny Rogers, all love songs. The words of the songs were beautiful and both their hearts filled with love for one another. Joanna was silent but Giovanni didn't mind. He liked a woman who could keep quiet and didn't feel that she had to talk all the time like some women do. They just give you headaches. His mind was on tomorrow. He'd ask his mother to help him prepare a picnic basket for their lunch. He was going to see Joanna in a bathing suit. His heart raced at the thought. Was her body as beautiful as it appeared to be? He'd find out. She was going to see him in bathing shorts, also. He wasn't worried, his body was still young looking and his muscles were not sagging. He didn't look his age but much younger. Tomorrow was going to be a great day.

They were almost in San Diego.

"Did you have a good time, Cinderella?"

"Yes, I did. The best. Thank you so much Giovanni, for everything."

"Don't mention it. Thank you for going out with me."

"I am so sleepy. I wonder if Maria is still up. I can tell her we went out, right?"

"Yes, you can. She doesn't work at the restaurant, so it's all right."

They arrived at Maria's apartment. Joanna took the roses and her purse. She gave Giovanni a kiss on the cheek, said thank you again and left. Giovanni waited till she got inside the building then drove away.

Maria was up watching the news. As Joanna came in she whistled.

"Flowers, how romantic. You look great Joanna; where did you go?"

"To Del Mar, to one of Giovanni's friends' restaurant. Then we went for a walk on the beach. Maria do you think there is something wrong? He never tried to kiss me, not even once."

"No, I don't think there is anything wrong. Actually it is a good sign; that means he respects you and doesn't want to rush things. Did he touch you in any way?"

"We held hands while we were walking, he put his arm around my shoulders, and he held my hand at the restaurant for everybody to see. Does that mean he likes me?"

"Yes, it does. Why would he ask you out otherwise? He is fifty-five. He could be your father. A man of fifty-five has wisdom, he doesn't act like an irresponsible person. I am sure he has thought it all through and knows what he is doing. That slap on his face was the best thing you could have done for him. It must have shaken him up. I bet he won't kiss you again until you are engaged and ready to get married. I want to be the Maid of Honor and the godmother to your child. Promise me."

"I promise. I have a date with him tomorrow; we're going to Torrey Pines. Have you been there?"

"Yes, I have. The hike is beautiful. If I weren't so lazy I would have painted it. Gorgeous colors. Divine. You'll enjoy it."

"Maria, I borrowed your sweater, I hope you don't mind."

"I don't mind."

"About tomorrow, we're going swimming but I don't have a

bathing suit. Would you, by any chance, have a spare one that I could borrow?"

"My bathing suit is too big for you. I have one of my daughter' Elizabeth that you can borrow. It's a two-piece; you'll look great in it. Let me see if I can find it."

Maria got up and went to the storage room. Joanna heard her moving things around. It took her five minutes but she was smiling triumphantly when she came out holding a skimpy bathing suit of a brownish color.

"That's too small. I am too bashful to wear that, I'll be practically naked."

"Do you want this man, Joanna?"

"Yes, I do, you know that."

"Then wear this bikini. Show him what you got but don't let him have it. Not unless he marries you. That's the game, baby. We're talking about your future, the rest of your life. Go for it."

"All right, you convinced me, but I'll be blushing all over."

"No, you won't. Maybe at first you will but when you'll see the power you have you'll feel like a goddess. Let him melt in your presence, give him a thrill, make him feel young again."

"I can't wait until tomorrow. Can you put the alarm clock for seven-thirty tomorrow morning? I am afraid I will over-sleep without it."

"Yes, I'll do that. Don't worry Joanna everything is going to be just fine. Now let's go to bed and call it a night. I'll see you tomorrow."

"Can we say a little prayer before we do?"

"Sure." They both went to the shrine.

****

They left the car in the parking lot at the bottom of the hill. It was nine forty-five. They must have been the first ones there because there was no other car in the parking lot. Holding hands they started to walk up the hill. After about fifteen minutes climbing the ground leveled off. The vegetation was composed mostly of shrubs with wildflowers scattered here and there. Giovanni had brought a camera and he took two pictures of Joanna as they were climbing. She was wearing jeans and a pink halter top, which made her look very sexy. Giovanni was wearing kaki shorts and a white t-shirt.

Joanna gasped as they arrived on top of the hill. She knew now why Maria would have wanted to paint the scenery. It was beautiful. The colors were magnificent. The blue of the sky melting with the blue of the sea, the orange color of the exposed sides of the hills, the green of the shrubs, made a picture perfect postcard. Joanna asked Giovanni if he would take a picture of her in that spot. He did. Joanna had a huge smile on her face; she was happy, truly happy. What a great day it was. She thanked Giovanni for taking her there. He put his arm around her waist and gave her a kiss on the cheek.

"It does my heart good to see you smile. You're always so serious. I am glad you're here with me."

"So am I."

They kept on walking. There were benches along the path. After a while they decided to take a rest and sat down. The benches were situated so that the hikers would have a full view of the sea below. They both took deep breaths wanting to take everything in. They sat in silence not wanting to break the spell. It was almost a religious experience. In that moment Joanna felt closer to God as never before; she told Him in her mind how much she loved Him and thanked Him for everything. At the same time Giovanni was thankful to God for bringing Joanna into his life. He felt inebriated by the clean, fresh air, by the colors, and by the sound of the waves battering the rocks below.

"A penny for your thoughts," he said.

"Two pennies for yours," replied Joanna"

"I was thinking what a beautiful day this is and how happy I am to be here with you, Pumpkin. Are you as happy as I am?"

"More. I am unbelievably happy; I wouldn't have missed it for the world. How far down is this trail?"

"Just a couple hundred yards. Let's go, let's start walking again that way we can go down to the beach and have a scrumptious lunch. My mother prepared it."

"Uhm, I can't wait. All this fresh air has given me an appetite."

They walked down the trail and back. The way down was much easier and it didn't take them long to get to the bottom of the hill where the car was parked. Giovanni took out of the car a big cooler, which he handed to Joanna; a smaller cooler with wine and sodas inside; a blanket and a big tote bag with towels and suntan lotions. They took the whole lot to the beach, which was few yards away. By this time they were not the only ones around. Other cars were parked in the parking lot and there were about thirty people on the beach. They picked a spot near the rocks where Giovanni laid out the blanket, smoothing it away making sure no sand would get on it. Giovanni opened the big cooler. Inside there were sandwiches wrapped in aluminum foil. He handed one to Joanna and took another for himself. "What is it?" asked Joanna, unwrapping hers.

"*Eggplant Parmigiana*," replied Giovanni. "Eat it, it's good."

"Uhm, this is good. I got to ask your mother for the recipe."

"Better still, ask her to show you how to make it, it's one of my favorites."

Giovanni took two glasses out of the cooler and poured some red wine. They both drank. "When was the last time you went to the beach?"

"Many years ago, with the school. We went on a trip to Lake Superior in Minnesota. It was fun; I love the beach. I remember I got sunburned. By the way, do you have suntan lotion? I should really put some on. My skin is so fair that I sunburn really fast."

"Yes, Princess. It's in the tote bag."

Joanna pulled the suntan lotion out of the bag and put some on her face and neck. She handed the bottle to Giovanni when she was done. He put it aside.

"Aren't you going to put some on?"

"Later. I am a roughneck; my skin can take it. I don't want the smell on my hands till we're finished eating."

He took some pears and watermelon out of the cooler and offered some to Joanna. She ate with gusto enjoying the fresh taste. When they finished eating Joanna started to get nervous. Now they had to undress. She wondered if she could find an excuse not to, but no excuse would come to her mind. Giovanni took his T-shirt and shorts off. His body was taut and muscular and he looked even more handsome, if it were possible. He gave her a look as if to say "Well, aren't you going to take your clothes off?" and Joanna blushed, uncomfortably.

"Is something wrong?" asked Giovanni.

"No, why do you ask?"

"No reason. Do you have a bathing suit under your clothes?"

"Yes," said Joanna. She slowly removed her top and her jeans. She was afraid to look around. She felt all eyes on her, especially Giovanni's, as if she had just performed a striptease. She was gorgeous in a bathing suit and she was right, all eyes were on her. Her stomach was flat, her breast firm and her buttocks full. Giovanni could not believe his eyes. It was in that moment that he decided he was going to marry her.

"Lie on your stomach and I will put lotion on your back," he said. Joanna did as she was told, laying flat on her stomach. Giovanni squeezed a generous amount of lotion into his hand and applied it unto her back. He started from her neck and slowly worked his way down her body. Her skin was soft and smooth under his hand. He was a little intimidated when he got to her buttocks. Desire stirred within him, he could hardly contain himself. Surprising himself he said: "Will you marry me, Joanna?"

Joanna jumped up halfway. "Are you serious?" she asked.

"Yes, I am very serious. Will you marry me?"

"I wasn't expecting anything like this. Will you give me time to think about it?"

"Sure." He was disappointed. He continued to apply lotion. When he was finished Joanna rolled unto her back and applied the lotion unto the front of her body. She was giving sideways glances at Giovanni. She saw he was perturbed and felt sorry for him.

"I will let you know when I come back from Minneapolis," she said.

"Take your time, Pumpkin, I don't want to rush you into it."

They spent the next hour sunbathing, saying nothing. Joanna's mind was working overtime. She was under shock from what had just happened. Thinking positive thoughts, she saw herself married to Giovanni and carrying his baby. She knew all along she was going to say yes, but she wanted to wait a while to tell him so. She was very lucky; so many changes in her life in such a short time. Jesus was truly changing her life around.

Who would have said few weeks ago that she would be laying next to a rich, handsome man who would ask her to marry him. *Wait till I tell Maria*, she thought. Sweet Maria, she hoped that one day she could repay her.

Giovanni was immersed in his thoughts too. He was sexually aroused by his nearness to that goddess and he was glad that she was lying down so she wouldn't notice the bulge in his shorts. It had been a long time since he had felt this way. He wished to take her into his arms and make love to her, but this was hardly the place or the time. *"I hope she says yes,"* he told himself. *If she says yes, she won't be a dishwasher anymore. No woman of mine is going to do that. I will promote her to hostess while we're engaged and then to manager when we get married.* He felt sure in his heart that she was going to say yes so he relaxed languidly, baking in the sun, thinking of all the different ways he would make love to her, a virgin.

After a long while they decided to go for a swim to cool down. Giovanni swam far out leaving Joanna behind who could not swim. When he got back he splashed her, teasingly. They hugged each other enjoying the feeling of wet skin against wet skin. Joanna's firm breasts were pressing against Giovanni's chest bringing him to a paroxysm of desire. She didn't know the power she had over a man, which was dangerous. He wished she was already married to him and he told her so. She didn't reply, only smiled. When they got back on the beach he repeated the ritual of the suntan lotion on her back. He didn't want her to burn; besides he enjoyed doing it. This time, after he was done, Joanna put lotion on his back. She too felt a stirring within herself and rubbed lovingly, taking her time.

He hasn't told me he loves me yet, she thought. *Does he love me*, she wondered. *He must; why, he wouldn't ask me to marry him if he didn't. Jesus, I can hardly breathe. I am afraid that if I relax it's all going to disappear: Giovanni; Maria; the dishwashing job. I am afraid I'll end up back on the street with no friends, no home, no nothing. This is a dream but I don't want to wake up. Heavenly Father, hold me still, don't let me make any foolish mistake. I want to be happy because I have never known happiness. Let me make it up to myself. I deserve to be happy. All those years of sexual abuse; the loss of my brother and my mom; so much pain in my life; so much loneliness. Giovanni is a good man; give me a chance God. I want to make him so happy, even happier than he was with his first wife. I want to give him a child, a beautiful baby boy.*

"You can do the front too, if you like," said Giovanni.

"Uhm?" Joanna had been so lost in her thoughts she hadn't realized that she'd been rubbing his back for a good ten minutes.

"I am sorry, but you can do the front for now. I'll do it next time we come to the beach," she said hoping that there would be a next time.

"Okay Princess. I am going to hold you to it." Giovanni remained on his stomach. He didn't want to turn around because he was afraid she'd see how her massage had turned him on. Her touch was so gentle, so relaxing. He regretted having spoken. Who knows how long she would have massaged him if he hadn't said anything.

Oh, well, I guess I better take her to the beach again, as soon as she comes back from Minneapolis. A thought hit him. What if she decided not to come back? What then? *I guess I better hold my breath for the next week. She is so innocent; I don't want anything bad to happen to her. I will protect her; I'll be her knight in shiny armor. Hopefully I'll be her husband.*

"Giovanni, what would your mother say if we got married, would she approve?"

"She already has. She likes you, Joanna."

"I am so glad because I like her too. A lot. Do you think she would mind teaching me how to cook? Judging from the *eggplant parmigiana* she is a wonderful cook. I bet she could write a book about it. That's an idea, we could write a book together."

"I don't know. I'll ask her about it. I know she is very jealous of her recipes, but now that she is older she might be willing to share them. Plus it'll give her something to do. That's a good idea Joanna. I hope it works. What kind of food do you know how to cook?"

"Hardly any. I never really had to cook. Felicia always cooked for me, and now Maria is the one who always cooks, I just help her out every now and then."

"I can teach you how to cook too. Most all the food we serve at the restaurant comes from my recipes. I learned a lot from my mother."

"I'll take you up on it, Giovanni. It'll be a great pleasure to learn from you."

Joanna was rejoicing inside. She felt she was so close to having her own family; she was going to burst from happiness. But the fear of loosing it all stayed inside of her; she held her breath and let the fear go. *I will be happy,* she told herself.

"What you say we're going to see a movie tonight? If we leave now we'll have time to go home and get ready."

"I'd love that. I haven't been to a movie theater in ages. Yes, let's go."

They quickly gathered everything and left.

CHAPTER TWENTY-THREE

Maria was in the kitchen fixing her cappuccino. All of a sudden she felt two arms hugging her from behind.

"Congratulate me," said Joanna. "You are seeing the next Mrs. Grimaldi. Giovanni asked me to marry him."

"Oh, Joanna, that's wonderful! What a great news. When did it happen?"

"Yesterday, at the beach. I couldn't believe it when he asked. I thought he was going to flirt when I took my clothes off but instead, he asked me to marry him. I am so happy, you can't believe. I have to let him know when I come back from Minneapolis if I accept or not."

"You mean you haven't said yes yet?"

"No, I didn't want to give the wrong impression. If I said yes too quickly he might think I am after his money. Besides it'll be good to have few days to think about it. Mrs. Grimaldi, what a sweet sound."

"You're not going to change your mind, are you?"

"Not for anything in the world. I've been praying for this to happen. I am so happy. Thank you Maria, for everything. If it weren't for you none of this would have happened. I'll never forget it. By the way, he will take me to the airport Sunday. If you talk to him while I am gone please don't say anything about Raul and about me being homeless. I don't want anybody to know that part of my life, especially Giovanni. I don't mean to deceive him but I like to keep it between us only."

"Sure Joanna. I understand. I'd feel the same way too; it's very painful for you, isn't it?"

"Yes it is, very much so."

"I toast to the next Mrs. Grimaldi," said Maria lifting her cappuccino cup. "May she be the happiest woman in the world and may I be around to witness it."

"Hear, hear," replied Joanna. "I'll let you get ready now, or you'll be late for work. I'll go back to bed and dream."

Maria had been pleasantly surprised by the news. She had her own daydreaming about being the Maid of Honor and the godmother to their children. She loved Joanna and there wasn't an ounce of jealousy towards her friend, only good wishes. She was thinking of what present to buy, what dress to wear. She imagined they'd get married right away so she was already making plans.

Joanna went back to bed but she couldn't sleep. She kept quiet till Maria left for work. Once she was gone she got up and went to the shrine. She lit the candle and sat in the lotus position. She thanked God, Jesus and the Holy Spirit. She thought of her mother and wished she could talk to her now. She sent her love from her heart and wished that somehow it could reach her wherever she was. She also thought of her brother John. So many thoughts were going on in her mind overlapping each other. She too thought that they'd get married right away and she was thinking about her wedding dress. Who was going to walk her down the isle? Wouldn't Giovanni question it when Raul wouldn't be there? How would she justify his absence? Maybe Alfredo would substitute Raul. She might tell Giovanni the truth about Raul being in jail but she would only mention him molesting Jackie, not her. She'd tell him that she hadn't said anything before because she was too embarrassed, hoping he would understand.

Giovanni, her soon to be husband. What kind of magic was being spun in her life? Jesus was the answer. She decided she was going to fast and pray the whole day as a thank you to Jesus. Jesus encouraged fasting and praying to receive healing powers from the Father. She wanted healing powers mainly to heal herself and hopefully others too. I am so glad to be part of your family, she told Him aloud. Thank you; thank you for everything, sweet Lord. You are the answer to my prayers, please be in my life forever more. She closed her eyes. She had visions of herself and Giovanni on their honeymoon. It was going to be in an exotic island, the Caribbean maybe or Hawaii. She preferred Hawaii. Long days of sweet lingering, doing nothing but kissing and hugging and long nights full of passion.

She breathed deeply. She remembered Jill Thompson's advice and as she exhaled she mentally cast out of her body Raul and the horrible things he made her do. She mentally washed out her body. She soaped it all from head to toe, made a thick, rich lather, scrubbed till it hurt then rinsed it all off. The feeling of dirt didn't go away though. It would take a long time and lot of therapy for that to happen.

The therapy. How was she going to justify that to Giovanni? She would tell him that she needed it to resolve issues about the loss of her mother and brother and being adopted. She was sorry about deceiving him but she saw no way around it. He must never know, period.

She said a closing prayer, blew out the candle and went back to bed. This time she fell asleep right away.

****

She woke up around ten-thirty but she didn't get up. Instead she remained in bed and went over in her mind to the happenings of the last few days. She thought of Joe Bellagio and what would have happened had she accepted his offer. She would have surely lost Giovanni's respect and she would have become a kept woman. She would have had material things but she would have become a slave. Slave to a man she didn't love and didn't like physically. She would have had to quit her job and so she would have not been able to see Giovanni anymore. She shivered and mentally patted herself on the back for making the right decision. She would not see Joe Bellagio until she came back from Minneapolis and by that time she would be engaged. That thought relaxed her a little but not completely. Men like Joe Bellagio were dangerous. What if he had her followed and found out about Raul? She would be extra careful on her trip to Minneapolis and see if anybody was following her. She told herself she was being paranoid, that Joe didn't have that much power. Besides, Jesus would protect her; He would not allow him to harm her.

She took another deep breath. Took the fear that was inside of her and threw it straight across the room. No more fears. With Giovanni she was safe. He would be the father she never had. He would be the husband she never had. What was she worrying about? Everything was going to turn out just fine. Think positive, she told herself.

The whole of that day and for the rest of the week she felt light-headed. She saw Giovanni in a different light. He was her soon-to-be husband and she felt almost intimidated in his presence. She was not more critical, but she was more perceptive of his moods, actions and reactions. Every night, when he took her home, they would chat for a little while before she'd go. He wanted to know more about her, about her past. What job she'd had, what men she dated. Joanna was always evasive and making up stories. Stories she hoped he believed. Of course he had no clue about the tragedy of her life so he believed everything she said. Had Joanna known him better she would have confided in him. He was a kind, compassionate man and would have felt sorry for her. He might have been enraged about the molestation, though, being a very jealous, passionate person, so it was good that she didn't reveal it to him. They would part with a light kiss on the lips, which always left Joanna with a desire to kiss more and to linger.

****

Friday morning Maria woke Joanna up at nine o'clock. She told her that she was going to La Jolla to get the money from Vittorio, the Italian hairdresser.

"Weren't we supposed to go last Friday?" asked Joanna.

"Yes, we did, but Vittorio called and he said he was going to be out of town. He was going to San Francisco, so I postponed it. Anyway, are you going with me?"

"Yes, of course, I love to go. Just give me half-an-hour to get ready and we'll go."

Joanna showered and dressed really fast and soon they were on their way. They walked to Fourth and Broadway and there they caught the number 34 bus going to La Jolla. It was a long trip and Joanna and Maria barely spoke. Maria was meditating and Joanna was busy looking at the view. Past Pacific Beach there were rows of very expensive homes. Gardens were filled with trees and plants of every kind increasing the value of the properties. Joanna was fascinated by so much wealth. Where did those people get the money? She would have loved to live in one of those houses. The colors were incredible, with the blue of the ocean in the background. Maybe once she and Giovanni got married she could convince him to move to La Jolla. She was still worried that somehow he would find out about Raul so she didn't make any more plans for the future. She was afraid that if he'd find out he would leave her so she was protecting herself from future disappointments.

Maria pulled the cord to request the bus stop. They got off at Prospect and walked towards the ocean. The salon was located at the corner of the street. It had a pink awning with the word "Bellissima" imprinted on it. As they approached Maria saw Vittorio outside, sitting on a bench, smoking a cigarette and talking to his girlfriend. She pointed him out to Joanna. When they approached Vittorio said: "*Signora, che piacere,*" and kissed her on both cheeks. Then he saw Joanna.

"Aren't you going to introduce me to your friend?" he said.

"Joanna, this is Vittorio. Vittorio this is Joanna," she said.

Joanna was impressed by Vittorio's looks and understood why Maria might have had a crush on him when she first met him. His hair was black, combed back and his eyes were green. In a way he reminded her of Giovanni but she decided that Giovanni was more handsome. He was dressed all in black and wore very expensive cologne. He talked to them ignoring his girlfriend. She was blonde, tall and very pretty. She didn't seem perturbed at all by the fact that he was talking to two women. He was a flirt and she was probably used to it. The receptionist came outside and told her that her next appointment had arrived so she put out her cigarette and went inside. She was a hairdresser too.

Vittorio was talking on his cellular phone so Maria and Joanna sat on the bench, patiently waiting for him to finish the conversation.

"I bet you he's going to keep me waiting for a couple of hours before he gives me the money. He always does that. He will wait for the moment when he thinks that no one is looking and then he will furtively put the check in my purse. He is paranoid that someone will find out that he owes me money and loose face. He is right, though. He wouldn't look too good if people found out that he takes money from women. I just find it exhausting having to come all the way here, having to wait hours for him to decide when it's the right moment then having to head back, waiting half-an-hour for the bus. It would be so easy and so simple if he just mailed me the money, you know?"

"I agree. It would bother me too," replied Joanna, sympathetically. "Can't he give you all the money he owes you in a lump sum?"

"No. He is always broke. He lives from week to week. He owes money to lot of people. I don't like him anymore. I think that more than not liking him I don't respect him. I never could respect men who use women. I think he uses his looks to entice people to do his bidding. That's despicable. Let's talk about something else. He's finished talking on the phone. By the way, you don't know anything about the money."

"Sure, no problem," replied Joanna. "We can't wait too long though, Maria. We got to get back in time for me to go to work."

"So, signora, how are you doing?" asked Vittorio, sitting on the bench next to Maria and Joanna and lighting a cigarette.

"I am doing fine, Vittorio. By the way, we can't stay too long," said Maria, hoping that he would get the hint.

"Would you like an espresso coffee?" he asked Maria and Joanna.

"Yes, sure."

Vittorio went inside the salon and told the receptionist to order three espresso coffees. He went back outside and lit another cigarette. His cellular phone was ringing so he got up and answered the call. He was gesticulating as he was talking and walking back and forth, looking important. Maria couldn't stand it. She just wanted her money and leave instead of having to endure that torture for the next couple of hours. The espresso coffees arrived. Vittorio, still on the phone, paid for them. Maria and Joanna sugared their coffees and sipped them slowly. Maria lit a cigarette and inhaled deeply.

"He is going to do this for a couple of hours. He's going to parade in front of us like a peacock, showing off and trying to look like an important businessman. It's all a show and for our benefit. He's broke and his business is not that great. Why don't we go for a walk, Joanna; I want to show you the La Jolla Cove and the beach. It's truly beautiful and besides, it will make time go faster."

"I'd love that, Maria. Let's go."

Maria told Vittorio, who was still on the phone and hadn't touched his coffee yet that she and Joanna were going for a walk. He gestured that it was all right and that he'd see them when they got back. Maria headed the way and Joanna followed.

They crossed the street and walked downhill to the La Jolla Cove. The view was spectacular. Sea lions were lying on the rocks below, as the seawater would splash against them. A multitude of birds were perched on the rocks and every once in a while would take flight passing over their heads. The air was crisp and clean and they both breathed deeply. Words were not necessary as both of them were engrossed with their thoughts.

Joanna was thinking that it would be nice to share the view with Giovanni and that she'd like to come back with him. Maria was thinking about painting the scenery and was looking at it in terms of colors, dark, light, and in-between.

Nature was a mystical experience for Maria. It was at those times that she felt closer to God and prayers would flow freely from her heart. Being an artist, she always felt inspired, and colors could really give her a high. She was always painting in her mind, always looking at colors with the eyes of an artist, always studying.

They stood there, silent, for a good while. Other people came to look at the view and broke the magic spell. They walked away from the Cove towards west. There was a little beach down below and they stopped to watch the beachgoers as they swam, scuba dived or just lay in the sun. They sat on a bench and just smiled at each other.

"Thank you for taking me here, Maria. This is truly beautiful."

"Isn't it so? The whole of California is this beautiful. I feel very lucky to live here, and we don't have to pay to see it."

"When did you come to San Diego, Maria?"

"In 1987. I was living in Hawaii at the time. George and I had already gotten a divorce in 1985. The Navy transferred him to San Diego, and he took Elizabeth with him. I had legal custody of Elizabeth but she chose to go with her dad. I didn't want to force her to stay with me so I let her go. It was hard. The day she left I was supposed to go with them to the airport but I felt so sick inside that I couldn't go. I said good-bye at the door of my apartment when they came to pick me up. Elizabeth was very sad and her face was pale. It broke my heart. Sometime later, Elizabeth told me that the Navy might send George to the Persian Gulf and that she might have to stay with me. She was afraid to fly by herself so I told her that I was going to move to San Diego. It was a brave thing for me to do. I left a good job and came here not knowing anybody, only George and Elizabeth. I stayed with them until I found a job and was able to take care of myself. The Navy didn't send George to the Gulf so I moved for nothing. On top of that George met someone and moved in with her. I rented a studio on Front Street, which was much closer to my job. As a matter of fact I was living right across from where Giovanni lives with his mom. Isn't that something? At any rate, Lisa, George's girlfriend didn't like me. She wouldn't even tell me where my daughter was going to school. One day I called her and asked her for Elizabeth's teacher's name. She wouldn't give it to me. She said: 'Why don't you leave her alone. Haven't you done her enough harm already?' I fell from the clouds as I realized that George must have been telling her lies about me. He was good at that. When I met him he told me horror stories about the woman he'd been living with before he met me. At any rate, after I hung up I called the police and told the policewoman what had happened. Bless her soul, she told me that since I had the custody I could take Elizabeth to come live with me, and if they refused to let her go, to just give the police a call and they would make sure she'd go with me. Encouraged by that I called George and told him that as of a certain date Elizabeth was coming to stay with me. He agreed without any fuss, so I was able to spend as much time with my daughter as I wanted to. I moved her to a school nearby and she made friends with some kids across the street.

We were happy in our little studio, just her and me. I was able to help her with her schoolwork and she improved a lot. Plus, she wasn't having any more nightmares."

"You had it rough, didn't you?"

"Yes, but I survived. And I am doing so much better now. I have a good job; my own place; I see a therapist; and I am taking better care of myself. Let's go back to the salon and see if Vittorio will give me the money. I hate this, having to wait around for so long, watching him showing off for my benefit."

They got up and slowly walked up the hill back to Bellissima. Vittorio was outside talking on his cell phone. He smiled at them as they approached. When they sat on the bench he sat next to Maria and furtively put the folded check inside her purse. Maria resisted the temptation to take it out and look at it. She lit a cigarette blowing the smoke away from Joanna. Vittorio lit a cigarette also and hung up the phone.

"So, signora, what has been happening with you? Is your job ok? How about your friend, who is she and how come I never met her before?"

"You haven't met her before because we just met few weeks ago. She is staying with me at my apartment until she can afford a place of her own. What's been happening with you? How is your business?"

"Oh, I have lot of problems. Things are delivered damaged and Customs is holding one of the shipments. Plus I have people staying at my place and I don't have a minute to myself. I can't wait till they leave but I can't just kick them out. They're business associates."

"Well, just hang in there Vittorio. We have to go now. I'll see you next month," said Maria kissing Vittorio on both cheeks.

"Goodbye signora. Don't say anything about the money to your friend," he whispered in her ear.

"Don't worry, I won't," lied Maria, pitying him.

They took leave and walked to the bus stop. "Thankfully it didn't take him very long to give me the check. Other times I have to wait for hours." Maria took the check out of her purse and looked at it. He had made it for $150, she noticed. Normally he would give her $100. Satisfied and frustrated at the same time she put it back in her purse.

The ride back to town was livelier than before. Joanna told Maria how scared she was about going to Minneapolis to testify against Raul. She also spoke about marrying Giovanni and becoming Mrs. Grimaldi. Maria let her talk, listening quietly. She was very sympathetic knowing that the trial ahead of her was complicated. *Poor Joanna*, she thought. *It's hard to be in her position but her life is definitely getting better. If she marries Giovanni she will be better off than me, but I don't mind. I am happy for her.*

Joanna's face was suntanned and it was very lovely especially when she'd talk about becoming Mrs. Grimaldi. She was very innocent, as a child would be and Maria felt sorry for her, knowing that in few days she would have to expose to strangers private, intimate matters. *That's all for the good*, she thought. *Once this is out of the way she'll be able to put it all behind and start afresh. She'll dedicate herself to Giovanni and start her own family, without any ghosts from her past, but Giovanni must never know. It would be a disaster if he did.*

"I wish I could come to the airport to see you off, but it is better that you go with Giovanni. He might want some time alone with you. I know it's only for a week but to him it will feel like months."

"I agree. He is so romantic. I bet you he will bring me flowers and candies. I can't stand to be away from him even for a day. A week is going to be very long for me too. I am just so sorry that I have to lie to him but there is no other way, don't you agree?"

"Oh, yes. I think it is very wise of you not to tell him anything. As far as I am concerned, my lips are sealed. Your secret is safe with me."

"Maria, you are the best friend I ever had. I don't know what I'd do without you. I will keep you in my prayers the rest of my life. Thank you for bringing me to Jesus; I feel so much stronger because of that, you wouldn't believe."

"I am much stronger because of Him too. You know, it's funny but I spent five years with the nuns and many other years in the Catholic Church but I never fully understood about Jesus and His redeeming powers. It took a big crisis in my life and feeling that I was lost to make me realize how powerful He is. It feels so good to be ready of all that guilt the Devil was making me feel, even for things I hadn't done. It's so liberating sometimes I just want to scream."

"I feel the same way. I don't feel guilty about Raul anymore. If I make a mistake I just ask Him to forgive me and I move on. Thank God for Jesus. Amen."

****

Sunday morning Joanna and Maria had been invited to go to church with Giovanni and his mother again. Maria declined because she wanted to give them as much time together as possible, so Joanna went without her. Mrs. Grimaldi looked lovely in a light blue, silk dress. Her accessories were a necklace and earrings of real pearls, a gift from Giovanni. She gave Joanna a warm smile as she entered the car. The Mass was an hour long. Joanna was on one side of Giovanni and his mother was on the other side. He felt real proud to be with two beauties. He looked very handsome himself. They held hands when the Lord's Prayer was recited. Giovanni kept Joanna's hand in his, after the prayer ended, and gave her a smile that made her weak in the knees.

I feel so lucky, Lord, Joanna prayed. *Please don't let it be just a dream. I want to make this man the happiest in the world; please let me.* She couldn't wait for next week to go by. Her anxiety was at a peak level, but she forced herself to appear calm so that Giovanni would not suspect anything. After the Mass Joanna had to decline Mrs. Grimaldi's offer to go to her house because she had to go home and finish to pack her meager belongings. She asked Maria if she could borrow her suitcase and a couple of sweaters. She packed in fifteen minutes.

When Giovanni came to pick her up, she was ready. She had worn her black dress with one of Maria's sweaters and she looked glamorous. As she entered the car Giovanni gave her seven red roses, one rose for each day she was going to be away, and a box of candies for Felicia. Joanna gave him a kiss on the lips, to thank him. They drove quietly to the airport holding hands the whole time. She only had one bag so it didn't take her long to check-in. They still had one hour before the flight so they went to the airport restaurant since they had not eaten yet. There was sadness in both their faces as they gave each other intense looks. They seemed lost and barely spoke. As the meal was over Giovanni asked for her telephone number.

"I am going to call you every day, Pumpkin," he said.

"Call me at night. We might be out during the day. Plus we can talk more at night."

"I'll call you from my office at the nightclub."

"I'll miss you, Giovanni."

"I'll miss you too. Think about my proposal while you're away, will you?"

"I will. I promise."

They walked out of the restaurant and went towards gate number 23. As the passengers started to board the airplane Giovanni took Joanna solidly in his arms and gave her a long, passionate kiss. "I love you," he said almost choking on the words.

"I love you too, Giovanni," and she was gone.

Giovanni walked out of the airport. He looked like a whipped dog. For a moment he didn't even remember where his car was parked. When he finally found it he sat there for fifteen minutes before he found the strength to move on. Never in his life had he been affected by a woman so much that he found it even hard to breathe. His chest muscles were all contracted and he felt a great pain in his heart. He directed the car towards his mother's house. He found her sitting in her bedroom watching television.

"So, is she gone?"

"Yes mom, she's gone."

"When will she get back?"

"Sunday, a week from today." Giovanni sat next to his mother on the couch. "I saved you your lunch if you are hungry. You left without eating anything and you didn't even have breakfast this morning."

"I am sorry mom, but we ate at the airport. I'll eat tonight when I come home."

"You miss her, don't you?"

"I can't lie to you, you see everything. Yes, I do miss her and I hope that while she's gone she misses me too and decides to marry me. I proposed to her but she said she needed time to think about it.

She'll let me know when she comes back."

"I hope she says yes. I want to see my grandchild before the good Lord takes me to be with Him."

"You will, mother, you will. I just know she's going to say yes, mark my words."

"Aren't you going to the restaurant?"

"Later. I want to take a nap first. They don't need me at the restaurant; I could be gone the whole year and business would be as usual. I just retire for a couple of hours, I'll see you later." Giovanni gave his mother a kiss on her forehead and went to his room. He lay on the bed without taking his clothes off. He put one arm under his head and stared at the ceiling. All he could see was Joanna's face. *How lovely she is*, he thought, *and so innocent, a virgin. I am a lucky man.* His eyes felt heavier and he was soon asleep.

****

Joanna ordered some wine to help her relax. She sipped it slowly; it wasn't as good as Giovanni's wine but it was all right. She quietly shed some tears looking outside the window. An older lady was sitting next to her, but she was snoring and didn't see her crying. The flight went smoothly all the way to Minneapolis. As they got closer her anxiety increased. She ordered some more wine. It did help her a little, and by the time they landed she felt light headed, almost happy. She wondered if she would recognize Felicia. Ten years had passed, who knows what she looks like now. She had changed too, no doubt. Would Felicia recognize her? She needn't worry; Felicia held a big sign with "Joanna Ruiz" written in big letters. She saw her immediately. She had changed; her hair was gray and she was wearing glasses. She was five inches shorter than Joanna and Joanna had to bend a little to hug her.

"Joanna, thank God you're here. Was your flight okay?"

"Yes, mom, it was fantastic, very smooth."

"Let's go get your bags and then let's go home. My, you look great, what have you done with yourself?" Felicia couldn't take her eyes off of her. She had left a young girl, and she was back a grown woman.

"I cut my hair, mom, that's all."

"You look so grown up. I've changed too; my hair is all gray and I have wrinkles on my face and neck. How do you find me?

"Beautiful as ever. Oh, by the way, my boss sends you this," said Joanna, handing her the box of candies.

"Do I hear wedding bells? Why would your boss send me anything unless he was taken with you?"

"I can't hide anything from you, can't I?"

"No, you sure can't. Tell me everything on our way home."

Joanna's baggage finally came around. She lifted it easily since it was light, and they were on their way, to the parking lot. Felicia's car was an old, white Sedan, four doors. They put the baggage in the back seat. Joanna kept the roses on her lap.

"Another gift from your boss?" said Felicia pointing at the roses.

"Yes, mom. He asked me to marry him and I have to let him know when I get back. What do you think, should I marry him?"

"Yes, you should. If you marry him I could finally rest and stop worrying about you. You have no idea how much I worried every-day these past ten years you've been away, wondering around the country."

"I am sorry, mom. I didn't mean to give you pain, but I just couldn't come home. You understand, don't you?"

"Yes, dear child, I understand. I just wish you had told me about it. I would have protected you."

"What would you have done, locked my bedroom door? Raul is a sick man. He would have found a way to do it anyway. But what's done is done; when this week is over we won't have to worry anymore. The monster will be behind bars, maybe for the rest of his life. I bet he pleaded innocent, didn't he? He will be shocked when he'll see me on the witness stand. So far he thinks he only has to worry about the little girl he molested. He has no clue that I'll be there. I am going to impress the look on his face in my mind so that I'll never forget it, as long as I live. This must be terribly hard on you, Felicia, how are you coping?"

"Oh, I sit on the couch and cry. I am so ashamed that I don't go out for my walks anymore. I don't want the neighbors to see me.

Even though I have a good reputation this terrible thing has brought shame on the house and everything in it, including me."

Felicia was a good driver. Even though the conversation was painful she kept a close eye on the road. It was late at night and there were few cars on the streets. Half an hour later they arrived at Felicia's house.

"Here we are. Is the house as you remember it or does it look older? We just had it painted last year."

"The house looks as I remember. Do you still have a vegetable garden? I'd love to see it tomorrow."

"You will. Here let me help you with your bag. Give me the roses and your purse."

Once inside the house Joanna went straight to her bedroom. She was surprised to find it exactly as she had left it ten years earlier. It was clean and dust free. The bedcover was the same, so were the books, the nightstand, her closet, and the pictures on the dresser drawer. Amazing. She went to Felicia and gave her a hug. "Thank you for loving me, Felicia. This is so touching. In ten years you have kept my room exactly as I left it. You must have wanted me to come home badly, didn't you?"

"Yes, dear child. I waited every day."

"What is it that smells so good? Don't tell me that you made my favorite dish?"

"Yep. Beef stew with carrots and potatoes, just the way you like it. Let's go heat it up and have us a nice meal."

They went into the spacious kitchen. Felicia turned the stove on to warm up the beef stew while Joanna set the table. She got a bottle of red wine and poured some for her, some for Felicia. Giving her the glass she proposed a toast. "To my coming home," she said. "Yes, blessed be today when I got to see my daughter again," said Felicia.

She kissed Joanna on the cheek and Joanna kissed her back.

"I only have one week. It's going to go by in no time, we got to make the most of it."

The beef stew was ready. Felicia served Joanna a generous portion. They ate slowly, savoring every bite. "Tell me more about your boss, what is he like?"

"He is very kind and very generous. He paid me for today also even though I didn't work. He is very handsome and very rich. He treats me with respect and is very much in love with me. I don't know how you're going to feel about this, but he is twenty-seven years older than I am but he doesn't look his age."

"I don't mind, Joanna. Maybe a mature man is what you need. At least he will be able to provide well for you and I will be able to rest. Have you told him anything about Raul?"

"No, mom, I am too ashamed."

"How are you going to keep him from finding out? When you get married he won't be there; what are you going to tell him?"

"I'll tell him after we get married; not right away. Hopefully I'll get pregnant soon after; that would put everything into perspective. He will be so excited about the baby that nothing else will matter. You know, his wife died five years ago of breast cancer. They didn't have any children. If I have a child with him the baby's future will be assured. I don't exactly know how rich he and his mom are, but I know they are wealthy. His father is no longer alive and he is the only child, so I know my baby's future will be secure, and mine too."

"Praise God. All my prayers are answered as far as you're concerned."

"Mom, do you believe in Jesus Christ?"

"Yes, of course."

"Then how come you never thought me about Him and you never took me to church?"

"Raul was against it. I used to wonder why but now I know. He had the Devil inside of him."

"He must have. How embarrassing this week is going to be. I bet all your neighbors are going to be in the courtroom. I wish I could wear a veil on my face. Where were you when he molested the little girl?"

"I was at the store buying grocery. I wish I hadn't gone. None of this would have happened."

"Mom, please don't blame yourself. He is a sick man. He would have found another opportunity to do what he did. People like him should not be allowed to live in society. They need to be locked up.

I feel sorry for you, but you have no need to be ashamed. You haven't done anything wrong."

"Would you like more beef stew?"

"Oh, yes please, mom." Felicia took Joanna's plate and went to the stove. She filled her plate again.

"Here, eat to your heart's content. I am so happy that you're here you can't imagine."

"Mom, tell me about your garden; what do you have growing?"

"I have tomatoes, lettuce, zucchini, eggplants, artichokes, hot peppers, herbs, you know, the usual. Tomorrow, when we come back from court I'll give you a tour."

"I love gardening. I hope we're going to have a big garden, Giovanni and I. Right now he lives with his mom. Should I suggest that we live with her or should we move to a place of our own?"

"I think you should find out what he wants to do first, before you make up your mind. If his mother is old he might not want her to live by herself. Just hear him out and then decide."

The phone rang. "Who could be at this hour?" said Felicia. "It's Giovanni, I bet you."

Felicia went to the living room to answer the phone. She came back five minutes later.

"It's for you, Cinderella," she said. Joanna blushed all excited and went to the phone. Half an hour later she went to the kitchen to find it all clean.

"Oh mom, I was going to help you. Why didn't you wait for me?"

"I was bored. I didn't have anything to do. We better go to bed, the trial starts tomorrow, we don't want to be late."

"You're right, as usual. I love you, mom."

"I love you too, dear child."

"Oh, mom, why were you on the phone for so long? What did you talk about?"

"Well, he introduced himself after I told him I was not Cinderella, then we just chatted. He wanted to know how the weather was, and how was my arthritis. You should have warned me. He thinks I am sick."

"Oh, my! I forgot. Did you give it away?"

"No, I understood right away and I played along. So, you're here to take care of your sick mother, you rascal."

"I am sorry mom, I didn't know what to tell them."

"Well, he is a very nice man, I approve of him."

"I am glad. Good night, mom." Joanna gave Felicia a hug and went to her room. She took a shower, put on her nightgown and slid under the covers. The linen smelled freshly laundered and she breathed deeply. Images of the day overlapped in her mind and she was soon asleep.

Monday morning Felicia woke Joanna up at six o'clock. Joanna's eyes wouldn't open and she had to drag herself out of bed. Freshly brewed coffee was on the stove. She poured herself a cup and sat at the kitchen table. She was wearing a robe from ten years earlier. It surprised her to find out that she hadn't gained any weight. The house was as she remembered; hardly anything had changed. She went to the window to look at the backyard. She could see rows of tomato plants and other vegetables growing. The garden was neat and well tended. Birds were eating seeds from a bird's house hanging from a tree. She watched them fascinated just as she had many years before.

"You know mom, if Giovanni hadn't asked me to marry him I would stay. It is so peaceful here."

"You're welcome to stay if things don't work out for you in San Diego. Maybe after you get married you can come to visit me for a longer period. Then you won't have to work."

"Oh mom, you're wrong. I'll be working more, helping Giovanni take care of the business. Plus there would be the house to take care of. I'll see if we can hire a maid to do the house chores. Mrs. Grimaldi is very independent, I am sure she can take care of herself. You know, I was thinking. Why don't you sell the house and come to live with us in San Diego?"

"Oh child, I appreciate your offer but this is my home. Everything in this house reminds me of something from the past. If I leave I'll be lost."

"We'll see. Maybe if you have a grandchild to take care of you won't mind leaving this behind. At any rate, you'll come to visit, won't you?"

"Yes, most definitely! How do you want your eggs?"

"Soft, on toast, please."

After they had their breakfast they went to their room to get dressed. At nine o'clock sharp they were at the courthouse in room number twelve where the trial was to take place. From what Joanna had gathered from Felicia the defense had no idea that she was going to testify. It was going to be a surprise move from the prosecution, and what a surprise.

A door opened and Raul, escorted by a guard was brought in. His dark skin looked pale and his face drawn. He looked much older than Joanna remembered. She didn't feel sorry for him and did not return his smile. Felicia tensed up as she saw him and didn't smile either. A puzzled look crossed his face at their reaction, a look that turned into worried. He exchanged few words with his lawyer and then looked at them again. He waved his hand and they nodded to acknowledge it, but no smile. His presence alone angered Joanna. The slime; he had no shame, no remorse and no sense of decorum. She wanted to assault him, to beat him with her fists and bloody his face; she wanted to castrate him. You ruined my life; she wanted to yell. I'll have no mercy on you, as God is my witness.

The judge came in and the trial started. Joanna wasn't called to testify that day. It wasn't till Wednesday that she finally was called to the witness stand. She poured out her heart. She talked about her childhood; how she was adopted; how she lost her mother and her brother; and how Raul had molested her all those years. She was crying as she recounted her story. Some women in the jury were crying also, and so were some of the spectators. Learning the details of her molestation broke Felicia's heart; it was in that moment that she stopped loving him. She would throw out of the house everything that reminded her of him. He was a monster. He deserved to rot in jail the rest of his life. No mercy for you Raul, no mercy.

After her testimony Joanna and Felicia left the courtroom. They didn't go back for the remainder of the trial. On Friday the lawyer from the prosecution called them. The jury had reached a verdict in less than one hour. Their vote was unanimous: Seventeen years in prison without the possibility of parole. "He's going to die in prison," said Felicia. Joanna did a pirouette around the living room.

She was elated. The monster could never touch her again. They decided they needed to celebrate. They had been working in the garden all morning and when the phone had rung they'd been drinking lemonade in the kitchen. They put away the garden tools and went to take a shower. They dressed real nice, put on make-up and looked at each other approvingly. "We should go to a fancy restaurant. What do you say?"

"I say, let's go for it, mom."

"How about Maselli, the Italian restaurant?"

"Mom, are you sure we can afford that?"

"No, but who cares. What we've been through deserves a treat, so let's do it."

So they went to eat at Maselli's, one of the top-rated restaurants in town. The elegant waiters treated them like royalty. They sat at a table near a water fountain adorned by plants and statues. It felt so good, so refreshing. They ended the meal with a *Tiramisu* and espresso coffee. They hadn't said one word about Raul through the whole meal. They were there to celebrate and to kill that ache they felt inside their hearts. Joanna was very excited. She monopolized the conversation. She told Felicia about Maria, Alfredo, Giovanni; about her job, her therapist, the dentist. She reminded Felicia of a little girl who's about to go to a splendid destination. She wished she were going with her. *I am too old,* she thought, *I'd just be in her way. I'll go visit her as often as I can.*

When the meal was over they left the waiter a generous tip and walked out.

"I want to buy you a present, Joanna. Tell me what you want and I'll get it for you."

"Oh, let's see. A sweater, I need a sweater. I borrowed Maria's to bring with me. That reminds me, I should buy a present for Maria. She's been so good to me, that's the least I can do."

"I agree. I'd love to meet Maria and thank her for what she's been doing for you. Next time you come to visit bring her along. She's always welcome in my house, or I should say 'our house'. It is as much yours as it is mine. That reminds me, I have to change the will. Everything will go to you when I die. Raul will surely die in jail; his heart is in bad shape. He's sixty now, he won't get out till he's seventy-seven. I don't think he'll last that long, praise God."

"Mom, if I marry Giovanni I am going to be a rich woman. Maybe we can sell this house and buy you a better one in San Diego. I'll tell Giovanni that you need to live where the sun shines all year long because of your arthritis. The weather there is perfect for you. You're not going to miss the cold and the snow, I promise you, plus you can become friend with Giovanni's mother, maybe even move in with her."

"God bless you, child. I need time to think about it. I feel so old, I am going to feel lonely when you leave."

"I'll call you every week, I promise," said Joanna with tears in her eyes.

They reached JC Penney and went inside. Joanna bought a black cashmere sweater for herself, which Felicia paid for, and she bought Maria a pair of gold earrings. When they got home Joanna asked Felicia if she needed help with cleaning or other chore but Felicia told her that she was fine. She was very healthy and kept the house immaculate. They went to Joanna's room. They opened a drawer full of photographs and Joanna asked permission to take some with her.

"Of course, child. They are yours. Take them all if you like, just leave me some to remember you by," said Felicia starting to cry.

"What's wrong, mom? Please tell me."

"I am sorry. It's the tension I've been under all this week and the thought of you leaving. It's more than I can bear."

"We'll be all right, mom, I know. Pretty soon I hope to call you letting you know when I am getting married and pretty soon after that to let you know that you're going to be a grandmother."

The doorbell rang. Joanna went to answer it since Felicia was not presentable. She opened the door and was faced by a group of six women, all neighbors including the mother of the little girl who'd been molested. Joanna let them in. One of them spoke: "We heard about the verdict and we're pleased about it. We're proud of you for speaking the truth. We've been praying all week at the church and God answered our prayers through you. Is your mama home? We need to talk to her."

"I'll get her, just a minute."

Joanna came back with Felicia whose eyes were red from crying.

"Felicia, we are so sorry about everything that's happened. We want you to know that we're not holding any grouches against you. You are a good woman. We've known you for years and you've always been the perfect neighbor. We want to invite you to our church this Sunday and every Sunday after that. Please say that you'll come."

"Oh, I'd love to, but not this Sunday. I have to take my daughter to the airport. She's going back to San Diego. I feel honored that you've asked me, I haven't been to church since the day I got married. Thank you! I am so sorry too for what has happened," she said looking at the mother of the molested child. She came forward and gave her a hug. Everybody was crying and hugging including Joanna. When the six women left Joanna and Felicia sat on the couch holding hands, without speaking, for a long time. Finally Joanna said: "God is great. Can't you see how He is pulling you towards Him? Now you won't be lonely anymore. Those church-women keep pretty busy all the time. Now I can leave and not worry about you. You're in good hands, God's hands."

"Praise God."

They spent the rest of the day chatting and watching television. Next day, Saturday, they went through all of Joanna's clothes. She tried them all and they all fit her. She hadn't gained an ounce since she was eighteen. She put aside those that were still fashionable and put back in the closet those that weren't. She needed to borrow another piece of baggage from Felicia so she'd have enough room to carry everything back with her. They went to buy some photo albums and spent the rest of the day arranging the pictures in them and drinking coffee. Felicia had made a cake so instead of dinner they had cake and coffee.

Sunday morning they got up real early. All Joanna had to do was getting dressed. She had taken a shower the night before. On their way to the airport they spoke tenderly to each other, express-ing concern for one another's well being while they were apart. They made promises to keep in touch more often and to write. They both felt like new women, free and lighthearted. A whole new life was opening in front of them, Felicia with the church and her neighbors and Joanna with being Mrs. Grimaldi. She couldn't wait to get to San Diego and let Giovanni know that she accepted his proposal.

The goodbyes were sad and tearful. Felicia hugged Joanna really tight and Joanna dried her tears, which were copiously flowing down her cheeks.

"Take care mom," she said looking at her in the eyes, hoping that she'd see how much she loved her.

"Take care daughter, keep in touch." One last look and Joanna was gone.

Giovanni had kept his promise. He had called her every night that week, from his office at the nightclub. Lying back in her seat she mentally went over all the conversations they had on the phone, how tender he had been. Of course she had to lie but she tried to keep the conversation about them and not about her family so that the lying would be minimal. Few more hours and she would see him again, kiss him again, and embrace him again. Giovanni.

CHAPTER TWENTY-FOUR

The plane landed safely at the San Diego airport. A big applause accompanied the landing and everybody let out a sigh of relief. Joanna was one of the first to get off the plane. She searched the crowd of relatives and friends waiting for the passengers to disembark, and then she saw him. He was standing a little back, a bouquet of roses in his hand. Joanna walked towards him with a big smile on her face. He embraced her and gave her a full kiss on the mouth.

"For you, Cinderella, how was your trip?"

"Just fine, Giovanni, and thank you for the roses. You are spoiling me."

"Nothing is too good for you."

"How is your mom?"

"She's fine. She sends you her regards."

"My mom sends you her regards too. She approves of you, and she thinks you're going to be a great husband."

"Are you telling me you're going to marry me?"

"Yes, Mr. Grimaldi. I'd be honored to be your wife if you'll have me."

Giovanni stopped and took her in his arms. "You won't regret it Joanna. This calls for a celebration, but first things first. We go tell my mom, and then we'll go out and celebrate. What would you like to do?"

"Well, we could go have dinner at some place romantic and then go for a walk by Seaport Village, by the water. What do you say?"

"I say fine. Your wish is my command."

They went by the baggage section to pick up her luggage. Giovanni noticed that she had two pieces instead of one so she told him that she had brought more clothes and photographs with her. He told her that he wanted to see the photographs.

"What about tomorrow? We can go to the La Jolla Cove and see them there."

"It's a date, Pumpkin. Let's go."

He grabbed the two pieces of luggage and put them on the cart. They drove to Mrs. Grimaldi's house holding hands the whole time.

"Mom we're home," yelled out Giovanni.

"I'm in the bedroom son. Come in."

"Congratulate us mom, we're engaged and we're going to get married."

"Well, congratulations, my son. Joanna I am very pleased. I hope you two can get married soon and give me a grandchild before I die."

"Hello' Mrs. Grimaldi, we'll do our best."

"I'll call Father Luciano at Saint Joseph's Cathedral to set up an appointment. That's where you'll get married, right?"

"Actually I was thinking of Our Lady of the Rosary Church, if you don't mind. I'll be happy if we can get married there," answered Giovanni.

"I don't see any problem. I'll just call Father Anselmo and set up an appointment with him. There might be some problems because Joanna is not Catholic but I am sure that they have provisions for that."

"Ok mom, if you make an appointment make it for Tuesday. We are busy tomorrow. Say, we're going out for dinner, would you like to come along?"

"Are you kidding? You two need time alone to know each other. Besides, I would just be in the way."

"Oh no, Mrs. Grimaldi, we'd be happy if you came along."

"Thank you children, but I already cooked my dinner. Besides I am a little tired, but thanks anyway, I appreciate the thought."

"Well, we'll be off then. Bye mom, I love you."

"I love you too, son."

"Goodbye Mrs. Grimaldi."

Giovanni took Joanna's hand and led her out of the house. "Where to, Cinderella?"

"How about Anthony's. I have been there with Maria and her friends from church and I liked it."

"Anthony it is."

They got in the car and drove the short distance to the restaurant. It was not full yet because it was still early. Besides them there were only two other couples. They asked to be seated by the window overlooking the bay. Giovanni was so happy he could hardly contain himself. He was beaming.

"Joanna, you made me a very happy man. I have news for you. As my fiancée you won't be washing dishes anymore and you won't work in the nightclub either. You are going to be the hostess of the restaurant. You'll work from eleven in the morning till nine at night with one hour for lunch and one hour for dinner. Your wages will be eleven dollars per hour, so what do you say?"

"I am so surprised. Are you sure Giovanni? What about the hostess that you have now, what is going to happen to her?"

"She's already told me that she'll quit by the end of the month because she's found another job, so there is no problem there. Another thing, as my fiancée you won't be wearing those skimpy skirts anymore, I want your skirts to be below the knee. Do you agree?"

"Oh, thank you Giovanni, I was so embarrassed having to wear them, you wouldn't believe. I agree. I agree with everything you say."

"Good. Waitress, could we have champagne, please? The best you have in the house. We're engaged and we're going to get married soon."

"Congratulations. How about Dom Perignon?"

"Splendid!"

Joanna was overwhelmed. She felt light headed even before she drank the champagne. So many good changes; she was overjoyed.

"How soon do you think before we can get married?" asked Joanna.

"Oh, I don't know, maybe a couple of months. Are you as eager as I am to get married?"

"Yes, oh yes, I can't wait."

They had a fine dinner of rice with scampi, a salad and dessert. They drank two bottles of champagne and were almost drunk by the end of the meal. They went for a walk in the cool air of the bay. Every once in a while they would stop and kiss. They went to Seaport Village and browsed through the stores. They stopped for a strong cup of coffee and sat outside to sip it. The village was full of people but Joanna didn't even notice. It seemed to her that there was only Giovanni; Giovanni drinking; Giovanni talking; Giovanni kissing; Giovanni, Giovanni, Giovanni. She felt light headed and smiled all the time, so much so that she felt stupid. *Say something*, she told herself.

"So Mr. Grimaldi, what have you been up to while I was gone?"

"The same as usual. You know my routine, work, work, work. By the way, tomorrow wear your bathing suit, we're going swimming. Right by La Jolla Cove there is the cutest little beach. We can look at the photographs there."

"I know, I was there last week. Maria took me."

"Oh, yea, how come?"

"She has an Italian friend who has a salon at Prospect. His name is Vittorio Malatesta. He owes her money and she goes there once a month because he won't mail her the checks."

"You're kidding, I know him. I used to take my mother there."

"It's a small world, isn't it?"

"So, he owes her money, ah?"

"Yea, over a thousand dollars."

"The swine, I am glad my mother changed hairdresser. Thank you for telling me."

"Don't tell Maria that I told you, ok?"

"Ok Pumpkin, I won't tell, I promise."

Tuesday morning Joanna, Giovanni and Mrs. Grimaldi went to see Father Anselmo at the Our Lady of the Rosary Church. His office was behind the church. It was a small room with a desk and some chairs. The secretary let them inside and told them to wait for Father Anselmo, that he'd be right there. Few minutes later a small priest appeared. He was bald, overweight and sweating.

"Mrs. Grimaldi, what a pleasure to see you," he said touching her hand slightly. "What is the occasion?"

"My son and his fiancée want to get married. We came to find out what they need to do. Joanna is not Catholic but she is not against marrying in the church."

"Well, Mrs. Grimaldi, that's a little bit of a problem. We can't marry them unless your daughter in law takes all the sacraments that she needs to take. Tell me Joanna, have you been baptized?"

"I don't know and I can't ask my mom because I was adopted. As far as I know I wasn't because I don't remember ever going to a church when I was little."

"You'll need to attend classes here at the church; we'll need to baptize you. Then you'll need to take the First Communion and the Confirmation and after that you'll be ready to get married. That will take about nine months."

"Nine months?" said Giovanni. "Can't it be done sooner?"

"We'll need to get a special permission from the church, but it can be done."

"How much sooner?"

"We can marry you in three months, but Joanna needs to come to lessons everyday."

"I'll do it," said Joanna. "I'll do whatever I have to do."

Father Anselmo took a handkerchief from his sleeve and dried the sweat from his forehead and his face. "Well, children, here is a list of all the requirements and all the documents that we'll need. I know Giovanni is a widower so he is free to marry again in the church. Of course I'll have to let Father Luciano at Saint Joseph know, because you belong to his parish, but that shouldn't be a problem."

"Thank you, Father," said all three in a chorus. "Here is a donation for the church, Father Anselmo," said Mrs. Grimaldi, handing him a check for one thousand dollars.

"How very generous of you, Mrs. Grimaldi. God will bless you for it. Would you like some coffee?"

"No, we better get going. So, it's all right if we make plans to get married three months from now, right?" asked Giovanni.

"Right. If you'd like I can recommend some people who can help you with the arrangements."

"Oh, don't worry, we'll take care of that."

They took leave from the priest and drove to Mrs. Grimaldi's house. Mrs. Grimaldi invited Joanna inside to have a drink to celebrate.

"I am so excited you can't imagine," she said. "Remember I want a grandson one year after you're married."

"We'll do our best, mom, don't you worry."

Mrs. Grimaldi took three glasses from a cabinet in the dining room and a bottle of orange liqueur. She filled the glasses three quarters full and handed one each to Joanna and Giovanni, reserving one for herself. "To my handsome son and his beautiful bride to be, Joanna Ruiz. May God bless this union and make it bountiful."

"We'll drink to that," said Giovanni. Joanna was near tears. She was so happy and incredulous by the way things were turning out that she could not speak. She took a sip of the liqueur then hugged and kissed Mrs. Grimaldi. "I'll make you proud," she said. "Anything you need I'll do it for you."

"Don't worry, Joanna. I might be old but I can still get around. Anything you'll need, come to me. It'll be a pleasure to be your mother-in-law. I have lot of experience and I can help you out."

"I am sure. Thank you!" They sipped their drinks then put the glasses in the sink.

"Say, how about the three of us fix lunch. We could have spaghetti with eggplant and tomato sauce, a salad, and *Veal Scaloppini* for second, all accompanied by our delicious Sicilian wine."

"You're the boss, mom. Let's start. I'll fix the salad; you and Joanna can fix the rest. Joanna needs to learn how to cook because she hasn't cooked much in her life. You can teach her mom. She will do the cooking for me once we get married."

Mrs. Grimaldi took three aprons from a cabinet and each of them put them on. Giovanni got out of the refrigerator all he needed to make a salad while Mrs. Grimaldi got the eggplants. Addressing Joanna she showed her what to do. "You cut the eggplants lengthwise without peeling them, then you layer the slices in a colander and lightly sprinkle them with salt. After you put the last layer, you cover them with a weight and put the colander in the sink for about half an hour. The reason you do that is that all of the black water from the eggplants, which is bitter, is extracted. While they are draining you prepare the tomato sauce and let it cook slowly. After half-an-hour you squeeze the eggplants really hard till all the black water is out, then put them in the tomato sauce. Let them cook for about ten minutes and it's done. For the *Veal Scaloppini* you beat the meat flat, you sprinkle it with salt and pepper, pass it in egg batter then pass it in flour. Coat both sides well then fry till it's golden."

Joanna wished she could write the instructions down on paper but she was too shy to ask. She watched attentively as Mrs. Grimaldi cooked, helping her out and following her instructions. Giovanni, who was almost done with the salad, poured some wine for all three of them. He brought into the kitchen a tape player and put on Sicilian music, the type you'd hear on the Godfather. They were hungry and couldn't wait to eat. While Joanna and Mrs. Grimaldi were cooking, Giovanni set the table. He went outside into the garden and clipped some roses to put on the table. They were all of different colors and very fragrant.

The meal was delicious. Giovanni kept them entertained by telling jokes and stories about his childhood. When they were finished Joanna and Giovanni washed the dishes and cleared the table. Mrs. Grimaldi went to her room to take a nap leaving the two lovebirds alone. They were both happy to be together, working side by side.

"Giovanni, do you have pictures of when you were a little boy? I'd like to see them," asked Joanna.

"I have tons of pictures. Wait till I show them to you. Promise you'll still love me when we're finished."

"C'mon, it can't be that bad. I promise I'll still love you, probably more."

Giovanni went to his room. He came out five minutes later carrying five photo albums.

"Before I show you let me make us some espresso coffee. We can drink it while we watch the photographs."

He went to the kitchen to make the coffee while Joanna watched him from the dining room. She was still amazed at how things had worked out. She'd pinch herself every once in a while to make sure she wasn't dreaming. She couldn't wait to tell Maria. She hadn't seen her since she'd been back having gotten home really late, founding her asleep. But tonight she'd see her and tell her the good news.

Giovanni brought two small Italian cups filled with espresso coffee on a tray with cream and sugar. They sipped the coffee slowly and began watching the photographs. There were pages after pages of photographs of Giovanni as an infant, toddler, teen, and full-grown man. Joanna couldn't believe how handsome he was. He got most of his good looks from his father of whom there were photographs on his fishing boats with crewmen or with his family. Mrs. Grimaldi was very pretty also when she was a young mother and a happy wife. She had a head full of curls and a very dark skin, typically Sicilian.

Giovanni sat by Joanna, patiently explaining to her when the photos were taken or what was the occasion behind them. They looked like an old married couple. Joanna noticed that there were no photos of Giovanni and his late wife. She understood that Giovanni wanted to keep that part of his life private so she didn't ask him about it. Giovanni silently noticed it and appreciated her sensibility.

"You should bring the photographs that you showed me yesterday here, to show my mother," he said.

"Do you really think that she'll like to see them?" she asked.

"Of course, she'd love to."

Giovanni wanted his mother to see them so that she'd know more about Joanna and come to love her too. He wanted to see if she felt like he had, watching that little adopted child and the sadness he'd seen in her eyes. Her face was serious in all of the photos; she hardly ever smiled. He wanted to put a smile on her face, see her rejoice and forget the ugliness of her past.

When they finished to watch the photographs Joanna felt as if she'd known him forever. He had been a happy, loved child. He was always smiling, mostly in photos taken with his mother. She would never get between him and his mother, Joanna decided. There was a strong bond between them; one she didn't care to break. He was so lucky to have grown up with his birth parents. She would never know what that felt like and she felt sorry for herself. She became sad and Giovanni didn't miss it.

"What's matter Joanna? Are you all right?" he asked worried.

"I wish I'd grown up with my parents. I feel a void in my life without them."

"I'll make it up to you, Cinderella. Once we'll get married I'll make you forget. I'll be your family; wait till we have a baby, then we'll be a real family and you will forget, I promise you."

"I believe you Giovanni. You are so sweet, so considerate. I am so lucky to know you, to be loved by you. I can't wait till we get married, I just can't."

They kissed passionately for a long time. Giovanni was tempted to ask her to go to his bedroom but he remembered his mother's warning of no sex before marriage, plus he decided he wanted to wait also. He wanted to be her first one and to wait till the night of the wedding. He got up, went to the kitchen and got a paper towel to dry his sweat. He was embarrassed by his arousal. Joanna smiled.

"I better take you home, Joanna or I won't answer for my actions," he told her. Joanna laughed, amused. He wasn't the only one to be aroused.

He drove her home. "I'll see you tomorrow at eleven. Tina, the hostess, will be there to train you. By the way, you will also be the cashier. You know how to operate a cash register, don't you?"

"Yes, I do. I worked as a cashier before, I know what to do."

"Good. I'll see you tomorrow then." He gave her a long, lingering kiss before he left.

Upstairs in the apartment Joanna unpacked. It would be another hour before Maria got home so she took her time. When she finished she went into the kitchen to prepare dinner. She wanted to surprise Maria by having dinner ready by the time she got home. She found fresh salmon, which she seasoned and wrapped in aluminum foil. She put it into the oven for half an hour. She found a mixed salad, pre-packed and pre-washed. She also found a can of green peas, which she cooked together with onions.

When Maria opened the apartment door she saw the table prepared for dinner with roses in the middle, the same ones Giovanni gave Joanna at the airport.

"Joanna," she screamed. "Finally I see you. Where have you

been these past two days?"

"I was with Giovanni," Joanna replied, coming out of the kitchen. "Congratulate me again, Maria. I will be Mrs. Grimaldi in three months. We went to talk to the priest of Our Lady of the Rosary Church this morning. Now all we have to do is make the arrangements. I hope you will help us. Of course you're going to be the Maid of Honor and I want Alfredo to walk me down the aisle. He doesn't know it yet but I am sure he will agree."

"Congratulations," said Maria, hugging her. "You deserve to be happy, Joanna. It does my heart good to see you this way. So what are you going to tell Giovanni about Raul not being at the wedding? By the way, you didn't tell me about the trial, how did it go?"

"Raul was sentenced to seventeen years in jail. I don't know what I am going to tell Giovanni. Maybe I'll tell him that he couldn't be here and I won't go into details hoping that he won't press me for more information. Of course Felicia will come; I'll send her the plane tickets. Could she stay here with you, while she is here in San Diego?"

"Of course, no problem. I'll be happy to let her stay here with me."

"Oh Maria, as the future bride I have been promoted from dish-washer to hostess-cashier for the restaurant. My pay will be eleven dollars an hour and I'll be working from eleven to nine starting tomorrow."

"Congratulations again Joanna. I don't think you're going to be homeless anymore. After dinner we should go by the shrine and thank God for your good fortune."

"I agree. Now let's have dinner before it gets cold."

Maria sat down at the table while Joanna served dinner. Before they ate they said a prayer with their heads bowed. The dinner was delicious. They accompanied it with warm Italian bread, which Joanna had put in the oven while the salmon was cooking. During dinner she told Maria everything about her trip to Minneapolis. Maria listened attentively while savoring the food. She had many questions in her mind but she didn't want to interrupt Joanna. By listening to her it was obvious to Maria that the week had been a very eventful one, both positive and negative. The negative would hopefully be left behind unless Joanna wanted those memories to linger, but she doubted it.

"So, tell me Joanna, will you become a Catholic?"

"I'll have to, if I want to marry Giovanni. He would not consider marrying anywhere else. It's very important to him because he is a very devout Catholic, and his mother also. Does it matter much where I get married? They believe in Jesus just like the Christians do, so what is the difference?"

"There is a lot of difference between the Catholic Church and the other churches. They do lot of things differently than the church we go to. They worship saints and the Virgin Mary. God forbids us in the first commandment to worship anybody but Him; the Bible also forbids us to call on the spirits of the dead. Easter and Christmas are not commanded in the Bible even though our church also observes them. Maybe you can still become a Catholic and don't do those things. My ex-husband was not Catholic and was allowed to marry me. All he had to do was sign a paper where he promised that he would raise his children in the Catholic faith, which he never did. He doesn't even believe in God. He thinks that aliens created us. I remember when we were going through our divorce he found me praying in front of the Bible. Very angrily he said:

'Why do you trust in God; why don't you trust me?' I told him: 'Because you're not God.' Do you know what he said to me? 'So, what if I have given myself to the Devil?' I said: 'That is your problem.' I was shocked. No one had ever said that to me and meant it. Plus I didn't see the logic of his thinking. We were getting a divorce and he was expecting me to trust him above God? He was insane. If he'd really given himself to the Devil it must have been because a gipsy told him that he'd die at thirty-two, in a motorcycle accident. He didn't die but maybe it would have been better if he had. This way he lost his soul and is forever separated from God, which is a lot worse than dying."

"Goodness, it gives me the shivers just to think about it. Your ex-husband must have been a really bad man. I am glad you divorced him."

"Yea, me too. If I hadn't divorced him I would not be so independent. I would still be a housewife catering to his every need.

That's all I knew how to do. Now I have a job, I am independent, I can do what I want and I don't need a man to feel complete."

"I am glad I have Giovanni and I hope you will find a companion too. It's lonesome without a man."

"I don't miss having a man in my life. I actually feel relieved, freer. I would like to have friends though, male friends, but it's hard to come across men who want that kind of relationship. Maybe one day I'll meet someone who feels the same way as I do. In the meantime I am happy as I am."

"I am glad. I hope one day I'll be like you, so strong, so secure. In the meantime I want to concentrate on becoming the best possible wife I can be to Giovanni. I hope you'll teach me, Maria. You know so much about Italian men. What are they like in bed? Raul molested me and made me do things for him, but I don't have any experience with Italian men. Are they hard to please?"

"No, they are not hard to please. They like to touch a lot; that's one way for them to show affection, and they like to make the first move, to be the leaders. They also get turned on by virginity, which you have, thank God. The less you know Joanna, the better it is. Let him teach you everything he knows, and be honest with him. Let him know what you like and he will do his best to please you. Participate in the lovemaking, don't just lie there and have him do everything. Learn what he likes, his sensitive spots; do lot of foreplay; be passionate. Once you live together you will learn a lot about him; take that knowledge to bed with you. You'll do just fine, don't worry."

"I hope you're right. We'll talk more about this after I get married. I am sure I will need your advice since you have so much more experience."

"I'll do my best. Now let's clean up and go to the shrine. We need to talk to our Father about all this and thank Him."

"I have started to put the whitening gel on my teeth at night since last Sunday. Do you see any changes?" said Joanna clearing up the table and giving Maria a big smile to show her teeth.

"Yes, I do. They are whiter. I guess it works; maybe I'll do it too. I just want to wait a couple of months to make sure they don't turn black like they did to Vittorio."

"Boy, that's scary. His teeth are really black. I don't want mine to turn out that way."

"They probably won't," said Maria soaping the dishes.

"Before I forget Maria, I brought you a present. Let me get it for you." Joanna gave Maria the earrings. She tried them on and noticed they were gold. She was moved and gave her a hug. "I am so happy you're my friend, Joanna. I hope we're friends forever."

"Me too, Maria."

The next three months were very busy for Joanna. In the morning she'd go to Catechism to learn about the catholic faith, then she'd go to work. By the end of the day she'd be exhausted. In her days off she'd go see her counselor once every two weeks. During the sessions she'd talk about Raul, about Giovanni, but mostly about her fears and insecurities. She was doing great at her job as a hostess-cashier. True to his word Giovanni had her wear a black skirt that covered her legs down to below her knees. She looked taller wearing it and very sexy.

Joe Bellagio had not given up on her. Ever since she stopped working in the nightclub he'd been coming over to dinner and he'd ask to be seated where he could look at her. That made Joanna feel uncomfortable, but since he was behaving himself there was nothing she could do about it. Then all of a sudden he stopped coming. Giovanni and Joanna started to get worried. Out of the blue Joanna received a letter at work from a lawyer. He wanted to see her in his office in two days. Giovanni went with her. He was just as puzzled as she was.

The lawyer's office was on Broadway. It was very rich with mahogany walls and antique furnishing. A very sophisticated receptionist asked them to wait while she would tell Mr. George Brunhill, the lawyer, that they had arrived. Five minutes later a middle- aged man, richly dressed, came towards them. "Ms. Ruiz," he said holding out his hand with a big smile on his face. Joanna shook it and introduced Giovanni as her fiancé.

"Ms. Ruiz, I need to see you privately. Mr. Grimaldi please don't take offense but what I need to tell Ms. Ruiz is of a very private nature. I hope you understand."

Giovanni seated himself again while Joanna followed Mr.

Brunhill into his office. He was not very tall and his stomach protruded a little. He had sparse, blond hair combed back and small blue eyes. He asked Joanna to take a seat in a very large, leather seat while he went behind his desk and seated himself in a rich, luscious armchair.

"Ms. Ruiz, Joanna isn't it? I have good news and bad news. Which one do you want to hear first?"

Joanna's throat was choked up by the anxiety she was feeling. She had no clue why she was in this rich office talking to this man. She cleared her voice.

"Tell me the bad news first," she said hardly breathing.

"All right. Joe Bellagio is dead. They found him hung in his house Monday morning. His maid found him. She also found this note by his body. Here, read it."

Joanna's hands were shaking. She took the note but had hard time reading it because tears were blinding her eyes. Mr. Brunhill gave her a tissue to dry them up. "Of course this is a copy. The police have the original."

"Dear Joanna," the note read, "I am so sorry for leaving you like this but life without you has no meaning. I wish you'd have accepted my offer to become my woman but you chose another man over me and I can't live with that. I sound insane and yes, I am insane. I could never lose. I decided to leave everything I have to you, to remind you of me every day of your life. I couldn't have you while I was alive, I'll have you while I am dead. Love, Joe."

"This is crazy," Joanna said. Her face was pale but she had no more tears in her eyes.

"Did he really leave everything to me?"

"Oh yes. That is the good news, my girl, five million dollars, the house and his car. He had the will made a month ago, with two witnesses and myself who would testify that he was of a sound mind. We want you to take it Ms. Ruiz. It would be in your best interest, believe me. Don't cross him while he's dead, that would be a mistake."

"Why, he can't do anything to me. He is dead."

"He killed himself. His soul is still earthbound."

"That sounds so creepy, it gives me the shivers. All right, I'll take it. Can I hire you as my lawyer? Please do whatever needs to be done legally. I'll pay you, of course. Please keep me informed." Joanna gave him her address and phone number and left the office.

Giovanni knew something was wrong the moment he saw her. She was white as a ghost and looked as if she'd been crying. He opened his arms and she nestled there.

"Oh Giovanni, it's terrible. Joe Bellagio killed himself because I said no to him and he left me everything he had. Isn't it crazy?"

"So that's why we haven't seen him at the restaurant lately. When did it happen?"

"Monday. His maid found him hung. What a horrible way to die, and all because of me. How am I supposed to live with that?"

"Joanna, don't do this to yourself. That's what he would want. He was a coward who couldn't take no for an answer. We just need to pray for him and for ourselves hoping that he won't give us any trouble now that he is dead. God knows he gave us problems while he was alive."

"But what can he do to us if he's dead? Even the lawyer said that. Tell me, please."

"Oh Joanna, you have no experience with this things. Let's go to my car and talk there. I don't want anybody to hear what I have to say to you." He took her by the hand and walked out of the office with her. His car was parked on the street. He checked the meter and saw that it had one more hour left. They sat in the car and opened the windows.

"As I was saying you don't have any experience with this things. The guy is damned. He is still on the earth. People who die with obsessions, especially sexual ones, try to attach themselves to the person they lust for. Now, I don't want you to have any sexual thoughts especially when you are alone. Tomorrow morning I will go to church with you and talk to Father Anselmo. He will know what to do. He might even have to come to the restaurant and your house to bless them. We'll see. How much did he leave you?"

"Five million dollars, his house and his car."

"Five million dollars? He was busier than I thought. I figured him for a million, but five millions? What are you going to do with it?"

"I don't know. I don't want to think about it right now. I need time to absorb it all in. I am very upset. I don't want to touch anything that is his yet. It gives me the creeps."

"I know how you feel. Well, business is waiting for us, let's go to the restaurant and get to work."

They drove in silence each absorbed in their own thoughts. A part of Joanna wanted the money while another part was horrified. It would always remind her of Joe Bellagio and the way he died. She couldn't live with that. She had a sinking feeling in her stomach, which grew more intense as she entered the restaurant and saw the table he used to sit at.

She could almost see him there. She would ask Father Anselmo to come to the restaurant and exorcize that spot, maybe then she could relax.

She went through the day like a robot. She was efficient as ever and nobody suspected how she was really feeling. Giovanni asked her a couple of times how she was doing and she said fine but she was lying. At six o'clock she jumped when a customer said hi. It was the time Joe Bellagio used to come to eat. A part of her still didn't believe that he had died. It was so unreal.

At nine o'clock she kissed Giovanni good night. She gave him appointment for next morning at the church at nine o'clock. Giovanni had bought her a Chevy Chevette so that she didn't have to catch the bus anymore. It was a used car but looked new. The engine had been rebuilt so everything was working fine. She got into the car and drove to Maria's apartment.

Maria was watching television. As she saw Joanna she turned the volume down and asked her what was wrong. She looked pale and upset. Joanna told her everything that had happened that day. She was in tears by the time she finished. Maria tried to alleviate her feelings of guilt and of being responsible for his death but Joanna wouldn't listen. She kept saying that it was her fault. How was she going to live with it?

"I tell you how you're going to live with it. Very well with the five millions he left you. You are going to have a grand time," said Maria.

"I don't know Maria. I have been thinking of giving the money to charity."

"No," screamed Maria. "Give them to me Joanna, please. Don't give them to charity. If you don't want them I'll take them."

"Are you serious?"

"Of course I am serious. Are you?"

"Yes, I am. After everything is put in my name I'll have the lawyer put it in your name."

Maria got up and hugged Joanna. She was overjoyed. Five million dollars; she wouldn't have to work the rest of her life. "What about the house and the car?"

"Those too; I'll give you everything he left me. Once I'll get married to Giovanni I won't need anything. I will still be working at the restaurant, helping Giovanni with his business and I'll have plenty of money."

"This calls for a celebration. You won't change your mind, will you?"

"No, I won't Maria, I am dead serious."

Maria went into the kitchen. She came back with two glasses half filled with red wine. She handed one to Joanna. "To the luckiest two women in the world. Cheers!"

"Cheers," said Joanna. She tried to look cheerful for Maria's benefit but she wasn't feeling cheerful at all. She went to bed saddened and tearful. After the TV and the lights went out she finally shed the tears she had been holding all day long. She thought about what Giovanni had told her, not to have any sexual thought and about Joe Bellagio still being on the Earth's plane. She prayed silently for protection and went to sleep holding the Bible.

Maria could not go to sleep; she was too excited. Five million dollars, a house and a car. She seemed to remember that Joanna had told her that he had a red Ferrari. She would love to drive it. With a red Ferrari she would have half of San Diego's male population after her. It was a very expensive car. Thank God for Joe's taste. She would sell the house. She didn't want to live in a house where somebody had committed suicide. She would buy another one, maybe in La Jolla and she would also buy one in Italy. She decided that she would not squander the money but that she would invest them wisely. She would give some to Elizabeth, so much per year so that she wouldn't get spoiled.

She felt that the world was hers. No more work, only a long, long vacation. First thing she would do was quit her job. Then she would get up at eleven every morning. She would get a cup of coffee and read the newspaper. She would have a maid, of course, who would come in every day till six in the afternoon and would fix her lunch and dinner. She would not lift a finger. She would finally go to a manicurist and pedicurist, she would have a facial and........She finally fell asleep.

****

Father Anselmo was surprised to see Giovanni and Joanna. "What's wrong, Giovanni?" he asked.

"Father, can we talk to you in your office?" Even though it was only nine in the morning and the air was crisp Father Anselmo was already sweating. He pulled a handkerchief out of his pocket and dried his sweat. "Of course, my son, of course," he said leading the way to his office. "What can I do for you?"

Joanna and Giovanni seated themselves on two chairs facing Father Anselmo's desk. Giovanni cleared his voice. "Father, someone we knew killed himself. He was infatuated with my fiancé. He was actually obsessed with her. He left a note saying that since he could not have her while he was alive, he would have her while he was dead. We've come to find out if there is anything we can do to protect her from him and if you can come and bless the restaurant and the nightclub."

"This is very serious. We must pray that nothing of that sort happens. I will come and bless the restaurant but I can't come and bless the nightclub. I hope you understand. Joanna, I will give you a booklet of prayers that you must recite everyday. That should protect you from his ghost. As you probably know, the church doesn't allow prayers for those who commit suicide. They are damned. If you feel a sensation in your nose, immediately close it with your fingers and say the Lord's Prayer. It might be him trying to get inside your body and possess you. Come to church every Sunday and partake of the body of Christ. That should protect you also. Other than that there isn't much more we can do. You might be in danger also, Giovanni. I see that you are wearing a cross; that's good. You should buy one for Joanna, also."

"I will. In fact we'll go and buy one when we leave here. Is it Ok if Joanna doesn't attend Catechism this morning?"

"Sure son, sure."

"Father, this is a donation for your church," said Giovanni handing Father Anselmo a check for five hundred dollars. He took it and put it in his desk drawer. He opened another drawer and took out a booklet, which he gave to Joanna.

"I will come to the restaurant tomorrow morning at nine o'clock. I will see you then." Joanna and Giovanni took leave from the good priest and went to a jeweler to buy Joanna a cross.

As soon as Mr. George Brunhill had put everything in Joanna's name she informed him that she wanted everything to be put in Maria's name. She took Maria to meet with Mr. Brunhill. Maria retained him as her lawyer and she also hired an accountant to take care of the taxes aspect of the inheritance. She had them deposit the money in her savings account so that she could start collecting interest right away. She sent Elizabeth a check for thirty thousand dollars, which she used to pay off her car and her credit cards. Maria told her not to tell her father anything. She didn't want him to know of her good fortune.

Elizabeth was very thankful and very excited and informed Maria that she wanted to come to live with her, to which Maria agreed only on condition that she would go to college. She said yes but she would do that the following year because she wanted to take some time off to just relax and do nothing.

Maria quit her job. She told Linda Suarez, her supervisor, that she was going to go live in Italy because her mother was getting old and she wanted to spend some time with her before she died. They gave her a big going away party with many people attending. She had been working there for seven years and everybody liked her. They were sorry to see her go. Maria didn't breathe a word to anyone at work about the money. If they only knew. Keeping the secret was a big kick for Maria; she took lot of pleasure out of it. She hadn't decided yet if she was going to say anything about it to her family. Maybe she would confide in her mother, but she wasn't sure she could keep the secret.

She went to visit the house. It was built on one-acre lot with a landscaped front yard, a swimming pool and fruit trees in the back-yard. It had five bedrooms, three baths, a living room, dining room, and a large family room; too big for a single person but Joe Bellagio had a taste for anything big. The furniture was contemporary and on the walls there were very expensive works of art. Maria liked it a lot and for a moment she considered keeping it but the thought of living with Joe Bellagio's ghost gave her shivers. She went to visit it alone, during daytime; it would have been too scary at night. She left as soon as she could. She hired a real estate agent after she'd had an appraiser to appraise the furniture and another to appraise the house. All together they sold everything for one and a half million dollars, but Maria didn't move out of her apartment yet. She was waiting for Elizabeth so they could both go house hunting since they were going to live in it together.

She wouldn't discuss the situation with Joanna because she considered it bad luck. She was still horrified of the whole deal so Maria didn't press the issue, but she was on seventh heaven. Every morning she'd wake up naturally, without the alarm clock. She would get up, have a cappuccino and read the newspaper. Joanna had already left for her Catechism lessons at the church, so she was alone. For the time being she hadn't hired a maid yet. She was wait-ing to buy a house first. She'd straighten up the apartment, would get dressed and go shopping; mostly she would buy clothes; only for herself, though, because Joanna didn't want anything to do with Joe's money. She had a manicure, pedicure and a facial. She went to the hairdresser and had an expensive haircut with light brown high-lights. She donated all the old clothes to the Goodwill store, ten bags full. She bought a bedroom set and got rid of the old mattresses that were lying on the floor. She wanted to buy a daybed for Joanna but she said no; she was fine sleeping on the futon.

While waiting for Elizabeth to come, Maria started to look at houses, mostly three bedroom houses in La Jolla and Pacific Beach. She was driving around in the red Ferrari and people assumed, rightly, that she was rich. Everybody was deferential after seeing her in the car and Maria just loved it. She had the car inspected by a good foreign cars mechanic and he said it was in very good conditions after he took it for a ride around the block. Maria was a bit rusty since she hadn't driven a car in so many years and she had to be very careful about stepping on the gas pedal because the car would switch gears very fast, but she got used to it in no time. She was a good driver and she never got a ticket.

When she went to collect her money from Vittorio Malatesta, the hairdresser, he was very impressed and wanted to go for a ride. He wanted to drive it and went all over La Jolla, showing off. A red Ferrari was his dream. Even though Maria had lot of money she still wanted the money that Vittorio owed her. After the ride he even agreed to send her the money in the mail every month. Maria didn't tell him that the car was hers, but that she was keeping it for a friend who was out of the country. Immediately he wanted to know who this friend was and how much money he had; maybe he would be interested in going in business with him but Maria told him no. She despised him and his smug attitude as if he was a big business man when in reality he was just a creep full of debts.

When she left he was outside the salon waving goodbye and looking at her with longing in his eyes while his girlfriend looked at him from inside. She thought he was a creep too, and that she was going to leave him soon. She was tired of him flirting with every woman in town and using his looks to make women do his bidding. She had no idea that he was taking money from them or she would have left him already. They had been together for five years and he had never made a commitment to her. She wanted to get married and have a baby, but he would always turn a deaf ear to that. He was already thirty-six years old and she was twenty-seven. She wasn't willing to wait any longer for him to make up his mind. She would leave him soon.

CHAPTER TWENTY-FIVE

Joanna and Giovanni were very busy all the time. They derived lot of joy working side by side and their bond strengthened as time went by. Joanna cared about his business as if it were hers and soon it would be. Their engagement was common knowledge at the restaurant and everybody treated her with respect. She was learning everything she could about the business since, once married, she would be in charge, Giovanni had told her so. Instead of eleven o'clock she would arrive at ten-thirty. She would inspect the supplies to make sure they were fresh. If they weren't she would send them back and call the suppliers telling them that she wasn't going to pay. They soon got the message. She was a tough customer.

Alfredo had been very happy to hear about her engagement with Giovanni and he told her so. He missed washing the dishes with her but he was glad that things had worked out the way they did. He couldn't even talk with the new dishwasher since he was Mexican and spoke only broken English. Joanna hadn't mentioned anything to him yet about being walked down the aisle by him. She would wait till the week before the wedding to do that, since she was sure that he would say yes.

Giovanni, reassured by her competency, left more of the business to her. The more he would watch her work the more confidence he had in her ability. He liked her honesty and the way she treated the customers. In fact, he heard lot of praises from the regulars.

Joanna was getting to know a lot of people. She was kind and caring and involved with their lives. They started to confide in her when she'd stop by her tables to make sure everything was to their taste. As a result more people started to come to the restaurant. Joanna looked great. Her hair was shiny and golden, her smile was bright and her body slim and sexy. A couple of the regular customers proposed to her, but she refused, of course. Instead of being jealous, Giovanni was pleased. That only made him surer that his choice to marry her was the right one. He would get turned on not only by being close to her when they were alone, but also by watching her work her magic around people. It was getting harder and harder for both of them to keep chaste and wait till the wedding night, but they were both determined to do so. It was part of their fairy tale.

Mrs. Grimaldi was also falling in love with her. She liked her humbleness and her shyness; it was as if she had acquired a daughter. She could still sense a lot of sadness in her and was convinced that there was a dark secret in her life, but she never got the nerves to ask. Instead, she loved to see how her face would light up when she saw Giovanni and how happy and outgoing she would become. Whatever her secret was she prayed that it wouldn't hurt her beloved son. Hopefully, with time, she would trust her enough to confide in her. Whatever it was she would keep the secret.

They had not discussed with her yet where they would live after they got married. She hoped they would live with her. They were never home anyway busy as they were at the restaurant. She looked forward to teach Joanna how to cook, and also to teach her everything she knew about Italian men and how to please them. Not in bed, of course, she could learn that on her own. She was very lonely so she would welcome the company.

Joanna had also been thinking where to live after the wedding. She wasn't against living with Mrs. Grimaldi, but she was waiting for Giovanni to approach the subject. She knew he was very close to her and that he was concerned about her being old and needing more company since she never went out except on Sunday mornings. Joanna was spending every Sunday morning with them and found it a pure joy. It was as if every time their bond grew stronger and more secure. She could feel God's blessing of her relationship with Giovanni and she grew surer and less fearful. She also enjoyed the lunch afterwards that Mrs. Grimaldi prepared for all three of them. The food was always delicious and Mrs. Grimaldi promised to start writing her recipes so that Joanna would learn how to prepare them herself. That would keep her busy and occupied since she spent many hours in her room alone, contemplating her past.

Giovanni had not discussed where they would live after the wedding because it was a given that they would live with his mother. But he failed to see that he needed to discuss it with Joanna and his mother because they didn't have a clue about what he was thinking. He realized it one day, at the shopping mall, as they stopped in front of a furniture store. Joanna was in love with the bed they had on display and she asked him if he liked it. He said yes but they already had a bed, and linens, and cookware. They didn't need anything. That's when Joanna asked him where they were going to live. "Where I am living now, of course. I am sorry Pumpkin I thought you knew. I never asked you, I hope you don't mind. My mother is old and I don't want to leave her by herself. She could use our company even though we're hardly ever home. If we lived somewhere else I would always worry about her. But don't worry; you won't have to take care of her. She is very independent and still does lot of things around the house herself even though we have a cleaning lady. She loves to iron my shirts so you won't have to do that. She says no one does it like her. You would do good to learn that because she won't be around forever to do it."

"I agree with every thing you say, Giovanni. It's just that I didn't know and the reason I never asked was because whatever you decided it would have been all right with me."

"You're so beautiful Joanna. You have a good heart; I can see why we're so taken with you. But don't worry; after we get married you go around the house and if there is anything you want to buy just say so and we'll go shopping. Until then all we have to worry is buying you a wedding dress and order the flowers."

"I wish Maria was here. Without her I feel kind of lost. I told you that she went to Italy, didn't I? She and her daughter Elizabeth went to spend a month there, but she promised to come back in time to help me with my wedding dress and the invitations. You know, her daughter Elizabeth is coming to live with her. That will be good so she won't be lonely after I leave. We've become like two sisters, she and I. I don't know what I would have done without her. We might never have met. I shiver only thinking about it."

"So Maria is going to be your Maid of Honor. That means I have to pick the Best Man. I was thinking about Alfredo, what do you think? I've known him for ten years and he is very devoted to me."

"I agree Giovanni. You couldn't have picked a better person."

So it was decided where they would live. On their days off, which were few, they went to talk to florists to see who could give them a better deal. They wanted roses for the church and gardenias for Joanna's bouquet. The roses were to be white and pink and they were to adorn the whole church. They ordered five hundred of them. The reception was to take place at Giovanni's and they spent some time making up the menu, which was going to be published on the invitations. The guests needed to RSVP with their choice of menu so the cooks would know what to prepare. There were going to be about one hundred fifty guests, mostly friends and family of Giovanni. On Joanna's side there were Maria, Elizabeth, Felicia, Penny and Theresa; no one else. This made Joanna feel very lonely, but not for long. At the wedding she would meet lot of new people, plus there were all the people she worked with at the restaurant. She was on good terms with all of them and even if they didn't love her, they respected her.

Two more months and she would be Mrs. Grimaldi. There was a splendid future waiting for her. Everything she had gone through in her life was worth it if it had brought her this wonderful happiness. She thought of Maria in Italy and wondered how she was doing. She didn't have to wonder for too long because she called her that night. She and Elizabeth were having a wonderful time. They had just gotten back from Rome where they had visited the Coliseum, the Forum, and Vatican City. The food was delicious and Maria was sure she was going to gain twenty pounds. Good thing she hadn't bought her dress for the wedding yet. They spent a good half an hour talking about the wedding. They decided they were going to wait till she got back to buy the wedding dress and to mail out the invitations. Maria's dress was going to be white and pink just like the roses. Joanna wanted white pearls on her dress and a long trail, which Antonio's children would carry. Joanna had bought the Bride's magazine and had seen a dress that she liked a lot. She described it to Maria in details and Maria asked her to wait till she got back. She wanted to see it with her own eyes. She told Joanna she wanted to pay for the dress and before she could say anything about not wanting anything from Joe's money she told her she was going to pay for it out of her own savings. So Joanna agreed. Maria also told her that she wanted to buy her the clothes for her honeymoon and she agreed to that as well.

"It must be nice to have money to spend," said Joanna.

"It sure is, darling. I saved a lot before you gave me the money so I can afford to be generous. Plus you deserve it Joanna, more than me. God bless you and keep you."

"Come back soon, Maria. It's not the same without you."

"Fifteen more days and I'll be there. We'll be there. Elizabeth will come back with me. She'll sleep in the bedroom so you don't have to worry. We'll have good time when I come back. We'll shop till we drop."

Alone in the apartment Joanna had hard time going to sleep. She called Giovanni at the nightclub.

"Hello' Pumpkin, what's going on?"

"Nothing. I couldn't sleep so I thought of calling you. What are you doing?"

"You know, the usual; talking to people, supervising the employees."

"Is the countess there?"

"Yes she is; with a new man, younger than her. I don't know where she finds them but she has a new escort every week. Maybe she pays them, that must be why they are not jealous when she flirts with me. You won't believe this but she actually touched my crotch and right in front of everybody."

"What did you do?" asked Joanna angered.

"I took her hand off and told her that 'it' was reserved. She got embarrassed and left. I hope I haven't made an enemy."

"So what if you did? We don't need her nor her money. The sooner she's gone the better."

"I hope she is not another Joe Bellagio. Hopefully she won't come back after tonight, but who knows. We have to wait and see."

"Well, I just wanted to talk. I let you go back to work. I hope I can go to sleep now."

"Good night Cinderella, I'll see you tomorrow."

Joanna tried hard to go to sleep but she couldn't. She tossed and turned. She didn't like darkness so she went into the bedroom and lit the candle. She laid down on Maria's bed hoping that sleep would overtake her there, but she was afraid the candle would burn the apartment down, so she got up and went to the kitchen to get aluminum foil, which she put under and around the candle. She went back to bed. She was tired, but wide-awake. She thought of the countess and hoped that she dropped dead. She then repented and hoped that she never came back instead. Giovanni was quite a catch she had to admit. The countess was not going to be the last woman to flirt with him. Others would follow. It was in her best interest if she took it lightly. As long as Giovanni was happy with her that's all that mattered. He was faithful and he showed it tonight. It was up to her to keep him happy so he wouldn't stray and find comfort in another woman's bosom.

Tomorrow they would set the wedding date. Joanna wanted to choose September 10, in honor of Maria because it was her birthday. She would surprise her with it, hoping that Giovanni would agree with her choice. If not it could be September 12, which was the Feast of the Virgin Mary. She wanted it to be a significant date, so that her marriage could have more meaning. She loved the Virgin Mary and sometime, in her mind, she would picture her as Maria, because of the dream Maria had about seeing herself dressed as the Virgin Mary, with a globe under her feet and a snake wrapped around it. Joanna thought that was awesome.

She wondered how she would feel had it happened to her. It was next to being God. But Maria was always her humble self, always nice and caring. She had a temper, though, and she could be very passionate when she cared about someone or something. She was fully human and Joanna knew that she had problems dealing with the whole issue of earth and heaven. The experience had wrecked her life and she had trouble staying afloat. Many times Joanna had heard her scream in her sleep, but didn't wake her up. Somewhere she'd heard that you shouldn't wake people who are dreaming, so she didn't. She knew she was fighting the Devil, so she prayed for her.

Maria had told her that the Devil was reading her mind and every once in a while he would hurt her right, upper leg or her heels because of something she had been thinking. This would anger her a lot and she would call him all kinds of bad names. That would make him stop. She felt frustrated at having to watch her every thought but it was working in her favor because she was very selective about what she'd think.

Joanna was paying more attention to her thoughts as well, since Joe Bellagio's death. She didn't like to be in the dark by herself and she was absolutely terrified of his ghost. She would think of him often. The "bird", as she called him in her mind, was always looking at her, especially at the restaurant. The priest had come to bless the place and she felt more relaxed because of that, but it was at night, in her bed that she would envision him more vividly. Tonight was no different. She saw him hanging, buried and roaming the earth, finding no peace. Her therapist, Jill Thompson, had suggested that she'd talk to him as if he could hear her and tell him that she was praying that he'd find rest. She was to be totally honest with him, telling him that she was engaged to be married to Giovanni, that she wished him well and that he'd leave her alone.

She got up and went in the living room to get her Bible. She took it with her to Maria's bed and hugged it tightly. The candle gave the room a soft glow. Joanna's eyes were wide open. She touched the cross on her necklace that Giovanni had bought for her. It was eighteen karat gold, very expensive. But that didn't matter. What mattered was the fact that it brought her comfort. Instead of talking to Joe she started to talk to Jesus.

"Dear Jesus," she said, "I am terrified. Please don't let Joe Bellagio near me, I beg of you. I don't hate him, but I don't like him. I didn't like him when he was alive and I like him even less now that he's dead. I didn't take his money because I didn't want to be connected to him. Please protect Maria and her daughter Elizabeth because they are the ones spending his money. Give Joe rest in his grave and if you cannot take him with you, at least keep him asleep so that he doesn't bother me. Maybe he can find a companion in the spirit world and he can forget about me. You are the Judge, Lord, I leave it to your wisdom, but please, please, please keep him away from me especially at night. I need to sleep because I have Catechism tomorrow morning and if I don't get some sleep I won't wake up on time. Watch over me.....ced" A gust of wind came through the window and blew out the candle. Joanna screamed, in panic and hid her head under the blanket. She was sure it was Joe Bellagio and he was mad at her.

She kept the blanket over her head not daring to move. She was hardly breathing.

"Oh God, dear God don't let him near me, please," she prayed. "I love you, Maria, Giovanni, his mother but I don't love Joe Bellagio. Tell me what I have to do and I'll do it."

She waited patiently as if God was really going to talk to her but, of course, no one spoke. She took a deep breath that made her feel better. She remembered a yoga exercise, of which she had read in a magazine article when she was eighteen. She was to take a deep breath and hold it till she'd count to ten; then another breath and hold it till she'd count to nine and so on until one. She did it and soon sleep overtook her.

****

It was one-thirty in the morning. Joanna came out of her dream with the distinct sensation that there was someone in the room. She was not fully awake yet but she could see the room through her fifth eye. There was someone in the room, an orange figure with the eyes like two burning coals. He was looking at her naked body lustfully, trying to touch her, but he could not because the light of the Holy Spirit surrounded her. Joanna was terrified and tried to scream but no sound came out of her mouth. She tried to move but she was paralyzed. Why was she naked when she had gone to bed in her nightgown? But that didn't matter. What mattered was the stranger hovering over her trying to get close. Her heart raced furiously as she tried to call for help. It was Joe Bellagio, she was sure. Why was he tormenting her? Why didn't he leave her alone? The words came out of her mouth in a slur. When she finally called for God in her mind the paralysis left her and she was able to utter, "God help me".

She was now fully awake. The room was in total darkness and she was under the cover with her nightgown on. There were no light surrounding her and no orange figure hovering over her. Had it been all a dream? She didn't think so. She was shaking as she got up to turn the light on. She went to the phone and called Giovanni at the nightclub.

"Giovanni, something terrifying just happened to me. Joe Bellagio was in the room with me, and he wanted to touch me but he couldn't. I am so shook up that I won't be able to go back to sleep. Can you stay on the phone with me for a little while until I calm down?"

"Sure Pumpkin. I told you his spirit was still around, didn't I? Do you believe me now?"

"Yes, oh yes I do. It was terrible. I couldn't talk and I couldn't move. If he'd touched me I would have gone crazy. Do you think Father Anselmo would come over to bless the apartment? I am so afraid that it might happen again, I don't want to be alone and in the dark. I will leave the light on the whole night because with the light on he is powerless. He belongs to the darkness and to hell. Jesus, protect me from him."

"Joanna, calm down sweetheart. Do you want me to come over for a little while?"

"Would you? Thank you so much Giovanni!"

Fifteen minutes later he was holding her in his arms, rubbing her back. She cried for a little while, and then she realized that she was in her nightgown, without any make-up on. She straightened her hair and blew her nose.

"God, I am a mess. I hope you still love me, Giovanni, after seeing me like this. It was so nice of you to come, I really appreciate it."

"Don't mention it, Cinderella. Now tell me exactly what happened."

Joanna told him about her experience leaving out the part where she saw herself naked. She was too bashful to tell him that. He listened quietly until she was finished. He was angry at Joe Bellagio even though he was dead. The man had been trouble when he was alive and he was trouble when he was dead. He felt powerless, not knowing how to stop him. He was bothering his girlfriend and Giovanni didn't like it one bit.

"Maybe you should come to my place for tonight. You could sleep on my mother's couch. Or I could stay here and sleep in the living room. Would you like that?"

"Oh, could you? Only for tonight. I am too shaken up. I don't know how I'd feel if I were by myself, I probably wouldn't be able to sleep at all and I have Catechism in the morning."

"Okay then. Fix me the bed, woman."

"Okay, master," Joanna replied laughing. She felt much better thanks to his kindness and concern. She was also relieved that she didn't have to spend the night alone and gave Giovanni a big hug.

"Let's not get too close or I won't be responsible for my actions," Giovanni said not wanting to be aroused. He gently pushed her away.

****

Maria and Elizabeth were having the time of their life. Fifteen days had already gone by since they'd arrived in Italy. So far they'd visited Venice, Florence and Rome. Maria was being careful not to spend too much money so that she wouldn't arouse anybody's suspicions. She had not told anyone that she'd quit her job and that she was now a millionaire. She was enjoying every minute of her vacation and she wished she could stay longer, but her friend Joanna needed her in San Diego. There was so much to do when she got back, but she looked forward to it, especially the thought of buying the wedding dress and the honeymoon clothes for Joanna. She loved spending money and now that she had plenty she was going to do just that.

Maria's mother was a loving and caring woman. She was seventy-two years old. Her hair was all gray and cut short. She was five feet two inches tall, the same height as Maria and she was a little plump. She had never worn a pair of pants her whole life and she had her clothes made especially for her by a seamstress. She wore no make-up. One of her main concern in life was that every-body in her family had had enough to eat. She was constantly asking if Maria and Elizabeth were hungry, and when they ate she gave them generous portions. The meals were very long and consisted of at least three courses. At the end of each meal they felt like they were going to explode and Maria was getting worried that by the time they left she might not fit into her clothes anymore.

After dinner, that night, they went to sleep. They were going to visit Capri the following day. Capri is an island off the coast of Naples and can be reached only by ferry. They prepared their bags at night so everything would be ready in the morning. Elizabeth, Maria, Serena, and her boyfriend would be going. Maria's mother would have the food prepared for them in the morning.

The following day they were ready by seven a.m.. After packing everything in the car, they said goodbye to Maria's mom and left. They drove from Onofrio to Naples where they parked the car in the port.

On the ferry they sat outside so they could see the coast of Naples as the ferry moved away from it. It was a beautiful, sunny morning and they could see the coast crystal clear. Maria hadn't realized how much she missed Naples until now. She loved the United States but this was where she had grown-up. She would still prefer to live in the United States though, because it was less crowded and, in her opinion, the standard of living was higher. She loved the English language and the diversity of people; the form of government and the fact that people seemed to be more obedient of the law. But she missed Naples, nevertheless.

They were approaching Capri. The island was beautiful, its waters an emerald green. From the Marina Grande they had to board a small trolley that took them to the top where there was the island's small square or *piazzetta*. There they sat outside a bar where Maria paid for refreshments. Tourists from various countries were there, either lounging in the sun, or taking pictures. It was the middle of the summer and the piazzetta was really crowded even though it was nine o'clock in the morning. It was very expensive to vacation on the island, but many people of lesser means would just make a one-day trip and bring lunch with them just as Maria had.

After the refreshments the group walked around in the area visiting the various shops. Souvenirs were very abundant and not very expensive. Maria bought two ceramic tiles with paintings of Capri, one for herself and one for Joanna. For Serena she bought a painting on a stone and for her mother a calendar with beautiful pictures, also of the island. Maria was charging everything to her credit card, not wanting to arouse suspicions about her new acquired wealth, and Elizabeth was close mouthed about it. She was the only one who knew besides Joanna and Giovanni.

From the *piazzetta* they walked westwards amid beautiful houses and gardens full of flowers until they reached Monte Solaro with statues built during the Roman Empire. There they sat under a tree to have their lunch and take pictures of the Faraglioni, rocks in the sea below, very famous and very characteristic.

The blue of the sky and of the sea was beautiful; it provided a perfect background to the many colorful flowers, plants, and Roman ruins. They rested in this colorful paradise for about an hour after their lunch. They then walked back to the piazzetta and caught the trolley to go back to the Marina Grande. From there they caught a bus to Anacapri on the other side of the island. They visited a church, a miniature replica of the island and shops. They then went back down and swam in the clear, refreshing sea.

It was soon time to leave. After they dried up they walked to the Marina Grande to catch the ferry that was going to take them back to Naples. They had a wonderful time and left the island with regrets.

When they arrived home that evening, even before they got out of the car, Maria's mother asked them if they were hungry. They all laughed and said yes. The dinner was already prepared so all they had to do was sit down and eat it. It was a clear, starry night so, after dinner, they sipped espresso coffee on the front porch and told Maria's mother about their day on the island. Maria gave her the gift she had bought, which she hung on the wall of the kitchen.

Maria asked her mother permission to call Joanna in the States. She called her at the restaurant since Joanna was at work and asked her how she was doing. Joanna was still shook up from what she'd experienced the night before and told Maria all about it. Maria replied that she'd had many experiences of that kind. She told her not to be afraid and if it happened again to call God for help and it would go away.

"That's exactly what I did, Maria. The moment I called God it stopped. You never told me you had things like that happen to you, why?"

"I didn't tell you because they are too weird. I told the doctor and he said I was schizophrenic. I didn't want you to be afraid, but now that you are experiencing it too I can tell you. I saw an orange figure also, one time when a friend was sleeping over at my place one night. The following day he told me about a good friend of his who had died in his arms. I said 'I saw him last night, he was here'. He was all shook up and started to cry. Don't tell anybody about it Joanna, only Giovanni and me. If you tell your therapist and your doctor they will say that you are schizophrenic and will put you on medication. You don't want that, do you?"

"No, I don't. Thank you for warning me. Listen, it's lunch time here and it's getting very busy; I can't stay on the phone so I'll talk to you next time you call me. Call me at home so we can talk longer. I love you Maria and I miss you. Bye."

"Mom don't worry about the phone bill, I'll pay it. I'll leave you some money for it before we go back to the States," Maria told her mother as she joined the group seating on the porch.

"Don't be silly," her mother told her. "It's only once a year, it's not going to break me."

"Mom, I insist. I don't feel right if you don't take the money."

"Okay, if you insist."

"So, Maria, what are we going to do tomorrow?" asked Serena. Serena was the fifth of the six sisters. She was five feet tall and had short hair like Maria. She was very slim and very active. She didn't live in Onofrio but in Monza, near Milan, where she worked in a hospital as an X-ray Technician. Her boyfriend Lorenzo was a co-worker. They shared an apartment and had known each other for five years. They were both on vacation.

"We're going to the beach with Susanna. Do you and Lorenzo want to go? Mom is going with us too."

"Yes, we'd love to go. Count us in. We're leaving now, Marta is expecting us and she'll be worried if we are too late."

Marta was the fourth sister. She was five feet two inches tall and had always been a little overweight. She had a beautiful face, which made up for her hair, which was sparse. She and her family lived in Naples in a beautiful apartment on the last floor of a building. She had two children, Giancarlo and Marina. Her husband, Lino, was a handyman and did most of the decorating work around the house. Serena and Lorenzo went to stay with them every time they came down because they were sleeping together but didn't want Serena's father to know.

Agostino Mariniello was a very old fashioned man and he would certainly not have approved had he known. He was a hermit. He never went anywhere, never participated in the family's activities. He had no friends and spent all his days between the kitchen, where he would watch television, and the front porch where he'd sit in a chair guarding the house and watch people go by. He was seventy-three years old and because of his lifestyle had put on lot of weight and had to be put on a special diet so he wouldn't even share the meals with the rest of the family. This was fine with Maria since he was very opinionated, would talk out of context and created arguments all the time. But she also felt sorry for him. He reminded her of a dog who couldn't talk and spent his days lonely, in a corner. He even spent nights outside. Tonight was no different. He stayed outside as the rest of the family went inside to go to bed.

Next morning Maria and her mother, Lucia Mariniello, got up at seven a.m. They made espresso coffee and sat at the kitchen table to sip it. Maria lit up her first cigarette of the day. "So, how are you doing?" asked Lucia. "We haven't had time to talk since you've arrived."

"I am doing fine, mom, why do you ask?"

"I haven't seen you in a while and I don't know what is going on with you. How is your job?"

"My job is fine. It couldn't be better." Maria was debating whether to tell her about the money but she decided against it. Her mother wasn't very good at keeping secrets, she'd learned in the past."

"How is between you and dad? Does he still beat you up?"

"No, he's changed with age. He doesn't make any scenes

anymore. He can barely walk and he doesn't have any energy to beat me up. We keep each other company; he's also stopped drinking."

"That's good. I am glad to hear that."

"How is your love life? Do you have a boyfriend?"

"No, I am not seeing anyone, but I have a roommate. Her name is Joanna and she is getting married in two months. I am going to be her Maid of Honor. When I go back I'll have to help her with the wedding arrangements and her wedding dress."

"How did you meet her?"

"We met on the trolley when I was going to buy a booklet about the rosary for Elizabeth; she was homeless so I took her in. She found a job at an Italian restaurant where she fell in love with the owner. He is a widower and fell in love with her too, so they decided to get married. Isn't it a romantic story, like Cinderella and the Prince?"

"Yes, it is, but you should be careful Maria about taking in strangers. What if they do you harm?"

"I am not worried about that mom. God is watching over me, he won't let anything like that happen, I just know it. Joanna and I pray all the time."

"I am glad you do because God exists. He is our strength and our refuge. Nothing is too big for Him. Every time you have a problem go to Him and He will see you through."

"How do you think I made it through the divorce and getting on my own two feet? Do you think I'd be where I am right now if it hadn't been for Him? There were times when I didn't know if I was going to make it through the next day. Only my faith in Him saved me and also fear of Him if I actually tried to kill myself, which I wanted to do a lot of times. I didn't tell you how much I suffered because I didn't want you to worry since we were so far apart, but I really had it rough, mom."

"You should have come home with Elizabeth after the divorce. I don't know why you didn't."

"I did it for Elizabeth. She would have fallen behind in school and would have had to learn Italian first before she could go to school here. Plus she loves her dad and it would have been rough on her. Also, since she is an American I don't know if I could have taken her out of the Country without her father's consent. He might have had me arrested for kidnapping. I didn't want to take that chance. Anyway, things have turned out pretty good for me. I love being an American and I have everything I want. I couldn't ask for more." Maria almost told her about the money, but she bit her tongue.

"Well, let's start cooking and have every thing ready by the time Susanna gets here," Lucia said. "Let's fix spaghetti pizza, peppers with olive and capers and friarielli with sausage. Do you think it's going to be enough?"

"Oh yes, more than enough. Let's not forget the fruit. Should we go to the store to buy some more or is this enough?" said Maria pointing at the fruit in a basket.

"More than enough, I think," said Lucia while putting on an apron. She gave Maria one also and they started cooking.

By eight-thirty everything was ready. Maria went to wake up Elizabeth since if she hadn't, she would have slept past ten o'clock. Elizabeth grumbled and put the covers over her head. "Wake up sleepy head, " Maria told her. "We're going to the beach and you better be ready by nine o'clock."

"Yea, whatever," said Elizabeth turning on her other side.

They were ready for Susanna to come back from work. She'd be bringing her son Lorenzo with her. She was the sixth sister, the baby of the family. She was a nurse and worked in a hospital in Naples. She was married to her second cousin Pasquale who was an English teacher and thought in a school in the suburbs where students called him all kinds of bad names. He was afraid to discipline them because their parents were *Mafiosi* who wouldn't hesitate to retaliate by slashing his tires or by giving him a beating. He would come home from his job red in the face and bewildered, incredulous at his pupils' conduct.

Susanna was five feet two inches tall, had olive skin and shiny, long black hair. She had lived with her parents till her son Lorenzo was nine years old, since Pasquale didn't want to marry her. Susanna took him to court and had Pasquale do a paternity test to prove that he was Lorenzo's father. The court ordered him to pay thousands in child support and that's when he decided to marry Susanna. She was very romantic and thought that he did it for love but Maria had her doubts. She didn't want to hurt Susanna's feelings so she said nothing. To make things worse Pasquale had a drug problem and was often in rehab. But marriage seemed to be doing him good even though they bickered all the time.

This morning they were waiting for Susanna to get off work so that she could drive them to the beach. Pasquale would be at work so she had the whole day to herself. A car honked outside the gate. It was Susanna and Lorenzo. Maria opened the gate so she could park the car in the courtyard.

"Boy, I am bushed," said Susanna getting out of the car. "Do you have any coffee made so that I can stay awake?"

"We'll make some fresh, just for you," said Maria. "Are you going to be all right? Maybe you should sleep for a couple of hours. We don't have to go to the beach right now. Besides, we're waiting for Serena and Lorenzo to get here. They are going with us too."

"No, I better not go to sleep. If I do I'll sleep the whole day. I am going to sleep on the beach if Lorenzo will let me."

"Don't worry, we'll keep him away from you. Why don't you go and get Elizabeth out of bed. She didn't want to get up when I went to wake her a while ago. Maybe she'll listen to you."

"Okay, I'll do that. Mom can you give Lorenzo some breakfast? I haven't had time to do it, please."

"Of course. Here Lorenzo, you sit here and *nonna* will fix you a *zuppa* of milk and bread," Lucia said pinching Lorenzo's cheeks and giving him a kiss.

"Maria we need some more bread. Why don't you go to your cousin Gaetana and buy a fresh piece. The money is in the kitchen drawer."

"Sure mom. I'll go right away before she sells them all." Gaetana was the wife of Maria's cousin on her mother's side. She made her living baking delicious bread and selling it to the community. She also sold it to stores. Her husband, Pietro, had bought a big truck and made his living transporting goods or material for people. They had five children. Together, with their trade, they had made enough money to build an apartment for each of their children. Gaetana used to have a cow and sold her milk, but it was too costly to feed her so she got rid of her. Beside the house they lived in they also owned a piece of land where they grew vegetables for the family and apples, which they sold in the winter. They made a good, simple living and they loved their family very much.

When Maria went to get the bread she found Gaetana in the oven room taking the bread out of the oven. Some pieces were already under the cover where they would sweat and make the crust softer. She took out one piece and gave Gaetana the money. After exchanging few pleasantries she went back home.

In the meantime Lorenzo and Serena had arrived. They were in the kitchen drinking coffee and smoking cigarettes with Susanna who had dark circles under her eyes for her lack of sleep. Elizabeth was eating a *zuppa* of milk and bread and drinking a cappuccino.

Maria couldn't resist the fresh bread and made herself a sandwich of *friarielli* and sausage. She told her mother that she wouldn't eat any at the beach, but she had to have some then because it was so good. Lucia laughed because she was pleased and told Maria not to worry, that there was plenty to eat.

It was ten o'clock by the time everybody was ready. They got into the two cars and headed for Licola. They parked at a private beach where they rented two umbrellas and seven lounge chairs. Everybody was carrying something because they had brought so much. They put everything under the two umbrellas and undressed. Lorenzo, Susanna's son, went into the water right away regardless of his mother's protest to the contrary. She wanted him to lie in the sun for a little while so that his body could adjust to the temperature but he wouldn't listen. Lorenzo, Serena's boyfriend went into the water with him and they played volleyball until, exhausted, they came back and lay in the sun.

All the women were lounging and talking as they put on sunscreen except Elizabeth who couldn't speak Italian. Every once in a while she would ask Maria to translate and she wasn't making any effort to learn the language because she had her mother to help her.

Elizabeth loved her *nonna*. She would kiss her cheek every chance she got, which pleased Lucia immensely. She would give Elizabeth money, which made Maria feel guilty because she knew her mother lived on a pension. She decided that she was going to send her money once she got back to the States so that she could not refuse.

Her mother was so giving that people, sometime, took advantage of her. There was a cookware saleswoman who would stop by Lucia's house almost on a daily basis and she would feed her for nothing until Susanna, infuriated, put a stop to it. She would always be concerned about others, especially her family. She was a true servant. She was now retired but she used to work at an elementary school where she would run errands for the teachers and do the cleaning after school hours were over. Anytime she was asked to do something she would say, "Yes ma'm, right away!" and the teachers loved her for it. They were sorry to see her go and Lucia missed her work because it kept her busy as if once she got home she had nothing to do. She had plenty to do. On her way home she'd buy the food to prepare dinner and once she got home she'd have laundry to do, straighten up the house, cook dinner, and anything else her husband needed her to do.

Agostino Mariniello stayed home everyday. He wouldn't even bathe or leave his bedroom except when it was time to eat or use the bathroom. There was a television in his bedroom, which he would watch all day long. He liked particularly American movies especially those of Indians and Cowboys. That was okay for the girls who were still living at home because he would stay out of their way. He was totally useless and wouldn't talk unless he was criticizing or rebuking them about something. Often times he would beat them, so they were glad that he stayed in his room. Maria told him one time, during an argument, "I have lost all respect for you" to which he looked perplexed as if what he was hearing was not possible. Why would she lose all respect for him? What did he do? He was living in his own reality, sometime distorted by alcohol, at which times he would insult his wife and spit on her face.

Poor Lucia, how much had she suffered at his hands. She was a Sainte. He would get terrible fits of jealousy. He was particularly jealous of one of Lucia's co-workers. He told her not to say hello' to him, to which Lucia replied that it was impossible for her not to say hello' and lack good manners. He beat her up and called her names like whore, slut, etc. The swine. Maria was fuming on her lounge chair, thinking about it, and she was amazed at how they were getting along now that they were older. She had the suspicion that the reason Agostino was behaving himself was due to fear. Fear that he was near death and would have to face his Maker soon. She repressed a feeling of compassion wishing that he'd go to hell and pay for all the suffering he had inflicted on all of them.

She wouldn't voice her feelings to the family because she knew that they loved him and had forgiven him in their hearts. Maria had not forgiven him and was constantly pushing away feelings of love, pity, and compassion towards him knowing that deep down he was the same cruel man, only older and without physical strength. As far as Maria was concerned, she didn't have a father here on earth, her father was God.

"Maria, Maria, are you listening?" Lucia asked.

"Uhm?" Maria came out of her thoughts.

"Do you want some coconut?" A beach peddler had stopped by selling fresh, cold coconut out of its shell.

"Yes, I'd love some but only if you let me pay for it," said Maria grabbing her purse. She bought coconut for all of them buying more for herself since it'd been a long time since she'd had any. She bit on it and lay back on the lounge chair savoring every bite.

Few minutes later another peddler stopped by selling beach-wear. He was a black man from Morocco and spoke a broken Italian. All five women gathered around him checking out the merchandise. Serena chose a skimpy bikini; Maria, Elizabeth and Lucia bought sundresses and Susanna a tank top. Again Maria paid for it insisting that it was a gift to repay them for all the kindness they had shown to her and Elizabeth. Lucia was touched and said thank you profusely.

She had her chance to repay Maria about half an hour later when a peddler selling jewelry stopped by. This time it was a man from Tunisia who spoke with a French accent. He was dark skinned but not black and spoke very suave words calling the women " beautiful ladies". Lucia chose a pair of earrings and asked Maria if she liked them, not mentioning that she was buying them for her. They were oval shaped, white with splashes of light blue. Maria liked them so Lucia bought them. She then asked Elizabeth to pick whatever she wanted and that *nonna* would pay for it, to which Elizabeth said thank you and kissed her on the cheek. She spent a long time deciding what she wanted and couldn't make up her mind. She finally asked her mother to help her choose between a necklace and a bracelet, both made out of beads. Maria told her to take them both and that she was going to pay for one of them. "Thank you, mom," said Elizabeth very pleased. That's all she was doing, nowadays, saying thank you to her mother and her grandmother. They were both so loving and so giving that sometime she felt guilty. She hadn't told anyone about the money, just like Maria had asked her to. She was good at keeping secrets, especially since her mother was sharing the bounty with her.

They spent the rest of the day sunbathing, eating, and swimming. Susanna had a chance to sleep since Lorenzo spent most of the time playing in the water.

Around five o'clock they gathered their belongings and drove home.

By the time they all showered it was eight o'clock and everybody was hungry including Agostino Mariniello, who had eaten some leftover from the day before. So Maria and Lucia got busy fixing dinner. It was not late by Italian standards since in Italy it is customary to eat dinner around nine o'clock.

After dinner Serena and Lorenzo took leave going to sleep at Marta's house and Susanna and Lorenzo went to their house. Her husband Pasquale had called complaining that he wanted his dinner and Susanna told him to grab something out of the refrigerator and eat it, not to bother her. He had gotten mad and hung up on her. So she took some of the food they'd had for dinner with her, knowing that he was waiting for her to eat. Lucia warned her not to fight with him when she got home as they said goodbye and for her to get some more sleep since she was still tired.

When everybody was gone Maria, Lucia and Elizabeth watched television until about eleven o'clock when they went to bed. Agostino Mariniello spent most of the night in the chair outside.

They spent the next week going to visit relatives and hanging around the house. Maria took Elizabeth shopping for clothes and shoes since she liked the Italian style. Elizabeth hadn't brought too much from the States just for this purpose since Maria had told her that she was going to buy clothes for her in Italy. They had a grand time especially Maria who could spend without restraint. It gave her an enormous joy to do so, not having to hide the fact that she had money to spend.

For their next outing with the family they went to Pompei about a week later. This time Susanna didn't go since she had to work. Lucia, Maria, and Elizabeth went in the car with Lorenzo and Serena. Lorenzo had never been there, since he was raised in Milan so for him and Elizabeth it was a new adventure. Maria, Serena, and Lucia had already been there.

Pompei was at the foot of Mt. Vesuvius, an active volcano, which had erupted in 79 AD, covering the whole city, killing all the people while they slept. For centuries there had been no trace of it until 1628 when the first ruins were discovered. Now a whole city lay in the sun and people from all over the world came to visit it.

It was sort of magic for Maria to walk on the same stones where people had walked two thousand years before. She wondered about their lives as they went from street to street and decided that she was happier living in the present era. They had to walk slow because of Lucia, but they didn't mind since they took their time admiring the houses, the statues, and the now dead gardens.

The lava and the hot ashes had preserved the city exactly as it was that night and, using a little imagination, you could almost see the active life that people had during that time. There were stores that sold olives, oil, wine, with the containers still intact; there was the Forum where all the public buildings were erect and where people would congregate to discuss their affairs; there were the houses of prostitution with beds made of stones with hay as mattresses; there were paintings and affrescoes adorning every wall; there were beautiful villas for the few rich, and the open theaters where they sang and played.

It was a beautiful, sunny day and they basked in the sun until they decided to go visit the church dedicated to Our Lady of the Rosary, which is located in the Valle di Pompei. Many people have claimed to have received miracles praying in this church, which is dedicated to pray mainly the rosary. Lucia immediately went inside to listen to the Mass. Serena and Elizabeth went to the church's store and Maria and Lorenzo remained outside. Maria had been forbidden to go inside because she was wearing shorts, so she sat on the front steps with Lorenzo where a gipsy started to harass her because she wouldn't give her any money. Since her harassment wasn't upsetting Maria, the gipsy finally tired out and left. After visiting the church they drove back to Onofrio.

So it was the end of another day. They were all very tired because of all the walking they had done that day and were glad to be finally home.

The remaining few days Maria and Elizabeth had left went by very fast. The day they left everybody was sad to see them go but they promised to be back within a year. It was at this time that Lucia gave Maria the earrings.

Maria wasn't sad. She was happy and looked forward to all she had to do with Joanna, and to the house hunting she'd be doing with Elizabeth. They said goodbye with a cheerful heart.

CHAPTER TWENTY-SIX

Maria was excited to see San Diego skyline from her window. The city appeared sparkling clean and she had the feeling of returning home. Joanna was waiting for them at the airport. They hugged and laughed, happy to see each other. Joanna informed them that Giovanni apologized for not coming but he was busy at the restaurant.

On their way to the apartment Joanna asked how their trip had been, to which Maria replied it had been wonderful but she was happy to be home. Once inside the apartment they opened their bags and started unpacking. Maria took out a small box and gave it to Joanna. She opened it with trembling hands. When she finally opened it she gave a little scream. There was a pair of white gold earrings that Maria had bought for her in Venice, in the shape of masks. She put them on and went to look at herself in the mirror. "They are beautiful, Maria. Thank you!" she said hugging her. Maria was very pleased.

"Wait till we go shopping Joanna. We'll have the most wonderful time. Show me that wedding dress you saw in the Bride magazine," she asked. Joanna took the magazine and flipped the pages until she found the dress she was looking for. "Look, isn't it beautiful?" It was indeed beautiful. White pearls, assembled in the shape of flowers, covered the corset. The material for the gown was white satin with white pearls cascading in rivulets from the waist to the hem. A long trail in the back measured at least five feet. On the head the model was wearing a short veil with strings of pearls adorning her forehead.

"Beautiful," Maria said. "And the price is very reasonable, but we should go to some of the stores here in San Diego and see what they have. I kind of had in mind a silk dress and if you want pearls on it we can ask them to customize it for you. What do you think?"

"I say yes, let's do it. It'll be fun to go shopping. We have to do it on my days off, though. Giovanni needs me at the restaurant."

In the next few days Maria made a list of all the bridal stores in San Diego so that on Joanna's days off they already knew where to go. Some of the stores were by appointment only and they had made reservations. They looked at hundreds of dresses and narrowed it down to three or four telling the clerks that they'd be back. They then looked at the dress in the bridal magazine again and compared it to the ones they'd seen. It was a though choice but they decided to order it. So the wedding dress was done with.

Now they had to buy the clothes for the honeymoon. They were going to Taormina, Sicily in the month of September. The weather was still warm there, with nights a little bit chilly, so she needed summer clothes with sweaters for the evening. They had the time of their life shopping, shopping, shopping. Maria bought Joanna everything, from the matching suitcases, to combs and brushes for her head. When they'd go home they'd put the clothes in the suitcases and when they were filled they stopped. She had everything she needed for a splendid honeymoon.

Joanna hadn't told Giovanni anything. She wanted to surprise him. She wanted to see the look on his face when she'd put on the new clothes and look like a million bucks, not to mention the bedroom clothes she had picked from Victoria's Secret and from Frederick's of Hollywood. Saucy.

Time was going pretty fast. Joanna and Giovanni set the date for the wedding for September 12, the day of the Feast of the Virgin Mary. They considered it good luck.

Joanna was baptized and received the sacraments of Communion and Confirmation. To celebrate she invited Maria, Elizabeth and Mrs. Grimaldi to eat at Giovanni's. They were all happy and had good time. Maria bought Joanna a beautiful Bible and had her name engraved on it in gold. Mrs. Grimaldi gave her a gold bracelet and Giovanni diamond earrings. Joanna didn't know whether to laugh or cry she was so thankful. It was all like a dream.

Everything was ready for the wedding. The invitations had been sent out, the menu chosen and given to the cooks, the limousine reserved and the photographer chosen.

One week before the wedding Joanna told Giovanni that Raul couldn't make it because of poor health. Giovanni was very understanding, he didn't probe her with questions and Joanna was relieved. She asked Alfredo if he could walk her down the aisle and he said it would be an honor.

Felicia arrived three days before the wedding and Maria's apartment was getting crowded. There were clothes everywhere, but she didn't mind since it was only for few days. For the wedding Maria had bought a pink, long, silk dress. She was going to wear a pearl necklace and pearl earrings with it. Her hair was cut real short so she didn't need to go to the hairdresser but Elizabeth did. They made an appointment for Felicia, Elizabeth and Joanna for eight o'clock in the morning so they could get their hair done. The wedding was set for twelve o'clock so they would have enough time to get ready for it.

While they were at the hairdresser Maria took a long, hot bath. She put bath oil in the water so her skin would be silky and smooth. When she was done she wrapped herself in a bathrobe and had some breakfast. She was nervous and had to remind herself to breathe every now and then. The same thing was happening to Joanna. Her thoughts were fixed on twelve o'clock. She was feeling so much anxiety she thought she was going to burst. She knew she wasn't going to be able to relax until the vows were spoken and the priest declared them man and wife. As the hairdresser was working on her hair she thought of the lie she had told Giovanni. She wasn't feeling right about it, in fact she felt miserable, but she decided that that was the only way to go. There would be enough time after the wedding for the truth. She didn't want for anything to be in the way of her happiness. This was too important.

Raul had already ruined her youthful life, she wasn't going to let him ruin her adulthood. She cast away flashes of memories out of her mind; today was not the time for them. She had to concentrate on the hours ahead.

She thought of Giovanni and his handsome face. God, she loved him. She still could not believe her good fortune. He was a catch. God must really be watching over her. Sweet God, she would pray to Him the rest of her life. She asked Felicia not to say anything about Raul being in jail while they were having their hair set. Felicia looked worried. She didn't feel right about it either but she went along with her.

After their hair was done a make-up artist did their faces. All three of them looked beautiful. On the way home they kept the windows of the car closed so the wind would not mess up their hair. Maria was still in her bathrobe when they got back. It was only ten o'clock, more than enough time to get ready. She fixed them a light breakfast because all three of them were starving. The mood was festive but also tense.

Joanna looked more beautiful then ever but every now and then she seemed to be gasping for air like a fish out of water. Even though she was hungry she barely touched her food. She told them she was going in Maria's bedroom for a while because she needed to be alone. She closed the door and lit the candle by the shrine. She kneeled as if she was in church and stayed like that for a very long time wanting to talk to God but unable to utter a word. She told herself that He knew what was in her heart and could understand her even though she didn't speak. She sat down and lowered her head. Few more hours and the dread of homelessness would forever perish. Even if something were to go wrong she would not be homeless anymore. She could always go to Felicia's; she thought of her biological mother and of her brother. How she missed them. She wished so much that they could be there today, but she knew she was wishing in vain.

She looked at her watch. It was ten-thirty. She blew out the candle, crossed herself and went into the living room. Maria, Felicia and Elizabeth were already dressed and were waiting for her. The photographer would be there soon, Maria told her, so she better hurry up. They helped her in the wedding dress and put on the veil. Maria asked Elizabeth to help her to straighten up the living room since the photographer would be taking some of the pictures there.

Joanna looked beautiful, so elegant and sophisticated. Maria couldn't help but wonder how strange life is, so full of surprises. Few months ago Joanna was a street person, derelict and destitute, but look at her now. She felt so happy in her heart she would laugh even though nobody said anything funny.

When the photographer arrived she quickly took charge. She had Joanna pose alone for several shots then she took group photographs of all four together. Felicia got to take pictures alone with Joanna since she was the mother of the bride. As Joanna followed instructions to pose she remembered Maria's essay about her wedding and she thought, "It is happening to me but it's as if I am watching a movie. One more hour and my life will change forever."

The white limousine arrived at a quarter to twelve. They all got in and silently were driven to the church. Antonio's children were waiting outside. As Joanna stepped out of the car they grabbed the back of her dress and followed her into the church. Alfredo, who was waiting by the door, gave her a kiss on the cheek and had her put the arm under his.

Joanna's legs were shaking, she was so nervous. Her heart skipped a beat when, looking ahead, she saw Giovanni waiting for her at the altar. He looked like a Spanish prince in his black suit and white shirt.

Giovanni was speechless. She was so beautiful all in white; she reminded him of an angel. Their bodies seemed to reach for each other. It took a lot of self-control for Giovanni not to run towards her and take her into his arms. *My angel*, he thought. She was close now and Alfredo took Joanna's hand and gave her to Giovanni who was visibly shaking from all the emotions he was feeling. Their hearts were beating fast and their heads were spinning but somehow they managed to look calm for all the eyes were focused on them.

The organ stopped playing and the priest started the Mass. Maria and Alfredo took their places by the altar as Maid of Honor and Best Man. They were filled with emotions too.

The church was filled with flowers especially by the statue of the Virgin Mary with the globe and the serpent under Her feet. Joanna had made a special request for that, for good luck. The audience was composed mostly of Giovanni's family and friends. His mother was sitting in the right front row together with Theresa, Penny, Elizabeth and Felicia. They all had tears in their eyes.

Felicia couldn't help but noticing how everything looked so rich, so expensive. She had never imagined it could be so luxurious, so elegant. She felt very proud of Joanna and wished her nothing but the best. She was already envisioning all the grandchildren she was going to have and unknown to her so was Giovanni's mother. They proudly smiled at one another as if on cue.

The Mass was long but the moment finally came to exchange the vows. The wedding bands were simple with inscriptions on the inside. Giovanni had given Joanna a diamond ring for their engagement so he kept the wedding bands plain. Inside it read, "Giovanni and Joanna Forever." Joanna's hands were beautifully manicured and so were Giovanni's. Ever since Joanna had stopped washing dishes she had visited a manicurist once a month so she wasn't embarrassed when she put forth her hand to receive the wedding ring. She almost cried when she put the ring on Giovanni's finger. *You are mine now*, she thought. She was filled with a sense of wonder and bit her lip to make sure she was not dreaming. When he lifted her veil and kissed her she was in seventh heaven and in her heart she thanked God, Jesus and the Virgin Mary. One special thank you went to the Holy Ghost.

At the end of the Mass they slowly walked out of the church with Antonio's children holding the trail of Joanna's dress. They were two lovely girls of six and five years old who wore crowns made of flowers on their heads and beautiful hand-made dresses of pink chiffon that Maria had had made just for them. As they got outside the church everybody gathered around to congratulate them. Joanna and Giovanni were holding hands while saying thank you to the well-wishers. Many of the people Joanna had never seen before and she assumed they were either friends or relatives of Giovanni. They made their way through the crowd and got inside the limousine with the two little girls. They were going to Balboa Park to take pictures for their wedding album. The guests were going to the restaurant to wait for them.

It was a beautiful, sunny day and being it Tuesday the park was not crowded with visitors. They took pictures in front of the Botanical Garden with the pond full of lilies and frogs, in front of the various museums and also inside the Japanese Garden. The two little girls were lovely and were included in many of the pictures.

****

When they entered the restaurant a big applause welcomed them. Two special seats had been reserved for them. Giovanni's mother was seated next to him and Felicia was seated next to Joanna. Maria, Elizabeth, Penny and Theresa were sitting at another table next to theirs. Appetizers were being served. Prosciutto and green melon, salami, black and green olives; *bruschette* with tomatoes, anchovies, olive oil, garlic and oregano; stuffed mushrooms, pickled veggies soon disappeared from the platters. Everybody was hungry since they hadn't had any lunch. Wine was abundant for Giovanni had made a special request to his relatives in Taormina, Sicily. Some of those relatives had flown to San Diego to be at his wedding. Some they would visit on their way there for their honeymoon.

Instead of hiring musicians for the wedding reception Giovanni and Joanna had decided to play the same music they played during the restaurant's business hours, because they could adjust the volume. A band would have made too much noise. They looked at the guests. Everybody was having good time, enjoying the food. Children had been seated at their own tables leaving their parents free to engage in conversation with other guests. The waiters and waitresses were very busy but they didn't mind since their services were a wedding gift to the bride and groom.

Every so often some of the male guests would approach the table and give Giovanni an envelope, which Giovanni would put inside a bag hanging by his chair. Joanna was curious about it so she asked her husband why. He told her it was the wedding gifts and that they would read the cards later, in their hotel room. Satisfied she gave him a big smile at which he gave her a full kiss on the mouth. Joanna blushed and Giovanni smiled at her shyness.

Wait till we're alone, he thought. That was exactly what she was thinking. For a moment she had the temptation to get up and run away, but it seemed that her body was stuck to the chair. She was both wishing and dreading for the moment to come when she would be alone with him. She was sweating at the thought and felt as if everybody was thinking about it to. She wanted to hide.

As if reading her mind Giovanni put his hand over hers and gave it a light squeeze. He then turned towards her and said: "You are my wife now, nobody can touch you." Instead of relaxing at those words Joanna grew even tenser. *"What does he mean 'Nobody can touch you,' does he know about Raul?"* she thought, but didn't say anything, only smiled shyly.

The dinner was composed of three courses plus the wedding cake. Champagne was served when Giovanni and Joanna cut the cake; even the children had a glass to celebrate. Somebody threw confetti in the air and the children left their tables trying to catch them. Everybody was in a happy mood, thanks also to the wine and the champagne. After the cake Joanna asked Maria if she would accompany her to Giovanni's office downstairs. She needed help to get out of the wedding dress and get into her honeymoon clothes. She also needed last minute advices.

"I am so scared Maria, I don't know if I can go through with it. What if I fail? I don't know what to do. Tell me something: Is it hard? Will it hurt?" she asked frantically, holding Maria's wrists till they hurt.

"Take a deep breath, Joanna. Don't panic or you'll make things worse. Like I told you before let him take the lead and he will show you what to do. Be open-minded and remember that he was married for many years before he met you. He has lot of experience so learn from him, ok?"

"You're right. Thank you Maria, I don't know what I'd do without you!"

"You'd be lonely and miserable wondering the streets."

"That's so true, but without me you'd still be working at a boring job four days a week, pinching pennies for your retirement. We're good for each other and we'll be friends forever."

"Amen to that. Now let's get you into your fancy clothes before everybody falls asleep out there. They're all dying to see what kind of clothes you are going to wear for you honeymoon. By the way, it does hurt but soon after you'll feel so good that you'll forget about the pain."

The outfit Joanna had chosen for the occasion was a silk pink skirt with tiny yellow flowers, a pink silk top with short sleeves and a silk and cotton white sweater to complete the ensemble. A white leather purse and white leather shoes accompanied the outfit and Joanna looked and felt like a princess. It made her feel good to wear new clothes, she felt new herself. Maria was folding the wedding dress, putting it away into a large paper bag. She looked at Joanna and silently stared at her with her mouth open.

"Do you know who you remind me of?" she asked.

"No. Who?"

"Wanna White on The Wheel of Fortune."

"You must be joking. She is so beautiful."

"And so are you, my friend, so are you."

"You're just saying that to make me feel good, because today is my wedding day."

"No Joanna, I really mean it and don't forget to go to a model agency to see if you can do some modeling. You are the type of person they're looking for."

"Oh, I don't know, I'll have to talk to Giovanni about it, see what he thinks."

"Of course, you do that."

"I am ready, Maria. Let's leave everything here, I'll take care of it when we come back from our honeymoon. Nobody comes in here because this is Giovanni's office. Only he and myself have the keys.Our bags are already at the hotel, all we have to do is show up. We don't leave for the airport till tomorrow, late in the afternoon. Who knows, I could already be pregnant by then."

"Ah, ah, very funny, Mrs. Grimaldi. I hope you are, for Giovanni's mother's sake. You told me how much she wants a grandson. Just make sure it's a boy. You are so set, Joanna, I am so happy for you, you can't believe."

"Let's go, bambina. They are waiting," said Joanna putting her arm under Maria's arm and walking together upstairs.

The minute they made their entrance a silence came over the room and all the eyes were on them. Then a big applause exploded in the room as people commented how beautiful Joanna looked and how lucky Giovanni was to have her for a *sposa*. Giovanni left her mother to walk towards her. He gave her a big hug and kissed her on the lips.

"You look beautiful, Joanna," he said. He couldn't wait to get away and be alone with her at the Hotel Marriott, by the ocean. If they hurried they could see the sunset from their window. He gently asked her if she was ready. When she said yes they said their good-byes and after taking a group photo they left in Giovanni's Jaguar.

"Giovanni, I forgot to throw the bouquet of flowers to the girls. Do we need to go back?"

"No, we don't. They are probably fighting over it by now. I'll ask my mom about it, when I call her later tonight."

At the restaurant Maria and Mrs. Grimaldi took charge of the situation. Maria had all the single girls line up in the middle of the room where she threw the bouquet of flowers left by Joanna. The girls screamed and pushed to catch it but only a lucky one did. It was Angelica, the daughter of one of Giovanni's cousins. She held the bouquet triumphantly in her hands while her mother tried to fix her hair and dress, which had been ruffled during the scuffle. Mrs. Grimaldi was laughing greatly amused and so was Maria. The waiters and waitresses were clearing the tables and the guests started to leave. They all stopped first by Mrs. Grimaldi to say goodbye. It pleased her very much to be shown respect and she hoped that the young ones would watch and learn.

Felicia was crying, sitting in her chair, all alone. Maria saw her and came close.

"I am sure those are tears of happiness, Felicia," she said.

"Oh, yes Maria, I am so happy. For ten years I did nothing but worry about her. You don't know what a relief it is to see her settling down."

"Don't talk so loud. We don't want Mrs. Grimaldi to hear. She and Giovanni don't know anything about Joanna's past," Maria asked her whispering in her ear.

"Holy Jesus, I forgot. I hope she didn't hear me."

"I don't think she did," said Maria, looking in the direction of Mrs. Grimaldi who was talking to some of the guests who were leaving.

"Anyway," she continued, "we better be going ourselves. Let me ask Mrs. Grimaldi to see if she needs any help and make sure she gets home alright," she told Felicia who had stopped crying. When she came back she told Felicia that everything was under control and that they could leave. Alfredo was to drive Mrs. Grimaldi home after he instructed the dishwasher boys to wash the dishes. He would come back to the restaurant and stay until they were ready to close. Giovanni had left him in charge for the whole duration of the honeymoon. He was going to take vacation from his other job so that he could stay at the restaurant full time.

Maria, Felicia, and Elizabeth caught a cab to go home after saying their goodbyes. Mrs. Grimaldi invited them all to her house for lunch the following day, and they accepted gladly. Felicia was going back to Minneapolis on the coming Saturday and she was glad to spend some time with her daughter's mother in law. So far, from what she'd seen, she seemed to be a very pleasant person. Her manners were graceful and she absolutely adored her son. Her son adored her also, you could tell by the way he talked to her, even if she didn't understand what they were saying, since they spoke a Sicilian dialect.

Once back at Maria's apartment they all took their shoes off first thing, then they changed into more casual clothing and sat down on the couch looking into space, going back with their minds to the day's events. It was about seven in the evening and nobody felt like talking, but it was too early to go to bed so they turned on the television and spent the rest of the evening watching CNN and then a movie on AMC.

****

It was ten past six p.m. when they arrived at the hotel. It took them five minutes to check in and get the keys to their room. All of their luggage, four big suitcases, was already in the room waiting for them. Before they got inside Giovanni opened the door, then took Joanna in his arms and carried her over the threshold as tradition demands. Once inside he kissed her passionately holding her very tight until she could hardly breathe.

She broke away. "Do you want to become a widower the same day of your wedding, Mr. Grimaldi?" Joanna said. "I could not breathe. Another kiss like that and I am dead."

"I am so sorry, Princess," Giovanni said apologetically. "It's just that I wanted to hold you all day long. I am afraid I got carried away."

"I forgive you, Giovanni. Look, they gave us champagne on ice. How nice of them; and these roses, they are beautiful. You did it, didn't you? You arranged it!"

"Yes, I admit it, I am guilty. But wait," he pulled back the curtains. "Look at this."

Joanna gasped. In front of her was the whole San Diego Bay. The sun, a huge fireball, was setting behind Point Loma and cast a warm glow over their faces and hair. Giovanni took two champagne glasses and poured the cold liquid into them. He gave one to Joanna and stood with her at the window without saying a word. It was a sacred moment. They stood there until the sun disappeared behind the hills.

It got dark in the room. Giovanni turned on a lamp by the bedside. Joanna didn't move. She was paralyzed by fear of the intimacy that was going to take place in the next few hours. She had all sorts of conflicting emotions. She had desired this moment to come for months and now that it was here she didn't know what to do.

Giovanni sensed her uneasiness. He lied down on the bed and asked her to lie down next to him. She did, after putting the glass by the ice bucket with the bottle of champagne inside. He stretched his arm and she nestled there.

"I won't do anything you don't want me to, Joanna. I can tell you're very nervous and tense, and I know that you are a virgin so I won't push you. When you are ready you'll let me know. How about we take a nice, hot shower. We've been out all day and our bodies are tired. A shower might perk us up a little. What do you say, Princess? Do you want to go first?"

"No, I might take longer, so you go first," replied Joanna.

While he was taking a shower she carefully selected a sexy, white nightgown from Frederick's of Hollywood. She took her toothbrush, toothpaste and a very expensive and delicate perfume to put on her skin after the shower. She didn't know it but she was going to drive Giovanni insane with passion. Everything she did turned him on, whether it was talking, walking or just plain sitting. She didn't know the power she had and that made her very sexy.

The light by the bedside cast shadows in the room. It wasn't very bright but Joanna didn't turn on any other light preferring it to be semi-dark. It was more intimate and she wasn't as shy as she would have been with bright lights.

Giovanni came in the room wrapped in a towel, which he let go to the floor remaining totally naked. Joanna let out a little scream and started to shake. He put the towel back on apologizing to her. Looking in his suitcase he found a silk pajama, which he put on his naked body.

While in the shower Joanna told herself to act like a woman and not like a silly girl the way she'd behaved a few moments earlier. *What's wrong with you?* She told herself. *Act like a woman.* She had no idea what a woman would act like but she knew it wasn't like she had before. After the shower she sprayed the perfume on her body, especially her intimate parts, brushed her teeth, combed her hair and put on the nightgown. She then sat on the toilet bowl taking big breaths, trying to find the courage to step out into the room. She heard a knock on the door. "Joanna, are you all right?" Giovanni sounded worried.

"I am fine, Giovanni. I am almost done," replied Joanna getting up as if she had been caught stealing. She looked at herself in the mirror and decided that she looked fine. Timidly she opened the door. Giovanni was lying in bed with the covers up to his chest.

"You look beautiful, Joanna," he said. "Come here by my side, Princess."

He was eating her up with his eyes. She was a very pretty sight and he still couldn't believe she was all his. He remembered his first night with his wife years and years ago, how they had both been inexperienced and fumbled with each other's bodies until they found some rhythm. He tried to call on his previous sexual experience to aid him and to make it the most memorable night of their lives together. No matter what was going to happen from now on that night they would remember forever.

He extended his arm on the pillow and as she had done before she nestled there finding comfort in his embrace. Her perfume caught him by surprise. It smelled divine; a mixture of roses and white ginger, it tickled his nostrils getting straight up to his brain. A strap of the nightgown fell off her shoulder leaving one of her breasts exposed. She didn't try to cover it up feeling the beginning of sexual arousal the way she had felt with Raul, at times. She told herself that the man next to her was not that horrible man, this one was her husband and she was supposed to have sexual relations with him, that she had everyone's blessing.

Giovanni was slow in his movements. He deliberately was taking his time because he wanted her to ask, no, to beg for it. He thought about turning the light off but decided to leave it on instead. He wanted her to overcome her shyness and he also wanted to see her face and body when she would climax. One of his hands grabbed her breast and squeezed gently, rubbing the nipple between his fingers making Joanna moan from pleasure. He whispered in her ears sexy words, knowing full well the power they had to excite. Joanna, despite the nervousness, felt herself melting. A strong desire was awakening between her legs. He took her breast in his mouth and sucked on it while his hand massaged the other breast. Joanna spread her legs unashamed. She took one of his hands and put it there. Giovanni didn't hesitate. He started to rub her clitoris, inserting one of his fingers in her vagina; few seconds later he felt her climax. He looked at her face; she was bewildered. She didn't know what had just happened and what did it mean. She looked at him as if coming back from a dream, a dream she wanted to go back to.

Well, Giovanni thought, *she has no problem when it comes to orgasm; I am going to make her come the whole night; I am going to give her as much as she can take. All these years of abstinence will work in my favor. I want as much of her as I can have.*

Joanna lied back with a smile on her face; her eyes were closed and her breath heavy; perspiration appeared on her forehead and on her lips, which Giovanni dried up with his hand. She wanted to tell him it was beautiful what had just happened, that never in her life had she thought that something like that was possible, but the words would not come out.

"Did you like it, Cinderella?" Giovanni asked apprehensible, since she was so quite.

"Oh yes, I did. Is that what they call heaven because I felt like I died and went to heaven. Can you send me there again?"

"Oh yes, I can, as many times as you want."

"What do I have to do Giovanni?"

"Just lie back and relax; you don't have to do anything but enjoy it." He took off her nightgown and his pajama leaving both of them completely naked. He looked at her body in total awe; it was so beautiful, he thought himself the luckiest man on earth. She was his and if any man dared to touch her he wouldn't hesitate to kill him. He hugged her tight covering her body with his, flesh against flesh. His member was turgid with blood, wanting to feel the moistness between her thighs, but he was a patient man, he could wait. He wanted to arouse her again until she begged him to penetrate her. That wasn't hard to do. He started with her ears, biting and licking on her lobes; he felt her shiver but he didn't stop. He moved down to her neck gently kissing it. His hands were rubbing her breasts, teasing her nipples with light pinches. Joanna felt in heath, open and willing, amazed and in awe. What kind of man had she married; only a wizard could create such alchemy. He must be a magician of the flesh. He was sending rivers of sensations through her body; her legs were parting as if they had a will of their own. She spread them wide drawing him in the middle, trusting her lower body upwards, emitting low moans of pleasure. Giovanni couldn't resist any longer. He thrust his penis into her vagina and even though he knew she was a virgin he was surprised to find resistance. Her veil would not let him penetrate her. He drew back and murmured, "I am sorry."

Joanna was confused; why was he sorry? He thrust his penis inside of her again, this time with more resolve. He did it again and again until the veil broke, all the time thinking, "I am the first, the one and only." Joanna's moans of pleasure had turned into moans of pain but as Giovanni moved inside of her the pain seemed to dissolve, replaced by spasms of joy. It felt so good each time he pushed in that she would lift her pelvis to make the impact go even deeper. She wanted to suck him in, instead she kissed his mouth inserting her tongue inside, moving it in and out in harmony with his penis.

But wait, what was she feeling? A warm sensation was starting to spread over her, concentrating in her belly and between her thighs. It grew stronger and stronger until it seemed that the sky had opened and a great white light engulfed her. Her brain was not in her head anymore, but she was everywhere, free and loved, with no pain, only joy.

Giovanni was pushing and pushing until a big moan escaped his lips and then he lay flat on her body, holding her tight.

After what seemed an eternity they broke apart kissing one more time. Giovanni got up, naked, and closed the curtains. He then went by the small bar and filled their glasses with champagne. He gave Joanna one and they both drank it as water, in one gulp, they were so thirsty.

Joanna felt like an explorer who had just discovered a new continent. This was great, why wasn't everybody happy, why wasn't everybody doing it? Had she known it felt so good would she still have been a virgin? She honestly didn't know, she only knew that this was the best thing that had happened in her life and that she was grateful to Giovanni for giving it to her. She considered herself a full-fledged woman now; she was married and no longer a virgin, Raul was in jail and Giovanni was going to protect her now and forever. What more did she want? She wanted no more; she was fully satisfied.

"Are you hungry, Giovanni?"

"A little; why, are you?"

"Yes. I didn't eat hardly anything at the reception. Now I am starving. Can we order room service?"

"Yes we can. Let me see, there should be a menu here, oh here it is. What would you like? This sounds interesting: Pepper steak with baby carrots and green beans, French bread and butter with flan for dessert and a bottle of champagne compliments of the hotel for newly weds."

"I can't wait; please call right away. I am going to take a shower again, I hope you don't mind."

"I don't mind. You go right ahead, Princess."

Giovanni lifted the phone and called room service. He was in a good mood because their lovemaking had been a success. It wasn't as if he hadn't worried about it. Even though he got turned on every time he was near her it had been five years since he had had sex and he had gotten older, not younger. With Joanna being twenty-eight years old he needed to perform at top level and he didn't know if he could do a good job all the time, but so far so good. He reached into his suitcase and pulled out a silk robe. He put it on. While he was waiting for room service to arrive he poured himself another glass of champagne.

Joanna went naked into the bathroom. She noticed that there was blood between her legs, not much but enough to have probably stained the sheets. She thought of the pain she had felt and decided that it was a small price to pay for the joy she had felt afterwards. It didn't hurt anymore; it just felt a little sore. She didn't know how lucky she was being able to orgasm during sex. She didn't know there were women who never felt it and had to masturbate afterwards. There was so much more she didn't know but Giovanni was a good, loving man who would teach her everything. She felt she loved him so much more now, that they were as one flesh. God blessed their union because Giovanni was a widower, not a divorced man, and she had never married before.

It was very important that she felt blessed by God because, even though she had just recently become a Christian, her faith was very strong. God came first, then Giovanni. She wondered if Maria felt the same when she had sex; she was going to ask her if she wasn't too shy. She practiced positive thinking and envisioned herself having a great marriage and three beautiful children. She could be getting pregnant that night for all she knew. Her period was due in two weeks. She'd wait and see. They'd have to have children right away because Giovanni was fifty-five already. If they had a child by next year Giovanni would be seventy-six years old by the time the boy was twenty. It had to be a boy to carry on the family's business even though if it were a girl it would be just the same. Women now a-days could do most everything men do, sometimes even better.

For some reason though, she knew that a boy would be like a trophy for Giovanni and that he would be incredibly happy to have any child since he had almost resigned himself to die without an heir. As the mother of an heir she would be incredibly spoiled both by Giovanni and his mother, not to mention by Felicia and Maria. She looked forward to that happening to her.

A knock on the door brought her back to reality. It was Giovanni letting her know that the food had arrived. She walked naked into the room, took the nightgown from the bed and put it on, then went to her suitcase and found a robe. She put that on as well. She looked very virginal all in white, even though Giovanni would have preferred to see her naked.

With the dinner the hotel had included two candles and a red rose at Giovanni's request. They lit the candles and turned off the lights. A soft music was coming from the radio by the bedside. It was perfect. Joanna was a little shy and didn't talk much, but she looked at him with adoring eyes.

"Thank you Joanna," said Giovanni out of the blue.

"Why, what for?" she asked puzzled.

"For being a virgin. It means a lot to me. Now a-days it's hard to find one. Virgins are as rare as diamonds, speaking of which I have a present for you. Close your eyes."

Joanna did as she was told. Giovanni went to his jacket and took a box out of his pocket. In it there was a diamond necklace. He went behind Joanna and put the necklace around her neck. He told her to open her eyes.

"Go by the mirror," he said to her. She did and she gasped. The necklace was beautiful. There must have been ten diamonds in it. Was he that rich?

"Thank you, Giovanni, this is so beautiful, I don't know what to say."

"You don't need to say anything, you look beautiful. Diamonds suit you."

She wanted to ask how much it cost but she refrained herself, not wanting to spoil the moment. She kept the necklace on even after they went to bed. They turned the television on and rented a movie.

"Do you realize we don't have to go to work for a whole month?" she said after the movie was over. "Yes I know. We'll have to keep busy or we'll get bored. We can stay up late tonight. Our flight to London doesn't leave till six in the evening tomorrow. We can stay in bed till three o'clock."

"Yes, we have to stay busy. Any idea Mr. Grimaldi?" Joanna asked teasingly.

"Yes, Mrs. Grimaldi. Let me show you," he answered turning the lights out and taking her into his arms.

It was two o'clock in the morning, when, finally exhausted, they fell asleep.

CHAPTER TWENTY-SEVEN

T hey woke up around ten the next morning. Joanna went to brush her teeth and returned to bed while Giovanni was stretching lazily under the covers. She kissed him on the head.

"Wake up Giovanni. Let's call room service and have a great breakfast in bed," she said to him.

"What time is it?" he replied.

"It's ten past ten. We slept eight hours straight. That's plenty of sleep. Wake up."

"You order room service. I want to be pampered, Mrs. Grimaldi," said Giovanni.

"I love to do that, Mr. Grimaldi. I want to pamper you to death and spoil you rotten," Joanna said picking up the phone and calling room service. She ordered coffee, grapefruit juice, scrambled eggs, sausage, bacon, toast and jam. She asked for a red rose like the night before because she thought the idea was very romantic.

The breakfast was delicious and satisfying. They showered and returned to bed where they made love, lingering and enjoying every minute of it. They lay in each other's arms for a long time afterwards, satisfied and content to just snuggle, each thinking their own thoughts of how blessed and lucky they were to have found one another, not wanting to break away not even for a minute for fear of losing the magic they had created.

Around one o'clock they got up. Joanna went to shower first.

While she was in the bathroom Giovanni took the sheet stained with blood off the bed, folded it neatly and put it in one of his suitcases. He then covered the bed with the bedspread so that Joanna wouldn't notice the missing bed sheet. He was sitting on the loveseat when she came out, suspecting nothing.

He went to take a shower while Joanna dressed. For their honeymoon they were going to Palermo and Taormina, in Sicily, via London. For the trip to London she chose to wear a very comfortable outfit, which Maria had bought for just that occasion. She had actually bought her two. She packed one in her carry-on bag and wore the other. The one she wore was navy and the other was sage. She would wear it from London to Sicily.

She took off her diamond necklace and put it in her purse. It wasn't appropriate to wear on a trip, more for a night out or a dinner party. She left on her diamond earrings.

Giovanni came out of the bathroom naked and comfortable as if they had lived together forty years. Joanna admired his strong body. Even though he didn't exercise the busy life he had at the restaurant kept him fit. He really didn't look fifty-five. She was so proud to be married to him. "Mrs. Grimaldi" sounded divine to her.

Giovanni wore jeans and T-shirt with a leather jacket. After he got dressed he called his mother to see if she needed anything before they left for their honeymoon. Alfredo was going to take her to church on Sundays and for this purpose he had given him the keys to his Jaguar. He told her that he was going to call her from Sicily to make sure she was all right. She protested that she was not disabled and that she could take care of herself. She told him not to worry and to enjoy their honeymoon. Joanna said hi also and she told her that she loved her for the first time. Mrs. Grimaldi was deeply touched and was glad that she had given her blessing.

After they hung up Joanna called Maria to see how she was doing and to say goodbye to Felicia who was returning to Minneapolis that evening. Maria was driving her to the airport in the Ferrari. Felicia asked Joanna to send her postcards and to call her every once in a while to let her know how things were. Joanna agreed and hung up the phone.

So it was time for them to check out of the hotel and head on to the airport. They called the porters for their luggage and went to the black limousine that was waiting for them. They were flying British Airways to London and from London to Rome. In Rome they would embark on Alitalia to Palermo. After going through check-in they still had two hours to kill before their flight would leave, so they went through the many shops to spend their time. Joanna bought two novels by Danielle Steel to read on the plane and Giovanni bought a book by Louis L'Amour. Together they also bought some magazines. Joanna was using the money she had from her paycheck and was curious to find out how her finances were going to be now that she was married. When they sat down she approached the subject with Giovanni.

"Giovanni, now that we're married how am I going to make a living? Am I going to get paid for working at the restaurant?"

"Of course you're going to get paid, Princess. How about you becoming the manager and be paid fifteen dollars an hour? That way you won't have to ask me for money all the time and can do whatever you want with it without having to explain to me. You'd be more independent, that way, you know what I mean?"

"Yes, you are right. What would I have to do as the manager?"

"You'd be in charge of the restaurant and I'd be in charge of the nightclub. Do you think you can handle it or is it too much?"

"No, no, it's fine. I can handle it Giovanni. Thank you."

"Of course if you need money for big things like buying furniture or a car we take it out of the profit we make at the restaurant, which reminds me of something. Start thinking of what car you want when we come back because I want you to drive a brand new car. The one you have is not good enough for you; it was just to manage till you became my wife. My wife has to drive in style so that people know that I am treating her with respect."

"I don't care what people think, Giovanni, but I accept the car. I too, want to drive in style like you and Maria. Oh don't worry, I won't ask for a Ferrari but pretty close. I promise to take good care of it, though. What do you think of a BMW?"

"Very good choice. When we come back we'll go shop for one. Give me a kiss to seal the promise." Joanna happily kissed him on the mouth, she then blushed because she saw people looking at them. She told herself that she was stupid for blushing; that she was married now and could kiss Giovanni any time she wanted. Giovanni smiled at her discomfort and prolonged the kiss to make her point. It was funny how Giovanni seemed to read her mind at times and at this thought she became nervous thinking about Raul and the lies she had told about him. She hoped that he wouldn't suspect anything, at least not until she became pregnant.

First class passengers were called to board the airplane first. They were flying first class on British Airways because they could fly straight to Europe without having to stop in New York or Philadelphia. They could afford the luxury and took it. Joanna felt as if she had died and gone to heaven. On their way to the airport, into the limousine, she had seen homeless people in the street and thanked God she was not one of them anymore. God willing, she had escaped that fate for the rest of her life. She was sure in her heart that their marriage would last forever, till death did them part. They walked hand in hand to their seats. Joanna wanted to seat by the window so she could see San Diego from the air. She was excited like a little girl and Giovanni experienced joy in his heart at seeing her reaction. He wanted to please her with everything he did and had every intention to make her happy for the rest of their life.

She had become his muse; he felt twenty years younger, energized by her presence and awed by her looks. It hadn't escaped him how other men looked at her and also other women. She had the kind of beauty you'd see in young women posing in a Playboy spread. Her body was perfect and he felt like a very lucky man to possess such a beauty. She was his and nobody else. He had been her first man and, God willing, he would be her last. He wouldn't forget that. He was going to transform her from the insecure girl that she was, into a full-grown woman, secure and sophisticated as if she was born to be rich. She deserved to be pampered.

Joanna was nervous because of the long flight ahead of them and was holding Giovanni's hand real tight. He advised her to take big breaths and exhale real slowly. She did that and was able to relax a little, not much. After the takeoff the stewardess offered them champagne and that made Joanna sleepy. She covered herself with the blanket, put the pillow on the reclined seat, gave Giovanni a kiss and fell into a peaceful sleep.

Giovanni awakened her with a gentle squeeze of her hand when the stewardess started to serve dinner. She ate, not because she was hungry, but because it would be a long time before they'd eat again. Giovanni did the same, commenting about the quality of the food, tasting better than he'd imagined.

"Who is coming to pick us up at the airport in Palermo, Giovanni?"

"My cousin and his wife, why?"

"How old are they?"

"I don't know, around my age. My cousin is the son of my mother's sister but I haven't seen him since my wife died five years ago. He came here for the funeral. We're like brothers and we talk on the phone a lot. He has three children. The oldest is your age. He is very handsome, I am afraid you'll run away with him and leave this old man."

"Oh, please hush. I don't want to hear you talk like that. You are not old and I will never leave you, not even for a king. I am one man woman and you will find that out."

"You make me happy, Joanna. Please don't change."

"I won't Mr. Grimaldi. You have no idea how important you are to me. You are my knight in shiny armor and I am the luckiest woman in the world. I wouldn't change my place with anyone, not even the Queen of England."

"Let's see what movie we can watch," Giovanni said picking up a magazine and looking at the programming list. Each seat had a small TV screen on the back, which could be programmed to show different movies by changing station. They each selected a different movie and fell silent. They held hands most of the flight like two teenagers.

In London they had to wait four hours for their flight to Rome. They spent the time shopping in the many stores in the international terminal of Heathrow Airport. Giovanni bought duty free perfume for his cousin's wife and for Joanna, and Joanna bought a navy sweater with "London" embroidered on the front. She also bought an old fashioned, white nightgown.

Hungry, they had lunch at one of the restaurants, taking their time. Giovanni hadn't slept a wink and if she hadn't slept a couple of hours after the champagne, Joanna wouldn't have slept a wink herself, so they both looked haggard. After lunch they went to the restrooms to freshen up. Joanna changed outfit and washed her face, putting on fresh make up. She looked wonderful when she was done. Giovanni complimented her on her looks and Joanna was really pleased.

There were TV terminals showing arrivals and departures in the middle of the terminal and they looked for their flight. It was on time and was starting to board at gate 56. They hurried so they wouldn't lose the flight and barely made it. Luckily, they had changed the time on their watches or they would have missed it completely.

Once in Rome they started to have a taste of the Italian culture. Giovanni seemed unperturbed by the commotion but Joanna was dumbfounded. People seemed to yell at one another instead of talking and they were gesticulating in a grand manner. It all seemed very theatrical and she kept looking at them, mesmerized. She was glad she was with Giovanni who knew the language and his way around, otherwise she wouldn't have known what to do. It was with relief that she boarded the Alitalia's flight to Palermo, holding Giovanni's hand.

The airplane was smaller than the other they had traveled in, but it didn't matter much because the flight seemed very short in comparison. As expected they found Giovanni's cousin and his wife waiting for them at the airport. Giovanni shook hands and hugged them, kissing both their cheeks. He introduced Joanna who was very shy and didn't know what to say. Giovanni hadn't taught her how to say anything in Italian so she was at loss for words. She wished she had thought about it early enough to learn at least the most simple words like "hi" or "pleased to meet you". As it was she extended her hand, which they shook. Then, without any warning they hugged her and said:

"Benvenuta" which meant welcome as Giovanni explained to her. She said thank you and looked at them.

Giovanni's cousin, Vincenzo, seemed his replica. They were the same height, had the same facial features except for the eyes.

Vincenzo's were brown. His wife, Amelia was shorter, maybe five feet four inches tall, had brown hair, brown eyes and was slightly overweight. She dressed very conservative like Vincenzo, who wore a pair of brown slacks and a white polo shirt. They had come into a rented van like Giovanni had suggested, so there'd be enough room for their luggage. Each one of them had two large suitcases plus the carry-ons. After they loaded the van there was barely any room left for them. The ride to their house took twenty-five minutes. They stopped in front of a two- story building. Three young men came out and helped them unload the van after each of them had hugged and kissed Giovanni and shaken hands with Joanna. They looked at Joanna admiringly and told their uncle that she was very beautiful. Joanna blushed when Giovanni told her. All the eyes were on her and she felt flattered by all that attention. The oldest son, the one who was her age, was devouring her up with his eyes but she preferred to act as if she hadn't noticed. He was extremely handsome but it didn't mean anything to Joanna who was madly in love with her husband.

Their house had two floors with five bedrooms upstairs. They gave their guests the master bedroom, which also had a bathroom. The walls of the house were two feet thick, even the internal walls. The house was beautiful, richly furnished. The tall windows had hand crocheted curtains, there were handmade tablecloths covering the tables, Persian rugs on the floor and a maid to take care of it all. She was in her fifties, all dressed in black because she was in mourning. Most women in southern Italy, especially in small towns, wore black all the time because they mourned for one relative or another. Assunta, the maid, was no exception.

It was nine in the evening and everybody was starving. Assunta had set the table for seven and announced that dinner was ready to be served. After a short visit to the bathroom everybody sat at the table to have dinner. The conversation was led mainly by Vincenzo and Giovanni who were discussing the state of their businesses. Vincenzo was a constructor who was very successful especially since he paid a high "tangente" to the mafia who would provide work for him and his crew. His first two sons worked with him while the third one was attending the university to become an engineer. They were very proud of him.

Joanna was listening attentively to the sounds the two were making but she failed to recognize any word. She ate everything that was put in front of her because she was very hungry and the food was delicious. Assunta was very pleased and she liked the "Americana" right away.

After dinner the men went to the studio where they drank whiskey and the women went to the "soggiorno" to have coffee. Joanna wanted to refuse the coffee because she would not be able to go to sleep since it was so late at night, but she didn't know how to convey her thoughts and Giovanni was not there to translate for her. She drank it slowly so that she wouldn't have to drink another cup. She felt openly eyed by Amelia who genuinely thought that she was beautiful and that Giovanni had made a good choice. She kept her hands on her lap and a big smile on her face to convey her feelings to her. She knew very little English. "You like?" she asked Joanna offering another cup of coffee. "No, no, thank you," said Joanna smiling back at her. "I sleepy," she continued, making the gesture of a sleeping face by bringing her cupped hands up to it. "Capisco," said Amelia. "Good night, cara," she said leading her upstairs to her room. She showed her the bathroom and left after giving her a hug and a kiss.

The suitcases were in the room and Joanna took out a night-gown. She went to the bathroom and ran the water to take a bath. She took off her clothes dropping them to the floor and stepped into the tub. Within ten minutes she was fast asleep and that's where Giovanni found her half an hour later.

Poor Cinderella, he thought, she must have been really tired. He bent down to kiss her forehead.

"Wake up Joanna," he said, gently taking her hand into his.

"Oh my God, I fell asleep; I could have drowned," Joanna exclaimed, waking up. She sat up straight.

"Let me help you get washed up. I want to shampoo your hair, then I am going to lather your whole body and then I will give you a first class massage once you come out of the water."

"Yes, that sounds absolutely divine. I am fully awake now and at your mercy. Do to me as you wish, my lord." Giovanni was surprised she was in such a good mood and willing to go along with his plans. He shampooed her hair making sure he didn't get any shampoo in her eyes. He then took a washcloth, poured bat gel on it making a rich lather and preceded to scrub her body with it. When he got to the lower section he asked her to stand up. She did so, amused. Washing her genitals he paused there long enough to arouse Joanna and waken her desire. She told him to hurry, that she wanted to make love.

When he was finished she turned on the shower to get the soap off her body and let him dry her up as if she was a little girl and he was her daddy. Raul came into her mind but she quickly chased him off by imagining that she bit his penis really hard and chopped it off. She would not allow him to ruin her life. What she couldn't do to him in real life in all those years, she was brave enough to do now with her mind encouraged by the love and respect that Giovanni was showing towards her. After he dried her up he kissed her mouth slowly pushing his tongue inside while grabbing and squeezing her breast. Joanna was enflamed and asked him to hurry and make love to her.

Giovanni was better able to control his arousal. He announced that he was going to take a shower and for her to start warming up the bed. Like a little girl Joanna obeyed. She had never felt this way her whole life; she had never wanted a man like she wanted him. She was totally taken by the pleasure she had discovered in her orgasmic vagina. She wanted it and wanted it soon. She put on a short, shiny rayon nightgown that revealed her magnificent breast, just for the pleasure she would feel when he would take it off. It took Giovanni ten minutes to shower after which he came in the bedroom, moisture still on his tanned skin. Joanna pretended to be dozed off while she was delirious with desire and couldn't wait till he touched her, which he did eagerly. It was very late when, finally exhausted, they fell asleep.

Joanna couldn't believe what was happening to her. Her body seemed to be new, as if it belonged to someone else that she was just beginning to know. She was afraid that it would all disappear and she wanted to make love every day just to reassure herself that it was all real, that she wasn't just imagining it. She adored her body for giving her such wonderful sensations; it was her new friend and she decided that she would lavish on it loving care by spending more time taking care of it, by massaging expensive creams into her skin, by exercising every day at least an hour, by paying more attention to her posture.

Next morning they woke up late. By the time they went downstairs it was ten-thirty and the whole family was waiting for them. Joanna looked very beautiful and the three boys were just eating her up with their eyes. The Americana was very cool in a white dress that exposed her tanned arms and legs. She was wearing a pair of white sandals, which made her legs look very sexy. They were offered cappuccino and *cannoli*, which they ate with gusto, regardless of the fact that five pairs of eyes were staring at them. When they finished eating they were consulted about making plans for the day. Giovanni would translate for Joanna and Joanna stated that whatever they decided to do was fine with her.

It was eleven o'clock and they still had two hours to go shopping or visiting churches or museums. Italian stores and businesses closed for siesta from one to four p.m. During the siesta most people went home to eat and sleep until they had to go back to work.

Since they were going to Taormina the following day they decided to take a grand tour of the city driving around, stopping at very old churches where Joanna had to borrow a shawl from Amelia to put over her shoulders since you can't go inside sleeveless. Amelia had brought the shawl specifically with that in mind and Joanna was grateful for that. Inside the churches' stores they purchased books and rosaries, which they were going to mail to the United States since there was no room in their luggage.

At one o'clock they went to eat at Luigi's, a restaurant near the water, which specialized in seafood bought fresh every day from local fishermen. Giovanni and Joanna were advised by Amelia and Vincenzo to order the seafood *zuppa* , a mix of different kinds of fish and shellfish cooked in a broth of water, tomato sauce and spices. Delicious. They also found on the menu spaghetti with tomato sauce and eggplant, which Mrs. Grimaldi had fixed for them in San Diego. They tried one serving to see if it was as good and decided that Mrs. Grimaldi's was better, although it wasn't bad.

After lunch they went back to the house for a nap since they were tired from walking and the weather was very hot. They woke up refreshed and looking forward to spending their second evening in Palermo. Giovanni was ready before Joanna and he went downstairs to spend some time with his cousin Vincenzo, to discuss business matters with him since they were going to be busy the following day.

They were engaged in business talk when Joanna entered the room. Both their mouths opened but no sound came out. She was a vision in a black dress, wrapping her body tightly, leaving her shoulders exposed. Her blonde hair framed her face, which looked angelic with subtle nuances of make up expertly applied.

"Is something wrong?" she asked.

"No, no, nothing is wrong dear, we were just admiring you. You look divine," Giovanni replied.

"Buon pomeriggio," said Vincenzo kissing her hand. He wanted to say that she looked beautiful but he refrained himself not wanting to arouse his cousin's jealousy. Amelia came in from the kitchen where she had been instructing Assunta about their dinner. Her mouth fell open too when she saw Joanna. She circled around looking at her from every side. *"Mamma mia, Joanna. Come sei bella,"* she said with a twinge of envy in her voice.

"What did she say?" Joanna asked Giovanni.

"She said you look beautiful," he replied.

He pointed to an armchair and invited her to sit down, which she did. They continued their business talk while Amelia and Joanna sat opposite each other not having the slightest clue on how to communicate; after five minutes of staring Amelia grew impatient and got up gesturing to Joanna to follow her. They went in the kitchen where Assunta was busy preparing dinner and asked for a lemonade. Joanna took it gratefully because she was really thirsty. Amelia gestured to her again and led her out into the garden. A gazebo with benches was in the middle of it and they went to sit down there. The sun was on the other side of the building and they enjoyed a nice, refreshing shade.

Joanna looked around, curious. Gardening was one of her passions and she wished she could tell Amelia that, but she didn't know how. She finished her lemonade and got up, followed by

Amelia. As she stopped in front of plants Amelia would tell her the name of the vegetables. She learned that tomato was pomodoro, basil basilico, celery sedano, parsley prezzemolo, zucchini zucchini, lettuce insalata, broccoli broccoli, origano origano, lemon limone, and other plants too numerous to remember. Amelia and Vincenzo were fortunate to have a garden. It was a luxury since they lived in the city and they got out of it as much as they could.

Joanna and Amelia turned around as they heard voices coming in the garden. It was the three boys or rather young men who were laughing amused at something one said. They stopped on their tracks as they saw Joanna and she became uncomfortable when she realized the effect she was having on them. Amelia was amused and scolded them for not saying good afternoon. They seemed tongue-tied and were very self-conscious as they were talking to their mother. She told them to go take a shower and get dressed for their early dinner. Normally they would have dinner around eight-thirty but since Joanna and Giovanni were used to dine around six o'clock they had anticipated the dinner to seven p.m.

They didn't see the young men for another hour when they showed up in the living room where Joanna and Amelia were look-ing at some photo albums. They had brought with them an English-Italian dictionary, determined to have a conversation with Joanna. Through the dictionary they learned that she was twenty-eight years old, worked at the restaurant with Giovanni, had an Italian friend named Maria who had a Ferrari, and that she came from Minneapolis where it snowed during the winter. They told her their names: Vittorio, Pasquale e Giovanni, and their age: twenty-eight, twenty-four and twenty-two. They liked to ride motorcycles and play tennis on their time off which wasn't very often. They would meet with friends in front of a local café' and would she like to go for a ride so she could meet them? Joanna looked at Amelia not knowing what to say. Amelia said, "Si, si, vai Joanna. Io dico a Giovanni," which meant, "Yes, yes, go Joanna. I will tell Giovanni."

She got up and followed them in the garage where their three shining motorcycles were parked. After a heated argument they decided that she would ride with Vittorio, the eldest. He got on the motorcycle and motioned to Joanna to climb on. She did and her dress left her legs exposed up to her thighs. They boys enjoyed the show while pretending not to notice. They drove the motorcycles through the streets of Palermo while pedestrians would turn to look at them, until they arrived at a big café' with tables and chairs outside.

The café' was crowded with young people who seemed to know everybody. You could almost feel their sexual energy just by walking through them. As the boys parked their motorcycles all the eyes were fixed on them. They were curious as to who was the blonde beauty and asked them to introduce her. Blonde women were a rarity in Palermo since most of the local girls had dark hair. Joanna's head was spinning with all the names of the people she was introduced to. Luckily one of them spoke English and he translated for her. She was offered a seat at one of the tables and an espresso coffee, which she finished in two sips.

She had never seen so many handsome people in one place, both males and females. She felt energized and laughed a lot, happy for all the attention she was getting. She felt unique, special and was glad she had taken special care in her appearance. Vittorio, Pasquale e Giovanni were proud of her and wished she could stay longer but they had to leave because Giovanni might be worried and wonder at their whereabouts. Joanna received hugs and kisses when she said goodbye and was surprised because she had just met them, but she would do good to get used to it because Italians were huggers and kissers and she would meet a great deal of them before their month would be over.

When they returned home they found Giovanni waiting for them with a worried look on his face. He kissed Joanna and asked her where they had been. She told him looking at his face intently to see if he disapproved but he didn't. He just asked her to wear pants the next time she rode a motorcycle. She apologized and gave him a kiss. He hugged her and they both walked inside the house where the family was waiting for them to start dinner.

There were fresh roses on the dinner table emanating a very inebriating fragrance throughout the meal, which consisted of trout, salad and calamari plus tiramisu for dessert. The food was delicious and Joanna was in seventh heaven still not believing her good fortune. No one knew about her past including her husband and she wondered what would they say if they knew. She was vitalized by their presence because they made her feel very special and treated her as if she were a goddess. The color of her hair seemed to fascinate people and distinguished her from everybody else. She felt as if she were an alien landed where everybody was darkly skinned and darkly haired, but she found them very appealing and handsome. She rejoiced for Giovanni who fit with all of them as a glove fit a hand. He was happy, laughing often and he conveyed all his joy to Joanna.

Their lovemaking that night was superb and they slept entwined in each other's arms.

The following day they left for Taormina accompanied by Vincenzo and Amelia in the rented van. The boys were staying behind, regretfully, because they wanted to spend more time with the Americana. They promised to visit the couple in the United States the following year after Giovanni, the youngest, would graduate from the university.

Vincenzo was driving but Giovanni would have liked to since the drive was exhausting for one person.

They took the A19, which extended all the way from Palermo to Catania. Joanna looked out the window the whole trip, fascinated by the small towns they were traveling through. When they arrived in Taormina she was gaping, it was that beautiful. The town was nestled on Monte Tauro and sloped down the Ionian Sea. In the distance Mount Etna framed the town beautifully. The colors were magnificent. Bougainvillea was growing in every garden adorning walls and fences, bringing splashes of colors to the green vegetation.

It was almost dark and the sun was setting when they arrived at Giovanni's cousin Antonio's house. He was the son of the late Mr. Grimaldi's brother. He was married and had six children, all married and living in the same neighborhood. In fact he had built each of his children a house and given it to them as a wedding present. He was wealthy and his wealth came from producing wine, which he sold throughout Italy. He also sent it to Giovanni's restaurant in San Diego. Giovanni had tried to convince him to market it in the United States but he had refused arguing that he was making a good living as it was and didn't want to disperse his energies by putting too much on his plate. He lived in a beautiful villa with a magnificent garden, which was tended by a full time gardener. The villa was a two-story house with ten bedrooms, eleven baths, a huge dining room, family room, living room, studio and kitchen. A swimming pool was behind the house and was screened by tall fences all around. He didn't want anybody to see his four daughters in bathing suits. His wife, Anna, was a lovely woman in her fifties who dressed elegantly but somberly. She was in charge of the household, which employed two maids, a cook and the gardener. They would all go home at night except the cook who lived in a cottage adjacent the house. She was in her sixties and had been with the family for twenty years. She had never married and was totally loyal to the family.

Anna and Antonio were waiting at the front door when Giovanni and the others arrived. They welcomed them with hugs and kisses on both cheeks, which did not surprise Joanna who was getting used to Italian ways of greeting one another. She actually preferred it, finding the American way more distancing. The Italian way of greeting immediately put one at ease and made her feel part of the family, welcome, accepted. She was hungering for love, the more the better.

After everybody said hi they all went inside. Anna showed them to their rooms and went downstairs to give orders to the cook to have dinner ready in half an hour. Joanna and Giovanni put their luggage in the room and went to freshen up in the bathroom. When they were done they changed clothes and went downstairs in the dining room where everybody was waiting for them to start the dinner.

Giovanni and Antonio had a lot to catch up and did most of the talking. Joanna concentrated her attention on the food since she didn't understand a word that was said. She also admired the furniture in the room and wished she could tell Anna so but she didn't know how. Everything seemed so abundant. The table was huge, seating twelve and she guessed it was because of the large family they had. She decided that she wanted a large family too, and wished to get pregnant right away.

The two maids served dinner. They had been asked to work overtime because of the guests staying at the villa. Joanna felt like royalty, being served as if she were someone important. What a change, she thought. God bless Giovanni and make him live till a hundred years. The wine was excellent. She had already tasted it in San Diego, and recognized it right away.

Anna was looking at her openly and smiled at her often not knowing how else to let her know her liking and acceptance. Joanna smiled back, a little shy.

After dinner Giovanni, Antonio and Vincenzo went to the studio while the women went to the living room. They were served a digestive liqueur, which Joanna found a little strong but ingested anyway not wanting to be rude towards her hostess. Anna gestured for her to sit down on the couch and brought a big photo album to show the family to her. By the time they were done looking at it, Joanna's head was swimming with names of children and grand-children. She couldn't possibly remember them all.

She said so to Giovanni, later on when they were snuggled under the blankets. He told her not to worry; she would meet them all tomorrow. The next day, while they were strolling in the garden, after breakfast, a procession of cars stopped in the driveway. Anna called out to them to come say hi and they directed their steps there. The hall was filled with people. There must have been twenty of them between children and grown ups. Joanna was introduced to all of them and they all shook hands and kissed her on both cheeks. To her surprise and delight, some of them spoke English and she didn't feel out of place anymore.

CHAPTER TWENTY-EIGHT

Two weeks later Joanna realized her period was late. It was supposed to have started a week earlier. Also, in the morning, she had been feeling queasy in her stomach, which scared her. She thought she had caught a bug, maybe by drinking the water. She told Giovanni, who told Anna asking if she could take Joanna to see her doctor. He was very concerned since she had never been sick the whole time he had known her. Anna made an appointment right away and told Giovanni he needed to go with them because she didn't know how to speak English and she needed an interpreter to communicate to the doctor what was wrong. To their surprise the doctor spoke English and told Anna and Giovanni to stay in the waiting room. He was a man in his fifties with thick moustache and black hair. He definitely looked Sicilian.

"So madam, what ails you?" he asked Joanna as he closed the door. He had a very thick accent. "My period is late and I feel really sick at my stomach in the morning. Maybe I have a bug or something," she said looking concerned.

"I will need to examine you," he said opening the door and calling to the nurse to come in. He asked Joanna to take off her underwear and to lie on the examining table. He knew she was pregnant the minute he felt how tender her womb was but didn't say anything because he wanted to run some tests first to be sure. The nurse gave Joanna a sterile container for the urine and accompanied her to the bathroom where she left closing the door. When Joanna came out she gave the container to the nurse and went to the waiting room joining Giovanni and Anna who got up as soon as they saw her.

"What's wrong, Joanna, did the doctor tell you?" asked Giovanni.

"No, he said he wants to run some tests before he tells me. He told me to wait here with you until he knows for sure." So they sat down prepared to wait for a long time.

To their surprise they didn't have to wait very long. The doctor asked Joanna and Giovanni to follow him to his office where he motioned them to sit down. Giovanni was very worried and wished for all the gallantry to stop and get to the heart of the matter.

"I have good news, dear friends," said the doctor. "Mrs. Grimaldi you don't have a bug. You are pregnant."

Joanna's eyes filled with tears and she looked at Giovanni to see his reaction.

Giovanni's face was white, drained of all color. He was speechless. He knew he was supposed to say something but the words wouldn't come out. It was a miracle. For years he had wanted a child but his first wife could not conceive and now, being married only two and a half weeks, she was already pregnant. What a blessing. He was going to be a father at fifty-five. He got up and hugged Joanna who was drying her tears of joy. They both thanked Jesus in their hearts.

The doctor was silent watching the scene with professional detachment. He was waiting for them to compose themselves, which they did. He gave Joanna vitamins and some pills for the morning sickness, with his congratulations. They thanked him profusely and left accompanied by Anna who was still in the dark. When they got to the villa, Giovanni gathered everyone around and gave them the good news. Anna hugged Joanna and told her, "Auguri, auguri, che bella notizia," which meant, "Congratulations, what a wonderful news." The men patted Giovanni on the back and shook his hand. There was a spirit of joy in the room and Joanna knew it was because of her. She was so happy she was crying. Her eyes were puffy and red and she had to blow her nose. Giovanni hugged her and kissed her on the mouth in front of everybody. What a magnificent creature she was. She was turning his life upside down and he felt twenty years old again.

The dinner that night was livelier than usual with Giovanni laughing at every little thing as if he were inebriated with wine. After dinner the men went to the studio, as usual, to have a drink and the women went to the family room.

Vincenzo had doubts in his mind circa the paternity of the child growing in Joanna's womb. It seemed suspicious to him that she got pregnant so fast and he pointed that out to Giovanni. Giovanni was so happy that he failed to take offense and told Vincenzo that he could prove to him that the child was his. He left the room to return five minutes later with a package wrapped in newspaper. The four men were speechless not knowing what he was up to. The mystery was over when Giovanni unwrapped the package and took out a bed sheet. It was the same bed sheet he and Joanna had slept on at the Marriott Hotel in San Diego when he had deflowered her. He opened the sheet and showed to their unbelieving faces the spot stained by Joanna's blood. They blushed and apologized to Giovanni who congratulated himself for having thought of bringing the bed sheet with him to Sicily. He was aware of the local custom of having to show the bed sheet the morning after the wedding to prove the virginity of the bride. He hadn't mentioned anything to Joanna to not offend her; she was so simple and so pure of mind and heart that she would have been totally upset had she known, and that's why he would keep it a secret. He asked the four men to keep it a secret too and they agreed to it.

That night, in their bedroom, Joanna and Giovanni embraced each other the minute they closed the door. They made passionate love and as they lay exhausted in bed Joanna decided it was time to tell Giovanni about Raul being in jail. She was stumbling at first, but took courage as she went on. She only revealed about Raul molesting the little neighbor; nothing about her molestation. Giovanni let her talk without interrupting. She was tearful as she told him the story and was stunned by what Giovanni told her, when she was through.

"I know Joanna," he said.

"You know? What do you mean you know?"

"Remember when you went for a week to Minneapolis because

your mother was allegedly sick?"

"Yea?"

"I had a private investigator check on you the whole time you were there. Not that I didn't trust you, but I had a suspicion about you not wanting to answer some of my questions when I'd take you home after work. Also, I wanted to know what made your eyes so sad at times and what I found out told me a lot about it. Believe me, love, I only did it for the good of our relationship."

"So what did you find out?" Joanna asked with fear in her voice.

"Everything. How Raul molested you for all those years. I have it on tape if you want to listen to it. Believe me, that bastard will pay for all he did to you. You wait and see."

"What do you mean?"

"Don't worry about it. Just wait and see." He didn't want to tell her that he wanted Raul murdered in jail because he hadn't decided yet. He was angry enough to want to kill him but didn't know if he had it in him to actually go through with it. He was not a murderer. He knew, though, that child molesters were not very popular in jail so maybe somebody would do him a favor and kill him. Just wait and see, he told himself.

"Now, beautiful mother of my child, you better catch some sleep so you can be beautiful in the morning. Nothing but the best for you, my love," Giovanni said kissing her on the lips one more time before turning on his side to go to sleep.

Joanna got on his back, trying to go to sleep but sleep wouldn't come for a long time. What he had revealed to her left her speechless. He had known all along about Raul and still had married her. How lucky can you get? He was truly a saint to her. Good, kind, loving man; bringing his child into the world was truly an honor. She would serve him the rest of her life. After God, he came next and she thanked Jesus in her heart. She felt a little guilty for not having prayed or thought about Jesus in the last few weeks but she attributed it to all the new things happening in her life. She made up for it by praying long after Giovanni fell asleep until, exhausted, she fell asleep too.

It took many days for the beautiful news of being pregnant to sink into Joanna's consciousness. It only took few seconds for

Giovanni. The next day they went shopping for baby furniture. They bought a wooden cradle hand carved by a famous local artisan and had it shipped to the United States together with a lamp and a hand made wooden train. Money was not a problem. They next went to Catania to shop for baby clothes where they bought tons of it and had it mailed to their house too. They were very excited

and Joanna started to research for a name to give the baby. Relatives suggested names of their ancestors, which she wrote in a baby book to be considered in the future but Giovanni had already chosen a name if it was a boy. It would be Giovanni Jr. If it was a girl they would call her Amelia after Giovanni's mom. He didn't even ask Joanna if it was ok with her, just made up his mind that it was going to be so. He wasn't sure but assumed that it was going to be all right with his wife, which it was.

Joanna was very pliable where he was concerned; he was her savior after all. During their stay in Taormina they visited all of Giovanni's relatives at their houses, while they came to visit them before their departure. They brought presents and souvenirs, which had to be mailed also, because there was no room in their suitcases.

They were all in love with the Americana even though they didn't understand why Giovanni hadn't picked a wife from his own people. Joanna would always be an outsider as far as they were concerned even if they liked her. She didn't fit in, although she tried, poor thing. Giovanni saw all this psychically and it only made him love Joanna more. He tried to protect her in every way he could, even by lying to her when she'd ask him to translate, occasionally, something someone said that she thought was about her. She liked all of them implicitly because they were Giovanni's relatives and had no idea about the situation.

All the women wanted to give her advice when they found out she was pregnant, but didn't know how. They didn't want to ask Giovanni to translate because they were embarrassed to ask questions of a feminine nature. Feeling frustrated by the inability to communicate Joanna determined in her heart to enroll into an Italian class as soon as they returned to San Diego. She told Giovanni.

"Why do you want to go to school, I can teach you, Princess," he said afraid that she might meet a younger man at school.

"I think it would be fun. In school I'd learn the real Italian, not the dialect that you speak."

"I can speak real Italian. I'll teach you," and that was it, end of the argument.

Joanna was upset. She wanted to go to school and didn't understand why he didn't want her to go. She had no clue that he was jealous. She pressed the issue.

"I also want to go to college to take a business class to help me run the restaurant better," she said hesitantly.

"Why are you behaving like a child, Joanna? I can teach you to run the restaurant. I am fifty-five and I never needed to take a class. Look at me: I am successful because I learned from my mistakes, not because I have gone to school. Give me credit, will you?"

He got up and as he got at a safe distance he lit a cigar. Joanna had tears in her eyes. She had never seen him this angry and towards her, of all people. Apparently her husband had something against her going to school. At a loss for words and heartbroken she went inside the house. As she passed the telephone she thought of calling Maria in San Diego and tell her what had just happened. It was lunchtime in San Diego and she hoped to find Maria at home. The phone rang four times before it was answered.

"Maria, this is Joanna. Do you have five minutes?"

"For you I have my whole life, Cinderella," Maria told her. "What happened, you don't sound too good."

"I just had an awful argument with Giovanni. I mentioned that I wanted to go back to school to learn business and Italian and he got all upset and walked away. I can't stand him being upset with me, what can I do?"

"Nothing, I am afraid. Just go along with him. I think he's afraid that if you go back to school he will lose you to a younger man. Don't forget that he is fifty-five and you are twenty-eight."

"I would be crazy to leave him. How can he doubt me now that I am pregnant with his child? Oops," she said realizing too late that she had spoiled the surprise. They were planning to tell Maria and Giovanni's mother that she was pregnant at a lunch reunion when they got back.

"You are expecting? Oh my God, this is huge. Wait till I tell

Elizabeth. So maybe that's why Giovanni doesn't want you to go to school. He might be afraid that you might lose the baby if you do too much. I agree with him. Just wait till you have the baby, then you'll know you can't go because you will be too busy. Why did you want to go back to school for?" asked Maria.

"I wanted to get more education but he said he can teach me so I have no reasons to go except that it hurts when he is mad at me. I think he's being bossy and unreasonable but I am going to give in because nothing is worth this heartache I am feeling right now. What if he never talks to me again? What if he leaves me? How would I support myself and the baby?" Joanna was hysterical; she had lost sight of reality and was exaggerating.

"Calm down, Joanna," said Maria. "You are making things worse than what they are. I tell you what you are going to do; you are going to tell him that you see his point and that you much prefer to learn from him than to go to school. Tell him that having the baby and running his business means more to you than taking a couple of classes. Tell him that you are only having this baby once, but you can go to school anytime later. See if it works, Joanna. Let me know."

"Ok, Maria. Thank you for your advice. I'll do what you said. I'll see you in a couple of days. I'll go now because I don't want to run up the bill here. Bye."

"Bye Joanna. Call me as soon as you get here, ok? Bye."

Joanna went to the bathroom to wash her face so that Giovanni wouldn't see that she had been crying. She composed herself and went outside into the garden looking for her beloved husband. She caressed her belly as she walked and when she was near she took his hand and put it on her belly too. They looked into each other's eyes for a long time seeing the pain they were experiencing there. Slowly the pain dissolved giving way to a feeling of love and compassion they had never experienced before. They embraced each other kissing on the mouth for a long time, oblivious to anything around them. She didn't have to say anything, he knew and she was thankful.

That night their lovemaking was slow and gentle. There was someone else with them there, even if in the embryonic stage. It made no difference to them. Afterwards they fell asleep into each other's arms. They only had a couple of days left before their vacation was over. They said their goodbyes to all of their relatives. Most of them gave them money, which is customary to do for a wedding present and Joanna wrote all of it in a book so that in the future they would know how much to send if anyone got married.

Amelia and Vincenzo had left after a week because Vincenzo had to go back to work. They wanted to give them money also, as a wedding present, but Giovanni said no, since they had done so much for them already. And the same went for Antonio and Anna who had been such gracious hosts. They invited all their relatives to their house in San Diego and many said they would come after the birth of their baby, which was due in June the following year. They were all so nice to Joanna and when they had parties they would talk and look at her as if she were a being from another planet. Joanna was used to it and it didn't bother her. She hoped that the next time she saw them her Italian would be good enough for a social conversation. They might accept her as one of their own, then.

The last night Giovanni and Joanna spent in Taormina they went out after dinner to buy ice cream at one of the famous gelatiers in town. Antonio and Anna accompanied them. They walked instead of driving. The night was clear, with a full moon high in the sky. It shed light and long shadows in the narrow alleys. They were happy and laughed a lot, walking arm in arm. They were not the only ones taking a stroll. In fact, the streets and cafes were alive with tourists and they would be open till two in the morning.

Business was good in Taormina, with floods of tourists coming down from north European countries and north Italian cities. Roman ruins were adorned with bougainvilleas and if you drove up Monte Tauro you could see the ruins of the Greek-Roman amphitheater down below. In the distance the blue of the Ionian Sea made the scene breathtaking. Joanna had taken many pictures to take home and show Maria, her best friend. She had the camera with her during their stroll and took pictures till she finished the roll. By the time they returned at the villa they were very tired and went to bed soon after.

The next day, Antonio and Anna drove them to Catania's airport.

They shed tears when they parted, promising to come back again when the baby was one year old. Joanna and Giovanni didn't speak much during the trip back to the United States. It was as if they were assessing at what point they were in life, thinking about the past thirty days and what lay ahead of them. Joanna was physically and mentally in the clouds. She was having tender thoughts about the life growing within her womb. She imagined the baby, a boy, learning to speak, walk, and laugh. They would teach him to speak both Italian and English of course and she mentioned that to Giovanni who agreed with a big smile on his face. He was thinking about the baby too. Ever since the doctor had given them the good news he had been filled by an immense joy. If he loved Joanna before, he loved her a thousand times more now. He took her hand in his and held it tight, then turned his head and gently kissed her lips.

"Thank you," he said.

"What for?" answered Joanna, surprised.

"For making me the happiest man on the face of the earth," he replied.

"I love you so much Giovanni that I wish to make you happy every day of every year. Just tell me what makes you happy and I'll do it for you. If you want a baby a year, I'll give it to you. How's that?"

"You're a sweetheart Joanna. Sure, let's make a baby every two years till I am seventy-five. That'll give us ten children. We can afford it. I can't wait to tell my mother; she'll be so happy, she is going to cry. You wait and see."

"Giovanni, we're going to need another room for the baby's nursery. There is no room in your mother's house, maybe we should find a bigger house and rent the one we're in now."

"I'll discuss it with my mother. We can buy a house in La Jolla with a big garden for you and a couple of extra rooms for our other babies you're going to have after this one. We're going to need a five-bedroom house. Once we settle down for a couple of months we'll go house hunting before you get too big. I don't want you to exert yourself too much. If you get tired working at the restaurant let me know. I will put a large sofa in my office so that you can rest during the day."

"With a husband like you I can sleep easy every night. Thank you, Giovanni for being so loving and considerate."

Joanna was living a dream. If Giovanni had met her few months' back he would have barely looked at her, she was that pitiful, dirty and living in the streets. Now she was Mrs. Grimaldi and people respected her. She owed it all to Maria. She was glad she had given her the money; no one deserved it more. Now they could go house hunting together, be neighbors, be friends for the rest of their lives. She was part of her family, an older sister, sister in Christ. *Lord, you've been very good to me*, she said in her heart, *I thank you for everything, especially for the new life growing inside of me. I know it's a boy, don't ask me how but I know, you wait and see. I want to call him Giovanni Jr. and I am sure Mrs.Grimaldi will agree with me. He is going to have nothing but the best; the best home, clothes, school, father, mother, grandmother. His future is already assured, with your blessing. We'll baptize him in the name of the Father, the Son, the Holy Spirit. I'll consecrate him to you, Lord, so that he might grow holy and precious in your sight.*

They were almost in San Diego and the airplane had started its descent. *Thank you Jesus for having brought us here safe. San Diego is beautiful*, Joanna said to herself. From their window they could see San Diego skyline. It was night but the city was full of lights. Even though they had visited many beautiful places in Italy, they were happy to be back. After they had retrieved their luggage they got into a cab heading home.

It was nine in the evening and Mrs. Grimaldi was still up waiting for them. Typical of an Italian mother she had dinner ready and after they had embraced and put their luggage in their room she told them to sit down and served the dinner, which was delicious.

"Mom, do you still have that bottle of wine from 1937, which you saved for a special occasion?" asked Giovanni.

"Yes, I do. Why do you ask? What's going on?" she answered, tensing on the chair.

"Well, we have the news of the century, ma. Joanna is pregnant," he said watching her face attentively.

Mrs. Grimaldi brought her hand to her heart and her face became pale.

"Are you all right, ma?" Giovanni was really worried. He thought she was having a heart attack.

"Oh Blessed Mother, Precious Jesus, thank you, thank you, thank you. My prayers have been answered," she got up and hugged Joanna.

"Welcome to the Grimaldi's dynasty, child. Now you are really one of our own. Blessed be thy womb and the child you carry in it. We have lot of things to do in the next few months but now you are tired. We'll talk about it in the morning," said Mrs. Grimaldi looking at both of them tenderly. She wiped tears from her eyes with a silk handkerchief, with her initials embroidered in one of the corners.

"What about the wine, ma?"

"Oh yes, the wine. I forgot. Wait here and I'll go get it," she said walking to her room. She opened a cabinet and extracted a bottle of home made wine that her mother had given her and which she had never wanted to open before. She was now nearing the end of her life and decided it was time that it'd be drunk. She was smiling big as she entered the dining room.

"Here it is, my beloved children," she said handing the bottle to Giovanni who took a knife to cut the cord holding the cork into the bottle. As soon as he had cut the cord the cork shot out of the bottle and red foam spurted out. Joanna was ready with her glass and the bubbling, rich liquid filled it to the rim. It was then Giovanni and Mrs. Grimaldi's turn to fill their glasses.

"We want a speech, Mrs. Grimaldi," said Joanna holding her glass. The old lady was at loss for words and she began to stumble but taking a deep breath she soon regained her composure and gave a wonderful speech. Joanna was crying by the time she was through and felt like the heroine of a soap opera. Mrs. Grimaldi made her feel as if she had climbed Mount Everest using only one leg. A little more and she would have knelt in front of her and kissed her feet. She made her feel like magic, as if she had done a miracle and in a way she had.

Giovanni had always known that the reason he and his first wife had had no children was not his fault, but since he was the faithful kind the thought of impregnating another woman had never crossed his mind. Now he had Joanna, sweet Joanna and she was going to give him a child every two years. He meant it too. The fact that she could conceive made her a miracle come true. While it was impossible before, now he felt that he could have a child just by willing it. That's how God must feel, he thought, as he lay his head on the pillow falling into a deep sleep.

Next morning they woke up smelling the espresso coffee Mrs. Grimaldi had brewed. They put their robes on and joined her in the dining room. Joanna's eyes were swollen and so were her feet. She passed her hand into her ruffled hair to straighten it out and suddenly felt like throwing up. She ran to the bathroom but nothing would come out except some stomach fluid. When she returned to the dining room she found Giovanni with a worried look on his face, while Mrs. Grimaldi was ecstatic.

"Are you all right, Pumpkin?" he asked.

"I don't know. I guess I better take those pills the doctor gave me in Italy for morning sickness. It's awful, I don't like it."

"I want you to take the pills too. You look awful. I hate to see you like this. When you finish the pills we'll go to the doctor and get some more. Actually we should go to the doctor soon anyway. Mom, do you know a good doctor I could take Joanna to for this kind of things?" he asked his mother.

"She could see my gynecologist. He is very experienced and I've known him for years. He'll treat Joanna as if she were his daughter," she answered.

"Thank you mom," said Joanna.

"Can you make an appointment for us?"

"Sure, I'll make one as soon as they open. Do try to get some breakfast if you can. I remember when I was pregnant with Giovanni. I was sick as a dog the first three months; they didn't have medication back then so I had to endure the whole thing. Then it suddenly stopped and I started to enjoy my pregnancy when I could feel him move inside of me and kick every once in a while. He was a good boy even so early on."

"I love you mom, and I love you Joanna. You two are the most important people in my life. My life would be empty without you. Now let's plan the day. First, mom you make the appointment with the doctor. Joanna and I are going to get dressed and go to the restaurant for few hours. We'll bring lunch here and take a nap after we eat, to make up for the sleep we lost during the trip. After our nap I want all three of us to go to the Our Lady of the Rosary Church and give an offering as a thank you for Joanna getting pregnant. Is there anything you want to do Joanna?" he asked.

"Well, I want to call Maria and let her know that I am here. Maybe I can go visit her after we finish at the church, for a couple of hours, then you can come to pick me up and we can have dinner here with your mom."

"That sounds fine. So let's get going and shower. You first, me first?"

"You first," said Joanna who wanted to choose the clothes she was going to wear. She chose the black, sleeveless dress that clang to her body like a second skin. She looked wonderful in it with her skin still tanned from the beach in Taormina. Her hair was lighter too and it made a nice contrast with the dark skin.

All the employees at the restaurant welcomed them with hugs and even some tears. They had been really missed and the staff couldn't wait till they would return full time. Joanna and Giovanni stayed at the restaurant for three hours as they had planned. Things seemed to run smoothly and the profits were just as good as when they were there. Mrs. Grimaldi had been at the restaurant three or four hours each day while they were gone just so one of the owners would be present and keep everybody in line. Giovanni didn't know that and was really surprised when they told him. *My sweet mother, God bless her,* he thought.

When they went home for lunch Joanna called Maria and they agreed to visit at five that afternoon, after the church. When Joanna rang Maria's apartment at five, she was very excited and couldn't wait till she told Maria every detail of her trip. Maria practically ran downstairs to meet Joanna halfway to her apartment. They both let out a scream when they saw each other, hugging and kissing one another. Tears rolled down Joanna's face. She hadn't realized how much she had missed Maria even if only for a month. They walked upstairs hand in hand. Elizabeth was at the door waiting for them. She hugged and kissed Joanna then went in the bedroom to play some CDs.

"So congratulations Joanna. You're going to be a mom. Remember that I want to be the godmother, you promised me."

"Of course you're going to be the godmother. I wouldn't let anybody else do it. So, how have you been? Have you found a house yet?"

"Elizabeth and I have been looking at some houses but we have not found one that we like yet."

"About the house, I want to tell you that Giovanni and I are going to be looking for a house too, because the one we have now is not big enough for us and the baby. I thought that maybe we can look together and find houses near each other so that we can be neighbors. What do you think?"

"I think that it's a wonderful idea. I'd love for us to be neighbors. When do we start looking?"

"Giovanni said in a couple of months, but you can start right away. We want to move to La Jolla. Does it agree with you?"

"I love La Jolla. It's one of my favorite places. We have to let the realtor know that we want two houses next to each other. It might not be that easy, but maybe we'll be lucky and find what we want. Now tell me about your honeymoon. How was it?"

"Oh Maria, it was beautiful. Everybody was so nice, I wish you'd been there."

"I know Taormina. I went there for my honeymoon too."

"No kidding, I didn't know that."

"Yea, it was in 1975, a long, long time ago. I really enjoyed it. Did you eat pasta with tomato sauce and eggplant?"

"Yes, did you eat it too? It must be a classic of the area. Did you go on Mount Etna?"

"We tried but when we got to where you catch the cable to go to the top we were told that the station was closed, so we didn't get to see it. Too bad."

"Giovanni and I had the best of time. I have never been so spoiled in my whole life. I felt like a queen, being served hands and feet. All of Giovanni's relatives are wealthy and they all have maids. I didn't have to lift a finger the whole time we were there. I am going to suggest to Giovanni that we hire a maid full time and when the baby comes to have a live in maid. I can take the baby with me at the restaurant part of the day and I can put a cradle in Giovanni's office downstairs so that the baby can sleep. The first few months, as you well know, babies sleep all the time and in the office I can breastfeed him, while he is awake. I am so excited, so happy. God, I feel like I can touch the sky."

"I am so happy for you, Joanna and I thank you for sharing it with me. If there is anything you need just let me know and I'll do it for you, especially now that you are pregnant. I'd love to go shopping with you for the baby and help you prepare the nursery, once we find a house."

"Yes, let's make plans."

CHAPTER TWENTY-NINE

The four men were sitting at the table of a restaurant on Avenida Revolucion, in Tijuana, Mexico. From the top floor they had the view of the street below and could see if someone was watching them. Their names were Juan, Miguel, Ramon and Rocco. Rocco Bandini was Italian; the other three were Mexican. They were all drug dealers. Rocco had requested a meeting and they agreed to meet at the restaurant. The Mexicans didn't trust the Italian because he belonged to the Mafia from New York and were suspicious of him, but they agreed to meet with him out of curiosity and also because their boss had sent them to see what he wanted.

They were drinking margaritas and making small talk to warm-up and break the ice. Rocco was nervous because he was outnumbered and felt like a fish out of water. But his resolve made him look self-assured. He had a master plan and was intentioned to see it through. He was acting independently and no one had sent him. He knew there was a huge market for drugs in San Diego but it was hard to break into because Angelo Bonifacio was opposed to drugs. The drug dealers trafficking there were not part of the clan and were often arrested because Bonifacio's men would squeal on them to the police.

Rocco was not going to use any man from the clan but Mexicans. He wanted to pocket most of the money. His plan was to market the drugs to nightclubs in San Diego, which meant he had to invade Bonifacio's territory. He wasn't scared, he knew that Bonifacio hated violence and would not do anything to him. Maybe warn him, that's all, or try to send him to jail, but a good lawyer would take care of that. He wanted to become a Don and for that he needed money to buy good clothes, an expensive car, a nice house, men to serve his needs and do collections. He had saved money for ten years so that he could purchase a good amount of drugs and increase his revenues one hundred fold. It would be easier after that; he would be rich.

He was doing the Mexicans a favor. He wanted them to consign the merchandise to him in the U. S. He didn't want to smuggle it across the border himself and run the risk of being arrested. The three Mexicans were mostly listening to him make his requests without saying yea or nay. They were not the ones to make decisions. Their boss was.

Rocco was sweating even though it was November and the air was chilly. He was wearing a dark blue business suit with a white shirt and gray pants. His dark hair was combed back and he had a scar on his face right below the left eye. He could easily pass for a rich Mexican. He was forty-three years old and was neither engaged nor married.

He had come from Palermo, Sicily at the request of one of New York's dons. Smuggling and selling drugs was his specialty. He had ten years experience. He made his requests looking at the three men straight in the eyes. He decided at what price he wanted the drug, how often and how much. He was sure he could do good business in San Diego, so he was not afraid to invest his money.

"So what do you think my friends, do we have a deal?" asked Rocco.

"We have to ask our boss, Rocco, we can't make a decision. We'll talk to him and let you know," replied Ramon.

"Don't take too long. I have the cash and I can go somewhere else."

"We'll talk to our boss today, so we should be able to tell you tonight or tomorrow. Give us your cell number so we can reach you."

Rocco gave them his cell number, put a twenty-dollar bill on the table and left.

"What do you think?" Ramon asked Juan and Miguel once they were alone.

"I don't trust him, but he has the cash, like he said. Better him than someone else; he's got good experience with drugs so he's not likely to make foolish mistakes. I'll recommend him to the boss," said Juan.

"I think we can trust him," said Miguel. "He is eager to make money so we don't have to work so hard to push him. He is ambitious and that's a good thing. I'll recommend him to the boss too."

"Well, since you both will recommend him so will I and let's hope that everything will be all right since we'll have to deal with him personally," concluded Ramon.

****

Maria was looking through the Union-Tribune at classifieds when the phone rang. It was Joanna. "Do you want to go look at houses this weekend, Maria?" she asked.

"Yea, I was just looking in the paper. When do you want to go?"

"Saturday from about nine through eleven, because I'll have to be at the restaurant after that."

"Ok, I'll pick you up at eight-thirty then," said Maria.

"No Maria, I'll pick you up. I don't want to ride in that car; you know why."

"Right, I keep forgetting. Ok, I'll be ready at eight-thirty. See you then."

Maria called her real estate agent after she hung-up and asked him if he had two houses nearby each other in La Jolla for her and Joanna to see. He said there were two but he was the agent for one and someone else was the agent for the other. She asked him if he could call the other agent and have her show them the house that Saturday at nine a.m.. He quickly made the phone call and let her know that she agreed to it. Maria also asked him to show them the other house at about ten, figuring that one hour would be enough time to see one. He agreed to meet them at ten.

When Saturday came around Maria and Joanna were both excited, but they curbed their excitement so that Ms. Ross, the real estate agent, would not increase the price. The house had six bedrooms, sauna, swimming pool, gym, seven bathrooms, family room, dining room, living room, studio and kitchen. The big bay windows overlooked the ocean and in the backyard there was a bungalow for the maid right by the swimming pool. The price was a million three hundred fifty thousand dollars. Both Maria and Joanna suppressed a feeling of surprise; they could both afford it.

They had many questions, which the agent answered. Just by looking at them she wasn't sure they could afford it; she hoped they weren't just wasting her time. They weren't, as she would soon find out.

At ten o'clock they met Maria's agent, Tom Brussell. The house was just next-door, separated by a green edge. It too had a swimming pool, a sauna, and a gym but it only had four bedrooms, which was just perfect for Maria. The view was the same. This house had a deck, which Maria thought would be perfect for her to paint on. She hadn't painted in long time but this house made her want to. She was deciding in her mind to paint white and blue paintings to match the blue of the ocean with the white of the interior. The dining room and family room were open and she could see in her mind how much she would enjoy spending time there entertaining or just reading. The current owner's furniture was still there but Maria's taste was different than theirs. She would paint the whole house white with splashes of color all over the place, Mediterranean style. That was one of her dreams. The price of this house was one million dollars. Maria said, "I'll take it, if Joanna gets the house next door. She'll have to ask her husband and mother in-law but I think they'll say yes."

"Well, I have been showing this house a lot and a couple of people said they'll let me know. Without a down payment I can't hold the house for you, so your friend must decide pretty soon."

"She will, she will. Isn't it true Joanna?"

"Yes. I'll talk to my husband tonight and bring him here tomorrow. We should be able to give you an answer by tomorrow afternoon. Is that soon enough for you?"

"That would be wonderful. You'll be happy here. The properties will increase in price very soon, so it will be a good investment for you. Make sure you tell your husband that, Mrs. Grimaldi."

"I will, Mr. Brussell," replied Joanna.

That night, at the restaurant, while they were having dinner, Joanna finally had a chance to tell Giovanni about the house. Giovanni was very interested and when she told him the price he didn't flinch. He said they would need to get a loan from the bank but that shouldn't be a problem considering all the assets he and his mother had. They could pay cash for it, he said, but he preferred to get a loan to continue building their credit.

"Can you go with me tomorrow morning to see the house, Giovanni? Maria has to give her answer for the house next door and she won't take it if we won't buy this house. Maybe we could go at about nine so that we could be back in time to go to Mass with your mother. She needs to see the house too since she would be spending most of her time there."

"Yea, make the appointment for nine o'clock. I'll love to see it and my mom will love it too. Tell her when you go home tonight, so that she can get ready for tomorrow."

"Ok, I will," said Joanna. Ever since they'd been back from their honeymoon she had been at work by eleven o'clock in the morning. She would stay through lunch and dinner then, after eating with Giovanni, she would go home at about nine p.m. Giovanni would come in around five p.m. and help her get everything ready for the nightly customers. The dinner with Joanna was the highlight of his day. He didn't let her stay at the nightclub anymore; she had a long day as it was.

He would sleep till about eleven in the morning, have a light lunch with his mom, then he would help her with the accounting for all her properties and get ready to go to the restaurant at five p.m. They had gotten into a routine and things were running smoothly.

Joanna had a new car, a silver BMW with black leather interior. She was paying for it out of her own paycheck, she insisted with Giovanni that that's how she wanted it. She was very proud of herself for earning that money and gladly paid her bills. She hadn't forgotten her poverty; it would always stay with her like a monster hidden in the closet of her past.

She went home earlier that night so that she could speak to her mother in-law. She told her about the house and she was excited to see it, so excited that she didn't sleep a wink. She thought about the grandchild she was going to have and his nursery; how she was going to spend time with him while his parents were at work and buy him presents. She hadn't felt so alive in a very long time. She liked Joanna a lot. She was proving to be an exceptional wife, definitely a good choice by Giovanni. She was hard working, honest, serious, loving.

She had been to the doctor and he had found her in very good health. He gave her vitamins and pills for her morning sickness and he wanted her to come see him once a month. So far she had already seen him twice. He was in his sixties, white hair, a very attractive gentleman. His name was Ross Friedman but he insisted his patients call him Ross. He had been Mrs. Grimaldi's gynecologist for the past thirty years. He had an assistant, younger than he, by the name of Sam Sullivan who would do mostly deliveries and would spend most of his time at the hospital. He would be the one to deliver Joanna's baby.

Next morning they were at the house at nine o'clock. Mrs. Grimaldi wanted to see the grounds before going inside the house and she was sold by the time she was through even before seeing the inside. The agent, Ms. Ross, was waiting for them patiently. She had a good feeling about this deal and already counted the commission she was going to receive from the sale. She was right on the mark.

"We'll take it," said Mrs. Grimaldi.

"That's wonderful, but don't you want to see the house first?"

"Yes, we'll see it but the back yard is lovely and I am planning to spend most of my time gardening or exercising in the pool. Ok, let's see the house then."

Ms. Ross gave all three of them a tour of the house, which they loved. She told them to go by her office on Monday to do the paperwork and they all left.

After the Mass Joanna called Maria and told her that they were going to buy the house and Maria called Tom Brussell and told him that she was going to buy her house as well. He was very happy and congratulated her on a wise decision.

Joanna was the first one to move. Maria and Elizabeth helped her since Mrs. Grimaldi was too old and Giovanni was too busy at the restaurant. Of course she had movers carry all the furniture and other items; they only had to unpack. Maria enjoyed it a lot because she got to see everything Mrs. Grimaldi owned. Joanna mentioned that they needed to go shopping for furniture because they didn't have enough to fill all of the rooms and Maria volunteered to go with her. She loved shopping.

Maria moved a month later and she too needed to go shopping for furniture and other items. She donated all of her furniture to the Salvation Army because she wanted everything new. She was starting afresh and she was going to decorate the house herself. She knew exactly what she wanted; she had painters paint all the interior walls in white and she was going to hang very colorful paintings on the walls, some of which she would paint herself. On the floor she would lay expensive Mexican rugs and she would buy beautiful houseplants to put in each room except the bedrooms and the kitchen.

The house was in very good condition because it was fairly new so she didn't need to spend a lot of money fixing it. Elizabeth was overjoyed because Maria gave her the credit card and told her to buy whatever furniture she wanted. Elizabeth liked Ikea so she went shopping there. The end result was very practical and functional without lacking good taste. She was also thankful to Maria for paying off her car and her credit card, but Maria wanted Elizabeth to go either to school or to work because it wasn't good for her to spend idle time. Maria told her that she needed to have a plan in life, to give it a sense of direction.

"Mom, I just want some time off, to rest my mind," Elizabeth told Maria when she approached the subject. "I'll go to school next year, in the meantime I can figure out what I want to do. I was thinking about drama school because I like to act."

"Ok, we'll check about schools in the area if they have a drama program. You might have to move to Hollywood. That shouldn't be a problem since I can pay for your tuition and cost of living, which I would do gladly, as long as you accomplish something in life," said Maria patting Elizabeth on the back.

Maria was very lenient towards Elizabeth but what the heck, she was her only child and she enjoyed spoiling her. Maria wished she had been as fortunate while growing up but it was no use to have regrets especially now that she was a millionaire. She didn't go crazy when she got the money; she was very conservative and only spent money when it was necessary. She was planning to live on that money the rest of her life; she kept it in the bank and only spent the interest earned every month.

She loved beautiful things and made her house a place she loved to be in, comfortable, practical, dream like; her dream. She had a greenhouse built on the back of the house and she filled it with plants. In one corner she put a huge wicker chair with a cushion on it; on the side a small water fountain made a trickling noise. That's where she would go to read and meditate. It was so peaceful there, that she would often fall asleep. Elizabeth wanted cats, so Maria bought her two Siamese kittens. They loved cuddling up on Maria's wicker chair while she read. On the side of the chair there was a small table with a basket attached full of magazines. A cordless phone sat on the table.

While Joanna was in Italy Maria had quit smoking so there were no dirty ashtrays around. Instead there were colorful ones filled with marbles of every color. She loved colors and created around herself masterpieces, whether it was paintings, furniture or other objects. She felt elated when she looked at colors and got many ideas, which she would store in her mind to create paintings in the future. In fact she was planning to go back to college the following spring to get a degree in art. She was also planning to go on an artistic vacation organized by a travel agency. She had seen the ad in a travel magazine and had replied that she was interested in going. It was a class to be held in Hawaii in February; it would last five days and consisted of field trips to paint the beautiful landscape and seascape in acrylic.

Ever since she got the money she had tried to make most of her dreams come true. So far she had a dream car, a dream house, a dream trip to Hawaii. During her meditation she would concentrate on her inner self: what made her happy, what she wanted to do, what she couldn't do without, who she wanted to meet. She hadn't told anybody about the money, only Joanna and Elizabeth knew about it. When she moved to her house in La Jolla she told her friends that she was house-sitting for a very rich couple who lived in Europe most of the time and that they let her use their car.

She helped Joanna decorate the nursery and they had the best of time. It almost made Maria want another baby but she knew it was impossible because she was going through menopause. She was so excited about Joanna's baby that she couldn't wait till he was born. She accompanied her to Lamaze classes and was going to go with her in the delivery room, when the time came. Giovanni was too old fashioned and didn't think he should be there.

Mrs. Grimaldi had brought all the furniture with her from their previous house since she was very attached to it and so was Giovanni, to tell the truth. Their furniture was handmade in rich mahogany by an Italian artist who was dead now. They cherished it because they knew it couldn't be replicated. The house looked a little odd because it was modern but Joanna hired and interior decorator to bridge the gap between their old furniture and the new one they were going to buy. It wasn't cheap but she thought that since they were spending so much on the house they might as well do a good job while they were at it. Joanna adjusted really quickly to the fact that they were wealthy but she always consulted with Giovanni before a penny was spent. Giovanni loved her for her wisdom and was happy to see that the sadness had disappeared from her eyes. His mother, Amelia Grimaldi, had noticed it too because she commented to her son about it. He replied, "She is safe now and she has all the reasons in the world to smile," without telling her the details of Joanna's molestation.

As far as their religious life was concerned they had the priest come and bless the house and they asked Maria if she wanted to have her house blessed too but Maria declined saying that she was going to ask the preacher from the church she attended. They were always attending Mass on Sunday and established a strong routine, which solidified their lives. Giovanni felt like the luckiest man on earth and there was only joy that he could foresee in the future.

Joanna called Felicia in Minneapolis and invited her to come over for Thanksgiving and stay through Christmas; she accepted gladly. Thanksgiving and Christmas were the busiest times of the year at the restaurant and they would cater to people who were alone and to families who preferred not to cook. Their celebrations were to be spent at the restaurant where Giovanni and Joanna had a table reserved for all of them. All together it was nine people and it included Maria and Elizabeth; Mrs. Grimaldi and Mrs. Ruiz; Giovanni and Joanna; Alfredo; Philip and his wife with their baby. The waiters and waitresses could take a break after the customers left and could have anything on the menu.

The gift exchange at Christmas took place downstairs in Giovanni's office. As the presents were opened they could hear screams of joy. Maria had bought gold watches for Joanna and Giovanni; a gold medal of the Virgin Mary for Mrs. Grimaldi since she was devoted to her; sapphire and diamond earrings for Felicia; and a $250 gift certificate for Elizabeth. Elizabeth didn't have any present for them because she was penniless and depended entirely on Maria for everything. She was flying to see her dad the day after Christmas and would stay with him for a month. Maria had rehearsed with her what to say to her dad since they were keeping the money a secret. As far as he was concerned she was still working to support herself and Elizabeth.

Joanna and Giovanni gave Maria a beautiful painting by Wyland, a large giclee with whales and other fishes. They knew she admired his works and she was immensely pleased by it. The overall blue colors would fit perfectly in her family room. For Mrs. Grimaldi they had a silk shawl that she could use at church as a veil over her head. For Felicia they had a picture of them in Taormina set in a silver frame and for Elizabeth they had $100 bill inside a Christmas card. Maria had told them to give her money because she needed it to buy presents for her other family. She wouldn't give her money for that purpose because she was angry at them for the way they had treated her. They would have been very envious had they known her circumstances but she preferred to keep them a secret. She didn't need their envy.

Elizabeth was very beautiful but she was very shy and insecure. Maria had to encourage her often to have faith in herself. At the moment she was dating Oliver, who painted houses for a living and was the neighbor at their old apartment. He was twelve years her senior and very handsome. His parents were Dutch and he had lived in Holland as a young boy. Not everything was well between them, though. Elizabeth wasn't one hundred percent satisfied with her relationship but she wouldn't tell Maria why. Maria didn't press her.

Joanna was three months pregnant but her stomach was still flat. She gave Giovanni a cup with "The Best Dad In The World" written on it and Giovanni gave her a small statue of the Virgin Mary holding baby Jesus as a way of saying that he adored her just like he adored the Virgin Mary. It was a great gift and it meant a lot to Joanna. She felt he was putting her on a pedestal but she didn't mind. She was going to prove to him that she was worth his respect by working hard, making money for him and conducting herself as a married woman in love with her husband.

Pregnancy was good for Joanna. Her skin had a subtle glow of a peach color and was soft to the touch. They gave the news to their employees shortly after they got back from Taormina and they all looked at Joanna as if she were a creature from another planet, as if she were the first woman ever to get pregnant. Joanna didn't complain. She loved the attention and was pleased to know that they loved her. God knows she needed it.

Maria had strange feelings about the Virgin Mary and she told Joanna so when they were visiting at her house on her day off.

"Somebody knows about me being the woman of Genesis 3:15 and of Revelation 12:1 because a couple of years ago, as I was going to bed at two-thirty in the morning a man shouted from the park across the street: 'Mary, you bitch, when are you going to appear?' I thought at the time that the Catholic Church was behind it somehow, but I had no clue about who the man was and how he expected me to appear. As far as I was concerned I appeared March 15 at 3:15 in the afternoon, in 1985. Psychic people and angels must know about it because it happened in the psychic world. But it has only brought me sorrow and persecution so far. The Bible says the woman was persecuted by the Devil for three and a half years but this Devil just won't quit. It's all politics, I believe, because there is lot of money and power involved. Lots of deception. Also envy because lot of women in the world think they are the Virgin Mary."

"I hope you marry again, Maria. It is not good to be alone; that might be why those cowards are bothering you. You need a companion. Maybe now that you have money you can pick and choose. Someone with money will be good too. Don't get somebody lesser than you; your relationship wouldn't last. You need someone artistic and intelligent, just like you; somebody different than your father who was brutal and violent while you were growing up. We should pray about it and put it in God's hands. Let's pray."

They held hands and prayed for Maria to find a good husband, also for Elizabeth, she needed to find a good husband too. After praying they made some coffee. The kitchen was full of light accentuated by the walls painted white and yellow. They were both in their housecoats since it was only ten in the morning. Maria had come through the backyard where they had built a door to connect both gardens, so that they needn't go out their front doors. Sitting on bar stools they read the newspaper swapping sections as they read them.

Giovanni was still sleeping but Mrs. Grimaldi was in the backyard working in the garden. The swimming pool was empty and covered to prevent leaves from falling into it. Around it there were pots filled with geraniums and desert plants, where lizards would lay in the winter sun. It was a mild February morning and Joanna was five months pregnant. She was definitely showing and Maria was overjoyed watching her grow bigger each month. They had both been working in the nursery, choosing the wall colors and designs, toys, bed, clothes and other furniture. Instead of resenting Maria, Giovanni was grateful to her because he didn't have the time to go out shopping with Joanna. Every time they bought something new they would show him to get his approval, which he gave wholeheartedly. Occasionally they would bring Mrs. Grimaldi with them who insisted that she wanted to pay for it since it was for her grandchild. She didn't have to insist very hard. She came inside around ten-thirty and joined them in the kitchen where she made herself a strong cup of espresso coffee; a small cup to be exact.

Joanna had grown to love and admire her. She liked her resourcefulness and wits, her business acumen, which had made her the owner of many properties. Now that Joanna was pregnant she had changed her will. She wanted to make sure her grandson had a secure future regardless of his father's business. Joanna convinced her that it was going to be a boy and she left everything she had to Giovanni Jr. except for few properties, which she left to Joanna and Giovanni Sr. She could die tomorrow in peace knowing that she had left her house in order. She was grateful to Giovanni for helping her daily to manage her properties. Even though she was advanced in age she still put in a ten-hour workday. She only required a two-hours nap in the afternoon from two to four. She still ironed her son's shirts and pants while the fulltime maid took care of the rest of the house and the laundry.

They only occupied two of the six bedrooms and the nursery. Of the three other rooms, Felicia had occupied one while she was visiting during her month and half stay at their house. In the future they were planning to hire a live in nanny for the baby and she would occupy one of the other bedrooms.

Maria had been knitting and crocheting baby outfits, small, tiny socks with embroidery on them and she was secretly making a baby christening dress. She was taking a chance because they might not like it but in the magazine it looked beautiful. She was also making small blankets the size of the crib because, even though it was going to be warm when Giovanni Jr. would be born, the nights were still cool and he was going to need a light blanket.

Mrs. Grimaldi asked the girls if they wanted breakfast and they said yes, they did. She fixed eggs over toast with ham and sausage on the side. She had the stamina of a young woman and both Maria and Joanna wished they'd be like that at her age. But her secret was working, being active every day, feeling blessed for the small things in life and having an indomitable faith in God through Jesus Christ. She knew both Joanna and Maria believed in God and she left it in His hands to guide them on the right path. She did not preach to them but every Monday, at about six p.m., they would get together and read passages from the Bible and comment on them for about an hour. At the end they would have dinner in the dining room where there were always fresh flowers. Elizabeth would sit in, in silence, bored by the whole thing, much preferring to be in her room listening to her CDs.

Maria felt responsible for her attitude because she had neglected to bring her to church as they traveled from one place to another when she was still little, but she had faith in Jesus Christ to save her, regardless.

The weekly Bible sessions gave all of them the strength they needed for the following seven days. As long as they stayed in the Word of God they felt safe and secure. Occasionally Giovanni participated and when he did he would hold Joanna's hand, otherwise he would be in the kitchen preparing dinner.

****

Rocco Bandini had been frequently to Giovanni's nightclub and had gone out of his way to befriend him. Giovanni didn't trust him and Philip, the bartender, didn't like him but they would always smile politely. Of course Rocco had his reasons for being nice as Giovanni soon found out. Rocco asked to talk to him privately and once in his office he asked Giovanni if he could sell cocaine to his patrons. He wouldn't have to do anything, just pocket a percentage of the sale. Giovanni told him that it was out of the question and asked him to leave. Once he came out of his office Giovanni seemed perturbed and Philip asked him if something was wrong. Giovanni told him about the conversation he just had and Philip became angry, wanting to break Rocco's jaw. Rocco had the good sense to leave but he wasn't done with Giovanni yet. He would just wait a reasonable amount of time then go at it again. He was doing really well with other nightclubs. The owners were eager to make extra money especially since they didn't have to do anything. Drugs were a very profitable business and one steady source of income. You'd have to be crazy to say no to that kind of money.

****

It was the month of May and Joanna was eight months pregnant. She went downstairs to lie on the couch in Giovanni's office. She put up her legs, which were swollen, and laid down her head on a pillow. She noticed the light was on, on the huge tape recorder and out of curiosity she turned it on play. What she heard left her speechless. A man was threatening her husband that if he didn't agree to selling drugs he would have to convince him otherwise. He said, "You have a beautiful wife who is pregnant; you wouldn't want anything to happen to her, would you?"

"What do you mean, you bastard, you stay away from my wife or you'll live to regret it. I don't want you to sell drugs in my night-club, and that's final."

Joanna turned off the tape recorder and lay on the couch trying to calm her heartbeat. She remembered that lately Giovanni had seemed distract and very quite, not his usual self and she knew the reason now. She was going to tell him about what she had heard and ask for an explanation. She didn't want him to be alone in this.

That evening, at six o'clock, as she was having dinner with Giovanni she said, "I was in your office earlier and I noticed that the tape recorder was on. I turned it to play and I heard something that chilled me to the bones. Who is this man who has been threatening you if you won't let him sell drugs in the nightclub? Tell me or I'll find out from Philip."

"Joanna, you weren't supposed to know anything about it. I don't want anything bad to happen to you but I don't want to profit from drugs either. Maybe you should stay here with me at night and sleep on the couch until we close, that way they won't catch you by yourself. I am afraid they might put a bomb in your car. I am unsure whether I want to go to the police about this but the only proof I have is the tape recording. I am going to wait a little longer and see what Rocco Bandini is going to do. I have a safe deposit box with other tapes about other conversations including those of Angelo Bonifacio. I also have a letter in it. I will give you the key and if anything happens to me I want you to give it to the captain of the police downtown, captain Steve Harrison. He will know what to do. Sorry, angel, for putting you through this but it's not my fault."

"I am glad you confided in me. We share everything, capito? I am your wife and you can tell me whatever is bothering you, anytime."

"Thank you, sweetheart, it means a lot to me. Let's not tell anything to my mother, though. She would lose sleep over it and at her age I don't know if her heart could take it."

"Don't worry, I won't say a word. What about Maria, can I tell her?"

"You better not, she might come at the nightclub to see what the fuss is all about. I don't want her to be in any danger. I am afraid we are alone in this. Maybe I should go talk to Angelo Bonifacio and see if he can talk to Rocco Bandini. I don't think he works for him; he hates drugs, he wouldn't be supporting him."

"You don't know this for sure. What if the mafia backs Rocco up? You would just be putting yourself more in danger. Let's just wait and see what happens. In the meantime I'll sleep here at night and we'll go home together when you close."

"Ok, let's do that. I love you, Princess!"

"I love you too Giovanni."

"Princess I forgot to tell you something. I am afraid is more bad news. Someone called me today. It's about Raul. Someone strangled him in jail, in the bathroom. They don't know who did it." Giovanni thought Joanna was going to be hurt by the news.

"I am glad. That's what the bastard deserves. You said he was going to pay, didn't you?" Joanna was excited and truly happy.

"Yes, I did. I don't even think we should pray for his soul. I hope he goes to hell and stays there."

"Amen to that. Praise the Lord." They gave each other a light kiss on the lips.

CHAPTER THIRTY

Juan, Miguel, Ramon and Rocco were sitting at the same restaurant on Avenida Revolucion on the top floor. Rocco had called the meeting to talk about business and about Giovanni Grimaldi. He was angered by the fact that he had made threats and resolved nothing, not even an inch. He had humiliated himself to the point of begging and did not like it one bit. The more he thought about it the angrier he became. Giovanni Grimaldi was going to die. He would use him to scare off others who might think of getting in his way, preventing him to reach his goal. He wanted to be a boss and a boss gets respect. He wanted to instill fear in people's hearts to the pointing of shaking in his presence; he wanted people to kiss his hand; he wanted to be a godfather, but didn't tell anyone, that was his secret. So his strategy was to kill Giovanni Grimaldi and drop hints around that he was behind it; just hints, that would be enough.

When he told the other three why he wanted to kill Giovanni Grimaldi they immediately agreed. Anybody against selling drugs was their enemy and deserved to die like a dog, no mercy. Of course they had to clear it with their boss but they were sure he would give the go ahead. It wouldn't be the first time they killed, they said. Killing was a high to them and they looked forward to it. They weren't afraid of the mafia; once they'd kill they would come back to Mexico and nobody would suspect them. So they had to discuss how they were going to carry on the murder.

It was decided that Juan, Miguel and Ramon were going to cruise outside the restaurant where Rocco would be talking to Giovanni, at eleven o'clock at night. When Rocco would see them pass, after two minutes, he would walk away from him so that he wouldn't be killed by the bullets sprayed at Giovanni, the second time the car would come around. Rocco would then get into his car and leave. A very simple plan. The three would be supplied a car and a machine gun and Juan was going to do the shooting.

****

Two weeks had gone by and Rocco had not approached Giovanni about drugs so he started to relax thinking that he had made his point and that Rocco wasn't going to do anything about it anymore. That night, in the nightclub, he saw Rocco talk to some friends and approached the group to say hi. They welcomed him and offered to buy him a drink.

"Come, paisano, have a drink with us, here, sit down."

Giovanni smiled and took a seat at their table. "This is a nice place you have here, paisano, if I say so," said one of the customers. He was Italian as were the other three men sitting at the table, including Rocco.

"Thank you," replied Giovanni. "Here, let me buy you guys a round. It's on the house, anything you want."

The place was crowded and smoke filled the air. Joanna was talking to Philip when she saw Giovanni sitting at the table.

"Who are those guys, Philip?" she asked.

"They're guys from up north, not from here."

"One of them wouldn't be Rocco Bandini by any chance, would he?"

"Yes, it's a matter of fact he is; the one wearing a striped suit on the outside, talking to Giovanni. How do you know about him?"

"Giovanni mentioned his name and told me he was from Sicily." She didn't want to say too much for fear of revealing something she wasn't supposed to, unaware that Philip knew everything.

"I don't like the guy," he said. "He wants to sell drugs and Giovanni won't let him. I am keeping my eyes on him, don't worry.

What is he up to now?" said Philip seeing that Rocco was whispering in Giovanni's ear. The two got up and walked past the bar. As they passed Giovanni said, "I am going to be outside talking to Rocco, Princess. Don't worry, everything is ok," and he gave Joanna a light kiss on the lips. Rocco was annoyed but he hid it well because he smiled a big smile. The two walked upstairs and outside through the restaurant's door. After a minute Joanna walked upstairs too and looked outside through the window. It was eleven o'clock.

A car went by. What looked like Mexicans were in the car and they looked towards Giovanni and Rocco with a grin on their faces. Something shiny caught the attention of Joanna but she thought she must be mistaken because it looked like a machine gun. The car just drove by, so she relaxed.

Giovanni and Rocco were talking more animatedly now, with Rocco gesticulating with his hands. He made a gesture of surrender and started to walk away. Joanna was so intently watching them that she didn't see the car with the Mexicans come by again. It wasn't until the spray of bullets and Giovanni falling to the ground that she saw them. She looked at the car plate as she ran outside. Terror was on her face. In a second their whole life together passed in front of her and her future all blackness now. She ran to Giovanni's side. Blood was everywhere soaking Giovanni's clothes and forming a pool on the ground.

Joanna could barely see through her tears and was calling his name over and over. A couple with a cellular phone stopped by and called 911, just as Philip and some customers came out of the restaurant and grouped around them.

Giovanni was dead. Philip put his arms around Joanna who was sobbing uncontrollably and tried to pull her away but she took Giovanni's head and pulled it close to her face not caring that his blood was soaking her. All of a sudden she gave out a scream and held her breath. "Oh my God," she said. "The baby, Philip, the baby. He's coming, call an ambulance." She was holding her belly, on her knees, while a pool of water got mixed with the blood. Philip got on his cellular and called 911 asking them to send a delivery team because a woman was about to give birth on the street.

****

Joanna opened her eyes slowly, trying to shelter them from the bright light above her head. She had an awful headache, which made her movements very painful. She turned her head to the left and saw Mrs. Grimaldi and Maria standing by her bed. Mrs. Grimaldi was holding her hand with tears in her eyes that were rolling down her cheeks like small rivulets. She was very dignified in her pain and her tears were silent ones.

"My baby, where is my baby? Is he all right? Did you see him? Oh God, please let him be all right, I can't take another loss," Joanna said crying.

"The baby is fine," said Maria. "Wait till you see him, he looks just like Giovanni. You're going to fall in love with him. I am going to tell the nurse that you're awake so she can bring him to you. You were right: It's a boy, and what a boy. I love him already; he's going to have all the girls in San Diego after him."

"Oh please do tell the nurse that I am fine and to bring me my son."

Maria left the room and walked to the nurse's station. She told the nurse that Joanna was awake and wanted to see her baby. The nurse went to Joanna's room to take her temperature, blood pressure and talk to her to make sure she made sense because she was very distraught when they brought her in. After a short conversation she decided that she was fine and went to get her baby. Joanna couldn't contain her emotions. She sat up in bed and kept her eyes on the door. The minute she saw the nurse she extended her arms and almost threw herself out of bed. She practically snatched the baby out of her hands.

"Oh Giovanni, you are so beautiful, just like your daddy. Don't worry little one, mommy is going to take good care of you together with your grandma and your aunt Maria. We'll take care of you, yes we will."

Joanna was on an emotional roller coaster. Her husband' death, her new baby, her life without Giovanni were churning her inside. She wanted to laugh and cry but could do neither. Maria and Mrs. Grimaldi were watching her closely to make sure she was all right.

When the ambulance arrived at the shooting scene the doctor declared Giovanni dead on the spot. Joanna was taken to Merci Hospital, which was very close, in another ambulance. She was under shock and later barely remembered about giving birth. The doctor gave her a sedative so she could get some sleep, hoping that, when she awoke, she would deal better with her situation.

Since no family member was present at the shooting scene, the police interrogated Philip and through him they contacted Mrs. Grimaldi. She in turn called Maria and asked her to go identify Giovanni's body with her. The old lady thought she was going to have a heart attack; she found the whole process extremely painful. If Maria hadn't been there to support her she would have surely fainted. She had been asleep when the police had rung the bell of her house. It took her a while to respond because she was slow and afraid to open her door at that time of the night. She dialed Giovanni's cellular but there was no answer and she learned why when she answered the doorbell. She left the screen door closed and didn't let the police in. She was mad at them for bringing her such awful news. Giovanni, her beloved son was dead; her only son was gone; she would never talk to him again, never see him smile; he would never wear his ironed shirts again. Her life was over; there was only a dark tunnel ahead of her. She wished she had died instead of him. She thanked the police and closed the door. Once alone a flood of tears streamed down her face. *Giovanni, oh Giovanni, why? How can it be, you never hurt anyone. I brought you up in the love of God, how could anybody do you harm?* She was almost insane with pain.

She called Maria and asked her to come over. Maria was worried sick by her tone of voice and the few minutes it took her to walk next door seemed like an eternity. What could have happened? The instant she saw Mrs. Grimaldi she knew something horrible had taken place; maybe a burglary; someone had raped her? No, it was much worse, Giovanni was dead. Oh no, dear God, it can't be, not Giovanni, not him. What was Joanna going to do?

She drove Mrs. Grimaldi to identify the body and then to the hospital to see Joanna. They both sat next to her bed waiting for her to wake up. They looked like beaten up dogs, silently whimpering and mourning, eyes swollen, mouths dry.

Tears were falling from Joanna's eyes down unto Giovanni Jr.'s face finally. His little face was red and he was still swollen from the stress of birth. It was still too early to breast-feed him so Joanna just held him tight. Her memory came back and she remembered Giovanni's body lying in a pool of blood, his face white, not responding to her pleas. She was crying convulsively now and Mrs. Grimaldi took the baby from her arms and held him tight. To hold him was like holding Giovanni again and she thanked God in her heart for his birth. *God giveth and God taketh away*, she thought bitterly, angry at those who had so brutally killed her beloved son. Now all the work would fall on Joanna's shoulders: The baby, the restaurant, herself. She was dependent on her for most things now, but she would do her best to help by not being a burden.

Maria was holding Joanna's hand trying to console her but it was useless. Her tears would not stop and she cried louder and louder attracting the attention of the nurse who came by and took the baby away. She asked Joanna if she would like to be sedated so that she would not feel the pain and Joanna just looked at her as if she were stupid. Sedate the pain? How do you sedate that pain? *Are you making fun of me*, she wanted to say but she just swallowed her tears and told her she would be fine. The nurse told her that the police wanted to talk to her when she was ready. Was she ready? Yes, Joanna said, she was ready. She might as well get it over with.

Captain Frank Harrison came as soon as the nurse called him. Maria and Mrs. Grimaldi had left to go home and get some rest.

"Hello Mrs. Grimaldi. Joanna isn't it?" he said nicely. "I am Captain Frank Harrison. Sorry to bother you at such a time but we're working very hard to catch whoever killed your husband. Do you know who did it?"

"Yes, I saw them. It was Mexicans driving a green Sedan with 1XAB222 license plate. I was watching from the window because I didn't trust Rocco Bandini. He had been trying to sell drugs in the nightclub and Giovanni wouldn't let him. I am sure he's behind his death. He was talking to my husband when the Mexicans drove by and as he saw them he walked away. He saw Giovanni fall to the pavement, yet he got into his car and left. I tell you, it was him who killed my husband, just as if he'd pulled the trigger himself. Giovanni was afraid that he might do something that's why he gave me the key to his safe deposit box. Here, give me my dress, it's inside the cabinet, and I'll give it to you. He asked me to. He taped conversations that happened in the restaurant and in his office. I hope you can arrest all of them, do a clean slate that way I won't have to worry about those sharks."

Captain Harrison took Joanna's dress that was inside the cabinet by the side of the bed. Joanna looked inside the pocket and took a small coin purse out. She unzipped it and took out a key.

"Here, Captain. Please let me know what you find inside the box. I want a complete list. Just take what you need for your investigation and give me the rest. You can come to my house; I am sure I'll be out of here by tomorrow. Here is my business card with my cell phone number. I'll help you any way I can. I want you to catch those monsters that killed Giovanni."

"Thank you, Mrs. Grimaldi, we really appreciate it. I better go now so you can get some rest."

"Thank you, Captain. Let me know."

Joanna was left all by herself. She didn't like it because she kept thinking about Giovanni lying dead in a pool of blood. Silent tears rolled down her face onto her neck and the hospital gown. It was only the day after but she felt like a hundred years had gone by, she felt that old. She rang for the nurse and when she came in she asked if she could have her baby. Her breast was full and she wanted to breast feed him.

Giovanni Jr. was crying but calmed down as soon as Joanna held him in her arms. She didn't have to work too hard to breast feed him. He went right for her nipple and sucked avidly. What a beautiful baby he was. His hair was jet black and Joanna was hoping for his eyes to be green. He looked so much like his father it made her heart ache. This was supposed to be their happy event, to share together. Now his son would grow up without a father and she would never marry again. She could only love one man and that man was Giovanni Sr.

She would dedicate herself to being a good mother. There was the restaurant to run; she would close the nightclub. She never liked it anyway ever since she had to wash glasses wearing a mini skirt. She would report anybody who would contact her about giving money as payoff, no matter who it was. They would find out that she wasn't intimidated easily. She had Captain Harrison to protect her now; she would make sure he would know everything that happened to her of a suspicious nature.

A wave of joy swept over her as she watched her son nurse. She mentally thanked God for a healthy son, considering the circumstances of his birth and she prayed for peace and strength to do everything she needed to do. After an hour of bonding the nurse came to pick the baby up and take him to the nursery. Joanna asked if she could leave the following day and the nurse said yes, if she was feeling up to it. She advised Joanna to seek counseling to deal with the death of her husband. It was very important that she did that to find some closure and lead a healthy life. When the nurse left she called Felicia to give her the bad news. She asked her if she could fly to San Diego to give her a hand with the baby until she got into a routine at the restaurant. Felicia was devastated by the news and told Joanna she would be on the first flight out.

Next Joanna called Maria and asked if she could come to pick her up at noon the following day.

"Don't come in the Ferrari," she said. "Take Giovanni's Jaguar. Ask Amelia for the keys. Giovanni had a spare set by the bed. Have her look for it, then drive by the restaurant and pick up the car. Please go by my mother in law and tell her to wait for us in the afternoon. Tell her not to worry, that we are both fine and that I am praying for her. I can feel the strength of Jesus right now Maria. He is so strong, and He is giving me some of His strength. Pray for me; tonight is my first night without Giovanni and I am going to miss him terribly. I thank God for my new baby. I got to be strong for him and for Amelia, my mother in law. Thank you Maria for everything. I'll see you tomorrow."

Next Joanna called the restaurant and asked to speak to Alfredo. She asked him to oversee the running of the restaurant while she was away, to run business as usual. They would close the day of the funeral to show respect. She offered Alfredo the job of manager because he was faithful, trustworthy and loyal. She didn't care that he was a dishwasher. Somebody else would have to do the dishes. Alfredo agreed and told her not to worry about a thing, what he didn't know he would learn and he would quit his day job so that he could concentrate on helping her. He told her how sorry he was for Giovanni's death. He felt like he had lost a brother and was in mourning. Joanna asked him to tell all the nightclub patrons that the nightclub was closed for good and to please ask Philip to call her tomorrow to talk about severance pay. She felt sorry for him but was sure he could find a job elsewhere especially with a great recommendation from her.

She got off the phone and lay in bed just staring at the white wall for a while. There was a television in the room and she turned it on to watch the news. As she expected they reported about Giovanni's murder. They showed the restaurant and the blood on the sidewalk. They said the police had some leads they were following and that the murder might be mafia related. They didn't mention her at all and Joanna thought her employees must have been close lipped, not volunteering any information.

She turned the television and the light off. There was absolute silence. Flashes of the night before appeared in her head and she cried all alone. *Giovanni, my love, I am going to miss you so much. You're the first man I loved and you will be the last. Give me strength and watch over your son and me from heaven, because I am sure that's where you are*, she prayed in her heart. She was going to ask the priest at Our Lady of the Rosary to say a Mass for his soul and was going to light some candles. She felt desperate and inconsolable. This was her first night without Giovanni and she missed him so much. She could almost sense his presence in the room and a couple of times had felt a gentle, invisible touch on her cheek. She couldn't wait to go home and bury her face in his clothes; clothes that she was never going to wash or give away. She wanted to be reminded of him every day of her life, to have him as her silent companion.

She suddenly remembered that her clothes were stained with blood and she couldn't possibly wear them to go home the next day so she called Maria and asked to pick up a pair of pants, shirt, underwear and shoes to bring with her the following day. They would need to go to the restaurant to pick up her purse, which was still in Giovanni's office.

The next day, after the doctor's round, she was given clearance to leave the hospital. She called Maria and told her to come to pick her and the baby up. She asked the nurse for a bag to put her belongings in so she could take them home. Her hands were shaking as she touched the bloodstain on her dress. She brought it to her lips and held it there for a while as images of Giovanni's dead body came to her mind. She felt nausea, the pain was so strong. The nurse brought the baby to her room and Joanna realized that she didn't have any clothes to dress him up with. Maria had already left so she told herself that she would have to take him wrapped in the hospital blanket.

When Maria arrived she was pleasantly surprised to find out that she had thought about picking an outfit for the baby and a white blanket that she had crocheted herself. She had never seen it before and it was beautiful. Overcome by emotions she hugged Maria tight and just held her for a few seconds. She was ever so thankful that she was there for her. *It is true*, she thought, *to have a friend is to have a treasure.*

Maria wanted to dress the baby and Joanna let her watching as she did so. Giovanni Jr. looked beautiful in his light blue outfit. She had fed him early before the doctor's visit and she would need to feed him again soon but she wanted to go by the restaurant to pick up her purse. She would feed him in Giovanni's office.

When they got to the restaurant, even though they were very busy (the restaurant was filled completely by people who heard about the shooting on the news and were showing up for support), all the waiters and waitresses, including some of the patrons, got around Joanna to look at the baby. They all took turns to hug Joanna and tell her how sorry they were for her loss. Joanna was fighting hard to hold back tears, which finally streamed out of her eyes. One of the patrons gave her a tissue and she composed herself a little.

Maria and Joanna left the baby with a waitress and went downstairs in Giovanni's office. Joanna checked the tape recorder and it was empty. The police must have taken the tape that was in it. She found her purse where she had left it, inside the desk drawer, but she noticed things out of place and guessed the police must have gone through it too. Maria and Joanna were both experiencing the tragic loss of Giovanni but they both felt immense joy anytime they were around the baby or thought about him. It was bittersweet and it felt odd.

"Joanna, I know this is hard, but we have to think about the funeral. We have to set a date and let everyone know so they can come," said Maria.

"I know. We have to wait until the police releases the body, then we decide."

"Do you want me to go get the baby so you can feed him?"

"Yes, would you?"

"Of course. I'll be right back."

Joanna lay on the couch disheartened. This was harder than she'd ever imagined. How was she going to ever deal with it? Her face lit up as she saw her baby. He was the answer. "Come here little angel. You've come to save your mom, haven't you?" She unbuttoned her shirt and took one breast out of her bra. She would have to buy nursing bras, she told herself. Giovanni Jr. was starving and attached himself to her full breast.

When they had arrived at the restaurant Joanna had checked the sidewalk as if she could still find her husband's body lying there. Her heart beat really fast and she had to take deep breaths to calm down. She noticed that someone had tried to clean the blood- stains from the pavement but had not succeeded completely, some of the stains were still showing. Alfredo knocked on the door. Joanna covered her breast with Maria's baby blanket and they let him in.

"Hello' Joanna. How are you doing?"

"I am hanging in there, Alfredo. How about you?"

"I want to thank you again for the job. It means a lot to me and I'll do my best to do a good job. We've had a full house since yesterday and we didn't know how to react. There was nobody to give us direction so we just did business as usual. I hope you don't mind, Joanna," he said apologetically.

"Oh Alfredo, I don't mind. I am proud of you all for keeping your head out of the water. Do you need anything from me?"

"Yes, I need to know when are you coming back because we have checks to write to our vendors. Some of those bastards are already calling. I think they are afraid that with Giovanni dead they might not get paid."

"I'll come by everyday around two p.m. and stay for a couple of hours. Leave all the invoices on this desk and I will write and mail the checks. That's all I can do right now. As the baby grows older I will stay longer but now I need all of my energy to take care of him. You know, we need to hire someone to be here early in the morning when deliveries are made and to go to the market to buy food. I can't expect you to do it. Do you think Philip would be interested in it?"

"I don't know. It's very busy in the morning and he is used to work at night. I guess you need to ask him yourself."

Just then there was a knock on the door. It was Philip.

"Hello' Philip, what a coincidence, we were just talking about you," said Joanna surprised.

"One of the waiters called and told me that you were here, so I have come to find out about my future," he said concerned. "I've also come to see the baby and to tell you how sorry I am about the loss of Giovanni. He was the best employer I ever had."

"I know Philip. Thank you! I guess you know that I want the nightclub closed so I don't need you as a bartender anymore but I do need someone to work with the supplies early in the morning until about eleven. Would you be interested in the position? You won't be making as much as you did as a bartender but it's some-thing in the meantime, until you find a better job."

"Thank you Joanna, but who was doing it before Giovanni died?"

"Giovanni and I would take turns. It's a very demanding job, don't be fooled. You have to make sure the food is fresh and in the amount we need. Sometime the vendors will try to cheat you so you have to be very alert and stand up to them."

"I can do it," said Philip. "I'll be helping you and that means a lot to me, lass."

"Great! You'll be paid eleven dollars an hour for five hours each day except Mondays and Tuesdays. Thank you in advance, Philip."

When Philip and Alfredo left Joanna put the baby on her other breast. Joanna hadn't told Philip because Maria and Alfredo were present, but she was planning to give him five thousand dollars severance pay for the bartending job in the nightclub.

"Joanna I am so proud of you for how you are holding up through all this situation," said Maria. "Giovanni would be proud of you too. I think we better go home and comfort Amelia, your mother in law. She doesn't have anyone with her and Giovanni was her only son. I am worried about her. At her age her heart might give up if the pain is too great."

When Maria and Joanna arrived home they found Father Luciano in the living room with her. They were both reciting the rosary but they stopped when they saw them. Amelia extended her arms to receive Giovanni Jr. and she brought him near the priest to receive a blessing. They talked about his christening, about saying a Mass for Giovanni and about the funeral. He would be buried next to his father's grave.

****

That afternoon Joanna received a call from Captain Harrison. He asked to see her and she invited him over. He came right away.

"I have good news," he said at the door. "We found a treasure in the safety deposit box; enough to put people in jail for the rest of their lives. We're holding Rocco Bandini based on the evidence we found on the tapes. It's only a matter of time and he'll confess, the punk. The remaining content of the safety box is for you," he said giving her a paper bag filled with jewelry and envelopes. One of the envelopes was from Giovanni and she waited for Captain Harrison to leave before she opened it. "Dear Joanna," read the letter, "if you read this letter it means that I am dead. I know you'll be hurting just like I am hurting now only thinking about it, but you have to be strong; for me, for our son. Look after him and after my mother. I hope you'll run the restaurant in my memory because it cost me my life and it took me years to build up. Don't be afraid; if you have problems go to Captain Harrison. He is a good ally to have. I think Angelo Bonifacio will go to jail after the police listen to all the taped conversations he had at the restaurant, so you can't depend on him for protection anymore, but that also means that you don't have to pay anyone every month anymore either. I have three life insurances, one million dollars each. That's the best I can do for you. Manage the money wisely, but you don't need me to tell you that. You are very wise and very beautiful and I love you forever. Goodbye my love. Your husband Giovanni."

Joanna was crying very hard, alone in the room. Her heart ached and she thought it was going to burst. She found the three life insurance policies and put them aside. She also found jewelry and photographs, things that had meant something to him enough to put them in a safety deposit box. She would give some to Amelia and would treasure the rest.

****

One month after the funeral life was starting to become a routine for Joanna and Maria. Maria was out of school for the summer and she'd been spending every day at Joanna's house. Joanna would go to the restaurant at two in the afternoon and leave Giovanni Jr. with Maria, Felicia and Amelia who would take turns in taking care of him. All together he had four moms. He was growing very well on Joanna's milk and Joanna made an extra effort to eat the right foods and be in a good mood, which wasn't very hard to do when he was near.

Felicia was growing very attached to Giovanni Jr. and had started to think about selling her house in Minneapolis and moving to California to spend her old age in the company of her daughter and her grandchild, since Raul was dead. Plus she and Amelia bonded really well. There was a lot of love in their house and somehow they all stuck together, looking out for one another. Giovanni was missed a lot by all. He would have approved of her moving since they had plenty of room in their house. Everybody had their own room and Felicia and Amelia, at their ripe age, had more energy than teenagers. They would exercise in the morning, go for a swim, sauna, before nine o'clock. By that time Joanna and the baby would be awake and they, including Maria, would have breakfast in the huge kitchen, drinking coffee, reading the newspaper and listening to the news on television.

It was a stress free life and that was exactly what they all needed. But their misfortune had not ended yet. One sad morning Felicia waited for Amelia to join her in the exercise room, then in the pool, sauna and the kitchen. She was concerned but didn't want to disturb her in case she was still sleeping. She might have had a bad night. When Joanna woke up she asked where Amelia was and Felicia told her she hadn't seen her all morning. Alarmed she knocked on her door. When she got no answer she went in. It was dark in the room so she switched the light on. As soon as she saw her she knew she was dead. Her beautiful, wrinkle-free face was white and cold as marble. Joanna started to whimper and called Felicia to come, quick.

"What's wrong, Joanna?" she asked alarmed.

"Amelia is dead, mother. She is dead. What are we going to do now? First Giovanni, now her; the whole family is dying. Lord help us, I can't take this."

"You have to be strong Joanna, for the baby. She probably died heartbroken for her son. The baby wasn't enough to keep her alive. Her heart just gave up. Poor Amelia, she was such a good company. I'll really miss her." Felicia knew she had to move, now. She couldn't leave Joanna and the baby alone in that big house. She hadn't hired a nanny because she had three people to take care of Giovanni Jr. If she left now she'd only have Maria and it wouldn't be fair to impose on her.

"What do we do now? Do we call the hospital, the police, what?" Joanna asked. Maria, who'd just come in, realized the situation in the blink of an eye.

"We have to call an ambulance," she said. "They will verify that she has died and then they will do an autopsy to verify the cause of death. Poor Amelia, she was such a beautiful lady; I am going to miss her very much. Let's call 911."

Maria and Felicia went in the ambulance to the hospital, where Amelia was declared dead by the doctor on duty. They sent the body to have an autopsy, so Maria and Felicia went home in a cab, after making a statement for the police.

****

Joanna was feeding Giovanni Jr. when they got home. They were all very sad. As they had done when Giovanni had died, they called all the relatives in the U.S. and Sicily to notify them of Amelia's death. Maria was the one to make the calls to Italy because she spoke fluent Italian and Joanna called all the relatives in the U.S. They said they'd let them know the date of the funeral, so they could fly over if they chose to come.

The funeral for Amelia was even bigger than Giovanni's funeral. The church was filled with flowers and people Joanna had never seen before came by to express their sympathy. When all was over Maria, Joanna and Felicia were exhausted. They retired in the kitchen and poured themselves a good drink, except Joanna who couldn't drink because she was breastfeeding. They were too tired to even cry so they just sat in silence. After about half-an-hour they retired to their rooms and Maria went home.

The day after the funeral Joanna received a call from Amelia's lawyer. He asked her to come by the office to open Amelia's will. Joanna's heart was beating fast when she sat in the leather chair, in the lawyer's office. She knew Amelia had a lot of properties but she had no idea how much she was worth. When the lawyer opened the will, in her sole presence, she learned that Giovanni Jr. had inherited everything. All of Amelia's assets, which had all been paid for, where to go in a trust managed by Joanna until the boy was eighteen years old. The total amount of the assets was eleven million dollars and their value increased every year. They speculated that by the time Giovanni Jr. was eighteen years old the total value would be fifty million dollars. Joanna was elated. Her son's future was taken care of and she had to thank that sweet lady who had been her mother in law.

After the lawyer she went to Our Lady of the Rosary Church and stood under the statue of the Blessed Mother. She lit ten candles and put a one hundred dollar bill in the donation box.

"Thank you sweet lady for protecting my son. Please shelter all of us under your mantle and protect us from all evil. Pray for us to your beloved son and ask Him to forgive us our sins. Forever, amen."

She felt comforted just by being there. She had suffered two losses in such a short time and she should be devastated. Instead she was filled with peace and an incredible love for everyone and everything. She remained in the deserted church for quite a while and didn't go home until feeding time for Giovanni Jr.

When she got home Felicia and Maria were worried and curious at the same time. When she gave them the news they hugged and kissed her happy for her son. Although they were all still hurting they saw a happy future in front of them and rejoiced greatly. It was then that Felicia gave her the good news about selling her house and moving in with her. Joanna screamed and hugged her tight. "Thank you, thank you, thank you," she said grateful. She asked Maria if she could have a word with her in her office. Maria followed her worried about her serious tone of voice.

"What is it Joanna?"

"I went to church before I came back and I stood in front of the Blessed Mother for long time. As I was standing there an idea came to my mind," Joanna said worrying Maria even more. "We should go in business together. What do you think?"

"What kind of business are you thinking of?"

"The restaurant, Maria. I am asking you to become my partner. Will you?"

"Gee Joanna, thanks to you I don't need the money and it is pretty hard work. I don't know, give me a minute to think about it."

"You don't need to think about it, just say yes. We are destined to grow old together. You are my best friend; we've been through so much already. Please say yes. You don't even have to come by the restaurant, just help me out with paying the bills and keeping the books. You can still go to school and do whatever you want but we'll be together."

"Ok, I can do that, that's easy. You're right; we are destined to grow old together. When do we start?"

"Right now, just give me a big hug, sister."

"Yes, sisters in Christ."

Printed in the United States
22820LVS00004BA/37-510